THE MOON FIELD

Judith Allnatt is an acclaimed short story writer and novelist. Her first novel, *A Mile of River,* was a Radio Five Live Book of the Month and was shortlisted for the Portico Prize for Literature; her second novel, *The Poet's Wife,* was shortlisted for the East Midlands Book Award. Her short stories have featured in the Bridport Prize Anthology, the Commonwealth Short Story Awards and on BBC Radio 4. She lives with her family in Northamptonshire.

www.judithallnatt.co.uk

THE
MOON FIELD

JUDITH ALLNATT

THE BOROUGH PRESS

The Borough Press
An imprint of HarperCollins*Publishers*
77–85 Fulham Palace Road,
Hammersmith, London W6 8JB

www.harpercollins.co.uk

This paperback edition 2014

First published in Great Britain by
HarperCollins*Publishers* 2014
1

Maps © John Gilkes 2014

A catalogue record for this book
is available from the British Library

ISBN: 978-0-00-752297-2

Set in Minion by Palimpsest Book Production Limited,
Falkirk, Stirlingshire

Printed and bound in Great Britain by
Clays Ltd, St Ives plc

MIX
Paper from
responsible sources
FSC™ C007454

Find out more about HarperCollins and the environment at
www.harpercollins.co.uk/green

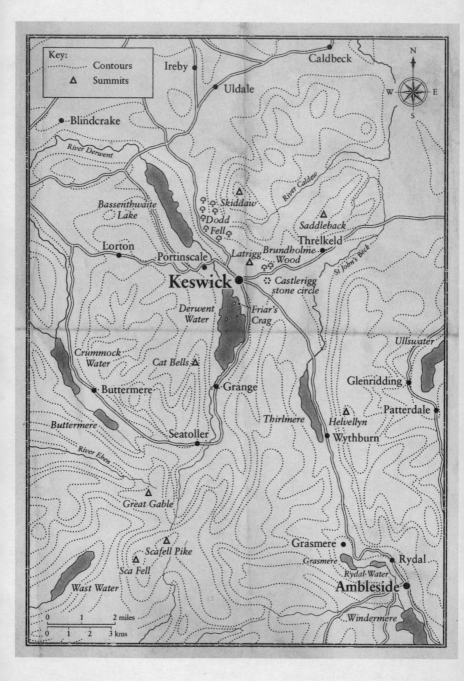

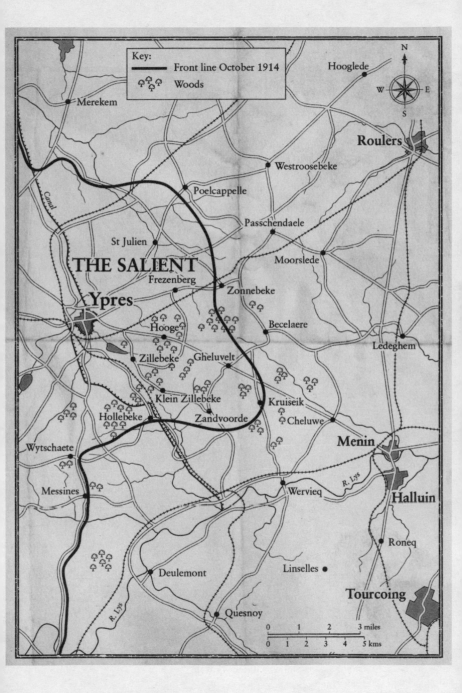

Contents

No man's land is a place in the heart: pitted, cratered and empty as the moon . . .

PROLOGUE

The lid of the tin box is tight; you have to move from one corner to another, prising and pushing with your thumbs. Green paint peels from its edges as though time has been gnawing at it. Brown patches of rust have pockmarked its surface, but you can still make out the picture: a man and a woman in a rowing boat, oars shipped, he with a fishing rod, she with a red parasol, the gentle slopes of tree-lined banks, the river calm, sun-dappled. 'Jacob and Co's "Water" Biscuits' reads the legend, as if the biscuits were meant only to be enjoyed when boating, conjuring lazy, sun-filled days suspended in the lap of the water, with time to drift, to float . . .

The lid comes loose with a faint gasp of released air. Inside are papers and objects, loosely packed. There is a bundle of letters, the expensive blue writing paper tied, oddly, with a bootlace. A pack of Lloyd's cigarettes has a faint smell of tobacco and an even fainter trace of roses. There are photographs: stiffly posed family portraits of men and women in high collars; a girl playing tennis, one hand bundling the encumbrance of her long skirts aside as she reaches for her shot; hand-tinted postcards of lakeside views.

The heavier objects have found their way to the bottom: an amber heart, a pocket watch, a set of keys, and an ivory dance-card holder with a tiny ebony pencil. Lifted, each one fits your hand, makes a hieroglyph: the shape of the past against your palm. *This was real; I was there*, they say as you feel their weight and smoothness.

Beneath them, lining the tin, is the stiff paper of a water-colour painting, slightly foxed and with its edges curling a little but still with its landscape greens and blues, the texture of the paper showing through the brushstrokes of some unknown hand.

PART ONE

FIRST POST

1

WATERCOLOUR

Today would be the day. George touched the bulky package in the breast pocket of his postman's uniform as if to check, one more time, that it was there. His best watercolour was pressed between the pages of his sketchbook to keep it flat and pristine, as a gift should be. He felt his heart beating against the board back of the book. All morning it had been beating out the seconds, the minutes and the hours between his decision and the act. Today, when he went on the last leg of his rounds, he would present Violet with the painting over which he had laboured. 'As a token of my esteem,' he would say, for, even to himself, he dared not use the word love.

In the sorting room at the back of the post office, he greeted the others, hung his empty bag on its hooks at the sorting table so that it sagged open, ready to be filled, and leant against the wall to take a few moments' rest. The late-morning sun slanted down through the high windows, alive with paper dust that rose from the table: a vast horse-trough affair with shuttered sides. Kitty and her mother, Mrs Ashwell, their sleeves rolled up, picked at the choppy waves of letters, their pale arms and poised fingers moving as precisely as swans dipping to feed. Every handful of mail, white, cream and bill-brown, was shuffled quickly into the pigeonholes that covered the rear wall, each neatly labelled street by street.

'I see Mrs Verney's Christopher has a birthday,' Kitty said as she pressed a handful of envelopes into '20–50 Helvellyn Street'.

'He's reached his majority,' Mrs Ashwell said. 'Let's hope he's soon home to enjoy it.'

Mr Ashwell, the postmaster, came in carrying a sack of mail over his shoulder. He nudged George and thrust the sack into his arms. 'Dreaming again, George?' he said. 'You left this one by the counter right where I could trip over it.'

'Sorry, sir,' George said quickly.

Mr Ashwell made some show of dusting off his front and pulling his waistcoat down straight. 'Concentration, young man,' he said, giving George one of his straight looks. 'Concentration is needed to make sure that work proceeds in an orderly manner.' He stroked his moustache with his finger and thumb while continuing to fix George with his gaze. George felt his cheeks begin to burn.

Mr Ashwell said, without looking at his wife, 'Very busy on the counter today, Mabel. Tea would be most acceptable. Arthur's assistance sorely missed.'

Mrs Ashwell's hands stilled amongst the letters and her back stiffened as if to brace herself against the thought of her son, so far from home. Through the doorway between the sorting room and the shop, she could see Arthur's old position at the counter. The absence of his broad back and shoulders, of the familiar fold of skin over his tight collar and the neatly cut rectangle of brown hair at his neck struck her anew each time she let her glance stray that way. It was as though someone had punched out an Arthur-shaped piece of her existence and pasted in its place a set of scales and a view of the open post office door and the cobbled street beyond.

Sometimes, when the post office was closed and Mr Ashwell busy elsewhere, she would stand in Arthur's old place and rest her elbows where his had rested. She would bow her head and finger through the set of rubber stamps as if they were rosary beads. At these moments, she tried not to look at the notice-board on the side wall. Amongst the public notices of opening hours and postal rates was the sign that her husband had insisted be displayed, just as all official documents that were sent from head office must be. An innocuous buff-coloured sheet of paper that one might easily overlook, thinking it yet another piece of dull information, it read:

POST OFFICE RIFLES –
The postmaster's permission to join must be sought.
Pay is equal to civil pay for all Established Officers plus
Free Kit, Rations and Quarters.
GOD SAVE THE KING.

The detailed terms and conditions followed in smaller print below.

Mrs Ashwell thought about the boredom of the counter job on a quiet afternoon, of how Arthur's eyes must have run over and over all the notices: 'Foreign packages must be passed to the counter clerk.' 'Release is for one year's service.' 'This office is closed on Sundays and official holidays.' 'Remuneration will be at an enhanced rate.' She imagined the phrases repeating in his mind as he tinkered with the scales, idly building pyramids of brass weights on the pan.

'Tea,' she said, under her breath. Then more determinedly: 'Tea,' and went upstairs to their living quarters to make it.

George hefted the sack up on to the table and upended it, spilling a new landslide of mail that re-covered the chinks of oak board that had begun to show through.

'Is that the last bag?' Kitty asked of her father's retreating back.

'Better ask George if he's left any more lying about,' he said and closed the door behind him.

Kitty rolled her eyes at George. 'He's been like a bear with a sore head ever since breakfast. We got Arthur's first letter,' she added.

George came round to her side of the table and they sorted side by side, their heads bent companionably together, George's fair hair ruffled where he had run his hands through it in the heat, Kitty's springy, pale brown hair tied back neatly out of the way. George waited for her to elaborate about Arthur but Kitty bent her head to her work and pressed her lips together. After a while, when the job was almost done, George said in his slow, gentle way, 'It must be a terrible worry for your father.'

Kitty snorted. 'Quite to the contrary; Arthur is travelling further afield than Penrith and preparing to tackle the enemy, whereas Father is still chained to the counter like a piece of pencil on a string.'

'Aah,' said George, pausing to look at her more closely. 'And how about you, Kitty? How are you bearing up?'

8

'I miss him, but it makes me sad to see Mother miss him even more and it makes me cross that Father won't let the subject rest.' She tapped the letters in her hand smartly on their side to line them up, shoved them roughly into a pigeonhole and then, seeing her mistake, pulled them back out again.

George laid his hand on her shoulder. 'Oh, Kit,' he said. 'I'm so sorry.'

She gave him a half-hearted smile. 'Never mind. What was it we used to say at school on bad days?'

'All manner of things shall be well,' George said slowly.

'Exactly.' She looked again at the address on top of her pile of mail and placed it carefully into the correct wooden cubbyhole. 'Here, give us your bag,' she said. 'I'll fill it up.'

He held the bag open while she put in the packages of post to be delivered to the villages; then she parcelled up each street with string and dropped them in on top. She helped him on with the bag, reaching up to lift the strap over his shoulder and then settling the weight at his back.

'Sorry it's a heavy one,' she said.

'It's cutting down the number of deliveries that's done it. Bound to be heavy.'

She buckled the bag and gave it a pat. 'See you later,' she said. 'We've got plum bread for tea. I'll save you some.'

George nodded and went out through the post office, past the dour looks of Mr Ashwell and a queue of chattering customers and into the brightness of the day. The market place seemed just as busy as usual; almost impossible to believe that the country was at war: shoppers were choosing vegetables, lengths of cloth and ironmongery from the carts lined up in rows in the centre of the square, each cart tipped forward to rest on its shafts, the better to show the goods. The calls of the vendors mixed with the barking of dogs and the rumble of a

9

motor charabanc passing along St John's Street. The sky was a hazy white and the green flanks of the hills rose in the distance behind the tower of the Moot Hall, their lines as familiar to him as the lineaments of his own face. Taking a deep breath to clear his lungs of the indoor smell of the post office, he caught the musky odour of horse dung and the sharper tang of motor oil. He paused to adjust the strap of the postbag and loosen his tie a little; then he turned down the alley at the side of the post office to collect his bike. He wheeled it out, leaning its saddle against his thigh, and went on in this fashion, bumping over the cobbles, past the Moot Hall and into the narrow streets beyond.

The bike was a heavy, black, iron thing with a basket the size of a lobster pot and when George first got it, he'd not been able to manage it on the steep inclines. He'd needed to get off halfway up a hill and walk it up the rest, sweat darkening his fair hair and sticking it to his forehead. He had persevered though, pedalling a little further each time, thinking of his body as an engine that would benefit from work, and taking pleasure in the healthy ache of his muscles at the end of a day. His uniform jacket had needed to be let out along the back seam to allow for the growing breadth of his shoulders, and his mother, fitting the jacket on him, had called him an 'ox of a man' and made him smile. Now, by standing up on the pedals he could force the bike uphill, clanking and complaining, his solid frame bent over the handlebars, shoulders hunched and front wheel wobbling as he slowed for the steepest slopes. Having the bike meant that he could deliver to the farms and hamlets. His spirits lifted as soon as he got out among the fells and he happily left the younger boys to divide the rest of the town between them and deliver on foot carrying lightly loaded bags and returning more frequently to the office to refill them.

George forced himself to walk at his usual pace along the street and up and down the steps of the guesthouses. There was no point hurrying, he told himself sternly, because if he arrived at the Manor House early she would still be lunching and he would have to deliver the family's letters to the gatehouse, and would miss his chance again. No, he had to do everything as usual and must not leave the town until the Moot Hall clock struck one. That would bring him to the grounds around two o'clock, just as she set out down the lane from the house to take her walk but before she turned off right for the fell or left for the fields and the river.

It had been at the bridge that he had first seen her. He had almost not noticed her in the dappled shadows of the alders that grew beside the river, right close against the stonework of the bridge; only the brightness of her white blouse had given her away, she was so still. She was holding a brown box in both hands and leaning against the parapet. George was struck by the way her straight brown hair was caught in a twist that sat neatly at the nape of her neck and how her posture, leaning forward to focus intently on something below, accentuated the slenderness of her waist. He slowed the bike, thinking to pass on the far side of the narrow bridge without disturbing her but the crackle of the wheels over the grit caught her ear and she turned, her hands still holding the object in front of her and looked at him as if puzzled for a moment. Her face . . . pale, with dark eyes, forehead slightly drawn, as if coming round from sleep, high cheekbones and full lips, which ran into upward indentations at the corners suggesting the tantalising possibility of a smile that was at odds with the serious expression of her eyes. Without even thinking, he put one foot down on the ground and stopped dead.

11

'What are you doing?' he said, blurting it out into the moment before she could turn away.

'Preparing to take a photograph,' she said.

He got off the bike and wheeled it over to her. His family had only one photograph, a studio portrait of his parents: his mother seated, wearing her bridal gown, veil and circlet of flowers; his father standing stiffly behind her, one hand resting on her shoulder.

She said, 'I want to catch the way the light is reflecting off the water on to the rock,' and pointed at the boulders that were tumbled midstream, the current divided by them into shining cords that glittered and threw up shifting patterns on their undersides.

He nodded and they stood together watching the movement and listening to the rush and trickle of the water over the bed of smaller stones.

'Can you see a pattern in it?' she asked.

'Nearly . . .' he said, for it seemed that there was a pattern though it was complex and hidden just beyond his ability to grasp it.

She turned to him. 'You're right,' she said. 'A nearly pattern. It's just a little too quick for us to follow.'

She held the camera up again and looked down through the viewfinder. She sighed and passed it to him, saying, 'What do you think? It'll be impossible to catch the sense of motion, of course.'

The viewfinder had a greyish tint and George looked through it at a scene transformed in an instant to cooler tones. Gnats showed like grey dots above the surface of the water, their dancing as complex as the lights on the rocks beside them. Without the glare, the shifting lights were softer. He could see, on the shady side of the stones, dark bars beneath the water.

12

'There are trout,' he said, 'lying up out of the heat.'

'Are there? Where?' She peered over the parapet at where he pointed. 'Are you an angler?' she asked.

George shrugged. 'I fish a bit. Mostly I just look a lot and so I see things.'

She gave a little smile and he blushed as if he had said something stupid. He gave the camera back to her. 'Will it be in colour? The picture?' he asked, making an effort to conquer his shyness.

She nodded. 'The new film still isn't as close to a natural palette as one would like; it's better than monochrome though.'

'Except for in the snow,' George said.

That smile again. George's heart turned over. 'I prefer painting,' he blurted out; then, fearing he'd been rude: 'I mean you can get the real colours then, all of them. I like going up on the fells in the evenings when there are greys and purples and the rust of the bracken, not just green, the slopes aren't ever just green . . .'

She looked at him then. Not as if he was being dull, as his little brother, Ted did, or as if he was unhinged as Arthur had once when he spoke to him about painting, but as if she was really, truly listening. She said, '. . . and clouds aren't ever only white any more than the water's ever only blue. Do you go down to Derwentwater to paint?'

'Sometimes,' George said, 'and out on the tops: Cat Bells, Helvellyn. But I haven't always got paints; sometimes I sketch. It's expensive, you know.'

'I don't always take the camera,' she said, 'sometimes I just sketch too.' She held out her hand. 'Violet Walter. I live back there.' She pointed towards the trees, beyond which, George knew, lay only one house, the Manor House with its grey roofs and many chimneys, impressive even against the rising ranks of evergreens that finished like a tideline halfway up the huge bulk of Ullock Pike, which over-towered all.

'George Farrell,' he said, taking her pale, perfectly smooth hand in his, then letting it go quickly in fear that she would think him too familiar. 'P-P . . .' he stuttered over the word 'postman'.

'Painter,' she said and smiled.

That had been in May. The first month he had looked for her often but his searching had been in vain because he had later learnt that she had been away. She told him that she had been staying with Elizabeth Lyne, an old school friend in Carlisle: describing another world of tea taken on the lawn, with white cloths under spreading elms, and dancing after twilight, music spilling like magic from the open throat of the gramophone.

He had kept looking and had eventually been rewarded. Sometimes he just glimpsed a distant figure on the hillside as he passed with his bike and bag along the road below; then she would raise her hand to him and he to her, in salutation. Sometimes she would be coming towards him from home with her camera in its leather box slung across her shoulder and he would give her the letters for the house. Almost every day, in among a sheaf of bills in brown envelopes, there would be one creamy envelope for her with a Carlisle postmark. She would shuffle through the letters until she saw it and then stow it in one pocket and put the rest in the other. He imagined that she must miss her friend badly and feel the isolation of the spot after her companionable stay in the town.

When he had passed over the letters, he would turn around so that he could walk with her a while. He would wheel the bike alongside; her camera stowed with the post in the basket so that she might have a hand free to hold her long skirt clear of the dusty road. If she had letters of her own to send, in the pale blue envelopes she favoured, they would walk first to the postbox before strolling on, out into the countryside. Sometimes, the best times, when he climbed a track to one of the lonely hill farms, he would come across her leaning on a gate looking out over the valley and he would join her to share the view. They talked of the way the clouds chased the light over the hills, and of the hawks nesting in the copse near the house, which hovered, dark specks in the heavens, giving perspective and making the piled clouds mountainous.

George learnt that she was older than he was by three years. 'An old lady of twenty-one,' she said. An only child, she had been educated at a boarding school in Carlisle, then a finishing school in France. She spoke of its beauty: the French countryside softer than Cumberland with hedges rather than walls, low slopes and wide plains of rich pasture and standing crops. She described the rocky coast of Brittany, its crashing waves and spume-filled air, and a Normandy beach with a wide arc of sand, which she had walked from end to end, slipping away from her school party to watch the gannets dive like black arrows into the sea. Her eyes lit up as she told him of such things and she motioned with her hands to trace the sweep of the bay or the birds' headlong plunge. Once he told her that looking out over the lake from the top of the fells was what made him certain that he had a soul, and she had touched his arm and said, 'Yes, yes.'

He had told her how it had been at his school. How he was different, always in trouble when the master asked him a question and he was unable to answer because he had been staring out of the window at the clouds, making dragons and faces and genies from their ever-changing shapes. He had said less and less the more he grew afraid that he would get it wrong, until the other children called him 'moony' and 'idiot' and 'simple'.

'You're far from simple, George,' she said. 'They mistook the distraction that comes from hard thought for no thought at all, and that's their error.' She touched his sleeve again and he thought his heart would burst with pride because although Kitty and his mother had always said such things this was different.

When she spoke of her parents, she always had a note of worry in her voice. Her father was often abroad attending to his business interests, leaving the land and Home Farm to the estate manager, and her mother to her own resources. Mrs Walter, too much alone, suffered 'sick-headaches' and fatigue and often withdrew to her room. Violet once let slip that her father, even when back in London, frequently stayed at his club and George wondered what had caused the breach between her parents, but asked no further, guessing at the hurt that a daughter would feel to know that she was not enough to tempt a father home.

From her room, Mrs Walter instructed the housekeeper, Mrs Burbidge, and took her lunch on a tray. Afterwards she wrote letters, but later in the afternoon, she required Violet's company, wanting her to sit with her and talk or read aloud. As the sun grew hotter in the afternoon, George would notice Violet glancing back at the copse within which the house was hidden or at her silver wristwatch. He would rack his brain for a question. 'What was the town like, where your school was? What did you sketch on your picnics?' Anything to stop her saying the words he dreaded: 'I must go.'

George rattled the latch of a garden gate and then stood stock-still to listen, in case he had missed the Moot Hall bell.

16

He heard nothing but nonetheless quickened his pace, the bike wheels juddering as he turned into Leonard Street where he lived. As he bumped the bike to a stop outside the house, his mother came to the door to meet him carrying a package wrapped in paper and with Lillie hanging on to her apron and sucking her thumb.

'I thought I heard you; you made such a clatter,' his mother said. 'Have you got a bit behind?' She passed him the package of sandwiches and a billycan of cold tea.

'Carry!' Lillie said and let go of the apron to lift her arms up to him.

'You mustn't get behind, George. Mr Ashwell's a tartar for punctuality.'

'Carry!' Lillie said again, imperiously, and George put the food down on the step and lifted her under the armpits: a bundle of warm body and petticoats. He put her on his shoulders where she grabbed on to handfuls of his hair.

'Ow! Lillie!' he said and loosened her fingers, laying them flat against his head.

'Horsy! Horsy!' Lillie said and George held on tight to her skinny knees and jogged obligingly up and down the street.

The sound of the Moot Hall bell reached him, a single sonorous note, and he lifted Lillie down, detaching her fingers from his ear as he did so, and handed her into his mother's arms.

'You'd better cut along,' she said. 'You'd think it was a holy calling the way Mr A. goes on about duty and professionalism and "the mail must get through in all weathers . . .".' But George was already on his way, billycan rattling from the handlebars and the corner of the sandwich packet clamped between his teeth as he ran with the bike to the end of the road, threw his leg over the saddle and freewheeled down Wordsworth Street.

He pedalled along the road towards the park and left the

17

buildings behind him, out into the elation of open space and over the bridge where the river flowed shallow and glittering and ducks and moorhens pecked at the trailing green weed. He passed the bowling greens where men in whites and straw hats were playing a tournament, while the ladies and elderly gentlemen watched from the benches, and then he took the back paths through the exotic trees, keeping out of sight of the park keeper, who would curse at him and make him get off his bike and walk. Then he was out on Brundholme Road with open fields either side, the sun hot on his back, soaking through his dark uniform jacket like warm water, the material prickling through his shirt.

By the time he had delivered the mail to the village post offices and to the scatter of farms beyond, he was starting to worry that he would arrive too late and took the last farm track down from the hill at a rate that rattled his teeth. A mile or so further on along the main road to Carlisle he reached the familiar gatehouse and turned in to the drive through the wood, his way lined by the dark glossy leaves of rhododendrons and the straight boles of Scots pines. Here and there, copper beeches made a splash of colour against the massive bulk of Dodd Fell that rose up behind, cluttered with rocks and strewn with sheep: small, pale dots on its upper slopes.

As he rounded the bend to face directly into the sun, he was dazzled momentarily; he put his hand up to his brow and squinted. A familiar figure, carrying a brown leather box, was making leisurely progress along the drive towards him. His pulse quickened. He felt a sensation run through him like a current through a wire making his grip on the handlebars tighten and his sense of the board back of his sketchbook in his pocket keener, as if it had imprinted itself on his skin. He forced himself to slow, to sit down on the saddle, to rehearse his speech in his head. He would greet her as usual, turn the bike around as usual, give her the post for the house and then, just casually, as if it were something extra he'd just remembered, take out his sketchbook, slip out the painting and say to her, 'This is for you, as a small token of my esteem.' She would thank him in her solemn voice to show that she took his gift seriously, and would look at it and exclaim to see that it was her favourite view – from Dodd Wood, out over the lake – and perhaps admire the workmanship. Here his stomach made a strange kind of tumble, as if he had swung so high in a swing that he thought he might fly right over the top of the bar. Perhaps she would put it carefully into her camera case and say she would treasure it . . . The bike jounced into a rut that nearly unseated him. He swerved and squeezed on the brakes; then he took a deep breath and got off the bike, just as she raised her free arm and waved: a wide, expansive gesture that made his heart lift. He forced himself to walk slowly towards her, concentrating on the soft shushing that the tyres made on the drive.

'Hello there, I don't suppose you have anything for me?' she said with a smile as he reached her and swept the bike round in a circle to walk back with her the way he had come.

He handed her the sheaf of letters that he had saved until last. Straightaway she picked out the cream envelope and tucked the rest into her pocket. She felt the letter between her thumb and forefinger and frowned as if surprised by its thinness. She turned it over as if she were about to open it, but then turned it back and started to walk alongside him.

He glanced sideways at her but she didn't turn to look at him and the words he had planned to say deserted him. 'Do you have anything to send?' he asked instead. She shook her head. 'Nothing from the house today, and I . . . I'm not sure. Perhaps I should read this one first.'

'Where are you planning to walk today?' he asked. 'It's very hot once you're out in the sun, you might find it tiring.'

'I thought I'd go up through Dodd Wood. I can take advantage of the sun and get a view of it brightening the lake without getting overheated.'

George nodded, pleased that he could go with her for most of the way as Dodd Wood was on his route back. 'I know a good spot where you can see the different colour of the shallows and the deeper water,' he began, thinking to turn the conversation to lake views in general and from there to painting them and then to one painting in particular, but the thought was enough to cause him to break into a deep blush and he found himself suddenly rushing to jump ahead, 'In fact I've brought something, as a token—'

'I'm sorry, George,' she said, fingering the letter. 'Forgive me, but I feel that I can't wait; I must open this. Would you mind?'

George shook his head dumbly; a sense of misgiving filled him and he knew that he would not now take out the sketchbook from his pocket; that, indeed, he felt afraid that its angular lines must show through the material, its bulky shape exposed, as if he carried his feelings like a foolish badge for all to see.

Violet took a few quick steps and then stopped; he drew to a halt a little behind her. She slit the envelope with her thumb, pulled out a single sheet of paper and bent over it, quickly scanning the page. Her hand dropped to her side.

She turned to him. 'It's Edmund,' she said. 'He's being sent away for more training, then he'll be posted abroad.'

'Edmund?' he said.

'Edmund Lyne, Elizabeth's brother.' She looked at him as though he were being obtuse. 'We were going to be engaged,' she said flatly. 'I was hoping to see him again when he got leave, to have one more visit to Carlisle before . . . before . . .' She looked away, into the trees, unable to trust herself to speak.

'I see,' George said as he began to understand. What a fool, he thought, to have imagined all those letters were exchanges between school friends: gossip and girlish confidences. Of course – they were love letters; of course they were. The phrase 'a token of my esteem' floated through his mind as though his brain was working minutes behind and had finally located the words he had so carefully chosen. An engagement! He swallowed hard; he mustn't let her even glimpse his feelings. 'I'm sorry,' he said; then, taking a deep breath: 'Is there anything I can do?'

She didn't answer but refolded the letter and then folded it again into a thin slip. Slowly, she returned it to its envelope and carried on folding, turning the letter into a small rectangle that fitted into her closed hand. 'He writes in haste; they're to travel to a training camp, and then be sent abroad. That's all they're allowed to say. He says he'll write again.' She nodded twice and wiped her cheeks with the back of her hand. At last she looked at him and her face was blotchy, her eyes reddened. 'So silly of me,' she said. 'Perhaps I had better go back to the house.'

'I'll walk back with you,' George forced himself to say although he longed to get away so he could be on his own, where no one could see him, where he could *think*.

'No need, I'll be fine,' she said and took in a huge breath. 'I'm sorry about all this.' She half turned but then seemed to remember something. 'Did you say you had something else for me?'

'It was nothing, really,' George said, trying to keep the misery from his voice. She was looking at him more closely now, her brows furrowed in puzzlement.

'George?' she said and he could see her expression change to concern as she scanned his face.

'I told you; it was nothing!' George said more loudly than he intended, his voice coming out hoarse and strained as he yanked the bike straight and moved past her. 'George, I didn't think, I'm so sorry . . .' she started.

He could hold on no longer and threw himself at the bike, nearly overbalancing as the postbag swung sideways. He pushed off and stood up on the pedals to gain speed, forcing it along the rutty drive and away from her in a spatter of grit. Gasping for breath, he looked back only once as he reached the bend. She was standing looking after him, silhouetted against the light at the end of the tunnel of trees, her camera slung across her shoulder so that it bulged at her side, her shoulders drooping and her fist still closed over the letter. Then he swung away into the trees that would hide him from view.

2

AT THE TWA DOGS

When George regained the road after leaving Violet, he wanted to be alone and so he turned the opposite way from home and rode out towards Carlisle. He cursed himself as a fool to have harboured affection in the first place for someone he knew to be so far above his own station, and called himself an idiot not to have guessed that she would have an admirer. He imagined how he must seem in her eyes: a callow boy, not yet a man, a lackey, someone you had to be kind to . . . Yet, when he thought about her tears, the feelings he had were not boyish: he felt fierce, angry with anyone or anything that could dare to hurt her. He wished, more than anything in the world, that he could wipe the tears away, and that he could comfort her and hold her in his arms. It had been weak to run away! Yet, now that he had run away, now that she must think him a cad, how was he to face her again? The thought of the way they had walked and talked together, the camaraderie they had shared and the feeling that this would never be recaptured weighed upon him; he rode on and on, seeking to blank out emotion with physical sensation, pushing his aching muscles further, seeking relief through sheer fatigue.

He rode and rode until he eventually came to the suburbs of the town, where dirty redbrick terraces crowded straight on to the roads and children dodged unnervingly in and out between the carts and cycles and motors. He turned out of the mêlée and into the haven of a leafy park where he sat on a bench for a considerable time, thinking about Violet and her sweetheart.

After a while he realised that Kitty would be wondering why he hadn't come back for tea. Three young men were kicking a football around on the lawns and larking about. The light began to wane and he remembered that his mother would be worried, yet he sat on, idly watching them and feeling dispirited.

One of the young men, showing off, kicked the ball high into the beech tree above him, showering him with leaves and breaking his reverie. He listened to them daring each other to get the ball down and watched as they threw sticks, unsuccessfully, until eventually two of them shinned up the tree. There they jumped up and down to shake the branches and urged each other to go higher and further while the third shook his head in disbelief and sat down on the bench next to George. He introduced himself as Ernest Turland, and said to George, 'One of the bloody fools is going to break his head. Probably Rooke,' he added. 'Haycock's taller and stronger.' The bigger chap triumphed at last by hanging from the branch where the ball had lodged, his boots appearing alarmingly in mid-air as he swung. The branch creaked ominously but the ball fell with a sound of snapping twigs and rustling leaves just as a park keeper appeared and started to lock up the tennis courts. Catching sight of them, he let out a shout. Turland scooped up the ball and had taken George's bike by the handlebars before George had even worked out that he would cop it too if he stayed.

'Come on!' Turland said and George got on the bike and pushed off, standing on the pedals with Turland perched on the seat with his legs dangling and the ball held tight against his stomach. Behind them, the others clambered down, dropped to the ground and then took off running after them.

'Go to the Twa Dogs!' Haycock called out as he swerved between two metal bollards and along a footpath, leaving the bike to take the road.

'Left! Go left!' Turland said as they made it to the wrought-iron gates at the edge of the park. George glanced back and saw the park keeper standing with one hand above his eyes peering after them, dazzled by the low sun. He cut left and then followed Haycock, who had re-emerged further along the road, down a series of side roads and back alleys between the terraced houses. When they reached the pub, Turland showed him where to stow the bike behind the privy at the rear and pressed him to come in for a drink. George, carried along on a wave of bonhomie that was new to him, readily agreed. Triumphant after their escape, jostling each other, faces flushed, they all crowded inside.

Turland ordered beers and they squeezed around a table, Rooke pouncing on spare stools and drawing them over. The place was full of men in their working clothes, some sitting at tables, some standing or leaning on the bar and a group playing shove-ha'penny at a board in the corner. The only female was a young woman with a figure that was beyond buxom, who was squeezing between tables to collect up the glasses. She paused beside a swarthy, heavily built man in shirtsleeves and braces who sat alone at a corner table reading a newspaper. George heard him ask for whisky and push some coins over to her without bothering to look up from his paper. She went straight to the bar and returned with a whisky glass, before carrying on stacking spent glasses. A fug of cigarette and pipe smoke hung in the air; the smell of Capstans mixing with the fruity smell of the briar. The whitewashed walls of the room had been turned a glossy brownish-yellow by the smoke. The only decoration in the place was a handful of paper Union Jack flags in a stoneware jar on the bar and a couple of pen-and-ink caricatures in frames, their faded mounts scattered with thrips, trapped behind the glass.

Behind the bar, a balding man with a sour face was pulling pints. He nodded to a younger man who came in briefly to change a barrel and then rolled the empty one out, cursing as it stuck in the doorway and kicking it through.

'As I said, Ernest Turland, junior reporter.' Turland offered him a hand wet with slopped beer. 'And this is Tom Haycock, from the gas works, and Percy Rooke . . .'

'. . . of no fixed employment,' Rooke cut in.

'Currently delivery boy and general factotum at the *Cumberland News* but with an eye to advancement,' Turland said, punching Rooke lightly on the arm.

George introduced himself as George Farrell and, when pressed about why he had been sitting alone and mournful in a strange town, gave a vague answer about having had a disappointment and quickly asked how they came to be friends.

'Turland and I were in the scouts together,' Haycock said, 'and Rooke lives at Turland's lodgings.'

'Under the dragon's eye,' Rooke said. 'She even counts the toast at breakfast.'

'That's because she knows you pocket some for your lunch,' Turland said.

Rooke grinned and shrugged. He took a pack of dog-eared cards from his pocket and shuffled them adeptly, flipping through two piles with his thumbs, cutting and splicing them together and then spreading them out on the table like a fan flicked open and clicked shut again. They decided on pontoon and as they played George took the opportunity to observe his new companions.

Haycock and Turland looked around his own age, eighteen or nineteen, Haycock maybe a little older as he was stocky, wider in the chest and well muscled; he moved with the confidence of a man who works with his hands and knows the strength of his arm. He had fair, crinkly hair that reminded George of the wire wool he used to clean the spokes on his bicycle wheels. Turland, who studied his cards with great seriousness, was a good-looking young man with more delicate features, dark-haired and with brown eyes and an olive complexion that seemed darker than merely the tan of summer. George wondered if there was continental blood in his family.

Rooke, despite his predatory name, reminded George somehow of a mouse: he was so quick in his movements and he was small, surely no more than sixteen, if that, really still just a boy. His hair was slicked to the side, flat to his head, which didn't flatter him as his ears stuck out rather. His eyebrows seemed always to be raised, giving him a look not so much of surprise as constant alert anxiety, as though he was ready to take off at any minute should something untoward occur.

Rooke had suggested that they play for matches and he soon

had a pile of them in front of him, whereas George, who hadn't been giving the game his full attention, had only three and Haycock, who broke off every now and then to watch the girl collecting the glasses, had not fared much better.

'It's Farrell's round then,' Rooke said, poking George's pathetic cache of matches.

'That's not hospitable,' Turland said. 'He's a visitor.'

'It's all right,' George said quickly. 'I got paid today.' He took out his pay packet from his jacket pocket, slit it open with his thumb and began to pull out a note from inside. There was a lull in the conversation at the table beside them and Haycock leant over and quickly put his calloused hand over George's, crumpling both notes and envelope back into his fist.

'Are you daft, man? This isn't the place to show your money about.'

George, feeling confused, stuffed the money back into his lower pocket and automatically, without thinking, patted his breast pocket where the painting still lay between the covers of his sketchbook. With a sickening jolt, he remembered the humiliation and disappointment of the afternoon and placed his hand flat upon the table as if to keep it in view and prevent it from betraying his feelings.

Haycock stood up, saying, 'My shout. Same again all round.' He made his way between the tight-packed tables to the press of men at the bar.

Turland scooped all of the matches back into the centre of the table. 'You took some off Haycock again,' he said to Rooke sadly.

Rooke grinned. 'He's so easy; he can't keep his eyes off a bit of skirt.'

'You're incorrigible,' Turland said with good humour.

'What's that mean? That another of your newspaper words?'

28

'A hopeless case.'

Rooke just laughed.

When Haycock returned with the drinks, George put out of his head the Methodist teachings on the evils of drink that his parents and a lifetime of chapel meetings had dinned into him. He was surprised how easily he did it. He had never taken a drink before, and his only experience of public houses was waiting outside while tracts for the Temperance League were distributed by his mother and a group of chapel ladies. He was anxious not to let his naivety show: even Rooke seemed at home in the bar. How could he have thought that Violet might see him as a man when he lived the life of a boy? He drank fast, as if the golden liquid that he poured down his throat could fill up the empty space inside him where his hopes had once been. They played on and drank more: Rooke was sent up to the bar, grumbling, then Turland went again, refusing to let George take his turn as he was 'a visitor' and 'had got him out of a jam, courtesy of the bike'.

As they played, the conversation among the men around them ebbed and flowed but returned always to the war: the horses being commandeered – what would the brewery do for the dray-carts? The barracks at the castle were filling up with new recruits; since Mons, men were flocking to the country's aid . . . they said the Germans were doing unspeakable things; they said someone had heard engines over Cockermouth, Zeppelins spying out the land . . .

As he listened, George felt an uneasy mixture of excitement and fear. What if the Germans were to come here? It was all very well being an island but what if the navy didn't hold? He imagined the heavy tread of marching feet through the town. An image from one of the recruitment posters came into his mind: a woman and child at a window, and suddenly the woman's anxious face was his mother's and the child clinging to her skirts was Lillie.

His father said it was best to stick to simple principles: 'Thou shalt not kill', that all should 'beat swords into ploughshares'. George knew his own view: that he would protect Mother and the rest of his family with his life. He had heard his father preach at the Convention last year on the text of 'turn the other cheek'. He imagined how badly such a sermon would be received in this changed world, against a backdrop of flags and posters, and men in uniform on the move, singing en route to the war. A piercing doubt about his father caught him for a moment before he turned its shaft away. Surely, if the enemy were at the door his father too would defend them all – turning the other cheek would be the same as turning your eyes away! Feeling disloyal, he comforted himself with the words he'd heard his father speak to his mother: that it would soon be over, that Europe didn't have the gold reserves to fund a modern war, that it could only last months and that they should trust in the Almighty.

Turland, who had also obviously been listening in to the conversation of the older men, suddenly turned to Haycock and said, 'I've been thinking of going.'

'Signing up?' Haycock stopped playing.

'Someone's got to do something, don't you think?'

'But you've got a good place at the paper. Not like me, poking about in machinery innards all day at the risk of losing my fingers. Now I *have* been thinking about having a bit of a jaunt. What on earth would you want to go for?'

'Oh, I don't know,' Turland said. 'I want to do something worthwhile, I suppose, and we're needed: we can't let the Germans go striding around Europe picking up countries to put in their pockets, can we?' He rested his elbows on the table and leaned in. 'Doesn't seem *honourable* somehow to know the army's in retreat for want of men whilst I'm swanning around covering sports days and grand-opening sales.'

Rooke, who had been quietly gathering more of Haycock's matches, his voice a little slurred, said, 'Well, if you're going, I'm going. We'll be like the heroes in *Valour and Victory*. Champions to the rescue!' He put his hands up in front of his shoulder as if cocking an imaginary rifle, jerked them upwards and threw his body backwards as if taking the recoil. An older man with baggy eyes and a well-trimmed beard twisted round on his stool from the adjacent table saying, 'Well said, young man; that's the spirit! Give those Deutschers what for.'

Haycock looked at Rooke sceptically. 'Harry says they measure you, how tall you are ... your chest and what-all before they let you in.'

'Who's Harry?' George asked.

'His brother,' Turland filled him in. 'He was in the Territorials so he's already been mobilised.'

Haycock asked Rooke, 'How old are you anyway?'

Rooke flushed: a blush that reddened his cheeks and rose to the tips of his ears. He shot a swift glance at Turland as if to refer the question to him, which George thought very curious.

'Leave it, Haycock,' Turland said.

'It's just that you have to be eighteen to join, nineteen if you want to serve overseas ...'

Rooke stared fiercely at Haycock. 'I don't know how old I am.'

'Don't be daft.'

Turland said quietly, 'Shut up, Haycock. Now's not the time.' He tapped his cards on the table whilst he thought. 'We should go up to the castle together,' he said. 'Rooke might have more of a chance if they see us as a job lot.'

George imagined the three of them in khaki, swinging their arms as they marched together and suddenly felt awkward sitting there in his postman's uniform. The role he'd been so proud of was safe, civilian. He felt reduced to a mere message-taker, little better than an errand-boy, while the others would be part of something huge, a glorious endeavour, taking their places as men. He was tipsily aware that somewhere beneath the muddle of his feelings about England and honour and protecting one's family lay the unease he felt about seeing Violet again: a troubling mixture of deadly embarrassment that he had revealed something of his feelings, and shame that he hadn't behaved with more gallantry. He felt an unbearable awkwardness that he had no idea how to overcome. Then his mind flipped unaccountably to Lillie and the fragile feel of her small bones as he lifted her that morning, and he felt a lump form in his throat.

At the next table, the bearded man was nudging his neighbour and drawing the attention of his drinking partners so that all turned round to look. One of them, who had a kitbag slung on the back of his chair, said, 'You shouldn't have too much of a problem. You'll soon shape up, even the young 'un.'

Haycock spat on his hand and held it out over the jumble of glasses and cards.

'Are you in, Farrell?' Turland asked.

George hesitated. The scrutiny from the table behind had spread and even the men standing at the bar had turned to see what had caused the dramatic gesture.

'Soldiers in the making!' the bearded man called out, and with that, Turland and Rooke spat on their palms too and the three of them joined hands, fist over fist, to a chorus of approving voices. George leant back on his stool as if to move out of the bearded man's eyeline.

'Three soldiers and a postman!' the man shouted and the swell of congratulation died away into laughter as George hunched his shoulders and stared into his pint. Rooke bent beneath his downcast face and grinned up at him, saying, 'Cheer up, mate, plenty of time to change your mind.'

George shrugged and downed the pint in huge gulps until there was nothing left. He saw that he'd fallen behind the others; there was a full glass set ready in front of him. He tried to focus on the task of stretching out to pick up the glass but his hand seemed to move independently of his will, jerking forward and nudging the full glass so that it slopped a pool of beer on to the table. He stared at the beer still frothing on the dark wood.

'Steady,' said Haycock, setting the glass in his hand.

'You shouldn't have bought him that last one,' said Turland.

'Needs cheering up, doesn't he?' Haycock said. 'Spot of woman trouble.' He winked at Turland and dealt the cards again. Turland and Rooke picked up their cards and another game began.

George took a sup and put his glass down very carefully but waved Haycock away when he tried to give him his hand of cards. 'I'll pass this one up,' he muttered.

We must have been here a while, George thought, as the girl who had been collecting glasses reached across a table to open a window and he saw her reflection in the pane and realised that it was now fully dark outside. He hoped that there was a moon and wondered how he would make the ride home without mishap otherwise. A cool draught of air reached him. He breathed it in deeply and tried to ignore the queasy feeling in his stomach and the sensation that if he didn't concentrate very hard on the three of spades which lay abandoned in front of him, the room started to waver slowly on the borders of his vision.

The girl reached their table and began to gather up the empties. She had coarse features, hair the colour of brass and the high colour that often goes with it. Strands of her hair had escaped her pins and stuck to her brow and neck.

Haycock said, 'Where's Mary tonight then?'

'She's ill; I'm just filling in this once,' the girl said. She paused to roll her sleeves up, revealing plump, freckly arms. She leaned across the table to pick up the empty glasses in front of George, and Haycock tipped his stool backwards so that he could give her posterior a long, appraising look. 'Bottoms up,' he said and drained the dregs of his beer. George thought this uncouth. Haycock sat forward again and put his glass down but as the girl reached to take it he moved it further away. She shot him a glance as if to say 'I know your game' but still leant over further to take it, and when he wouldn't let it go and looked at her with a challenge in his eyes she laughed and drew it slowly from his fingers.

George, noticing as she bent forward that her figure beneath her blouse didn't have the corseted solidity that he usually associated with the female form, but instead a loose movement as if all below was only constrained by petticoats, dragged his eyes back to her face. Feeling the effects of the drink, he was aware of a delay between thought and action and realised that he was staring, yet was strangely fascinated by her blond eyelashes, which gave her eyes a red-rimmed, unfinished look.

'Your friend all right?' the girl said to Turland. 'He's looking a bit queer.'

'He's had a fair bit to drink.'

'Maybe more than he can manage,' Haycock said, knocking George's arm so that his elbow slipped off the table, jolting him into action. George sat up as straight as he could.

'I'm perfectly . . .' George found that even his lips now seemed

34

to be rebelling against him, with a numb sensation as he pressed them together and tried to form the words. '. . . fine. And it's my round,' he finished, fishing around in his pocket for some money. He tried to rise but had to put his hand on the table to steady himself.

'I'll bring them,' the girl said. 'You stay here.'

George subsided and she picked out some threepenny bits and pennies from the handful he held out, her wet fingers leaving the remaining coins sticky in his hand.

Haycock and Turland were talking about giving in their notice at work. Both felt that their employers wouldn't ask them to work it out; they would be released straight away if they had their military marching orders. Rooke said that when he decided to move out he just did it, although always on a payday – no point going without what was due to you. George stared into his drink; the conversation seemed too hard to follow. He very much wanted to go to sleep. He tried to marshal his thoughts by concentrating on what was before him; the beer reminded him of the colour of a beech hedge, 'a distillation of autumn'. He thought the phrase rather good but couldn't trust himself to share it in case it came out all wrong. The sound of the words moved through his head in a slow, pleasing procession. Why couldn't he just curl up somewhere warm and go to sleep?

The voices of his companions rose as they explored the heady excitement of being able to escape their normal humdrum lives so quickly. The anticipated freedom of having extra money in their pockets bred madcap plans for their return. Haycock would join forces with his brother to sell motors; Turland would move to London and try his hand at a job on a bigger paper, maybe even take up travel as a foreign correspondent some-where glamorous, 'Paris or New York,' he said grandly. Rooke said he would get the best cycle money could buy and eat out like a king every night. His ambition didn't seem to extend further than a more comfortable version of the life he knew.

The girl returned with four tankards on a tray and Haycock suggested that they 'down them in one' so she stayed for the empties, standing with arms folded and wearing an amused expression. Rooke put George's tankard in his hand, folding his fingers around the handle and ribbing him a little. Haycock counted them in, 'One, two, three . . .' and they lifted their elbows as one and threw their heads back.

With the first few swallows, George knew that this was a step too far. A horrible gurgling started up in his stomach and he set his glass down and put his head in his hands, trying to still the sensation that the room had begun to spin and that his stool was at the centre of the turning and seemed to be trying to buck him off. He heard the boys thump down the tankards and burst into a cheer at the same time as he felt the girl's hand on his back; he smelt a mixture of sweat and face powder as she bent over him.

'Not feeling too good?' she said in his ear. 'You come along with me.'

George was afraid to move or even look up, convinced that he would disgrace himself by either falling over or being sick.

'Come on now, gently does it.' She slipped her arm under his so that his whole forearm was supported. Once on his feet, she gripped his hand and he stumbled beside her, aware of a shout of, 'Steady, Farrell!' and the sound of his fellow drinkers drumming their fists on the table ever louder and faster. The girl ignored them and led him to the passageway that took them to the back door.

Outside, the air felt cool: his shirt and waistcoat were chill and damp with sweat. His upper lip prickled and his legs wanted to buckle beneath him as they walked into the yard. 'Here,' she said, pushing him towards the privy. 'In there.'

He went in and pulled the door shut behind him. The smell of piss rising from the hole in the wooden bench seat of the closet was the final straw. He barely had time to sink to his knees and brace himself against the plank before he threw up what felt like everything he had drunk or eaten that day. Eventually, he rested his forehead on his arm, exhausted. It was wholly dark in the privy. George couldn't abide dark, close places. Ever since his father had taken him, as a child, on an adventure down into the mine where he worked George had feared small spaces: the suffocating sense of enclosure, the tomb-like dark and the stale air pressing in on him. The tunnels, narrowing as they had gone further into the mine, were a source of wonder and admiration to his father, but they had terrified him. Their lowering roofs made his father stoop, casting a crooked shadow that stretched and shrank on the wet rock as he shuffled along in the nodding light of his lamp. Ahead and behind, the darkness was solid, as if they were moving through black treacle that parted for a moment before them only to ooze back behind them as they passed. He had known, even at seven years old, that he could never work in such a place, exiled from the sun and rain and wind, had felt that the earth and rock around him and the weight of the mountain above were pressing on his chest and stealing away his breath.

George stayed very still, waiting to feel a little better before attempting to stand up. Outside, there was a rustling noise, a shuffling against the wall, as if someone was trying to squeeze between it and the bushes. He thought of the bike, hidden behind the laurels, and hoped it was safe, but he hadn't the strength to do anything about it. After a while, he took out a handkerchief and wiped his mouth with a wobbling hand. He realised that he was kneeling on an earth floor. He levered himself up, steadied himself against the bench seat and tried to dust down the knees of his uniform trousers. Having got himself upright, shakily he felt for the door latch, lifted it and went outside.

The girl was leaning against the wall of the privy, her hands behind her back. George felt a sharp stab of embarrassment to think she had been there all the time. 'You needn't have waited,' he said. 'I was perfectly all right.' Then he thought that he had sounded ungrateful and added, 'Thanks for bringing me out.' He stuffed the handkerchief in his pocket.

'You still look pretty poorly,' the girl said, peering at him. 'You should stay in the fresh air a bit.' She took hold of his sleeve and moved along the wall, drawing him beside her. 'That's right, breathe it in.' George drew in a breath that smelt of damp leaves, the pitch on the privy roof and a faint tang of tobacco as though someone had ground out a cigarette butt nearby.

She took his hand and began to rub it between hers, at first as if to bring life back into his fingers but then she put her thumb in his palm and moved it in a circle, pressing it into the concavity of his hand. George felt a hot current run through him, a disturbing reflex reaction, as though his body recognised an urgent message that his mind was too slow to decipher. His fingers closed around her hand. In a sudden movement, she swung herself round to face him and her arms reached up to entwine his neck as she leant the whole length of her body against him. The soft, yielding feeling of her body beneath her light clothes undid him. He put his arms around her and bent to kiss her but she turned her head away, instead nuzzling her face into his neck, kissing and licking. She took his hand and guided it to her breast, slipping it between the sticky cotton of her blouse and the warm heaviness beneath which George

38

cupped, trembling, his head spinning, his body taking over. She pressed against him, moaning softly and he felt suddenly afraid, unable to stop himself, and thought that this was what she wanted him to feel. She was taking his hand again, pulling up her skirt. Oh God, he could feel the clip of her suspender beneath her petticoat. She was moving his hand up and down over the silky material, over her thigh and up to her buttock . . .

Suddenly a blinding light was in his eyes, so bright that at first they both turned their heads away.

'Well, what's going on here then?' a man's voice said, dropping the torch beam a little and running it over the girl's open buttons and the curve of her breast. George, blinking in the light, couldn't understand why she didn't move away, didn't cover herself. In his shock, George had the bizarre notion that they were caught in some music-hall tableau of static nudity, where the slightest movement would bring down the force of the law. Then, as if a moment of posing for a photograph were over, she pulled away and began expertly restoring her clothes to order.

'That'll be five shillings,' she said matter-of-factly.

'I'm sorry?' George said, not understanding.

'Five shillings,' she said slowly as though explaining to an idiot. 'You've had your pleasure, now pay up, there's a good boy.'

'But I didn't ask . . .' George started. 'You . . .' The sudden change of circumstances left him floundering. He couldn't grasp what was happening or quite believe what was being requested of him. He felt weak and pressed his head back against the wall as if its cool solidity could give his mind focus. He started to tuck his shirt in and then stopped, feeling ashamed.

'Come on, pay up,' said the man, and this time George raised his head as he recognised the voice of the chap who had sat in the corner with the newspaper earlier in the evening;

he squinted against the light, trying to see him. In an instant the torch was thrown down – he heard it hit the gravelly ground with a crunch – and the man was on him, slamming his head back against the wall and punching his fist into his gut. George doubled over, retching, a dry acidic heaving from the depths of his empty stomach. He sank down against the wall and slid to his knees, winded, unable even to shield himself against the man's boot as it met his ribs and tipped him on to his side. He lay groaning, his eyes scrunched up in pain. He felt, rather than saw, the girl bending over him and then, with her small fat fingers, quickly feeling into his jacket pockets, pulling all their contents out on to the ground and picking through them. He heard a heavy and a lighter tread as both of them walked away.

The side of his face was pressed against the sharp gravel and he could feel a long string of saliva dribble from his open mouth. His arms were folded across his stomach as if to hold him together and contain the burning pain in his gut and the pulsing throb of his ribs. He could think of nothing but the pain yet he knew that when it finally abated, what was beyond it would be even worse: the vague outline of thoughts that heaved at the edge of his consciousness would resolve into monstrous, shameful shapes.

He could no longer feel the weight of the sketchbook against his chest. Slowly he stretched out one hand, trying to trick the pain through moving by degrees; groping across the dirt, he felt the crumpled handkerchief, the coldness of a few scattered coins. He couldn't find it. He slumped back with a groan.

Across the yard, he saw the back door open, throwing a quadrangle of light across the steps and releasing the sound of voices and laughter into the air. A small figure came out and hesitated, peering around as if waiting for his eyes to get accustomed to the dark. George tried to call out but all the air seemed to have left his body and only a moan came from him.

'Farrell?' The figure came down the steps and picked its way towards him. 'Farrell? Are you all right?' Then Rooke bent over him, taking his elbow, trying to lift him up. 'What the hell happened?' He looked about him quickly, checking that whoever had done this wasn't still around. He managed to raise George into a sitting position. 'I'll get the others,' he said.

George hung on to his arm. 'My book. I can't find my book.'

'Never mind that, we need to get you out of here,' Rooke said.

'I need it.' George struggled to control his voice.

Rooke squatted beside him and felt around until he found the book. He put it into George's hands and then ran back to get the others.

The book's smooth covers were grainy with sandy earth. George brushed his fingers over them and put the book safe in his pocket, wincing as he lifted his arm. Rooke returned with the others who lifted him and got his arms over their shoulders so that they could help him along.

'We'd better take him back to our lodgings,' Turland said to Rooke. 'You get the bike.'

Rooke pulled it out from behind the bushes and wheeled it along beside them.

'Took your money, I suppose,' Haycock said.

George nodded.

'Did you see who it was?'

'No. He jumped me from behind,' George said, already forming the lie that he would tell and retell, already feeling the hot shame creeping through him, sordid and unclean.

3

DANCE CARD

When Violet had first arrived at the Cedars, Elizabeth's family home, Edmund had been away and she had been so busy, in the first week, meeting the Lyne family's cousins and friends for luncheon parties, picnics and concerts, that she had almost forgotten Elizabeth had a brother. After a morning spent boating with a group of relations who had failed to include sunshades in their preparations, Elizabeth had felt the worse for the sun and suggested that they withdraw to their rooms for the afternoon, the better to enjoy the evening's entertainment.

Violet, however, was unable to rest. Despite closing the drapes against the intense heat of the June afternoon and taking off her shoes and lying full length on the bed, her thoughts were too full of the unwonted excitements of the last few days, her mind a whirl of gowns and opera glasses, new faces, drives in the motor, parlour games and laughter. The room was stuffy, the satin quilt beneath her sticky and clinging, and at length she gave up, slipped her shoes back on again and decided to go in search of something to read.

Downstairs, the tall double doors of the library were open and Violet went in softly, glad that she wouldn't have to risk breaking the oppressive quiet of the afternoon by their creaking. The room was lined with books from the floor to the ornately plastered ceiling, and was furnished with library steps to reach them. Chairs, couches and occasional tables stood around for the convenience of the reader, some arranged in a group in the centre, some placed with their backs to the room giving a view from the long French windows of the sloping lawns, elms and cedars. A large desk, belonging to Elizabeth's father, stood to one side, littered with stamps, magnifying glass and glue pot and Violet felt that she was intruding a little and thought that she would choose something quickly and go.

Her eyes travelled over the books in the lower shelves, which were large, dull, leather-bound volumes of county history, and passed up through travelogues and heavy-looking biographies until she found a set of the Waverley novels on one of the top shelves. She wheeled the library steps along and positioned them so that they were well braced against the shelves; then, picking up the skirts of her afternoon dress in one hand, she awkwardly climbed up to find one that she hadn't yet read. The set, tightly packed together, wouldn't yield a volume easily. Getting a finger hooked into the top of the spine of the book in the middle, she pulled hard, dislodged several, then, juggling books, steps and skirts, tried to catch them and failed so that three volumes fell with an almighty thump on the polished wood floor.

There was a muttered curse of 'What the devil?' from one of the couches and a man sat up and rested his elbow on its upholstered back. He blinked and passed his hand over his face and through his dark hair, staring with a bemused expression as though unsure whether he was still in a dream.

Violet, still clutching a copy of *Ivanhoe*, said, 'Oh! You startled me!' and then flushed crimson, feeling foolish, as she had undoubtedly startled him first. Momentarily lost for words, she stared back. His tie was loosened, his waistcoat was undone and his sleeves were rolled back giving him a rakish look that was at odds with his neat moustache and candid grey eyes. 'I'm so sorry to have woken you,' she said, reaching to put the books that had fallen flat on the shelf back into position.

'Oh, don't trouble yourself about that. Here, let me help,' he said, jumping to his feet and coming to the foot of the ladder. He picked up the other volumes and passed them up to her. 'I'm Edmund, by the way. Who are you?'

'Violet. Violet Walter.' In reaching down to shake his offered hand, she almost lost the books again and he steadied her elbow.

'You're Elizabeth's friend, aren't you?' he said. He broke into a wide grin. 'She never mentioned you were such a big reader.'

Violet smiled as she put all but one of the books back. 'I do like to read,' she said, 'but for an afternoon's idle hour even I would find the full set daunting.'

'Well, you're welcome to as many as you can manage,' he said, helping her down from the steps. She turned at the foot and they came face to face. There was a moment when they both stopped and looked – a beat, barely a pause, but it seemed to Violet that something passed between them: a strange instant of recognition. Violet drew away first, suddenly aware of the impropriety of their situation: alone together – and at this proximity. She stepped to the side but before she could pass him he said, 'Must you go? Don't run away. Elizabeth's only told me a little about you; do come and tell me more. Please?' and before she knew what she was doing she found herself steered to an armchair. Edmund solicitously tucked a cushion behind her, saying cheerily, 'None of these chairs are comfy. They're lumpy old horsehair things but we're all fond of them just because they've always been here.'

'Thank you, I'm very comfortable,' Violet said, and then felt confused all over again as she realised that she should really be protesting that she must go.

Edmund said, 'I see you favour the classics. Do you read the newer works as well? Forster? H. G. Wells? I can recommend Wells; he has a knack of warning us of where our current follies may lead us.'

'I prefer Forster,' she said, considering. 'Wells's view of the future is a little too bleak for my taste.'

'We have the latest Forster somewhere; I'll look it out for you. Have you been enjoying your stay so far? I hope Elizabeth has been looking after you and showing you around?' Edmund tried to make this beautiful girl with the serious face feel more at ease.

'Oh, we've had the most marvellous time. We went to see *La Traviata* and we had a wonderful picnic by the sea at Cockermouth with your father and mother and some of Elizabeth's friends, and the cousins of course . . .'

'They're a jolly lot, aren't they? We usually see a fair bit of them in the summer. Are you able to stay for long?'

'A month, I hope, as long as my mother keeps well and can spare me from home.'

'Well, we must make the most of your stay,' Edmund said sympathetically, remembering what Elizabeth had told him of Violet's circumstances. 'What do you like to do the most?'

Violet told him about her photography and he listened carefully, asking her questions about shutter speeds and coloured filters, and suggesting places of interest locally where they could picnic and she could take some photographs. The conversation moved easily along as he told her of his recent studies at Cambridge and how much he had enjoyed the Officers' Training Corps with its outdoor life of riding, camping and shooting. He told her that he was applying for a commission and hoped that his uncle, who was in the local regiment, would be able to arrange something for him. Ideally, he said, he would have liked a cavalry commission but he would have to take what his uncle could get for him and the chances were that he would end up in the infantry. 'Foot-slogger more likely than donkey-walloper,' he said, making her laugh, which drew from him a broad smile in return.

As Violet began to ask him more, she heard someone approaching the room and stopped abruptly. A housemaid, holding a pile of tablecloths and napkins, stood uncertainly in the doorway looking from one of them to the other. 'Sorry, sir,' she said to Edmund, 'Cook said I was to lay for afternoon tea in here, sir, so's we could open the French windows and have the draught.'

Violet, suddenly aware of how odd this must look: a lady visitor, unchaperoned, sitting knee to knee with the young gentleman of the house, got quickly to her feet.

Edmund stood too, saying, 'Ah, yes, of course, Dolly. Miss Walter has just stepped in to find a book and I can see that I'm going to be in your way.' He gave the girl a winning smile and she bobbed a curtsey. He turned back to Violet with a mischievous look in his eye and said, 'I hope you'll enjoy Mr Scott's *Ivanhoe*, Miss Walter.'

'Thank you. I'm sure I shall,' Violet returned with equal formality and left the room. Behind her, she heard Edmund offering to open the French doors for Dolly, saying that they were rather stiff for her to manage. He engaged her in friendly conversation, distracting her with questions about the health of all below stairs and whether there had been any changes while he had been away.

Violet retired to her room and sat at the window with the book open before her. She had to admit herself charmed. She found herself recounting every step of their unconventional meeting and a strange sensation came over her once more as she thought of him helping her down from the steps and of his touch as he tucked the cushion behind her as carefully as if she were porcelain. She was not used to such attention, such cherishing, and certainly not to the way Edmund had made it so easy and natural to talk about herself. When Elizabeth put her head around her door an hour later to tell her that tea was served, she found that she had read two chapters of *Ivanhoe* without taking in a single word.

Entering the library once more, now freshened by a breeze from the garden, which sweetened the room with the scent of honeysuckle and fluttered the corners of the tablecloths, she was met by the sight of Mr and Mrs Lyne, Elizabeth, Edmund and three other houseguests. The party was assembled next to tea tables laden with sandwiches, ginger cake and a pale blue and gold tea service, while Dolly attended to a large urn on a side table.

'Ah, Violet,' Mrs Lyne said as the gentlemen rose, 'let me introduce my son, Edmund.'

Violet, taken by surprise, almost said, 'Thank you but we've already met.' She bit back the words as they formed in her mind and hesitated, casting around desperately for the phrase that she needed.

Edmund, now buttoned into waistcoat and jacket, stepped quickly forward, saying with a deadpan expression, 'Miss Walter, I'm so very pleased to meet you,' and shook her hand, while Dolly looked round sharply from the tea urn with an expression that clearly said, 'Whatever next?'

Violet subsided gratefully into her seat and Elizabeth began to tell her that she still felt a little muzzy and wondered about bridge tonight rather than an excursion. Edmund caught her eye over Elizabeth's head and raised his eyebrows, a small smile at the corner of his mouth. As she asked distractedly for Elizabeth to repeat herself, she couldn't help but smile back and in the moment's complicity, she knew that her heart was lost.

Over the following weeks, Edmund joined Violet and Elizabeth in their outings with cousins and friends, Mrs Lyne accepting their plans as long as the young people were in a large group, thereby playing chaperone to each other.

'Mother goes on the principle of "safety in numbers".' Elizabeth said, drawing up yet another long list of guests to join them for a country walk and picnic. Violet had noticed that however much the list varied, one name, Titus Emory, was always included, and that Elizabeth and he would often conspire to sit next to each other when dining or to share a boat when on the river. Far from feeling abandoned by her friend, Violet rejoiced in the opportunities it gave her to talk relatively privately with Edmund. They had become easy in each other's company at home, as the family played cards together or entertained one another at the piano in the evenings; but the conversation then was light and general and Violet longed for the more personal discussions that she and Edmund shared when they could. They had exchanged opinions on music and books, Edmund playing her Chopin's nocturnes and lending her his well-thumbed copy of poems by Yeats, which she loved and discussed with him at length. They had moved through personal anecdotes about school and university to confidences on deeper matters. Edmund told her of his belief that the old order must change, and his interest in the law as an instrument of reform to deal with working-class poverty, before social turmoil should get out of hand. Violet confided her worry about her mother and her frustration at being powerless to use her education or to affect anything beyond her own home.

For the latest outing, Elizabeth had invited a mixed group of ten and decided that they should motor out into the countryside. Violet, hopeful of some good views, took her camera with her. After parking and walking half a mile, the men carrying the wicker hampers and the ladies the rugs, they settled on a spot under an ash tree overlooking pasture, with a small stream leading into woods and in the distance the glitter of the sea. After picnicking, some of the party wanted to walk further and some to simply loll and enjoy the view. Elizabeth and Titus stayed behind for a few minutes and then strolled down to the stream; Violet and Edmund sat on, chatting, surrounded by rumpled rugs and tablecloths strewn with spirit lamp and kettle, hard-boiled eggs and Dundee cake.

'If you could do anything at all with your life,' Edmund said, lying back with his hands behind his head, 'what would you do?'

'Anything at all? Do you mean regardless of the fact that I'm a woman?' Violet asked dryly.

Edmund looked up into the green and blue of leaves and sky above him. 'Anything.'

'Travel,' Violet said, hugging her knees and looking out at the distant line of the sea. 'I'd explore and take wonderful pictures of Alps and ice floes and . . . Oh, I don't know . . . temples and pyramids, desert sands . . . I'd like to capture it all and bring it back for others to see.'

Edmund sat up, leaning on one elbow, and looked at her with interest. 'What would you do with all the pictures?'

'Publish them,' Violet said seriously. 'Sell them to magazines like the *National Geographic*.' She paused and fiddled with the fringe of the rug, waiting for Edmund to laugh. 'I suppose you'll think me a suffragette now,' she made light of it. 'Just a silly dream, I know.'

'Not silly at all,' Edmund said. 'I think it's rather admirable,' and he leant across and took her hand. He said in a low voice, 'I wish we could see them together,' and lifted her hand to his lips and kissed it.

Violet, her heart quickening, looked into his eyes and saw that he was regarding her tenderly. What did he mean? Surely he couldn't be toying with her; his expression was full of hope, as though he had spoken from the heart and now waited for her reply. The sound of voices reached them as Titus and Elizabeth made their way back, Elizabeth teasing Titus about his unending appetite for tea and cake.

'I . . . I should like that,' Violet said quickly as he relinquished her hand. Then, made bold by a heady rush of joy, she said, 'And you, what would you do with your life if you could do anything at all?'

Elizabeth was calling to her, 'Do we have more matches for the spirit lamp? Titus says I've talked at him so much I've made him thirsty.' Violet held up the matches, knelt up and smoothed out the cloth and started setting out the tea things.

As the others reached them and flopped down, Edmund leant close to her and said, 'I would take you to all of those places,' and Violet bent her head to measure tea from the caddy into the pot, to hide her face from the others.

Elizabeth took off her hat and fanned herself with it. 'Do you think the weather's set fair for a few days, Titus?' she asked.

'Mmm, I should say so,' Titus said, cutting himself a good wedge of fruitcake. 'For the rest of the week at least.'

'Then our garden party will be on Saturday,' Elizabeth announced. 'We can invite everybody: the cousins, our set from school, Edmund's set of officer types.' She lit the spirit lamp under the kettle.

'Hold on, old girl, don't go overboard with the numbers – in particular no need for too many officer types,' Titus said. 'Your mother might not want too much brouhaha.'

'Nonsense, Mother's a dear and you know I wouldn't choose any other tennis partner than you.'

Titus said, 'Ah, well, in that case . . .' and looked mollified.

'If it stays fine we can have dancing in the open air in the evening as we did last year. What do you think, Edmund?'

'I think that would be perfectly splendid,' Edmund said, looking straight at Violet.

On Saturday, the long sloping lawns beneath the cedars and elms were mowed and rolled. The horse pulling the contraptions had its hooves clad in leather overshoes to achieve a smooth, undented finish, although, as Edmund pointed out, the undulating nature of the ground always added an interesting dimension to ball sports, however much one rolled it. The formal gardens were tidied: hedges neatened, paths raked, the rambling roses around the arbour trimmed. Tables and chairs were brought outside and placed in groups under bright awnings and trestle tables with starched white cloths were laden with lemonade and ginger beer.

By four o'clock, the party was in full swing. Older guests, aunts and mothers chatted in the shade or strolled sedately around the grounds while children chased hoops or stood in line to climb through the great split trunk of the oldest cedar tree to jump down into the arms of obliging uncles. The young people had voted for tennis rather than croquet and the grass court on the least bumpy stretch of ground beside the shrubbery had been newly marked out and the net strung up. Despite Lucien Hilliard, a boisterous but conversationally inept young man, importuning Violet to partner him, Violet had sat out for the first few games, pleading the heat as an excuse. Edmund, as host, had held back until all the guests who wanted a game had played, but then, in the late afternoon, deftly suggested that the heat was waning and swept Violet into a game before Lucien could say anything more.

Violet and Edmund were playing Elizabeth and Titus, who were winning with panache: Titus having a powerful serve and Elizabeth a fiercely competitive streak.

'You're not trying hard enough, Edmund!' she called out to her brother as the ball hit a bump in the ground and flew off at an impossible angle.

'Oh come on, 'Lizbeth, no one could have reached that.'

Elizabeth smirked.

'Forty-love,' Titus said loudly, sweating and red in the face. He positioned himself to serve again and bounced the ball impatiently in front of him.

Edmund and Violet exchanged a smile. Violet settled her hat more firmly on her head and gathered her skirts in one hand, ready to return the serve. Titus threw high and hit the ball with such force that Violet had to duck. She turned to see Edmund running backwards in an effort to keep the ball in play. Swiping wildly at it, he missed his footing on the uneven ground, scrambled backwards, and finally sat down with a thump, pulling a clownish expression. Violet, overcome by laughter, subsided to her knees and the ball bounced away into the shrubbery behind them.

'Game!' Titus and Elizabeth shouted at the same time. Titus raised his fists in a ridiculous overplayed gesture of triumph and Elizabeth threw her racquet in the air and caught it, which made Violet turn to Edmund and laugh even more. She got up and ran to help him look for the lost ball. They pushed through the thick stand of bushes and trees and moved deeper into the gloom, Edmund sweeping away the twiggy undergrowth and last year's fallen leaves with his racquet. Spotting the ball at the same time, they both stooped to retrieve it and bumped into one another. Edmund put out his hand to help her up and mumbled an awkward apology but as they rose, his eyes were already searching hers. Violet knew with sudden certainty that he wanted to kiss her and, even more disturbingly, that she wanted to be kissed. From the court beyond, the sound of slow hand-clapping and calls of 'Play on!' and 'New game!' reached them. Her hand trembling, she picked up the ball and gave it to Edmund.

As they turned to go back to the game, Edmund said urgently, 'I need to be able to talk to you alone, properly. Sometime this evening do you think we could slip away?'

Violet barely had time to nod before they broke free of the bushes and out into view of the cheering audience.

As they played on, she felt aware of her body in a new way: how it moved, the strength of her muscles, her youth and vigour, and of Edmund: sensing exactly where he stood behind her, the degree of closeness as he moved forwards and back with the play, as if they were each surrounded by force fields that fizzed and sizzled as they touched. When the game finally ended, she and Edmund had made up ground and Elizabeth congratulated them on 'a much more creditable third set' as hands were shaken over the net. They retired to deck chairs to watch others playing. Lucien appeared at Violet's elbow bearing a tray with elderflower jellies and lemonade so that she was obliged to listen to a long and tiresome commentary on further games until she could decently withdraw with the other ladies to rest for an hour before dressing for the evening.

'I shan't let you go before you promise me the first dance,' Lucien insisted, and Violet had to agree gracefully.

Later, when Violet had rested and bathed, instead of ringing for Elizabeth's maid, she dressed herself with great care, choosing her pale lilac, an evening frock with tiered layers of flimsy lawn. She turned back and forth in front of the cheval mirror by the window to see how it would accentuate her movements when she danced. Tonight, she wanted everything to be perfect.

As she opened the domed lid of her Noah's Ark trunk to search for her best ivory evening comb, there was the tiniest tap on the door. Thinking it was Elizabeth, and with her head in the depths of the trunk, she called out, 'Come in,' but no one entered. She found the comb and put it on her dressing table; then she went to the door. There was nobody there. A row of closed doors stretched the length of the landing and the sweeping stairs at the end were deserted. From other rooms, faint noises of girlish voices, running water and clinking china suggested that others were rising but there was no sign of the person who had knocked, not even the distant footsteps of a disappearing maid in the hall below. As she stepped back to close the door, she glanced down and saw on the floor, pale against the rich reds and blues of the silk hall runner, a beautiful corsage: a perfect cream rose and two tiny buds against a wisp of maidenhair fern. Delicately, she picked it up and took it inside. Turning it in her hands, she found that there was a tiny scrap of paper behind the pin. She took it to the window to decipher the minute lettering and read:

For a glimmering girl . . .

She instantly recognised it as Yeats and knew it was from Edmund. She called to mind the verse from the mysterious poem:

> I went to blow the fire a-flame,
> But something rustled on the floor,
> And some one called me by my name:
> It had become a glimmering girl
> With apple blossom in her hair
> Who called me by my name and ran
> And faded through the brightening air.

Flushing with pleasure, she hid the note in her jewellery case and pinned the flower carefully to her dress, the heady champagne of hope rising in her that Edmund meant this as a precursor to a declaration. Her heart quickened; it must be tonight. He knew that she was to stay with the family only a few days longer. He had said that he wanted to speak to her alone . . .

There was a brisk knock at the door and Elizabeth bustled in, resplendent in pale blue silk. 'Are you nearly ready? Didn't Mary come to do your hair? Shall I help you with it?' She was fizzing with excitement. 'Aha,' she said, noticing Violet's corsage, 'I see you have an admirer.'

Violet, still half in her dream world of anticipation, visibly jumped in alarm. 'Sorry?'

'I see Lucien continues to pursue you at every turn,' she said.

'Oh, yes, Lucien,' Violet said faintly. 'He's a little over-whelming, don't you think?' She sat obediently at the dressing table and let Elizabeth tackle her hair.

Elizabeth brushed it smartly until it became flyaway and static, talking nineteen to the dozen all the time. 'Lucien *is* rather pressing, I must admit, and when it comes to dancing he's got two left feet, but he's clearly rather taken with you so don't be too hard on him, poor boy. He was positively dogging your heels this afternoon, wasn't he?' She wound and pinned strands of Violet's hair up into a soft arrangement of piled twists, and held it there while Violet anchored it in place with the ivory comb. 'If he gets too much for you, Edmund or I can always rescue you,' she said. 'Edmund's quite a good dancer. Well, I taught him actually, so at least he can waltz without tripping you up or standing on your dress.' She teased out a wisp or two at Violet's temples. 'There, you'll do,' she said, picking up her gloves and handing them to her. 'Shall we go down?'

As they passed through the hallway, thumps and male voices came from the music room where some of the young men were rolling back the carpet in case it should rain and the party be forced to come indoors. Outside, Edmund and his young cousin, Samuel, were carrying the gramophone between them. Violet, suddenly shy, hung back behind Elizabeth. The men set the machine down on a table, its brass trumpet gleaming in the hazy evening light. Immediately, the young men and women gathered round, pulling out records from leather carrying cases, peering at titles and exclaiming over their favourites. Edmund took charge, winding the handle and carefully placing the needle. The strains of 'Dreaming' wavered into the still air, the tenor voice lifting over the sweet sound of the strings as the music poured out and over the velvet lawns to lose itself in the trees and formal gardens beyond.

'This is for our hostess,' Edmund said. His mother looked pleased as his father stepped out and took her hand to lead the first dance. For the first few bars they danced alone, Mr Lyne ramrod straight with his chin held high, Mrs Lyne with a long-fringed shawl elegantly draped around her shoulders. Then others followed and the space between the great trees filled with moving figures, chattering voices and bursts of laughter as the twirling couples circled in a river of pale silks and evening suits.

Edmund was explaining the operation of the gramophone to Samuel so that he could take over. Violet hovered at the edge of the dancing crowd, beginning to despair as, one after another, friends of Elizabeth asked her to write their names on her dance card. She saw Edmund look towards her and his expression softened but then Lucien was beside her, saying, 'I trust you wrote me in for this first one as promised?' and whisking her into the dance.

As she danced with a succession of young men who led her rather over-enthusiastically and asked her the same set of predictable questions, to which she gave polite but less enthusiastic answers, she looked for Edmund. She feared that, as the son of the household, he might feel obliged to dance with every relative who was left sitting out a while but there was no sign of him among the dancers. He was no longer at the gramophone; neither could she see him in the groups gathered around the tables where refreshments were laid out: poached salmon and game terrine, cordials and champagne.

By the time Lucien returned and claimed his second dance, the shadows were deepening under the trees, stretching across the lawns like the fingers of long black evening gloves, and Violet felt taut with anxiety.

In the middle of the throng, Edmund suddenly appeared and tapped Lucien on the arm. He pointed over to the trees, saying, 'Do excuse me, but as Miss Walter is interested in matters of illumination, through her photography, I think she might enjoy lighting-up time.' Before Lucien could remonstrate, he had taken Violet in his arms and danced her away, moving lightly and swiftly with the flow of the crowd but guiding her expertly between the dancers so that as the music finished they found themselves at the edge and stepped out as if alighting from a carousel.

He placed her hand on his arm and walked her away from the milling crowd and over to the nearest cedar where Violet saw that under the spreading hands of the branches Chinese lanterns had been tied: white papery spheres, waiting to be lit, they hung like huge fruits.

'Do you like them?' Edmund asked. 'I thought we'd never get them all up.'

'They're beautiful,' Violet said.

'Would you like to light them? Here, look, I have tapers.' He picked up a long thin stick, struck a match in a splutter of flame and a smell of saltpetre and lit the end of it, which glowed a soft orange. He handed it to her and steadied her as she climbed on to the crooked roots and reached up to guide the flame carefully inside the lantern to the candle within. The flame caught and grew, filling the sphere with light that cast a pool of radiance over their upturned faces and the gnarled and shining roots below, and faded into shadows beyond them.

'I made a wish,' Violet said, smiling, but didn't tell him what it was.

They moved silently between the lanterns, sometimes separating and lighting them simultaneously, sometimes steadying each other on the slippery wood and guiding each other's hands. They went from tree to tree, cedar to elm, as the crowd danced on, oblivious. At the last tree, they stopped and looked back at their handiwork.

'They're like captured fireflies,' Violet said.

'Or little moons caught up in the branches,' Edmund said, and it was true: in the elms, twigs and leaves laced the globes with dark patterns.

'"The silver apples of the moon,"' Violet said dreamily, remembering the ending of the Yeats poem.

'Exactly,' Edmund said. 'Shall we walk?' He gave her his arm. 'I don't think anyone will miss us from the general mêlée.'

They slipped away across the lawn behind the trees. Dew had formed and underfoot the short grass was cool and damp, scattered with the closed eyes of daisies. The sun was now a mere line of gold on the horizon, a last gash in the twilit sky. Edmund pointed out the papery disc of a full moon, slowly gaining brightness and substance, 'As if one of our lanterns has escaped and floated away,' he said whimsically.

They came to the walled garden with its deep borders and turned along the walk towards the arbour. Violet was aware of every small thing around her: the shapes of peonies and larkspur; the smell of sweet peas; the faint strains of music; the warm solidity of Edmund's arm under her gloved hand. Every now and then, she felt that he glanced at her but didn't break his silence. They reached the arbour and sat down on the stone seat beneath a wrought-iron arch weighted down with a mass of balsam and roses. In the fading light, the garden had faded to monochrome, the flowers becoming pale, their beauty transformed to form and scent rather than colour.

'You look incredibly lovely tonight,' Edmund said, gazing at her.

Violet, unused to compliments, looked down at the flower pinned at her bosom. 'Thank you for the beautiful corsage,' she said, as if her appearance lay only in the adornment of her dress. She touched the flower self-consciously and he gently took her hand.

Slowly, without letting his gaze slip for a moment from hers, he took each finger of her glove in turn, pulling until he had freed it and could twine his fingers with hers and place warm palm to warm palm. 'Dearest,' he said, 'you must know how I feel about you. I realise that we can't be together straightaway, that I need something more behind me before I can offer you the kind of future you deserve . . .'

Violet looked into his dear eyes, hardly daring to breathe, her heart beating like a ragtime band.

'But only say you'll be mine,' Edmund said softly, bending towards her, 'and anything will be possible, because I shall be the happiest man on earth.'

Violet, moving into Edmund's embrace, closed her eyes and without speaking let her lips say their tender 'Yes'.

When Violet had opened Edmund's letter to say that he was being sent abroad she had felt all her hopes shrink, just as Edmund and the family had grown smaller as the motor had carried her away down the long drive at the end of her stay, receding to a dark dot against the stucco house. She had struggled, not entirely successfully, to compose herself in front of George but as he rode away, she felt panic at the hopelessness that threatened to engulf her.

She remained perfectly still as George rounded the bend. She felt that she should call after him but her throat was closed and tight with misery and she couldn't speak. She tried to get a grip on herself; she must make sure she asked him tomorrow about what he'd wanted to show her; it was thoughtless of her to have disappointed him through being so overcome by her news. The sound of the bicycle wheels clattering over the ruts receded and left only the hot, heavy silence of the summer afternoon. After a few moments, she turned and began to walk away. Instead of returning to the house, however, she veered into the wood and took the path that ran alongside the beck, although she was barely aware of its trickling and gurgling or the smell of greenness and fresh water. She walked slowly amongst the huge Scots pines, sun slanting on their tawny red trunks, the canopy high above her. Shafts of light fell on glossy rhododendron leaves and the white trumpets of yellow-stamened flowers, their petals with a bruised look this late in the summer, as if thinned by heavy rain, and the vivid green moss growing thick and soft as carpet on the trunks and branches of coppiced trees.

Thank God I have an hour or so before Mother will miss me, she thought. Her mother knew nothing of all this. Violet had kept her own counsel about meeting Edmund, afraid that her mother would not react well to the news. Even though Edmund had understood that they would have to make a home for Mother with them, Violet knew that Mother would fret dreadfully at the prospect of 'losing' her to a marriage and she didn't want to burden her with worry any sooner than was necessary. So she had said nothing of the talks she and Edmund had shared on country picnics, at the park, at the garden party. She had been non-committal when answering her mother's questions about the people she'd met during her stay. Instead, she had offered descriptions of the garden, the decor and the food in minute detail, to satisfy her mother's curiosity and take her to a place, any place, other than the house that her mother now hardly ever left.

In secret, she thought about the feel of Edmund's hand in the small of her back as they danced, or the way his moustache tickled when they kissed. Such things were private – no, *sacred* moments which could not, in any case, be unwrapped in the stuffy sickroom among her mother's bottles and potions. The very air, heavy with the knowledge of her father's neglect, would dull and tarnish them.

She and Edmund had stored up every minute that they could snatch together, knowing that there would be time apart to follow, as Edmund would be sent away to an officers' training camp. They had planned that once Edmund had finished the first leg, he would apply for leave and they would find some way to meet.

It's so unfair! she thought. Now he would have to go abroad and even if the whole conflict were short-lived, as people said it would be, it would be months before he was in barracks at Carlisle again. She tried to stifle these selfish thoughts, and think instead of troubled Belgium, threatened France, honour and the King. Over the past few months, the whole country had been speculating on German expansionist policies and the likelihood of war; it should be no surprise that now it was here it was going to affect everyone's life, even hers.

War. The word reverberated through her mind as if it were a cold gust shaking the little wood and rattling like a dry shiver through its leaves.

What if he were hurt? It had not been until she had fallen so headily in love that she had realised that it was possible to feel the same tenderness and care towards the body of another that she felt towards her own. She thought of the way the outdoor summer life had browned his forearms and tanned a V at his throat; of how she imagined the rest of his skin, pale beneath his clothes; and of the vulnerability of the body that she loved. She squeezed the letter even harder in her hand and quickened her step. She would go to the little church at the lakeside where she could be private and alone.

She reached the edge of the wood, swung open the iron gate and stepped out into the brightness. The beck ran on through the parkland, rushing and gurgling beside the path, on its way down to the wide sheet of water. Before her was an open view over the fields to the lake and hills, interrupted only by a scattering of sessile oaks and a lonely church that stood encircled by a dry-stone wall, a quiet grey against the surrounding green.

She walked towards the church. Despite the heat of the day, a stiff breeze blew from the lake, carrying the sound of sheep bleating from further fields and of the water lapping fast against the shore. She felt exposed as she walked across the empty parkland, aware of the house in the distance, angled to take in this vista. She imagined her mother at the window watching her solitary progress and wondering where she was going with her camera slung across her shoulder, when she had taken photographs a-plenty of this view in every season. She hurried across the field to the church and let herself into the churchyard. Tall blond grasses and thin purple thistles grew among gravestones with their memorial verses obliterated by the scourings of the weather.

She went into the church and pushed the heavy wooden door shut behind her. Despite the fact that the leaded window was clear rather than stained glass, it took a moment for her eyes to become accustomed to the dimness. Ahead of her, the sandstone font, at which she and generations of Walters before her had been christened, sat squat and solid. Above the arch opposite the door, a wooden plaque, muddied dark brown with age, bore the images of a lion and a unicorn facing each other in regal poses. The painted banner above them read 'Dieu et mon Droit'.

She sat down in a pew at the back, so that the light from the window would fall over her shoulder, and slowly unfolded Edmund's letter again. It had been softened by the moistness of her hand. She spread it out on the dark material of her skirt and read once more:

My dearest Violet,

I am so sorry, my love, to have to tell you that I have received my orders. We are to be dispatched today for further training in mapping and signalling then on to a different camp to meet up with our draft of men, and to embark for active service. My dear, I know that this is a setback to our plans, but believe me it is only that and I hope and trust that I'll be back soon and we will be able to be together at last. Before we met, I was never done badgering my uncle to get me a commission so that I would be ready, if called upon, to serve, so I must remember now that it's an honour to fight for my country, put aside my own desires and do my best to step up to the mark and make my family proud.

You must not <u>worry</u>. I am fit and well thanks to the Officer Training Corps and the boxing (not to mention all that tennis we played!). Although one shouldn't swank, I've been told at rifle practice that I'm something of a crack shot too. Sam Huggins and Lofty are in the same battalion so I shall be in the best company and we will give Old Fritz something to think about.

I wish that I could have come to you to say goodbye in person – it has all been so fast. I'm writing this in a corner of the mess, which, despite the clatter of plates and knives and forks, is the least chaotic place in camp. I wonder where you are at this moment. I always somehow imagine you in a garden. Perhaps it's because of my memory of how I came

upon you once at home, with the honeysuckle spilling over
the pergola and your head bent over your book and the sun
painting copper lights in your hair.

In my mind's eye, I see you reading in a garden. Your
long, slender fingers reach to turn the page and I bend
towards you and cover your hand with my own. How I wish
that I could pluck a flower to mark your place, take your
hand in mine and lead you away. <u>I must not do this.</u> <u>It is</u>
<u>hard enough already</u>.

I have your letters, which I will keep by me at all times so
that I can always hear your sweet voice in my head. I will
write again as soon as I can and let you know how to
address your letters so that they will find me. Please do write
as often as you can. You know that you have my heart in
your safekeeping.

Ever yours,
Edmund

Violet put her forearm down on the ledge of the pew,
amongst the hymn books, and rested her forehead on it,
breathing in the musty smell of old, damp paper. 'Please, keep
him safe; I'll do anything; I'll be a better person,' she prayed.
'I won't be irritable with Mother when she asks me to read the
interminable household articles in her women's paper, nor leave
the planning of dinner so often to Mrs Burbidge. I won't pester
Mother to let me visit Elizabeth, or long for company, or feel
sorry for myself, stuck here, where there is no one younger
than forty. Only let Edmund be all right and I'll be a model
daughter and a better housekeeper and I won't even be angry
at Father any more for going away and leaving us here . . .'

In tears all over again, Violet stopped praying as the old hurt
overcame her. The hollow, empty feeling that thoughts of her

father brought on began to bear down on her, black as the darkness under her eyelids where her face pressed into the crook of her arm. Why did he not write? Why did he never come home? He hadn't been near the place since before she went away to finishing school and then he had been cold to her mother and horribly formal with her, as if she had done something terribly wrong. The litany of questions ran through her mind as it always did. If he had loved her even a little, he would have visited her at school. No, it was not merely his estrangement from her mother that kept him away; it was something about her. It was somehow her fault.

If only Edmund could be here. His smiles, his small kindnesses and consideration somehow made her real, as though she was only brought into being when someone looked, really *looked* at her: as if his attention were an artist's pencil sketching her lightly on a page. She thought of him holding her and how nothing else beyond them had existed, the hurt all blotted out, his eyes on her face conjuring her from drawing to sculpture, willing her into three dimensions so that she was solid and firm and glowing like bronze under the spotlight of his gaze while, all around them, everything that was other just fell away.

She sat up and stared again at the letter. How could she stand it? How was she to bear it? Soon she would have to go back to the house. She would have to swallow all this down into herself and keep it there, carrying on as though nothing was wrong, exchanging meaningless conversation, arranging the unremitting round of domestic life: the repetitive menus, the cycle of cleaning and gardening and maintaining the grounds, forever preparing for the visit from Father that never came, moving through days whose friction was slowly, inexorably, rubbing her out.

4

MEASURING UP

George was woken by the noise of a milk-cart in the street outside. The milkman's whistled rendition of 'Hearts of Oak' went through his head like the shriek of an engine with a full head of steam. He lay very still, gritting his teeth until the clink of bottles into crates was over and the clop of hooves on cobbles faded into the distance. He found that he was lying on top of a bed rather than in it and was still in his clothes, although his jacket and his boots had been removed. Gingerly, trying not to groan at the tenderness of his rib cage, he rolled over to face into the room and found Turland, sprawled asleep in an armchair with a pillow under his head and a washed-out green quilt over him, from which his legs protruded, showing a large hole in the heel of one of his grey socks.

Recognising Turland, everything about the night before came back to him in one huge wave of misery. How was he to explain that he had lost his wages and had no board money to give to his mother? He knew how much they needed every penny and that it was all accounted for as soon as it came into the house. He remembered the lessons at chapel on 'the demon drink', and how his mother had always said in her milder way that it 'led to errors of judgement'. As a child, he had thought of God's Judgement and wondered how God could possibly make a mistake. Now, as though he could hear his mother's voice in his head, the true implication of human frailty sank in and he recognised his own weakness. He was angry and disgusted with himself.

There was nowhere in his thoughts that he could turn for any comfort. If he thought of Violet, her gentle eyes, her quiet manner, her lovely smile, it was as though a picture of the girl from the pub stood between them. The memory of the girl's piggy eyes with their fair lashes and the feel of her pudgy, soft hands made him feel grubby, as though to think of Violet as existing in the same universe was to besmirch her. He had sunk *low*. He had let himself down and behaved like an absolute beast. He thought of Kitty scolding him over some minor foolishness in the past and the way that she would eventually shake her head and say, 'You are a *lost cause*, George Farrell!' and he would know he was forgiven. He had always been able to tell Kitty everything yet the thought of this made him wonder how he could look her in the face again.

There was a tap at the door and Rooke opened it a little way and put his head round it. 'Breakfast's started,' he said.

Turland woke, stretched, and scratched his head. 'Righto, I'll be down in a minute.' He glanced over at George and then added, 'Here, Percy, see if you can put your filching skills to use and get something for Farrell, will you?'

Rooke nodded and withdrew.

George said, 'Thanks for giving me the bed – very much appreciated.' He slowly swung his legs down, using their weight to lever himself into a sitting position, and then braced himself by leaning on his hands, pressing his palms down on the edge of the mattress and straightening his arms to release some of the pressure on his bruised ribs.

'No trouble. Everyone was in bed so we smuggled you in without a hitch. The bike's down behind the basement railings.' Turland pulled on his clothes and sat down again to tie up his shoes. 'If you want to use the lav you should be all right while everyone's at breakfast. There's only Mr Anstey on this floor and he always goes fishing on a Saturday so he'll be out by now.' He chucked George a towel and hurried off to breakfast.

George crept along the landing to the bathroom where he splashed his hair and face with water and then stripped, washed and towelled himself down briskly. He rinsed the foul taste from his mouth, dressed and tried to make himself look respectable once more. He rubbed at the grubby knees of his trousers with a dampened corner of the towel and disposed of his soiled handkerchief in the bin marked 'Laundry'.

When he slipped back to the room, Turland and Rooke were standing back to back comparing their height.

'Turland reckons he's five foot five. How much smaller am I?' Rooke asked.

George obliged by putting his hand flat on Rooke's smooth, well-oiled head. He marked where Rooke came up to with the side of his hand against Turland's head. 'Well, you're about half a head shorter.'

Turland said, 'Come on, Percy, you have to make five foot three to get in.'

Rooke pulled himself up to stand even straighter.

'You're still about three inches shorter,' George said uncertainly.

Rooke's shoulders sagged. Turland turned round and gave him a friendly punch on the arm. 'Buck up, Rooke. Everyone knows our lads are desperate for reinforcements. I bet they'll take you on, even at bantamweight.'

Rooke looked pleased and straightened his tie and collar.

Turland turned to George, and eyed his height and broad shoulders. 'How about it, Farrell? Fancy changing your mind and coming along to make up the numbers? They'd snap you up, you know.'

There was a silence. George felt pleased that Turland thought so well of him and that the lads wanted him to come along as one of them. He'd always been outside the gangs at school, just him and Kitty muddling through, never feeling part of a group, never really belonging. Not like this: friends, comrades, brothers in arms. He thought about the extra pay he'd get, a shilling a day, and how it would help him make things right at home. He thought about casting off the self that he saw as grimy, weak, despicable, and replacing it with the aspiration of glory and honour and being a man. It would be like diving into a clear lake and emerging a new person: fitter, stronger. He imagined them all returning together, victorious: bronzed and battle-hardened men. Perhaps he would be able to do something half decent so that he could hold his head high in front of Violet again. His heart beat a little faster and his spirits lifted.

'All right,' he said. 'All right, I will.'

Turland nodded sagely, affecting a gravitas suitable to the occasion.

Rooke said, 'Oh, I nearly forgot,' and brought out from his jacket pocket a square package wrapped in a rather greasy-looking napkin. George opened it to find a round of toast with a thin piece of bacon pressed between the slices.

'Iron rations,' Rooke said. 'Eat up, soldier.'

They met up with Haycock and set off for the castle where recruitment was taking place. As they approached the centre of the town, they could hear the sound of a silver band in the next street. Haycock said, 'Eh up? What's this all about?' and they wandered over to the Botchergate to find out. The street, always busy with shoppers, was thronging with people who had been drawn by the music, a martial tune with a solid drumbeat and a brash melody in a major key. George craned his neck to try to see above the spread of caps and hats but the crowd was four or five deep on the pavement and he was too far back. Rooke disappeared into the press, ducking under a man's arm, and George followed suit, slipping through behind a nursemaid who was trying to manoeuvre a baby carriage.

He reached the others at the front and saw, coming towards them, a military band in navy dress uniform, striped with red ribbon: trumpets and trombones in front, polished to a glaring brightness in the morning sun, a euphonium and the huge bass drum behind. The drummer beat the taut skin with gusto and the sound reverberated as if caught between the high buildings. The rhythm was underwritten by the sound of the marching feet of the soldiers who followed on behind, carrying placards that read: 'Will You Answer the Call? Now Is the Time' and 'Take up the Sword of Justice. Enlist Today!' A wave of cheering from the crowd followed their progress. Behind the soldiers followed a mass of ordinary men in civilian dress, looking a rag-tag group in comparison with the orderly men in khaki. Some were laughing, some waving at friends in the crowd, while others made self-conscious efforts to fall into step with the marching soldiers. Every now and then, a man or two would break from the crush on the pavement and step out to join the procession and the volume of the cheering would rise as if to carry him forward on a swell of sound.

The band drew level with George and the others. A group of young women applauded but the sound mingled with the music, drowned out as the people all around took up the cheer. Turland plucked at George's sleeve. Haycock was watching with a broad grin on his face. Rooke took off his cap, smoothed down his hair and put his cap back on again. 'This is it, then,' Turland mouthed at George over the ear-splitting noise. The band passed and the rows of marching soldiers followed, four abreast. 'Ready?' said Turland.

George pulled at the bottom of his jacket to straighten it. As the volunteers came level with them they all stepped forward. The cheering seemed to George to echo around him. As he came forward out of the shadow of the buildings, he was intensely aware of the heat of the sun on his head and the clear blue of the strip of sky above him. Everything was shining: the glittering instruments; the plate-glass windows of the shops with their fancy goods; the boots and belts of the soldiers they were to follow. They fell into line amongst the men; someone clapped him on the back, others moved to make space for the four of them to march together. They passed on into Lowther Street. The tram wires above them seemed to vibrate with the sound of the band, men raised their hats from the steps of the Royal Temperance Hotel and everywhere people stopped what they were doing to listen to the music. A group of young women, gathered at the upstairs window of a tearoom, leant out and waved and Haycock waved back. One of them took a flower from the vase on the table and tossed it down to him and Haycock caught it.

'Who's that?' George yelled at him over the din.

Haycock shrugged and turned round; walking backwards, he held out his arms to the girl and made a great show of tucking the flower into his buttonhole. He pulled a mock-woebegone face and then turned back to march on.

The band took a sharp left turn in the direction of the main road. A gap in the line of carts and motors opened for them and they joined the road and marched on towards the castle, a queue of traffic quickly forming behind them.

The castle was a huge medieval pile. Built of red sandstone, everything about it was square: the shape of the gatehouse, the lookout towers and the crenellations along the ramparts. The thickness of the walls was such that it almost seemed to have been hewn from solid rock. As they passed beneath the massive archway that led into a wide parade ground, all four young men felt a little over-awed; even Haycock's swagger was less jaunty as he looked about him with curiosity. George thought about the soldiers who had passed through these barracks over centuries, all the feet that had drilled in this enormous, open square and marched out to do battle. He looked up at the corner towers and imagined the sentries posted there, scanning the surrounding countryside for the approach of opposing forces, preparing for a siege and determining to defend the fortress with their very lives. Wasn't it something to be part of this history!

The band stopped playing and began to empty out their instruments. The soldiers directed the men towards the recruiting rooms on the other side of the square and the crowd began to disperse towards them. George nudged Turland to indicate to him the queue of men at an open doorway; in unspoken agreement, they all walked around the perimeter of the courtyard to reach it, suddenly shy of crossing the open space on the diagonal and drawing attention to themselves.

The men in their queue were of varied ages and occupations. Most wore the flat cap of the working man or carried their cap folded. Some had the rough-handed look of the labourer, with worsted jacket and heavy boots, whilst others had stiff collars, neat ties and an air of confidence about them.

The line of men moved along until they entered the hall. George could see that men were being called forward one by one to a row of desks, and old memories of school and the humiliation of being called in front of Mr Bevinson to explain himself returned for a moment, making him feel nervous. He moved back a little in the group so that Haycock would reach the front first.

When George's turn came round, the corporal asked for his full name and occupation, and if he was willing to serve 'for the duration'. He gave his details and said that he was willing. When he was asked his age, he said, 'Eighteen years and three months.'

The corporal looked up sharply and said, 'I'm sorry, I didn't hear that. Did you say nineteen?'

George looked puzzled.

The corporal asked him, 'Do you want to join the war?'

George nodded uncomprehendingly.

'So you need to be able to take up service overseas, should the opportunity arise,' he said patiently.

George vaguely remembered the conversation of the previous night in the taproom. 'Sorry, nineteen and three months,' he said quickly and the man gave him a weak smile, took down his address, asked him for a signature and then told him to stand in another line to one side. As he left the desk, he heard Rooke step up behind him and declare, as confidently as you like, that he was Percy Rooke, an apprentice baker and that he was born in 1895.

Rooke came over, wearing a non-committal expression. George knew that he must be delighted to have passed the first hurdle and marvelled at his ability not to show it. Rooke seemed always able to blend into the background; he carefully avoided attracting attention and his knack of adopting a deadpan expression made him less visible than those with more animated faces.

'Why did you say you were a baker?' George asked wonderingly. Rooke's capacity for duplicity made him a mystery to George.

Rooke tapped the side of his nose. 'Scoffum,' he said. 'If I can get taken on in the cookhouse I'll always have plenty of grub.'

George wished that he had thought of that and wondered whether admitting to being a postman had been a good idea. Perhaps he would be asked to take messages. He didn't quite like the idea of scouting around alone along the front line; he hoped he could stay with all the others.

When they reached the front of the second queue, Haycock again went in before George. He emerged a few minutes later, straightening his jacket, and gave George a broad wink. Before George had time to ask him what had happened, the sergeant, a dapper man with a neat moustache, ushered him in. He closed the door behind him, saying, 'Take your clothes off and step on to the scales, please.' A doctor in a white coat was finishing making some notes on a form. George stripped. It was cold in the room. He placed his clothes in a little pile on top of his boots, as there seemed to be nowhere else to put them, and stood with his hands folded over his private parts. As he stood on the scales, he glanced down at his pale body and saw, to his consternation, that a huge area of dark bruising had come out on his left side. The sergeant raised his eyebrows but said nothing, simply noting his weight, and then quickly taking his height and chest measurements.

The doctor came over to examine him. 'Well-built lad,' he said over his shoulder to the sergeant and then asked the question that George had been dreading. 'How did you get this bruising?'

George didn't know what to say. He could hardly say that he had been set upon and robbed. He felt his cheeks stinging as he thought of his humiliation, how he hadn't even fielded a blow, much less aimed one in return. 'It was an accident, sir,' he blurted out.

The doctor looked at him keenly, clearly recognising a lie.

George heard the sergeant mutter, 'Fighting, more likely. These young men have no self-discipline.'

'Well, I don't know,' the doctor said mildly. 'The recklessness of youth, though a nuisance in peacetime, can have its uses in wartime. Let the army sort him out.' George, still smarting from being misrepresented as a roughneck, murmured a 'Thank you, sir.'

The doctor told George to get dressed and then asked him to read some letters on a white board. George could read all bar the very last row. The doctor wrote something down on his form before asking George to show him his teeth; like a horse, George thought; then, more alarmingly: 'I wonder if they can tell your age from your teeth?' However, the form was duly signed and George was told that he could go. He left, feeling that the strict eye of the sergeant was still on him.

When Rooke and Turland had been through the same process, the four gathered once more.

'I'm in,' Rooke said, rubbing his sides. 'I thought my ribs would bust, I took such a breath when my chest got measured.'

When a few others had joined them, they were taken into a room to swear the oath.

The adjutant who swore them in struck George as very fine. He had a strong physique and an upright bearing and his hair was cut very short and neat. His jacket was tightly fitted, and belt, boots and buttons were all polished to a high gloss. George was acutely conscious of the rip in his jacket pocket and the smear of soil on his rounded collar and longed to get out of his dirty clothes and become a proper soldier.

They stood in a row before the adjutant. He let his hand rest on a large, black Bible and stood to attention. He asked them to raise their right hand and swear to serve their King and country.

The room was very quiet afterwards. The officer let the silence linger to bring home to them the solemnity of the occasion and his eyes fell on each of them in turn, as if weighing up their character. George dared not glance around him but felt that every one of the group must feel as serious as he did. Then the adjutant relaxed his face and wished them luck. He gave them all a shilling and said that this was one day's pay and meant that they were now deemed to be soldiers and subject to the King's regulations. Rooke put his quickly in his pocket, as though afraid someone might realise they'd paid him three times his usual wage and take it away again. George thought that he would like to keep his as a kind of talisman but then remembered that he needed to give it to Mother.

The adjutant told them to come back on Monday morning and not to wait for their mobilisation papers because the paperwork wasn't keeping up with the huge influx of recruits. 'There's a great need for men, and training must commence as soon as possible,' he said. 'We'll be sending the next draft to camp on Monday so report here by eight thirty.'

They were ushered into a further room to be measured for their uniforms. Here, both men and women were working at sewing machines, treadles clattering as they sewed. Rolls of cloth stood on end, some neatly in line, some leaning at angles against the wall like a parade of tipsy soldiers. More bolts of cloth that looked like tent canvas were piled haphazardly together in a heap on the floor. George wished that he hadn't had the thought that they were like soldiers.

One of the men got up from his machine. He had a tape measure draped around his neck. He took each man's name and measurements and wrote them down; then he disappeared into a storeroom and returned with a pile of uniforms in a blue cloth and began to distribute them.

'They're the wrong colour,' Rooke said under his breath.

'What happened to the khaki?' Haycock said with disappointment in his voice.

The machinist said, 'There are too many recruits; we can't get the supplies so we're forced to requisition from the post office.'

'Might as well stay as you are then, Farrell,' Turland said cheerily.

George was relieved to be given trousers and a jacket, bundled together. Turland and Haycock only had trousers. He slipped the jacket on. It was a bit bigger than his post-office uniform and less tight across the back but the arms were a little short. He turned to find Rooke trying his and stifled his own complaint. Rooke was drowned in his jacket: the shoulders stood out well beyond his actual shoulders and the sleeves were inches too long.

The machinist tutted. 'That's the smallest we've got, I'm afraid, lad,' he said to Rooke. 'Get your mother to turn up the sleeves or they'll be getting in your way.' A woman whose needle had broken called him over and he went to attend to her machine.

Haycock said, 'Well, it fits where it touches,' and laughed.

Rooke scowled at him and took it off.

George took off his jacket and refolded it. They stood there, uncertain what to do next. The machinist, who had given the woman a new needle, turned and seemed surprised to see them still there.

'That's all,' he said, looking amused and gesturing to a door at the far end of the room. 'You're free to go.' He made a flapping movement at them with his arms and they trooped out feeling a little foolish.

In the parade ground, men were still queuing to enlist; others carrying bundles of uniform like their own were waiting around watching two horses being unharnessed from a cart and led away. The backboard of the cart was unfastened and its load of boots and shoes, of many different styles and clearly not army issue, was tipped out on to the paved ground. The quartermaster arrived and held each pair up in turn, shouting out the sizes. Men called out, 'Me, sir! Here, sir!' in return and he would toss each pair over, a scrum ensuing as men scrambled to get hold of them. Rooke, who took a small size for which there was no great competition, got a pair of boots fit for a farmer and said that they more than made up for the jacket, even though it was so big it stood still when he turned round. George decided that he would stick with his own boots. The legwork on his rounds had taught him the value of a pair of boots that were well 'broken in' and he had no desire to change.

Whilst the scrum was going on around the pile of boots, Turland waiting patiently and Haycock darting forward every now and then to make a grab, George noticed that a pair of fellows had detached themselves from the recruitment queue and were moving casually along the line to the edge of the square. Something in their manner made George immediately certain that they had changed their minds and sure enough they were making towards the gate. One of the men waiting in the queue spotted them and knocked the arm of his companion.

'Oi!' he shouted. 'Where you off to?'

One of the men glanced back, and then carried on walking, his gaze fixed firmly on the ground.

A ripple of movement ran along the line as men turned in curiosity.

'Enjoyed your march through town but had enough of the glory now, eh?' shouted another man.

A mutter rose from the line. The man who was leading the way to the gate said something in reply that George couldn't hear and he saw him stumble as someone shoved him. He recovered himself and for a moment squared up to his attacker, but then clearly thought better of it and stepped away from the line, beyond easy reach. There were boos and jeers from the crowd and shouts of 'Cowards!' and 'Turncoats!' The two men hurried away without looking back.

George felt his cheeks and neck burning as if he had been one of them. How horrible it would be to have everyone against you in that way. He almost hated the men for drawing down upon themselves the very thing that George dreaded most himself: that someone would see through him and realise that although he had been buoyed up by the glitter and the camaraderie, lurking close to the surface on which he floated was a current of dark, cold fear. Surely he wasn't the only one to feel it. He looked around at the others; Turland was smiling, and Haycock laughing as Rooke hopped around absurdly trying to pull on the second of his new boots. He took a deep breath, thought of the feeling he had experienced as he stepped forward in the street and looked up at the blue sky. The moment passed.

Rooke tied the laces of his old boots together and slung them over his shoulder. They set off companionably towards the gate. Haycock said goodbye. He said he was going to drop in at the gas works to let them know not to expect him next week and then go on to visit a few friends and say cheero.

George walked back with the others to retrieve his bike from behind the basement railings. He didn't relish the prospect of breaking the news of his enlistment to his family or the Ashwells. Nonetheless, now that he had overcome what he told himself was a fit of the 'collywobbles', he felt again the excitement of the great change that was to come. As he shook hands, first with Turland, who wished him a safe journey, and then Rooke, whom he joshed about his luck in squeaking into the army at all, he felt a little rebellious pride begin to grow, that he had instigated this and was being his own man. As he set off back towards the main road out of the town, the strains of the silver band reached him faintly once more and he found himself pedalling to the rhythm of imagined marching feet.

5

FRIAR'S CRAG

Feeling hot and dusty, George came through the gate into the yard, squeezed past the privy and the shed and propped his bike against the coal bunker. He took his new uniform out of the basket and tucked it under his arm. Lillie was sitting on the back step, surrounded by cooking pans. She was singing to herself and pouring water from one pan to another, using a broken-handled cup.

'Hello, our Lillie,' George said and squatted down opposite her. 'What have we here? Is it a tea party?'

Lillie offered him the cup and he started to drink from it.

'No, no,' Lillie said crossly. 'P'tend!'

George pretended to take a sip and said mmm. He was rewarded by a pat and a smile. Lillie's 'Fums Up' doll lay on the ground with its painted lick of baby hair and rosy cheeks, looking up with a cheeky expression from the dandelions growing in the cracks in the brick path. George picked her up, put the cup between her hinged arms so that she held it and swivelled them up as if she were drinking. Lillie started to laugh. His mother's voice came from inside saying, 'What's tickled you, Lillikins?'

George put his finger to his lips and passed the doll and the cup to Lillie. 'There you are,' he said. 'You feed Baby.'

He stepped round her and went into the scullery. His mother was in the kitchen beyond, standing at the table with her back to him, buttering the end of a loaf of bread. Her frowsy hair was pulled back into a plait; it hung down her back rather than being pinned in a coil in her usual manner. George noticed the dull grey hairs that were curlier than the brown and had escaped to form a soft edge to the silhouette of her head against the light from the window. Her apron strings were coming undone and the bars of her shoes were unbuttoned as if she'd slipped them on in haste. Such was George's scrutiny as he hesitated to speak that, as if she had sensed it, she made a small sound of irritation and paused to slap at the back of her neck as though she felt a midge bite.

George steeled himself. 'I'm back,' he said.

His mother wheeled round. 'Where have you been?' Her face looked pinched; the two worry lines between her eyebrows that he knew so well were drawn tight. 'You stayed out all night!'

George, unable to tell the truth without eliciting further questions that he didn't want to answer, simply said, 'I've joined up.' He walked into the room and put his folded uniform down on the table.

'Mind! Crumbs,' she said automatically, moving it further over, away from the breadcrumbs and smudges of butter on the oilcloth. 'What do you mean? Whatever did you want to do that for?'

'I . . . I lost my wages. It was careless of me; I must have put them in my trouser pocket so they fell out when I was riding the bike. I know you always tell me to put them in my breast pocket. I'm sorry.'

'Well, that was foolish, but never mind that, George. What do you mean you've joined up? Not enlisted?' She looked again at the folded clothes on the table; then she reached out and touched the cloth as though trying to believe that it was real.

George said nothing.

'It's not right,' she said. 'We've taught you that since a baby.' She looked him in the eye. 'You know better than to get involved. Think how your father will feel about it; it's not Christian!'

George shifted uncomfortably. 'Well, I've done it,' he said. 'I've signed the papers.' He reached into his pocket to look for the shilling.

'But it's dangerous!' A plaintive note came into his mother's voice. 'Surely you're too young . . . They won't send you overseas, will they? How long have you signed up for?'

'The duration.'

She sat down at the table and pushed away the breadboard, which chinked the butter dish and the muddle of plates together. 'That's good, better than signing up for years, that's not so bad . . . it'll be training,' she said as if to herself. 'It'll all be over soon – before you're old enough to go. Well, that's something . . .' She rested her forehead on her hand, her action belying her words of self-comfort. She looked as though she was about to cry.

George said, 'Oh, don't, Mother, please don't.' He touched her shoulder but she wouldn't look at him. 'I'm very sorry about the money.' He produced the shilling, saying, 'Here, I know we'll still be short but I'll get this every day so we'll soon catch up again.'

He held it out to her but his mother just shook her head and looked away from him.

George was unsure what to do; he wished that his father were at home. Even if it meant facing his disappointment, it would be worth it to have him know what best to say to Mother.

'Well, I suppose you must just look after it for me until I come back then.' He put the shilling down on the table beside her elbow. He kissed the top of her head, picked up his uniform and went slowly upstairs.

It was stuffy in the bedroom with its sloping ceiling under the eaves. George changed out of his postman's uniform and put on a clean shirt and trousers. The uniform would have to go back to Mr Ashwell but he didn't feel that he could ask his mother to sew up the ripped pocket and he knew he would make a mess of it if he tried to do it himself. He put it on a clothes hanger, opened the window and hung it from the sash to air. He wished he had asked Mother for some of that bread.

Ted's bed was unmade and still had the dent in the pillow where he had slept. George lay down on the smooth coverlet of his own bed, his head propped against the wooden headboard that his father had made for him when he was a child. He had been so proud to have this crude piece of carpentry from his father that he had scratched his initials in the corner. The marks were there still, though dulled by age and polish. It felt strange to look around the little room that was still so full of his childhood and know that he would be leaving it in just two days. All his things had been handed down to Ted so the shelves still held his old games: Ludo, Railway Race and Magnetic Fishing; his eye wandered over the boxes, their cardboard lids softened and dog-eared with use. Piles of *Boys'*

Best Story Papers and *Funnybone* comics, which he had reread time and time again, were stuffed higgledy-piggledy between a book on scouting and a pair of shin pads. George thought that he hadn't taken Ted to play cricket for a long time and felt a pang of regret.

On top of the boxes was Ted's newest acquisition, a 'panorama' of Captain Scott's expedition. The little theatre had a scarlet proscenium arch decorated with gold acanthus leaves and inside was a snowy scene with tiny stand-up figures. In the foreground, Scott himself shouldered an ice pick while behind him fluttered the English flag, and men, horses and dog sleighs crossed the snow between the spread of tents and the mountains. He thought of the boldness of the expedition, how courageous it was to brave those unknown wastes. He thought of the aching cold, the labour of moving all the equipment and making camp, the fear of breaking ice. How arduous the enterprise and how glorious the attempt! He felt a shiver go through him at the romance of it all. Soon he would be starting out on an expedition of his own that was equally serious in intent, and which would demand just such manly qualities. He got up, retrieved his sketchbook from his jacket pocket and tucked it under his pillow. He closed his eyes and let all the strain, and the events of the last two days, drift into the background. He daydreamt of the time when he would return from the war. He would visit Violet, upright in his uniform, perhaps with stripes on his sleeve, and with his own tales to tell of distant countries . . .

Ted shook him by the shoulder to wake him to tell him that tea was ready. He groaned as the movement made his tender ribs ache. He could hear the clatter of plates and his mother's voice telling Lillie to wash her hands at the tap.

'Are you really going for a soldier?' Ted said. 'With a rifle and everything?' He bounced down on the end of the bed.

George groaned again and said, 'Te-ed.' He rubbed his eyes. 'Is Father home?' he asked.

'Not until around ten. I heard him tell Ma at lunchtime that he's going on to choir practice after the meeting with the Elder. Where's the rifle then? Go on, show us it.'

'I haven't got it yet and anyway it wouldn't be safe to have it lying around in a bedroom,' George said in an authoritative tone.

Ted, rather stung by what he saw as George acting 'above himself', said, 'Huh, not much of a soldier then; you haven't even got a proper uniform.'

George shuffled up the bed and slowly lowered each leg to the ground, wincing as he did so. He had stiffened up and his ribs felt as though someone had taken a hammer to them whilst he slept.

'What's the matter with you?' Ted said grumpily. 'When you've gone, I'll be able to use your fishing rod. And your cricket bat,' he added meanly.

George said, 'If I show you, will you promise not to tell?'

Ted nodded.

George pulled up his shirt and Ted said, 'Holy Mother!' – an expletive that he didn't fully understand but knew to be Very Bad.

George pulled his shirt back down again. 'Not a word, now.' He gave Ted a nudge. 'And I don't mind if you use my rod and my bat as long as you catch all three-pounders and only hit sixes.'

At teatime, the atmosphere was strained. Lillie was fractious after having spent too long in the sun, which had made her arms and legs pink. She scrambled up on to her mother's lap and then down again, and wouldn't be comforted. Ted started asking

George more about how he had come to join up but soon realised from George's frowns and his mother's hurt silence that this was not a topic to pursue at the table. Finally, overwrought with tiredness, Lillie took to throwing herself backwards in Mother's arms so that it was all Mother could do to hold on to her, and she decided to put her to bed early.

'She's about done up,' Mother said, standing and hefting Lillie to her shoulder, 'and I know just how she feels.'

George began to stack the tea things on to a tray. His mother turned at the door. 'Oh, I forgot to say, George, Kitty called round while you were sleeping to see if you were all right; she'd been concerned since you didn't drop back to the post office after your round yesterday. I told her you were home safe . . .' She tailed off as though uttering the word 'safe' brought all her fears once more to the surface. Lillie wriggled in her arms and began banging her head rhythmically against Mother's shoulder. 'I told Kitty your news, and I'm sure she'll pass it on,' Mother said, holding Lillie tighter and stroking her hair.

George appreciated his mother's attempt to break the news to Mr A. on his behalf; he hadn't been relishing the prospect of telling him himself. 'How did Kitty seem?' he asked.

'She looked rather stricken, to be honest. It seemed a bit of a shock to her. Well, I expect it was, Arthur having gone so recently and now they'll be another man short.'

George felt a stab of anxiety as another uncomfortable conse-quence spread from his action, a ripple from the stone he had dropped into the calm pool of his own ordinary life.

'You know you must go and see Mr Ashwell anyway, don't you? It's only polite,' his mother said abruptly and, shushing Lillie, carried on upstairs.

*

'Well, it's very inconvenient,' Mr Ashwell said. He stood with his arm resting on the mantelpiece in their best room 'above the shop'. George was seated, along with Mrs Ashwell and Kitty, on the pretty, floral parlour chairs that Mrs Ashwell draped with antimacassars to protect the treasure of her upholstery from Mr Ashwell's hair oil.

'I'm sorry, Mr Ashwell,' George said with downcast eyes.

Mrs Ashwell said in a mild tone, 'I expect your mother and father are very proud of you – making a stand for poor Belgium and supporting the King.' She risked a glance at her husband.

Mr Ashwell snorted. 'It's all very well, everyone gallivanting off, but why on earth couldn't you go about it in the proper manner, like Arthur? You could have applied to the Post Office Rifles. We could have had time to plan!'

Mrs Ashwell opened her mouth to suggest that she make a cup of tea but Mr Ashwell held up the flat of his hand and continued: 'As it is, I'll now have to take the cart to the station as well as all my other responsibilities, and from tomorrow we shall have to put two of the younger boys on to your duties until we can get a replacement, that's if we can get one at all.'

George made a great study of the rug. It was a proper woven one, not like the lumpy rag rugs they had at home but smooth and with a trellis pattern and twining, stylised roses.

The lack of an answer from him seemed to annoy Mr Ashwell even more. 'You realise that your hot-headed decision will mean extra work in the sorting room for Mabel and for Kitty?' he asked.

George shot a quick look at Kitty, who had her hands clasped in her lap and was looking miserable.

Mr Ashwell, feeling that he had scored a winning point, said, 'And what if I'm ever ill? Are we to send Kitty out with the horse and cart? Whatever next?'

Mrs Ashwell felt that her husband had breached the bounds of propriety in speaking in that manner to a guest in their home. Seeing that her husband had worked himself up until his eyes were staring and his face was red, and knowing that these signs meant that she would be treated to a reiteration of these arguments until bedtime and probably beyond, she stood up. 'Kitty,' she said in a louder voice than she had meant, 'perhaps you and George should take the opportunity to have a walk, as the evening is so lovely and George's time with us so short.'

Kitty and George both rose. Mr Ashwell, still watching George with a hawkish expression, picked up his pipe from the mantel and began to tamp tobacco into it. Mrs Ashwell ushered them to the door and George turned back into the room to mutter 'Goodnight, sir', as they left. Mrs Ashwell nodded. 'Give my best to your parents, George.' She glanced back at Mr Ashwell, who had lit his pipe and was now sucking so hard on it that he was working up a fearsome glow in the bowl. She said, 'And we wish you the best of luck in your endeavours,' loud enough for her husband to hear. 'Keep safe,' she said, quietly, as she shut the door softly behind them.

'Where would you like to go?' George asked as they walked out into the balmy air of the warm evening.

Kitty shrugged. 'Down to the lake, I suppose. That's where we always seem to end up.' They walked across the market place, where cabbage leaves and bits of torn paper were strewn from the Saturday traders' carts earlier in the day, and then on past the shops. When they came to Abraham's Photographic Studio, George found himself stopping and peering into the window at the pictures of climbers roped to walls of rock and postcards of lake views, fells and waterfalls. He had seen them all a million times before and yet today his feet had simply refused to pass them. It's because of Violet, he thought, that's why, and he pictured her with her camera over her shoulder, setting off on her walk alone, and felt that his heart would break.

'Are you coming?' Kitty had stopped a few yards further on and was now looking at him impatiently.

George hurried to catch her up. 'Are you angry with me too, Kitty?' he asked. 'Is it because of the work, as your father said?'

Kitty made a tutting sound and gave George a look which seemed to say: 'Don't you understand anything?' They turned down Paraffin Alley past the ironmonger's shop, Kitty striding away from him until they reached Lake Road where she slowed down a little to match her pace to that of the couples and families, tourists and locals strolling down towards the lake and its surrounding circle of quiet hills.

George held out his arm to her but she didn't take it. Instead, she said, 'You didn't come back for tea. We waited, but you didn't come. I thought you'd had an accident or something.'

'Oh, is that all!' George said. 'I'm sorry, by the time I remembered it was too late to get back, I was in Carlisle you see . . .' Too late, he realised that he had meant to keep off that subject.

'What took you to Carlisle, then?' Kitty said.

'Oh, I don't know, I'd heard about other chaps joining up and I thought I'd just go and see. Just find out.'

'It was a bit sudden, wasn't it?' Kitty said, looking at him with that look she had which seemed to go right through you. 'You never said a word about this before.'

George, aware that, apart from matters to do with Violet, there had been barely a decision in his life he hadn't talked over with Kitty first, felt uncomfortable. He put his hands in his pockets and hunched his shoulders. 'It was on an impulse,' he said quickly.

'George,' she said, 'that is *not* like you.'

They had reached the tearooms, which were still open, making the best of the last of the sunshine that brought folk out to stroll or boat or fish. The sound of muted talk came from the tables on the terraces, as if the stillness of the evening and the calmness of the water demanded that voices should be low and soft.

'Would you like to go in?' George asked. 'We could have ices.' The moment he offered he realised that he had, in fact, no money, and the memory of how he had lost his wages came back sharply, causing his stomach to knot up and his mouth to dry.

However, Kitty shook her head and they carried on walking until they came to the lake itself and took their usual path alongside the pebbly shore that would bring them to Friar's Crag. Across the lake, Cat Bells and Maiden Moor were bursting with the green of summer, wide swathes of bracken girdling the fells. They towered above the waters and the reflection of the line of the hills against the sky was beautiful in its unbroken symmetry; the mirror image lent the lake a depth the measure of both earth and heavens. At the landing stages, the last boats of the day were being hired and the splash of oars and the sound of youthful laughter carried over the water in the still evening. George thought of the many times that he and Kitty had taken a boat out to one of the tiny islands that dotted the lake and spent the day building dens, or simply lazing on a rock in the sun and chatting the day away. Now he couldn't even tell her what had happened, never mind how he was feeling.

'Do you remember when I went swimming and got cramp?' he asked. 'You thought I was larking around?'

She gave him a weak smile. 'Well, you usually were.'

'You didn't realise I was really drowning until it was almost too late,' he said.

She looked at him as though she was finding it hard to fathom him out.

They entered the wood of sparse trees: alder and birch. Kitty kept waving away the clouds of midges that hung under the branches and danced around their heads. Usually George would have teased her for her fussiness but he said nothing.

They reached Friar's Crag, a rocky point protruding into the lake like the prow of a ship to give a panoramic view of the expanse of water and its thickly wooded islands. Kitty sat down on a tree stump and looked out. George climbed down a little way until he found a flattish rock and sat down with his knees drawn up and his forearms resting on them to relieve the ache in his ribs. The sun laid a glittering path on the water that one could almost imagine walking and George thought, I'll store this up; I'll keep this like a picture and remember it precisely as it is. He closed his eyes and opened them again, committing to memory every curve of the hills and every tone of the palette: the worn grey rocks, the shades of green, thick upon the islands, the pink undersides of the clouds and the gold on the water.

'George?'

He turned his head to find Kitty regarding him seriously.

'Are you sure about this?'

'What do you mean?'

'Well, fighting. You're not exactly the fighting sort.'

George shrugged and turned away again and Kitty fell silent.

His parents had taught him that the Good Book said you should turn the other cheek and at school he had tried to ignore the teasing and pinching of the nastier set. He had been aware that he was a strong child and that he could beat any lad of his age in a fight but his mother had taught him to be gentle, to try to be fair to his younger brother, and to always keep his fists to himself, even when provoked.

George thought about Charlie Spragg and Silas Norris, the worst boys at school, and about how he and Kitty had come to be friends: the fat girl and the dopey boy teaming up to find safety in numbers and sticking together because no one else wanted them.

Kitty was quicker-witted than he was. She had always had a sharp tongue and could give short shrift when someone shoved her or called her 'lardy'. She saw off her enemies but her tartness and prickly demeanour made others wary of her and left her with no friends. This had made no difference to George. He took everyone as he found them, so when he found himself seated next to the chubby girl with a suspicious expression he simply looked out of the window as usual and waited for her to speak to him. It had taken two whole days but eventually, seeing that Mr Bevinson was making his way round the class to check their sums, she had whispered, 'Look out!' George had only done the first two sums before embarking on a drawing of a galleon in full sail; she had turned his page over and pushed her book towards him so that he could quickly copy her figures down. After that, she started to talk to him, and George didn't mind if she was sharp or impatient when he was slow. At some level, he recognised that their minds just worked in different ways and to different rhythms, that was all.

At the end of that week, Spragg had put dog dirt in George's desk and then waited, sniggering, for Mr Bevinson to discover where the smell was coming from. Mr Bevinson had sworn under his breath and been about to haul George out to the front to give him the stick when Kitty stood up, all red in the face beneath her freckles, and said she'd seen what had happened.

George had been able to put up with a lot after that: the name-calling, Spragg setting him up to take the fall for writing an obscenity on the privy door, even the feet stuck out to trip him in games. He had been able to put up with it all as long as he had Kitty to sit next to in class and to walk home with at the end of the day.

For Kitty, even when she had lost her puppy fat and become merely curvaceous, the taunting continued, simply shifting its focus, picking instead on the fact that, as the postmaster's daughter, she was well turned out and knew some long words. Suddenly she was 'snooty' and 'born with a silver spoon in her gob'.

There had only been one time when George had actually snapped and that had been over Kitty. He'd been thinking about a plan he had for a painting of the Lodore Falls and how the tumbling water looked like ropes and wondering how you could do that in paint and yet still keep the lightness and the shine of water: he had been kept behind for not paying attention in class. By the time he got out, Kitty had had to go on ahead.

He found her sitting on a boulder down by the river. It was the only time he'd ever seen her cry. Spragg had taken her beloved piano music and trodden it into a puddle. When she'd tried to get it back, shouting at them that she needed it and that she didn't have it by heart yet, they had pushed her over and when she stood back up and shouted at them they had thrown stones and Spragg's had cut her lip. George had taken her home and then, filled with a cold white rage that blanked out all rational thought, he had run to the park where he knew the boys hung around after school and waited behind the toilets until Spragg came to take a piss. Then they had fought and something had come over George that he didn't like and that he didn't ever want to happen again. After George laid into him, Spragg stopped trying to hit him and put his forearms up in front of him, which anyone knew meant he was done, but George hadn't been able to stop. He kept pummelling Spragg until his nose bled and he was in a ball on the ground shouting, 'Stop it! Stop, you mad bastard!' George stood over him, panting and trembling. Then he walked away and left him there with his face smeared with blood and snot. Spragg had been away from school for days. Kitty knew nothing about any of it.

He heard Kitty get up and scramble down the rocks. She sat down nearer to him.

'No, really, have you thought about what it'll be like? Arthur says they have to do bayonet practice and stick the thing into sandbags as if it was a person's stomach.' She pulled a face. 'It's so you can do it when it's real. I mean, how will you manage?'

'I'll manage,' George said, though the thought made him feel sick. He felt stung that she thought him a coward.

Kitty said nothing more.

The noise of the pleasure boat setting off to bring the guests back from the town to the Lodore Hotel carried across the lake and soon it came into view, ploughing a frothing wake through the darkening water, bedecked with spots of yellow light from oil lamps that swung and bobbed with the motion of the boat.

Kitty began picking out the small pebbles strewn between the cracks in the rocks and throwing them into the water. 'It's going to be horrible without you,' she said quietly, almost too quietly for him to hear. 'Just me and Mother and Father and no Arthur. I shan't have anyone to talk to.'

He knew that she meant him to confide in her, to share their feelings as they had always done, but what could he do? He couldn't tell her the sorry tale of what had really happened and he couldn't – wouldn't – lie. Not to Kitty.

It was growing colder; Kitty held her elbows and then rubbed at her arms. 'There's something you're not telling me, George,' she said. 'And I wish you would.'

George, panicking at her persistence, said, 'It's really none of your business,' and immediately wished he had bitten his tongue.

He saw Kitty's shoulders stiffen and she raised her chin as she always did when someone hurt her. He braced himself for her sharp riposte but none came. He was left at a loss.

'Come on, you're cold. We'd better be getting back,' he said, trying to soften the harshness of his last words. He stood up slowly and climbed past her back to the path.

She sat on until she had thrown the last of the pebbles and then followed him. As they passed back under the trees, it was difficult to see her face. She made no further attempt at conversation and they walked silently together, the only noise the slap, slap, slap of the water lapping against the pebbles of the shore, the distant result of the steamer's wake.

By the time they'd reached the town and walked back through the darkening streets to the market place, Kitty still hadn't spoken. George began to feel that he had managed very badly and that he was actually very miserable. He tried to put himself in Kitty's place: it would be hard for her, caught in the middle of the stresses and strains between her parents, and lonely with only the younger post boys for company, who were surely a trial to endure, with their cheek and their practical jokes. Now she would have him to worry about as well as Arthur . . .

As they came level with the last street lamp before the post office, he touched her arm and bent round to try to look at her face. 'I'm sorry I'm going away and that you'll be lonely . . .' he started but tailed off when he saw her expression.

Kitty moved her arm away. 'Oh, you have a high opinion of yourself, George Farrell, if you think I'll miss you that much.'

'But you said you would be lonely!' George said. 'You said, just now, on the rocks!'

Kitty took a long quivering breath. 'I shan't be on my own; I have a follower,' she said and began to walk quickly towards home.

George caught her up and stood in front of her, saying, 'Who? Who are you seeing?'

'It isn't anyone you know,' she said shortly. 'In fact – it's really none of your business.'

The words hung between them like a thread stretched too thin.

George swallowed hard. 'Well, shall I write?' he managed to say.

'I expect you'll suit yourself,' Kitty said; then, without even shaking his hand, she walked past him and went inside.

When George got home, everyone had gone to bed. He could hear the murmur of his parents' voices from upstairs. They were talking quietly so that they wouldn't wake Lillie, who slept in a cot at the foot of their bed. When he locked the front door and pulled the bolt across the voices stopped so George deduced that he was the subject of the discussion. He climbed the stairs slowly so that he wouldn't make another sound and give his mother a reason to call out to him or come to say goodnight. He paused at the top of the stairs and overheard his mother tell his father that when he had come home that afternoon she had smelt drink on him. He crept past the door hoping that he could postpone conversation with his father until the morning. He was still feeling jangled and shaken up by the strange exchange with Kitty and unready for a discussion with his father. He slipped into his room and undressed in the faint light that came from the rectangle of the window. His mother had taken the uniform away, he noticed, and he hoped that she would mend it and return it to the post office for him. Ted stirred as George pushed his shoes under the bed where he wouldn't trip over them but then turned away towards the wall and subsided again into sleep. George got into bed and lay still, trying to calm his thoughts. The last he heard was the continuous murmur of his parents' voices as though bees were in the wall behind his head.

6

FEATHERS ON THE STREAM

George's father, Frederick Farrell, was a conscientious man. He worked hard all week at Force Crag, mining ore for the zinc, and he worked hard in his spare time to support his wife, Maggie, in the raising of their family and in the service of God. The work at the mine was dirty and dangerous: the ore lay in veins that were almost vertical within the side of the hill and were worked by a series of cramped tunnels driven straight into the fell side, which were linked inside by shafts and ladder-ways. The ore had to be dislodged with explosives in such a way that the veins were cut away in steps, leaving huge blocks of mineral in place to act as supporting pillars. Frederick, having been a miner all his working life, knew the fragility of human flesh in the face of roof falls, moving hoppers or the jaw crusher:

a piece of mill machinery that began the process of breaking down the ore. His belief was that life was difficult enough with all the illness and injury that comes uninvited, without men taking up arms against each other.

Frederick had stayed awake until the small hours thinking about his eldest boy and how best to approach the matter of his desire to go soldiering. George was a man now and could be stubborn in his views. Frederick had prayed a little and had eventually gone downstairs, lit the gas in the parlour and spread his books on the table, turning to the words of the Church for understanding and guidance. He skimmed through an index, found the page and ran his finger beneath the tiny print:

> The United Methodist Church supports and extends its ministry to those persons who conscientiously oppose war and who therefore refuse to serve in the armed forces. However, the Church also supports and extends its ministry to those persons who conscientiously choose to serve in the armed forces or to accept alternative service. The Church also states that 'as Christians they are aware that neither the way of military action, nor the way of inaction is always righteous before God'.

He sat back, frowning at the passage, which clearly presented the decision as a matter for individual conscience. Surely, he thought, the Bible was adamant on this; what could be clearer than 'Thou shalt not kill'? Although, on the other hand, it was true that there were battles in the Old Testament 'by the word of the Lord'.

He read on, studying one book after another until he had

exhausted both himself and the subject, and then returned to bed with cold feet, feeling that, in all conscience, he could not forbid George to join the army but that he would do his utmost to dissuade him.

He slept fitfully until dawn and was glad when the light began to creep through the gap in the curtains. He dressed by the dim light without waking Maggie and Lillie and went quietly to the boys' room. George was sleeping on his side, and Frederick noticed that he had one hand under his cheek, just as he used to sleep as a child. Look at the length of him! He never ceased to be amazed at the fact that George was a head above him. Maggie put it down to the off-cuts they'd had for free from her father's butcher's shop. Well, it was probably true. There had been little enough meat to be had in his family, to be sure. He touched George on the shoulder and waited for him to wake.

George scratched his head and squinted up at him. 'What is it?' he asked, his voice thick and croaky.

'Do you want to go fishing?' Frederick whispered.

George sat up, surprised that his father should suggest fishing on a Sunday, which was usually kept for church, rest and reading scripture. He glanced towards Ted but Frederick shook his head and pointed first to himself and then to George to indicate that it should be just the two of them this time. He went downstairs to the kitchen, leaving George to get up and gather his fishing rod and reel.

Frederick opened a tin of corned mutton and made sandwiches. He wrapped them in paper and packed them into his knapsack amongst a jumble of spare reels, scraps of line and tins of fishing flies. When George came down, Frederick picked up the rod and landing net that he had propped by the door and they slipped out into the back yard.

Dew still lay on the path and on the straggle of onion leaves and ferny carrot tops in the vegetable bed. It glittered on the webs that stretched from plant to plant making the invisible work of a thousand spinnerets suddenly appear in plain sight. Frederick took a deep breath of the cool damp air. It gave him the same pleasure that he found every evening when he came up from the mine and filled his lungs with air so clean it made him heady. He would walk down through the ramshackle scatter of rusty-roofed mill buildings, leaving behind him the slopes of dusty scree that surrounded the mine, and rest his eyes on the greenness: the comely form of the fells and the long straight valley of Coledale.

'It's a beautiful morning,' he said. 'Makes you feel like the First Man, getting up this early.' He turned to look at George with a smile. George nodded but without conviction. Frederick thought that he looked worried sick and his heart went out to the boy. He was hopeful that, with careful handling, he would be able to make him see sense.

They walked down to Blencathra Street and past the curtained houses shuttered in sleep, the Sunday quiet punctuated only by the noise of the sparrows and the sweet fluting call of blackbirds from gardens and yards. George glanced surreptitiously at his father. Why was he not saying anything? The look of sympathy in his eyes as they had left the house was far worse than if he had been angry. The great weight of his decision to enlist hung between them as if they were carrying a heavy trunk with each of them waiting for the other to suggest they lay it down and unpack it.

They emerged on to the road that ran parallel to the river, on the other side of which were the green lawns of the park. 'Once everyone's up and about, it'll be noisy near the park,' Frederick said.

'Shall we go upstream a bit?' George said.

'Up by the bridge then.' They walked on, accompanied by the busy noise of water over stones, past the wide shallows where the ducks stood, still with their heads under their wings, the slight breeze lifting and parting their feathers. They crossed the bridge and Frederick led the way down the steep incline at the side, grasping on to the shrubby growth to avoid slipping on the sandy soil. At the bottom, they reached the flat pebbly shore that was one of their favourite fishing spots. From this point, it was possible to stand with a firm footing or even cross to the glacial rocks that littered the shallows, and cast a line out into the deeper water. The far bank cut away steeply and trees overhung the water, casting a deep shade beloved by brown trout.

'Water's down a bit,' Frederick said quietly, seeing the tangle of roots that was exposed above the waterline. He sat down on a boulder and opened the knapsack. 'Shall we have some breakfast before we start?' He passed George the packet of sandwiches. Frederick, who had wanted George to broach the subject, decided that he needed a little help after all.

'Your mother tells me that you're considering a big decision,' he said tentatively.

George chewed on his bread while he thought what to say. 'I have decided,' he said, at length. 'I know that you'll say I'm wrong and it's against Bible teaching to take up arms but I think it's right and I'm going to do my bit.'

'I think you'd be ill advised to go on with it,' Frederick said mildly. 'You know, I've always taught you and Ted to be peace-loving and to treat others as you'd wish to be treated yourself. It's a philosophy I've always found to stand me in good stead.'

George snorted. 'I don't believe the Germans are following the Golden Rule,' he said with spirit. 'They even have a book, you know, called *World Dominion or Decline*. We can't just stand by and let them get away with it; besides, everyone says they're doing awful things in Belgium.'

Frederick pondered on the fervour of his son's response. Whatever Maggie had assumed about George joining up merely to go to training camp, Frederick felt sure that George was considering active service overseas. His own heart ached with worry. 'That's exactly my point,' he said. 'I don't think you have any idea what you'd be getting into, what it'll be like, the brutality and butchery of war . . .'

George seemed not to be listening. 'We can't let them have it all their own way.'

'It's not a game, George!' Frederick said, more sharply than he'd meant to. He took a deep breath to muster up the calm resolve he had gained through prayer in the long hours of the night. 'There's a reason why the Bible warns that "those who live by the sword, die by the sword", and it goes beyond a warning of the bodily risks.' He leant forward and looked George straight in the eye. 'It's not a small thing at stake; it's your immortal soul! What kind of father would I be if I didn't steer you from that path?'

George dropped his eyes. 'It's too late. I signed the papers.'

Frederick nodded slowly, taking this in. 'But you'll not go overseas. They haven't signed you up for that, at least? Your mother's terribly worried – understandably so.'

'I can't see any point doing it if you're not going to fight, and I told them I would.'

Frederick, seeing the stubborn jut of George's jaw, grew frustrated. 'George! We're talking about taking up arms against your brother, your fellow man . . . decisions like this can't be taken all hot-headed in the heat of the moment and certainly not in the sway of strong drink!'

George looked up quickly.

'Your mother smelt it on you when you came in, but that's by the by. Look, I'm asking you, please, to reconsider. I'm not blaming you: we all do foolish things when we're young; but you have no experience to draw on, no knowledge of injury or death. You have no idea . . .' He stopped, overcome by the ferocity of his desire to protect his son, and fought to control his emotion. 'You needn't decide now. Just say that you'll give it some more thought. Eh? To please me.'

George felt alarmed to see his father close to tears, as if the rock on which he was sitting, so deeply embedded in the soil, were suddenly about to shift and slide away from him. He nodded.

His father patted him on the shoulder, saying, 'That's the spirit. We needn't talk of it again for now. Let's do some fishing, shall we?' He took the rods and landing net and led the way a little downstream to where he had seen the brief disturbance of the water: the bubble and ripple that showed there were fish rising. Putting the net down on the stones, he said, 'We'll leave this here between us just in case either of us needs it!' He handed George his rod and walked back a little way upstream leaving George in the spot where he had seen the fish jump.

Frederick used the rocks scattered in the water as stepping stones to reach a large flat stone a third of the way out into the stream. The water gurgled and frothed around the obstacle and the rushing sound of the river filled his ears. He balanced his stance, braced his knees and cast his fly into the quieter water where it would be carried slowly downstream. He watched as George cast short at first; then reeled in and got his line in a tangle. He fought off the reflex urge to go and help him. He turned his attention to following the fly, half closing his eyes against the glitter on the foreground water; the sun was well up now and he could feel its warmth on his back. He tried to relax a little into the peaceful scene, his usual respite from the dark and dirt and ugliness of his weekday life, but the gifts of clear water and clean air weren't enough to quieten his sense of foreboding, the worry that sat like a block inside him. He thought that perhaps he had not been eloquent enough and that he should have spoken to the Elder and sought counsel and strength.

Suddenly, his line jerked, loosened and then pulled again. 'George! Fish on the line!' he shouted. George began to wind in his own line furiously whilst walking backwards towards the spot where the landing net lay. Frederick let the fish go for a little spell, then reeled in, then let it run again. It felt as though it was a good size. George laid down his rod, grabbed up the landing net and came galumphing over, slipping from stone to stone in his haste to get to the scene of action and ending up stepping right into the water up to the ankles. The fish began to tire; its runs were shorter and feebler. Frederick stopped playing out the line and the end of the rod bent down as he held the fish steady and then began to draw it in. George scrambled over the last few rocks and reached his side with the net at the ready.

'Is it a good one?' he said.

'It's lunch for all of us, I think,' his father said, the reel making a ratcheting sound as he wound it steadily in. They got their first view of the fish: a glint in the yellow brown water, then a flapping, flipping, silver shape as it was drawn out of the shallows and up above the rock. Falling into the familiar sequence of movements that they knew from long practice as fishing partners, George caught the fish neatly in the net and Frederick propped his rod against his shoulder and leant over to detach the fly from its jaw. Both heads bent together as he retrieved the barbed hook and vivid blue and yellow feather strands; then George took the rod while his father killed the fish with a sharp tap on the surface of the stone slab.

'It's a whopper,' George said with delight.

Frederick looked at George's broad smile, the very same that had won his heart from infancy, and felt his love for his son well up. 'You landed that very well, George, he's a big one all right. Now let's see you beat it.'

As they walked home, George felt overwhelmed by the enormity of his decision. How could he know whether he or his father was taking the righteous path? He tried to put aside his desire to escape from the events of the last few days and all their complications, but could not. It was too late to go back on it all now and too uncomfortable; he wanted to get right away. He needed to make a new start, make something of himself.

It was a just cause, he told himself, and there was no question in his mind that they would send the Deutschers packing. It might take months, now that no quick victory had been possible at Mons, but the BEF would prevail, everybody said so, and he would be back in a few months with just the experience that his father had talked about under his belt. His father had Mother and the children to think about, whereas he was a free agent, that was why their decisions were different. His mind was made up.

As they reached the back gate, Frederick paused with his hand on the latch and turned to look at George enquiringly. George's bullish expression told him all he needed to know.

'I want to do something to be proud of,' George said, wishing that he could go with his father's blessing. Instead, he saw how his father's face fell and how he struggled to recover himself.

'I was already proud of you, son,' Frederick said and turned away.

The rest of the day passed in its usual Sunday pattern, yet for George it seemed different, as if a bright light had been turned on to a picture that you usually passed with barely a glance. The knowledge that he was to leave home tomorrow seemed to heighten his awareness of all around him, as if he was unconsciously trying to commit everything to memory in the same way that he had tried to memorise the scene at the lakeside the night before. At chapel, he looked with a strange new fondness at the familiar faces of the congregation and the light from the high windows falling on to whitewashed walls and plain wooden lectern.

George had expected to see Kitty and hoped to make amends for upsetting her but she wasn't with her parents. He sought out Mrs Ashwell, who told him that unfortunately Kitty had been forced to stay at home with a headache. Mrs Ashwell's manner was formal and so different from her farewell to him the day before that George wondered if she was angry with him too. Perhaps she had witnessed Kitty coming in feeling upset. He didn't know how to respond and mumbled something about passing on his best wishes; then he excused himself and returned to sit with his mother. Father had asked him not to speak to anyone in the congregation about his departure the next morning to save his mother answering questions that she would find distressing. George took her gloved hand and gave it a squeeze.

After chapel they dined royally on the fish, and then George helped Ted with his homework and played 'bear hunt' with Lillie, who squealed with delight when he roared until she crawled under the table and hid. His mother reproached him, saying that he was getting Lillie over-excited and that she'd never get her off to sleep, but Father looked sad and said, 'Let them be a while longer.' Eventually George caught her, gave her a smacker of a kiss on both cheeks and handed her over to Mother for bath and bed. Later in the evening, instead of Bible study, they all played dominos. Father read a Charlie Chaplin story from *The Pluck Library* and they all laughed too long and too loudly at the jokes. Ted started yawning so Father suggested that they all turn in, as George would be up and away early in the morning to catch the milk train, and they all said goodnight with faces suddenly become serious.

In the bedroom, George's uniform was hanging on the back of the door together with a clean shirt that his mother had pressed and his father's knapsack, now filled not with the paraphernalia of fishing but with underclothes, comb, soap and towel and a photograph of the family. The photograph was one taken before Lillie was born, when he and Ted were several years younger. George looked at their grumpy expressions and remembered that their faces had been scrubbed until they tingled. George added pencils and writing paper, his smallest sketchbook and a few tubes of paint wrapped up in a cloth. He thought about taking some books but decided they were too heavy. As he was falling asleep, Ted asked him if he would lend him his best flies as well as his rod and George said yes.

George got up while it was still dark. Downstairs he found his mother cooking sausages and eggs for breakfast and Lillie, who had been fractious all night because of the sunburn, was hanging on to her skirts and grizzling.

'You need something that'll stick to your ribs when you're going on a journey,' his mother said, putting a plate down in front of him and plonking Lillie on his lap where she moaned and wriggled. George tucked her into the crook of one arm and told her that if she were very good and still he would make something for her. He took out his clean handkerchief and started to roll and knot it until it bore a passing resemblance to a sausage with two floppy ears. 'It's a rabbit,' he said.

In the corner by the stove stood his boots, stuffed with newspaper to make sure they dried out properly. Unable to settle down to eat, his mother picked them up, got the polish out and began to black them.

'Thank you for doing my uniform.' George began making the rabbit peep out at Lillie from behind his teacup while shovelling in his food with the other hand.

'Well, if you have to go, you're going to go well turned out,' she said, looking down and brushing the toe of a boot with unnecessary vigour.

'I've packed writing paper,' he said.

She nodded and said, 'Let me know you've arrived safely, won't you?'

Frederick came down in his work clothes, sat down in silence and started on his breakfast. He gave George some money. 'For the train and miscellaneous expenses,' he said gruffly.

Mention of the train made George feel nervous and he checked the clock. Father mopped up the fat on his plate with some bread and then said that he needed to water the vegetable bed and would be outside when George was ready.

His mother hefted Lillie from his lap on to her hip and handed him the boots, which were now gleaming, and he put them on and laced them up. He stood up and put his arms around them both and she pressed her face against his shoulder.

'Take every care,' she said. 'And always remember that I love you.'

George bent and kissed her on the cheek. He picked up the

knapsack, saying, 'I'll be back before you know it,' and did his best to produce a smile as she walked with him to the door. Lillie, picking up that something unusual was afoot, began to grizzle again and to reach out her arms to George. He gave her the rabbit, saying, 'For you to look after while I'm away,' quickly kissed her on the top of the head and turned away.

He followed his father down the paved path. At the gate, he turned for a last glance at his mother standing on the top step, and Lillie clutching the rabbit and staring after him. He raised a hand to wave but dropped it again because he could not bear to see Lillie waving back.

They let themselves out of the back gate and into the shadowy alley between the rows of terraced houses, and then walked at a smart pace through the quiet streets, down to Station Road. George felt queasy now with nerves and wished he'd not eaten such a hearty breakfast. As they reached the station approach his father said, 'You know how I feel about this, George, so I'll not say any more about it, but there are two things I will ask you to promise me and they both relate to your mother.' He looked keenly at his son.

George nodded to show that he was listening.

'We both recognise that drink had a part to play in all this. Now, whether you feel that it clouded your initial judgement or not, I'd like you to swear to me that you won't touch it again. No need to sign a pledge, just let your word be your bond.'

George, thinking of all the trouble drinking had led him into, though not of the type meant by his father, agreed readily enough.

'The other thing is to keep to yourself the fact that you're intending to go overseas, for as long as possible. There's no point worrying your mother any earlier than necessary.'

George coloured up. This was, in fact, something that he had already thought about but he was embarrassed to have been found out in a deceit. He mumbled something about upsetting anyone being the last thing he wanted to do.

The train was already in and the last churns were being loaded on to the rear wagons. The sky had begun to lighten in the east and George noticed, with a strange, heightened clarity, how the light caught the metal in flashes of silver as the men rolled the churns up the wooden ramp, and heard each deep rumble and creak of the planks as the heavy weight passed over them. The gas lamps on the platform waned to a tawdry yellow as the day crept in, the low sun glinting on the polished rails that stretched away into the distance.

The last churn was loaded; the guard secured the bolts and blew a piercing blast on a silver whistle. George embraced his father awkwardly and then got into a carriage and opened the window.

'Write soon and let your mother know that you're eating properly and are well,' Frederick said in a gruff voice. The train began to pull away and he walked alongside and called out over the noise of the engine, 'We'll be thinking of you. Take every care!'

As it got up steam and drew ahead, George leant out of the window and called out, 'Goodbye,' but his voice was lost in the rush of noise.

George watched his father walk to the end of the platform and stop. His last view was of him raising his hand, his shadow long in the low light, then figure and shadow diminishing, the station with its bright awning and flowerbeds shrinking to a blur of colour.

Frederick watched until the train rounded the bend. When its plume of steam was also out of sight, he stood on a little longer, listening as the engine noise died away and the call of birds seemed only to deepen the silence.

7

BLUE ENVELOPE

Violet timed her walk on Monday afternoon to be sure to catch
George, intending to apologise for losing her composure when
they last met. Although she counted George a dear friend, she
felt she shouldn't have let him know about Edmund's letter or
allowed her devastation to show. It had been a weakness; she
should have remembered his youth and awkwardness. The poor
boy had been completely out of his depth and had virtually
run away. She planned to put a brave face on things, to tell
him that she was quite in control now, and was sure she could
trust him not to mention her engagement to anyone. George
would understand; he knew a little about her situation and her
mother's illness.

As she reached the long walk down through the Scots pines

and rhododendrons, she remembered that George had been going to show her something and wondered whether he would have brought it again today or whether he had lost his nerve. She thought that perhaps it was one of his paintings; she had been trying to encourage him in his artistic endeavours and had asked him many times to show her his work. He was such a shy boy, she was annoyed with herself for having scared him off; now she would need to persuade him and build up his confidence all over again.

In the distance, a figure riding a bicycle appeared. Violet quickened her step but slowed again as she saw that it couldn't be George. This boy was much slighter and leant forward over the handlebars as if struggling to get both bike and bag along. He laboured towards her and as he approached, made a wobbly swerve to pass on the other side of the road.

'Excuse me.' Violet put her hand out to flag him down and the boy stopped abruptly, the bike, which was too big for him, falling to the side as he put his foot down on the ground.

'Sorry, miss,' he panted, straightening his cap, which had slipped to the back of his head.

'You're new, aren't you? Can you tell me what has happened to the usual boy?' Violet, anxious not to reveal her inappropriate friendship with George, adopted the haughty attitude that the boy would expect.

'He's joined up – gone off leaving us all in the lurch, miss. That's why I'm all behind; I don't usually deliver right out here. I'm sorry if I'm late, miss.' He rubbed his hand over his forehead, leaving a smear of bicycle oil above his eyebrow.

'Joined up?' Violet echoed. 'Why?'

The boy shrugged. 'Everyone's doing it, miss. Arthur, that's the postmaster's son, he already went weeks ago, so we're very short-handed.'

115

'Do you know where George has gone?' Violet asked, forgetting to feign a merely practical interest in the timeliness of her post.

'I'm afraid I wouldn't know, miss,' the boy said, looking at her curiously. 'Once you're in the army they can send you anywhere they like.'

'Yes, of course, they can . . . thank you,' she said distractedly.

'Is the Manor House straight on, miss?' the boy asked. 'Only if I'm late back I shall get in terrible hot water with Mr Ashwell.'

Violet pulled herself together. 'Don't trouble yourself to go right up to the house; I can take it.'

The boy took out a handful of letters but seemed reluctant to pass them across. 'I'm supposed to give them in at the door . . .'

Violet thought quickly. 'I'm the daughter of the house and I do prefer to walk down and pick up my post from you myself.' She reached into her pocket and pulled out a penny. 'It would save you time and perhaps you could let me know if there's any news of . . . of your boys who've enlisted?'

The boy eyed the coin, nodded and gave the letters to Violet. With a quick 'Thank you, miss' he turned the bike around and rode away.

Violet was nonplussed. There was no way that she could contact George; she didn't know where his family lived and she could hardly go and ask the postmaster for news of one of his boys. She would have to wait for him to write to her himself and let her know where he was and that he was all right. It struck her that what he had intended to show her might have been his army papers; he might have felt proud of joining up and wanted her to see that he was being a man. She felt awful that she hadn't given him the chance to talk to her about such a serious decision, nor to give him the blessing he might have been looking for, nor to express her affection with even so much as a 'bon voyage' . . . As she walked on towards Dodd Fell, worrying about both Edmund and George, she was aware of the mournful silence. She carried on into the wood with only the sound of her own footsteps for company.

Life at the training camp in the Midlands was a slog: digging trenches, bayonet practice and marching, marching, marching. On an unseasonably hot day in September, George and the others were on a route march. The muscles in his shoulders were burning hotter than his head under its thick cap as the heavy weight of kit pulled them backwards, stretching the tender ligaments around his collarbones as he forced himself forward. Fifty-six pounds! Carrying his kit was like giving Ted a piggyback but instead of a quick run and dumping the weight thankfully on the grass, you had to slog on for hours with it battened on to you like some kind of parasite.

At last it was time for the first rest break and the order came to fall out. The sergeant opened the gate into an empty pasture and the men poured through, slung off their kitbags and threw themselves down upon the grass. Burrows, who was one of the twelve who shared their tent, came over and flopped down beside George and the others, saying, 'Bloody hell, why does it have to be so hot? It's worse than August.' He, and two or three of the others whom they shared with, had already been in the camp a few weeks when they had arrived. They had passed on all kinds of useful information: how to rub soap on your feet to help against blisters, how deep to 'stick' a sandbag so that you could still get your bayonet out afterwards, and how to get out of camp and down to the village without anyone noticing. Burrows lounged back on one elbow, fanning himself with his hat.

There was the sound of a motor stopping in the lane and shortly afterwards three officers turned up: Captain Hunton with two younger officers whom George didn't recognise. Captain Hunton was an old campaigner; his face and hands had the dark, weathered look of a man who has lived a great deal out of doors. He held himself very stiffly, some said as the result of an old shoulder wound from his time in the African war. It was rumoured that it caused him constant pain and that this was the reason for the harshness of the discipline he imposed, and that he marched the men long and hard as if he had something to prove. George speculated that the two younger officers with him were probably also completing their training before going overseas. As they all went over to Sergeant Grice, George noticed how they walked a pace behind Hunton on either side, but otherwise didn't pay much mind to them.

He opened his water bottle, which was tied to his pack with string. He took a long pull, not caring that the water tasted of tin.

Over by the gate, Captain Hunton and the two lieutenants were looking at a map.

Haycock said to Burrows, 'D'you think it means anything, those two turning up?'

'It could mean a move's in the offing,' Burrows said. 'Maybe they're here to take a look at us and see what we're made of.'

'You think we could be off before too long?' Rooke, who had been drooping with his head between his knees, perked up.

Burrows looked at him sceptically. 'Well, when they ask, you can *say* you want to go . . .' he said, as though unconvinced. Rooke had come in for some heavy ribbing about his youth when one of the men had discovered that he was trying to grow a moustache and that his efforts were proving unsuccessful.

As if to prove Burrows right, the two lieutenants began to walk around the field, stopping here and there to say a word to the groups of men. George watched with interest, wondering whether they would fall under the command of one of the new boys. It struck him that they were very different in their approach. The stockier of the two seemed awkward with the men; he waited with a deadpan expression for them to scramble to their feet and salute him at attention before asking them questions. The other, who was tall, with fine features, put out his hand as he approached to let the men know to stay at ease and smiled as he made some comment to open the conversation. George noticed that although Captain Hunton was still standing talking to the sergeant, he was watching the young officers all the time. When they rejoined him, he said something to the taller one and George saw that his face fell as if he had been rebuked. The three took their leave of the sergeant and returned to the waiting motor and the sergeant gave the order to move.

They formed up in the lane once more and set off again, arms swinging.

George recognised one of the men behind him as belonging to the group to whom the stocky lieutenant had spoken. 'What did you think of the new officer?' he asked, to draw the man into conversation.

'He seemed all right,' he replied. 'Said his name was Lieutenant Carey. Asked us how long we'd been training. Said he and the other chap, Lyne, would be taking a draft overseas soon to replace wastage in the Second Battalion.' He paused to get his breath back.

George was so muddled by fatigue and heat that it took a moment for him to digest what he had been told. 'Lyne?' he said. 'Not Edmund Lyne?'

The man looked at him as if he were stupid. 'We didn't exactly exchange first names!' he said.

George fell silent. Of course, he thought, it must be! Why had it never occurred to him before? He knew that Violet had met Lyne when staying with the family near Carlisle; of course he would have joined up locally too, taken up with the same regiment. He tried to remember everything he could about the man. His height, his clean-cut looks, his easiness with the men were all a cause of anguish to him now as he compared his own youth and awkwardness. It made him feel even worse that in the moment when Captain Hunton had reprimanded Lyne, George had felt a kind of fellow feeling for him. Having thought that he seemed a likeable chap and, without recognising it consciously, even made the decision that he would rather be under him than Carey, it now felt very disturbing to find out that he and the imagined rival whom George hated were the same man. One thing he did know was that he wanted to find out more. He wanted to know everything about the man who had so impressed Violet; he wanted to know if he was worthy of her, but couldn't decide whether to hope that he was or that he wasn't.

They had reached a village where Sergeant Grice had arranged for them to be fed. As they turned into the football field beside the village hall, George caught the man he had been speaking with earlier by the sleeve.

'Did he say anything else about him?' he said. 'Anything at all about Lyne?'

The man looked at him strangely. 'What you on about? Had a touch of the sun?' He pulled away and sat down on the grass. He pushed off his pack and began massaging his neck, turning his back on George in a pointed manner.

George walked away and sat down on his own. He decided

that he would go along to the canteen tent later when they got back to camp; if he hung around perhaps he would see Lyne again. He would be bound to come in at some point to eat, as both men and officers used the same mess. He wanted to get a better look at him, close up. It occurred to him that if he could get near enough he might even hear something of Violet. He found it very difficult to have no news of her, there being no one at home he could ask. He remembered the way she had cried when she got Lyne's letter. What on earth had he put in it that made a girl cry like that? He had seemed very chipper, talking to the men. George thought that if he had been in Lyne's position and Violet was his girl he should be miserable as hell at having to leave her. For the first time he considered a new possibility: perhaps Lyne had told her that he wanted to finish it, as he had to go away. His heart lifted at the thought. He couldn't recall everything from that day but he knew she'd said, 'We were going to be engaged . . .' He remembered that. He had assumed she was upset because their engagement would now be postponed, but what if he had broken it off? George clutched at the possibility. Yes! Surely that would have been the honourable thing to do, if there were a chance a chap wouldn't be coming back: to release a girl from her promise.

As the others rejoined him, George said, 'Burrows was right, looks like we'll have the chance to get moving soon. I had it from a chap who spoke to one of those lieutenants.'

'Humph,' said Haycock. 'I know Hunton's a bastard but I hope he's coming too. I don't fancy our chances under two brand-new officers.'

Turland said glumly, 'There's not much hope we'll see any action anyway; we'll be "lines of communication", won't we? It'll be all loading, unloading and lugging stuff about. More pass it up and down the line than front line, I shouldn't wonder.'

Back in camp that evening, sure enough, the word came that the colonel was to speak to them en masse. They also learnt that their company, B Company, was to be commanded by Lieutenant Lyne. George, thrown into an even greater state of turmoil, didn't know which piece of news to worry about most.

The colonel, campaign ribbons across his chest and wearing a sword in a polished scabbard, gave a stirring speech about the ferocity and ruthlessness of the enemy's treatment of the Belgians and the need to protect their own homes and families. He reminded them that if they had no domestic ties and were over nineteen years of age they had every reason to relish the opportunity to be part of the show and should volunteer for service overseas.

George volunteered with the others, both he and Rooke keeping quiet about being under-age. They pinned their little silvery 'Imperial Service' badges on straight away. Afterwards there was a kind of euphoria in the camp; you could tell whether someone had volunteered without even looking for a badge. Those who had not sat quietly by: not joining in with the speculation about when, where and how they were to travel. Back at their tent, much to George's surprise, Burrows was one of the quiet ones. When Turland said that he didn't know what they would all do without his advice, Burrows tapped the side of his nose and said, 'I've got a girl, you see.'

Haycock, who also had a girl but didn't appear to see it as an obstacle to going off on a big adventure, said, 'You kept that quiet.'

'She's a peach,' Burrows said. 'You think I'd let you anywhere near her?'

'I take exception to that,' Haycock said, looking flattered.

George, realising that the short embarkation leave they'd been given wouldn't allow him to get to Keswick and back, decided that he would go down to the YMCA marquee, where it was peaceful, and write a letter home. He had kept quiet in his letters about planning to go overseas, as his father had suggested, but now he would have to break it to his mother as gently as he could.

In the YMCA tent there were little folding tables with writing paper and pens. The tables rocked a bit on the uneven grass and the light was rather dim unless you sat near an open tent flap but it was quiet and private and many men were there taking the opportunity to let those at home know their news. George took a seat next to one of the massive tent poles, pulled a sheet of paper towards him and began to write in his usual vein:

Dear Father and Mother,

I hope this will find you in the same health that it leaves me at present. I am all right and getting on very well. I hope that the money I sent has reached you safely and will make up for some of what I lost. I cannot say how sorry I am about that.

Mother, you mustn't worry but I am to go overseas in two days.

Here George stopped and sucked the top of the pen for a while. He didn't like to imagine his mother opening this letter. He thought hard and then continued.

There is nothing whatsoever to worry about; I shall be quite safe as we will be well behind the lines, organising supplies: food, petrol, blankets and that sort of thing. It would be very nice if you could send me letters regularly and perhaps some of your fruitcake. Not socks, as I have plenty.

Have you seen Kitty or Mr and Mrs Ashwell? Kitty still hasn't written to me although I've written to her. I hope that Ted is enjoying using my rod, and that Lillie's head has healed up after that nasty bump you mentioned in your last letter. Give them both my love.

We had another long march today and I am very fit and ready to take on anything.

Your loving son,

George

PS Give Lillie a kiss on that bump from her old George, a.k.a. 'Big Bear'.

George put the letter into the envelope, addressed it and quickly stuck down the flap as if to trap inside the wave of homesickness that had come over him. He doodled on another piece of paper, a little drawing of a stone bridge and a winding stream, and then, feeling unwilling to leave the peace of the dusky tent, a sketch of a kingfisher on a branch. He thought about Kitty and of why she hadn't written. Maybe she was taken up with her 'follower'. He wondered, for the umpteenth time, who it could be and when Kitty had started seeing him and why she had said nothing until now. It made him feel uncomfortable to think that she might be too busy with someone else to write to him. She was most likely still sulking over their argument and the fact that he wouldn't confide in her. Why did she always want to know everything? Well, he had written to her, hadn't he? Surely that was an olive branch. George tried hard to convince himself but knew fine that the letter he'd sent would not have been seen as such by Kitty as it was limited to enquiring after her health and that of her parents and an account of the food he was getting and the weather. He knew he wasn't very good at writing letters. Quite possibly she would see such a paucity of information as adding insult to injury. George sighed.

Looking up, he saw that he had been busy with his writing and reflections so long that many of the original visitors to the tent had gone and been replaced by newcomers. Leaning back in his seat he scanned the company for anyone he knew. He stiffened. Over by the main entrance, Edmund Lyne was sitting alone, writing, with papers spread out in front of him and a newspaper at his elbow. George sat up slowly and then leaned forward as if to reach for more paper so that he could get a better view. Without his hat, Lyne looked younger but also somehow more athletic. George envied him his loose-limbed, rangy build. He watched him for a while. His head was bent intently over his writing, and his hand moved across the page fluidly at a steady pace, without the stops and starts George experienced whilst trying to think up what to say. George hoped against hope that he wasn't writing to Violet. He would get a good look at him on the way out, he thought. He would be able to walk right past him.

Picking up his letter and his drawing, he set off, edging sideways between the closely packed tables. As he approached, his heart gave a lurch. The papers in front of Lyne included a pile of letters and poking out from the bottom was a blue envelope, of a shade he knew well, having seen it often enough in Violet's hand. He hadn't realised that he was staring but Lyne looked up and met his eyes.

'Did you want a glance at the paper?' he said pleasantly, mistaking George's interest. 'There's been another push.'

Panicked, George said, 'That would be jolly decent of you, sir.' He took it and, thinking quickly, turned to the casualty lists.

125

'Have you got family out there?' Edmund asked.

George shook his head. 'Just a friend.'

'Everything all right, I hope?' Edmund was puzzled by the way this young man was blushing, his colour rising as he watched. Perhaps it was a close friend, for whom he was concerned. He noticed the little silver badge above his breast pocket and wondered if his evident emotion was perhaps a funk about going overseas. He seemed terribly young: so many of them were.

'Thank you, sir. Everything's fine,' George managed to say, handing the paper back again.

'That's good, then,' Edmund said gently. 'Give my regards to Keswick,' he added, trying to lighten things. At this, the young man looked shocked, as if he had been caught doing something wrong. Edmund pointed at the envelope that George was holding, addressed to 26, Leonard Street, Keswick, and George's face cleared.

'Thank you, sir,' he said again.

George went out into the evening air. It struck him coolly, making him realise that he was in a lather of a sweat. He walked down to the post, hoping that the regularity of his steps would calm his beating heart. He felt shaken up and unable to disentangle his emotions. He had been near enough to just put out his hand and touch Violet's letter . . . His hope that Edmund might have broken off their engagement had been self-delusion. He tried to quell the rush of jealousy he felt. The man seemed a decent sort; what right had he to hate him or even harbour a grudge against him? Violet had always been beyond his reach, in any case. But it pained him so, to think of them together . . . Oh, why couldn't things be as they used to when he and Violet met and talked so easily together! He remembered the day when he rode out in the bright afternoon, the picture in his pocket: the release of leaving the cobbled streets and cramped buildings behind, the wide green spaces of the park and the freshness that seemed to rise from the moving river. He had ridden fast as flying, such joy was rising in him.

Everything had changed that day. He recognised that he would never capture that sense of limitless possibility again.

Edmund refolded his newspaper. What a strange young man, he thought. There had been something intense about him . . . Well, it had been an odd day and perhaps the news that they would be overseas in a couple of days affected people in different ways. He settled back to his letter.

On the morning of their departure, they arrived at the station and stood around at ease in the freight yard. The horses were brought in: a string of forty led along, roped together in eights. They were a fine sight: all light draught horses, chestnuts, greys and bays. Well groomed and with shining coats, they tossed their heads and snorted, some of them skittering at the unfamiliar noises of the railway, but they soon calmed as the leading group, chosen for their docility, slowed to a walk as they entered the far side of the yard. Haycock, whose father was a blacksmith, was fond of horses. He wanted to watch them being loaded and he suggested they move to the end of the platform to see the beasts walked up the ramp and into the covered wagons.

George was surprised to see that they were led into the wagons and left loose, with no head-ties, and commented on it to Haycock.

'In theory it'll be safer for them that way,' he said. 'They can't get entangled with each other and they can move a bit and get comfy, like, although if they're jammed in too tight they'll end up stepping on each other's hooves or pasterns and then there'll be biting and kicking.'

They stowed their kit on the parcel shelves to show those places as taken and then watched the horses being loaded, and the sliding doors shut and barred. Between the wooden slats were glimpses of flared nostrils as a horse snuffed the fresh air or a rolling eye as they jockeyed for the best position. George and the others got into the carriage and then a few more men from further down the train came looking for a seat and joined them. Turland and Rooke let George and Haycock take the window seats, as they were so keen on the horses, which meant they could watch when the train stopped for the horses to be watered.

A whistle blew and doors slammed as soldiers left the last embrace of wives and sweethearts and boarded the train. They started off, passing families waving handkerchiefs and little groups of women and children clinging to each other: small tableaux of grief.

Thoughts of the continent made George's stomach turn over, yet again, with the queasy mixture of anxiety and excitement that had beset him since he woke in the early morning. He had lain among the huddled, blanket-covered shapes of his companions, looking at the shadows of leaves on the tent canvas, and wishing someone else would wake up. Now he longed for the smell of bruised grass and unwashed socks that was at least familiar, a kind of temporary home.

The chaps who had joined their party were from Kendal and Penrith and the conversation turned to places they knew in common, and the fortunes of the local football teams, so that the first hour or so of the journey passed quickly. After a while, George's restless night and early waking caught up with him and he leant his head against the polished wooden frame of the window, closed his eyes and, despite the engine noise and the faint bumps and bangs from the wagon as the horses continually shifted and braced themselves, he soon fell asleep.

Half an hour later he woke as the train stopped with a tremendous jolt, throwing him forward in his seat so that he nearly landed in Haycock's lap. It was pitch black.

'What's happened?' he said. His voice came out higher than he'd intended, as the darkness, the closeness and the awful banging behind him shot him straight into panic. The familiar dread of being shut in overwhelmed him.

'We're in a tunnel, you idiot,' said a disembodied voice from the other corner of the carriage. 'God knows why we stopped so suddenly.'

With less engine noise, they could hear whinnying, and kicking and sliding noises from the horse wagon behind them.

'They're getting a bit restive,' Turland said.

'Why don't they get a bloody move on?' Haycock said. 'Those horses are all shod; they'll be kicking seven shades of shit out of each other in there.'

The train took another jolt forward and Rooke, who had been trying to light a match, dropped it as the movement jerked him from his seat. There was a moment's confusion as everyone tried to stamp it out at once; then as they sat back down they became aware of a regular and massive thumping in the wagon behind as if one of the horses was having some kind of seizure.

'One of them has gone down,' Haycock said. 'The others'll close over and take up the standing space . . .'

The rest of his words were drowned out by the approach of a train going the other way. It passed them in a flicker of lighted windows and a cloud of steam and soot, shaking their stationary carriages as it went. As the noise began to die away, a most horrible sound took its place: the sound of the fallen horse screaming.

George, who sat frozen in panic, put his hands over his ears and pressed out the terrible sound. His breath came short and quick; he was gasping for air . . . he had to get out . . . At last, the train jerked forward again and this time kept on moving until they emerged from the tunnel and into the light that revealed their anxious faces and George with his head between his knees and his hands clamped over his ears.

Turland put his hand on George's back. 'Are you all right?' he said. 'Here, look, we'll be out of it in a minute and they're sure to stop and sort it all out.'

Haycock's face was grim.

The train moved on slowly, gathered pace and then slowed again, and all the time they could hear the noise of the horse struggling to rise and others kicking and neighing. George couldn't seem to calm down. He stared out of the window trying to find something to focus on that would stop him picturing the panicking crush of horses in the dark wagon.

At last, they pulled into a station at the edge of a village. There were fields beside the station and an orchard with sheep beyond. They heard the sound of doors opening further up the train. Haycock pulled down the window and leant out and George stood up so he could see over Haycock's head. Some men got out ready to fetch water but hearing Haycock's shout and the noise from number-one wagon, they looked alarmed. The farrier sergeant and a private came straight over and started unbarring the sliding door of the stock car, the sergeant keeping up a steady stream of swearing; another man hurried towards the front of the train.

The horses nearest the door were led out by their halters, one at a time, and tied to the station railings. One had a bad bite on its neck with a big flap of skin hanging loose. They were jumpy, pulling and shying until more men turned up with buckets of water, then they put their heads down and drank. As soon as enough space had been cleared there was a scrabbling, thumping noise as the injured horse was helped to scramble to its feet.

Captain Hunton and the two lieutenants arrived as the men half pulled, half coaxed the horse from the wagon. It was a grey; blood on its withers showed bright against its light coat. The animal's hindquarters seemed strangely sunken and scrutiny showed that its back legs were buckling under its weight because of a bad injury above the hock; the flesh had sheared away right through to the bone. It stood shivering and then staggered as its back legs almost gave way. Captain Hunton walked around it, looking it over. He gave an order and Lieutenant Carey took its halter and led it, lamed and halting, down into the field. Hunton and Lyne moved to one side and seemed to be having quite a discussion. As George watched, it seemed to him that the more animated Lyne became, moving his hands as though sketching something in the air as explanation, the more impassive was Hunton. He heard Lyne out; then he looked over to where Carey was standing with the horse, its head drooping, and gave Lyne an order.

Through the bustle and movement of the men going back and forth with buckets, George saw Lyne join Carey. He ran his hand over each of the horse's uninjured legs in turn. Captain Hunton stood watching with a look of intense annoyance and fiddled with the fastening of the holster at his belt. Lyne stood talking to Carey, one hand on the beast's neck.

Suddenly, as if he had lost all patience, Captain Hunton strode down the platform and into the field. He said something to the lieutenants and George saw Lyne and Carey step away sharply from the horse. Hunton grasped the halter; then, as casually as if it had been his handkerchief, he took out his service revolver and discharged it into the beast's temple. It dropped as though its legs had been taken from under it. A spasm went through its body. Hunton had walked off before the last twitch died away.

It was all so quick that George could hardly believe it had happened, but there was Lyne, standing looking down at the horse as if stupefied, and Carey kneeling and taking off the animal's halter. He turned to Haycock.

'It had had it,' Haycock said, and sat back down in his seat as if to say 'the show's over'.

Captain Hunton came up the platform with his face set hard. He spoke to the station manager about the disposal of the carcass, asked the farrier sergeant how much longer the watering operation would take and then strode back towards the front of the train. Carey and Lyne returned and handed over the harness to the sergeant. They too began to walk back up the length of the train. George bobbed his head back into the carriage before they drew level; he didn't want to draw further attention to himself after his encounter with Lyne in the marquee.

When they had passed, George leant out of the window as if to check the evidence of his own eyes once more. All was quiet. A faint cidery smell of windfall apples hung in the air. A dark cloud of flies moved around the animal's head.

As they set off again, everyone was silent for a while. Eventually, Rooke suggested cards, one of the new chaps shared out some cigarettes and gradually conversation returned. The train sped on through fields of stubble, past canals and factories, villages and wooded valleys, taking them ever nearer the docks where the ships waited at quays scattered with limbers, water carts and rolls of wire, all bound for the Front.

PART TWO

FLANDERS, AUTUMN 1914

8

POLDERS

George and Rooke were lost. The track that they were following ran through pasture and fields of ploughed-in stubble, and was lined on one side by poplars that were meant to act as a windbreak against the storms that blew straight off the sea. Instead, over time, the wind had weeded out some of the trees and left the others leaning, all at the same angle in an uneven row. Between the trees, scrubby bushes merely sieved the sharp October wind: the steady rush of cold air chilled one side of their bodies, finding its way into sleeves and under collars.

They had been slogging along under their packs on their way to the Front. It had soon become clear that their duties would not continue to be limited to 'lines of communication', but were to include taking their turn in the line like everyone else. En route, they had fallen behind the others because Rooke was on his last legs and it was George's turn to stick with him. So when the low buzzing of the first Jack Johnson split the air, there was no one to shout out to in warning and they simply scrambled for the ditch as, *whump*, an eruption of soil shot up from the field on the right and pattered back to earth like dark hail. They threw themselves face down with their arms over their heads, their packs crushing them down so that bandolier and pouches stuck into their chests. The crumping explosions continued as the shells hit somewhere in the field beyond. George dug his hands into the soggy vegetation and held on tight; he thought that this must be how a spider feels under the shadow of a man's boot. He pressed himself into the damp earth, feeling the water well up from the clay soil and seep coldly through his clothes.

At length, the explosions ceased. At first, it seemed as if the quietness surged back and then George became aware of the small noises of the countryside once again. The rustle of the wind in the branches, a blackbird's fluting call from its singing post at the tip of a poplar, a pheasant croaking somewhere in the field.

Rooke lifted his head. 'What on earth are they shelling right back here for?'

'After our guns, I should think.' George wondered if the Alleyman thought there were guns being stored ready to be brought up to the Front. He hoped that the others up ahead were in a lane with a ditch and trees for cover too and not out on the road through the open fields. The polders were low-lying lands reclaimed from the sea. In this flat country, criss-crossed by canals and drainage ditches, the file of men would be exposed like a column of ants on a chequered cloth. He shuffled forward on his elbows and looked over the edge of the ditch. Dark holes pitted the field. Slabs and clods of yellow clay were scattered across its surface. An old wooden harrow that had stood abandoned had completely disappeared. The evening sky was streaked with vivid lemon and lavender close to the flat horizon, its tranquil mood at odds with the wounded earth below.

George turned round to find Rooke sitting up and holding his stomach.

'I feel awful; I think all that meat and biscuits has disagreed with me again,' he said ruefully.

George helped him up and handed him into the field where he disappeared behind the bushes. 'Keep your head down,' he called after him and, taking his own advice, he squatted back down in the ditch, nerves fraying further with every lost minute. If Rooke was ill, they were never going to be able to catch up with the others.

After some time, Rooke emerged, struggling along, bent double in pain. 'God, I feel terrible. I don't think I can get along,' he said.

'Well, we can't stay here, that's for sure,' George said. 'We could be blown to blazes. If we're not going to be able to catch up, we need to get off this road.'

Rooke sat down, drew up his knees and rocked backwards and forwards, moaning, 'I can't, I can't.'

Panicking, George said, 'You're going to have to, Percy. Come on, get up! We've got to move in case another lot come over!' He pulled at his arm. Rooke looked up at him, his face pale and drawn: the face of a frightened boy. Forcing himself to be patient, George spoke more gently, 'Look, we'll strike off over the field behind us – put a bit of distance between us and the road then look for some cover for the night.' He hefted up Rooke's pack and got his arm over his shoulder so that he could support him. They dragged themselves out of the ditch.

Keeping low, they stumbled across pasture. To their right, some miles away, lights flickered and bloomed against the lavender cloud as guns rumbled along the horizon. From nearby came the deep sound of a river and all around them the trickling of water in the dykes. They went along slowly, searching for crossing places, George supporting Rooke but all the time looking about him. For all we know, the Alleyman could have broken through, he thought; we've been told time and again that's what they're trying to do now they've got the Belgians cornered – get past us and down to the Channel ports. A new thought struck him: if they ran into some of their own troops, what if they were taken for deserters? Away from their own company they had no one to vouch for them. It wouldn't look good. As they struggled on, he strained his ears for the sounds of men, dreading the sound of a challenge.

They were edging along, following the line of a ditch and moving between the scrubby bushes, when Rooke stopped, letting his weight slump against George, saying, 'I can't go much further. I'm done up.' He sank to his knees and was violently sick, George squatting beside him to support him and telling him he would feel better once he'd got rid of it all.

George looked around desperately for cover for the night. There were no buildings of any kind but on the far side of the next field was the rounded hummock of a haystack. 'Come on, Percy. You're going to be all right,' he said, pointing it out. 'We're nearly there. One foot after another.' Rooke raised a hand weakly to say he was ready and George helped him along over the tussocky grass.

When they reached it George walked around the nubby shape of the hayrick. Half of it was tightly packed but the other side was a looser heap, pulled apart where the forkfuls of forage had been gouged from it, until it collapsed in on itself. It made easy climbing; George hauled the packs up and then helped Rooke up to the top. Once there, he dug through the outer layer, coarsened and greyed by past rain, to the golden-fawn beneath, releasing a smell of dust and clover, making room for them both to burrow in. It was a good vantage point with a clear view all around. In the twilight, the flat fields seemed deserted. George got out his field rations and ate in silence, concentrating on the process of filling his belly as fast as possible and washing the lumpy meat and dry biscuit down with swigs of metallic-tasting water from his canteen. Rooke took one look at the food and put his head down on his knees. George was so hungry he didn't care what it tasted like, he just wished there was more.

George let out an enormous sigh as he lay flat and felt the ache set up in his back in new places and then gradually dissipate as he relaxed his muscles. He touched his breast pocket with its pad of folded letters: long chatty letters from his mother, graver ones from his father, short ones from Kitty who had thawed only enough to reply to him but not enough to do more than ask after his health and give the most basic news. He wished she would write to him properly, in her own voice, with all the things she was thinking and feeling.

He turned to Rooke. 'How are you doing?'

'Not as bad now I can stay still. Very cold. My feet are freezing. Are you taking off your boots?' He sat up and began to loosen the laces of one of his own.

George considered how to put his answer without scaring Rooke. 'Best not, in case we have to leg it. You know . . . if we had some unwelcome visitors.' George imagined being woken by a prod from a bayonet or not woken at all but simply shot to blazes before you could even get your eyes open . . . He tried to block out the images. He felt sure he wouldn't be able to sleep at all.

139

Rooke was quiet for a moment; then he retied his boot and lay back down. After a minute he said, 'Here, there's another thing. This wouldn't count as desertion, would it? If we were found here, like this?'

With a confidence he didn't feel, George said firmly, 'Not if you make every effort to return to your company. We'll get up and off first thing and soon catch up with them. Either that or report to the first officer we see from another outfit.'

'Righto,' said Rooke, and George felt a pang at the way that Rooke trusted him and was so easily reassured, when he himself was unsure about everything, feeling unfit to take on the responsibility for another person that circumstances had thrust upon him. Rooke settled himself deeper in the hay, raising the dust and making himself sneeze. George was reminded of Ted and the way he would burrow right down under the blankets with only the crown of his head showing. Sometimes Percy seemed hardly any older, despite his quick wit and eye for the main chance.

'Percy?' he said. 'Why don't you know how old you are?'

There was no answer and the silence went on for so long that George began to think that he had gone to sleep.

'I haven't got a birth certificate,' Rooke said.

George digested this. It hadn't really occurred to him that you needed a birth certificate to tell you your age. 'But wouldn't your parents . . .'

'Haven't got any parents,' Rooke said. 'I lived at the Waifs and Strays for a while. They told me I was found stealing out of the bins and they took me in because I was sleeping in a doorway.'

'But you don't remember it?'

'No. I remember the Home. There were food and clothes but I didn't like the lessons and it was strict. As soon as I thought I'd have a chance on my own, I legged it.'

140

'So, you've got no one,' George said wonderingly.

'Only Turland,' Rooke said. 'I wasn't doing too well when I met him – lot of trouble with the law – but he got me the job at the paper and the room at the boarding house.' He sighed. 'I fell on my feet all right there. God knows why we had to go and decide to get caught up in all this malarkey.'

George thought of the warm fug of the parlour at home, the smell of cooking, his mother saying 'Go carefully – watch out for those motors' every time he set off on his bike. He couldn't imagine the cold emptiness that would exist without his family. Without thinking whether it would sound daft or soppy, he said, 'And me. You've got Turland and me and Haycock.'

There was a pause and then a muttered 'Thanks.'

The noise of the guns took on a new ferocity as the night's bombardment began to build. Rooke shuffled himself round to look towards the guns and George turned over on his stomach. Flashes of light split the darkness in a line that gave definition to an indistinct horizon, and grey puffs of smoke appeared and hung as smudges against the blackness before moving slowly in the westerly wind, lengthening and dissipating until overtaken by the next explosion.

'I bet the lucky bastards are in billets by now,' Rooke said.

'I expect so,' George said, and the thought that they might have gone forward into the line hung unspoken between them.

'George?' Rooke said. 'Apart from your family, have you got anyone waiting for you at home?'

'Kitty,' George said automatically and then stopped, remembering the frostiness of her letters.

'Is she your girl then?' Rooke asked wistfully.

'No, Kitty's just Kitty.' It was hard to explain his certainty that however much she berated him or gave him the cold shoulder, in some way he felt sure she would be anxious to see him back.

'I see,' Rooke said slowly, clearly confused.

'We've been friends ever since school and we had a falling-out because she didn't want me to enlist,' George said. 'I'm not much good at writing letters, not about feelings and that sort of stuff anyway, so I don't think she's forgiven me yet. I got her this though.' He dug deeply into his breast pocket and brought out a thick, cream-coloured postcard. He wiped his hands on his uniform and then held it by its edges for Rooke to see. In the centre of an embossed card frame was a gauze envelope embroidered with tiny pictures: purple and yellow pansies, a lady's fan, a swallow with a flower in its beak, and beneath, a banner reading 'TO MY DEAR FRIEND'.

'See, you put the address on the back and a little card inside,' George said triumphantly, taking out a tiny slip of paper. He held it up between his chunky thumb and forefinger. It had a picture of a soldier on the battlefield handing a letter to a winged child and a printed message that said at the top 'Happy Birthday Greetings' and below 'From a Soldier of the King'.

'Very fancy, I'm sure,' Rooke said in a lah-di-dah voice.

George grinned. 'It's her birthday soon. I thought she'd like it – as we both worked on the post, you know.' He put it back carefully, sandwiched between the wad of letters in his pocket. 'Hopefully she'll start writing me longer letters at least.'

'It must be nice to get letters but I suppose you have to be able to write them first – and you have to have a girl to write to, of course.' After a pause he said, 'It'd be awful to get shot up before you'd even, you know, been with a girl . . .'

'You can't think like that,' George said firmly. 'You might even meet someone while we're out here. If we free the Belgians

142

there'll be victory marches and girls galore taking buttons off your uniform!'

Rooke pulled a wry face and dug into the hay, shivering and pulling it over him. In the half-light he looked terribly washed out and George thought of Ted when he'd had flu and how his mother had sat up all night in their room with him.

George pulled his greatcoat more tightly around him and tried to stay awake to keep watch. That was what he was out here for, wasn't it, in a way, to protect Ted and Lillie from the same danger? The Germans must at all costs be kept from breaking through to the Channel ports; it was unthinkable that they should ever set foot on British soil. He thought of all at 26 Leonard Street sleeping peacefully as the fire burned down in the hearth downstairs and the last wisps of smoke eddied from the chimney.

The disc of a full moon and the cold white points of stars were now visible in the clear sky. The cold numbed his cheeks and jaw as though it beat down on him from the vastness above. With a pang of jealousy, he wondered if Edmund had sent Violet a sweetheart card: he had seen ones that said 'To my Dear Sweetheart' when he was choosing, and messages with crossed flags that said 'A kiss from France'. He closed his eyes, shutting out the flashing reports and the stars and thought of Violet as he first saw her when she was taking the photograph of the stream: the concentration in her eyes; the play of dappled sunlight reflected from the water on to her blouse as she leant forward.

George woke and blinked, feeling drops of water beading his eyelashes. He freed his arm from the pile of damp hay that covered him, wiped his face on his sleeve and pushed his hand through his hair; everything was cold and sodden. He lay still, trying to regain the blessed insensibility of sleep but as he recognised the humped shape of Rooke's back and remembered where he was, he felt afraid. How late was it? They had meant to set off at first light. He sat bolt upright and discovered a sea of whiteness. The hayrick was an island afloat in a thick ground mist that reached halfway up its sides and extended around it as far as he could see. The sky was a soft grey, the air still and damp, smudging the outlines of distant trees that stood knee-deep in a lake of milk.

There was an eerie quiet after the shelling of the night before but, in the background, George was aware of a muffled, regular sound that was familiar to him and yet seemed out of place. His mind, still muzzy with sleep, refused to make sense of it at first but as his ear became attuned, he recognised it as the sound of gently lapping water. He leant across and grasped Rooke's shoulder. Rooke groaned and tried to push him off but George shook him awake.

'Bloody hell, what is it?' Rooke said.

'We've been flooded, that's what it is.'

Rooke sat up, small and pale in his oversized greatcoat and with his hair sticking up on his crown and scattered with strands of hay.

The slow lapping and the sound of droplets from the edge of the rick dripping through the mist into water beneath were unmistakable.

George took an empty bully-beef tin and crawled to the edge of the stack. He dropped it through the whiteness and they heard the splash below.

Rooke joined him. 'How deep do you think it is?'

George picked up his bayonet and scrambled as far as he could down the sloping side of the rick. He took off his coat, pulled up the sleeve of his jacket and thrust the bayonet into the water, extending the length of his arm into the coldness. Loose hay floated on the surface and there was a strange smell, quite different to the smell of fresh river water at home. 'I can't feel the bottom,' he said, over his shoulder, 'but I'd say at least half of the stack is out of the water so it can't be over our heads.'

'I bloody well hope not,' Rooke said. 'I can't swim.'

George climbed back up and hefted his pack on to his shoulder, saying, 'Well, we're going to have to chance it. It's not as if anyone's going to come along and rescue us, is it?'

Rooke peered gingerly down.

'Come on; I'll go first.' George stowed his bayonet and picked up his rifle. He half climbed, half slid down the greasy surface of the wet haystack and entered the water in a stumbling rush as he raised his rifle in both hands above his head. The shock of the cold made his breath catch and his balls shrink. Through clenched teeth, he called up to Rooke, 'Come on in, the water's lovely!'

Rooke, seeing that George's head and shoulders were above water and free of the mist, got his stuff, shuffled slowly down on his backside and slid in, swearing. He followed George, who was feeling his way forward in a straight line away from the tumbled side of the rick.

'It smells funny, don't it?'

George sniffed. There was a smell of old drains and a tang of something else – he sniffed again. Salt. 'It's seawater!' he said.

Rooke, his teeth chattering, nodded. 'Is it rising?'

'Let's not stick around to see.'

They waded side by side towards the line of a fence, the square tops of its posts protruding a few inches above the surface like a string of stepping stones. George was painfully aware that they made a sitting target, dark and solid

145

through the pale mist that rose and drifted a little with their slow movement only to settle again behind them.

They followed the fence until it disappeared and then stopped, unsure whether they had just reached the end of the field or whether the land sloped away.

'I think the mist's thinning,' George said. It was true; the breeze from the sea had returned and the faint warmth of the early morning sun was breaking up the solid whiteness: opacity diluting to translucence. They could see the leaves and twigs that littered the water; an old sack floated by and a bucket caught against a fence post thumped woodenly in the tiny swell.

'D'you think some kind of sea defences could have burst?' Rooke asked.

'There was a full moon last night so maybe there was an extra high tide. I don't know; I don't understand it.'

'How far do you think it stretches?'

George shrugged. 'It's so flat it could be miles.'

Rooke was holding on to the last fence post with both hands. 'I've been thinking: what if we step right into a canal? We'd just sink – we'd simply disappear.'

George imagined suddenly feeling nothing beneath his feet, water closing over his head, not being able to breathe, the weight of his pack pulling him down, impossible for either one of them to pull the other out . . .

Rooke, pale and shivering, looked terrified, gripping the fence post as a drowning man would a raft. George thought he might not be able to shift him. He took a deep breath. 'I'll go ahead,' he said. 'You follow a little way behind, then if . . . anything happens . . . you'll know to turn aside. All right?' Before Rooke had time to answer he set off, taking a gamble that Percy would be equally afraid of being left behind. After a moment or two, Rooke waded after him.

Fifty yards out, George caught his foot against something submerged and stumbled, sloshing into the water up to his shoulders. He floundered and righted himself. With a gasp, he pulled his boot free and carried on.

He moved on through the debris: a rabbit hutch lying low in the water, branches, straw, and the empty tins that littered the sides of roads and railway tracks, discarded by troops passing to and from the line. An open newspaper floated face-up as though someone had just set it down for a moment during his breakfast. He fished it out but it was in French and yielded no information. He gave it back to the water, wondering at the mixture of objects, the lives of so many people who would never normally meet now thrown so close together that their belongings were mixed like vegetables in soup.

He paused to let Rooke catch up a bit and peered through the lifting mist, looking for a barn, a windmill, anything that might suggest higher ground. There was no sign of a building but he saw a straight line of trees in the distance. He thought that its thickness could mean that it was a double line and that, in turn, might mean that it was bordering either side of a road. He turned and signed to Rooke where they should go. As George made for the drowned road, something large and unwieldy lay in his way: a five-bar gate, flat in the water with a sodden mess of debris at the other side. As he paused, the gate drifted towards him and bumped gently against him. On the other side of it, the sodden object that lay heavy in the water washed up against the gate and, its progress impeded, rolled a little. The grey-brown cloth, which he had thought sacking, George now saw covered the shape of a man's back and shoulder. As the body rolled, he glimpsed a man's face, horrible in its bruised pallor. It grazed the side of the gate, insensible as the wood it touched. George could feel his boots sinking down into the mud yet he could make no move. In the split second before the body rolled back, face down, he had seen the hair matted like weed over the forehead, the flesh puffy and swollen around its vacant eyes and open mouth. As it settled in the water, George saw that the back of the head was strangely flattened and hairless: a grey the colour of old rubber. He gave the gate a push and it nudged the body further away; it floated stiff and solid as a log. The uniform was German. George felt only a deep revulsion that left room for neither hate nor pity. He glanced round quickly to make sure that Rooke hadn't seen. He forced himself to grasp the slimy wood of the gate and steadied himself against it, as he pulled first one foot and then the other free of the sucking mud. Hands shaking, he pushed the gate as hard as he could so that it and the body were cleared from his path; the gate seesawed wildly on the swell as it was swallowed once more by the mist. He moved away so that Rooke, following him, would not go near. He told himself that if Rooke didn't see it, if they didn't have to speak of it, somehow he could tell himself that he hadn't seen it, that it didn't exist. 'Come on, Percy,' he said in a shaky voice. 'We're nearly there.'

At last, they approached the line of trees and George pushed Rooke up a shallow bank where he stumbled, exhausted, to the top and slumped down at the foot of a tree. George in turn scrambled over the hard ridges of tree roots, water streaming from him as he emerged, first thigh-deep, then knee-deep, then finally free of the water as he attained the hard flat surface of a metalled road. He sank, panting, shoulder to shoulder with Rooke, his whole body shivering. He closed his eyes, feeling the warmth of the watery sun on his eyelids and seeing its light glow red through the veins of their thin skin. He tried to shut out the image of the dead man, the body swollen, its face the colour of the underbelly of a dead fish. He pressed his head back against the tree, and spread his fingers against its bark, feeling its roughness, the small crumbs of algae that came off against his palm. Don't let that happen to me. Let that not be me, he prayed.

'What's the matter with you?' he heard Rooke say. 'Don't say you're getting the same thing I've got. My legs are like two sticks of jelly.'

'Nothing, just feeling a bit done up.' He opened his eyes and began wringing out the cloth of his uniform. He felt inside his top pocket; the wad of letters and the special card for Kitty were a solid mass of soggy pulp. He wanted to put his head in his hands and weep.

The last shreds of mist were fading away and the sunlight glinted on the floodwater that spread over the land: the nearer fields were completely covered; then there were some with standing pools and stretches of higher ground where grass showed through like paddy fields. The road on its raised banks ran above it all and led towards the Front. Rooke was making a hopeless attempt to warm himself by wrapping his arms tight around his body. His hands were mottled with cold and his lips had a blue-grey tinge. 'Right,' George said, alarmed. 'Better keep moving.' He put his arm around him and hoisted him on to his feet; then he pulled Rooke's arm over his shoulder so that he could support him. 'We're going to have to risk the road; it's the only way we can get along.' Together they set off along the long straight road towards the guns.

9

STUDIO PORTRAIT

Sergeant Tate surveyed the two soldiers before him: Farrell and
Rooke. They had been brought in on an ASC lorry, the driver
having found them wandering about some miles behind the lines.
Muddy and dishevelled, they had obviously been sleeping rough.
He had seen this kind of thing before, boys who got in a blue
funk as they approached the line, backsliders who tried to get the
cushy jobs and side-steppers who hung back hoping to stay out
of trouble. It had to be nipped in the bud before it spread and
caused more serious breaches of discipline.

'You went absent without leave,' he said.

George stood up very straight. 'Yes, sir. Sorry, sir.'

He nudged Rooke who mumbled an apology. He looked
pretty ropey, George thought. Although he had slept for hours

in the lorry, he had woken complaining of a crushing headache and that chills were running up and down his back. He was standing to attention but George saw that every now and then he was swaying forwards on his toes and then righting himself again.

The sergeant eyed them suspiciously, wondering whether drink was involved. 'You'll have to explain yourselves to the lieutenant,' he said decisively and led them from the farm buildings that served as billets, stores and guardroom and out into a cobbled yard. An old seed drill stood beside the door and Rooke staggered against it, catching on to its rusty tines and then sinking down on to the cobbles as his knees gave way.

'Rooke's sick, sir,' George said.

Rooke's face had turned a putty colour and he was sweating. He put his head down between his knees. The sergeant put his square hand on Rooke's forehead and lifted up his head to look at his face, and then let it fall again. He made an irritated noise, clicking his tongue against his teeth, and called two men over who were shovelling horse manure into a cart.

'Take this man to the M.O.,' he ordered abruptly and they lifted Rooke and put one arm over each shoulder. 'You! Follow me!' he said to George and walked briskly away.

George followed him out of the yard and along a short path towards a stone farmhouse missing half its roof. The timbers sagged from one gable end; the covering of terracotta pantiles was patchy, as if a moth-eaten quilt had been thrown across. The other gable stood bare: a steep triangle of stones, unconnected to anything. They climbed over rubble through a gap in the garden wall, and picked their way through a plot of potatoes and leeks strewn with stones, shards of broken chimneypots and bits of tile and mortar.

'Wait here.' The sergeant knocked at the door and went in.

George took the opportunity to lean his back against the wall. Every bone ached and his clothes, un-dried, stuck to his skin in a cold and clammy embrace; he hugged his elbows to conserve as much warmth as possible at his core. Hearing the sound of several animated voices in discussion inside, he wished that Rooke were with him to corroborate his story. Shivering all over, he could feel his skin quivering like a dog's.

Sergeant Tate opened the door and motioned him in. A crude wooden stair went up from the hallway and above it chinks of light showed through gaps in the roof. Tate knocked on a door to the right and a voice called, 'Enter.'

Several officers were sitting around an old deal table spread with maps and papers. George recognised Lyne, Carey and Hunton but didn't know the other two men. He and Tate saluted smartly and Lyne told them to stand at ease before returning to discussion with the others as they pored over one of the maps.

The farmhouse kitchen was dim; the back window was covered in brick dust and the front had been blown out and was hung with sacking to keep out the wind. The smell of burning wood came from a stove where a pot of water was set to heat. It warmed the room and George longed to get nearer and thaw out his icy hands and feet. Makeshift beds stood along the walls: crude wooden frames supporting wire mesh on which were spread out bedding rolls and blankets, and under which were a jumble of belongings: boots, field glasses, balled-up sweaters, tins and packages from home.

Hunton was saying, 'It's the Belgians' weapon of last resort: to return the land to its natural state; that's what Flanders means, of course – "flooded lands".' He pointed to the coast on the map. 'They've opened up the sluice gates at Nieuport, and let in the sea.'

152

Lyne said, 'What intelligence do we have about the extent of the flooding and the German units deployed?'

'We're still waiting to hear,' Hunton said. 'But as a result of the inundations the Germans are bound to move south and bring their main force to bear on the Brown Wood Line to try to break through, with Ypres as their objective.' He tapped the map with his forefinger. 'We're going to be right in the thick of it, however you look at it.'

'What's the state of the artillery?' Carey asked.

'Plenty of guns but hardly any shells. Orders are, two per gun per day until further notice.'

There was a pause as everyone digested this.

George, whilst feeling agitated by what he'd overheard, was also glad that, for the moment, he had been forgotten. He hoped that no one would ask him what he knew about the floods as he had very little idea exactly where he and Rooke had been, and he had even omitted to ask the lorry driver what road they'd been on when he picked them up. He thought of the expanse of water he'd seen reflecting the drifting clouds and tried to imagine it reaching all the way to the coast: scenes of half-drowned trees and windmills and farms repeating over miles, the people forced to leave their homes and everything they'd built, the land ruined, maybe for generations. He stood very still, kept quiet and tried to keep the image of the drowned man from his mind, afraid that if he pictured it something would show in his face. It struck him that he should probably have looked for his pocketbook or orders, to find out which unit he was from. Yet again he had let the side down. The thought of touching the corpse, of searching through the slime-streaked material of his uniform, made him feel bilious. He kept his head down, staring at the cracks in the grey flagstones.

'When do we get a look at the trenches?' Carey asked.

'My opposite number, Captain Dalgleish, should be along any minute to take us down,' Hunton said. 'Get the lie of the land. You and Mallory can come with me.' He nodded at the young subaltern who was hanging on his every word. 'Parks, you'd better stay and inspect the men; I don't know if I shall be back in time, and Lyne, you get the stores return done and deal with this miscreant.' As if he had been fully aware of George all along, he fixed his eyes upon him. George jerked up straight.

Hunton kept up his steady stare. 'Do you know the punishment available to the courts martial for an absconder?'

'No, sir.' George held himself erect, though he could feel his fiery blood rising to his face.

Lyne broke in, 'Oh come on, surely not . . . They got lost, that's all.'

Hunton continued talking over Lyne. 'Hard labour, loss of pay and privileges,' he intoned, 'or field punishment number one: shackled to the wheel for a period determined by the court, or, if guilty with no extenuating circumstances, execution.'

Unable to believe his ears, George stared at Hunton's florid face, at his watery blue eyes and his sandy moustache where a fleck of spit had lodged. Beside him, he sensed the sergeant stiffen and heard him clear his throat.

Lyne said, 'They got a lift back as soon as they could find one, for goodness' sake.'

Hunton glanced sharply at him.

Lyne said, 'I mean they made every effort to return to the company, sir.'

Hunton leant back in his chair and began to inspect his nails. 'This is, of course, a disciplinary matter for you, Lyne,' he said with a cold smile. 'I shall be interested to see how you deal with it.'

'I know this soldier, sir,' Lyne said doggedly. 'I feel confident that he wouldn't have decamped. He's not the type.'

Hunton looked at George from under his eyebrows. These new recruits, he thought, their faces have a naked look, like something newly peeled: like soft-boiled eggs. This one was a stronger specimen than most; he'd watched them, stripped for baths or delousing, their thin chests, ribs sticking out, mere boys. If only he could be in charge of regular soldiers, the men who'd served under him in Africa: disciplined, battle-hardened men.

A rap at the door announced the arrival of Dalgleish and Hunton stood up and gathered up his gloves and hat, Carey and Mallory following suit and the others rising as a mark of respect. Other than Carey, whose uncle had served with him in Natal, he had little time for these young officers who had seen nothing but thought they knew it all. Look at Lyne with his chin up, thinking he's doing something rather brave, he thought. I despise them, with their talk of decency and honour. War isn't decent. It's the give of a man beneath a bayonet; it's flesh and bone and blood. It's quickness and precision and a cold efficient eye. He eased his back straighter, holding his breath through the familiar pain in his shoulder from his old wound. Settling his belt more comfortably on his waist, his hand automatically checked his pistol.

'As I said, Lyne, I shall be interested to see how you deal with the case.' He folded the map and handed it to Carey, signalling the end of all discussion, and then followed Dalgleish outside.

The door closed behind them and Lyne sat down again. Frowning, he sorted through the papers that remained on the table. 'Well, Tate, what evidence can you bring to bear on all of this?' he said.

Sergeant Tate, who had been thinking along the lines of

fatigues as an appropriate punishment, maybe taking rations down to the line or sandbag-filling, said quickly, 'Although I didn't see the wagon that brought them in, sir, there's no doubt that they did return under their own steam.'

'Quite. Is there anything else you can tell me that's relevant to the case?'

Tate thought for a moment. 'The reason given for lagging behind was the illness of the other soldier, sir, and that soldier is now with the M.O. P'raps the M.O.'s report would be useful, sir?'

Lyne turned to George. 'Who were you with, Farrell?'

'Rooke, sir.'

Lyne nodded. Now the whole situation was perfectly clear. Rooke was one of several on whom he was keeping a watchful eye: small, undernourished and probably under-age. To be honest, they had done pretty well to get this far. 'I'm of the opinion that we need every man we can get, sergeant, and that Farrell here is not a blind bit of use stuck in the guardroom. Perhaps you'd be so good as to bring me the M.O.'s report as soon as it's available?'

'Sir.' Tate stood to attention.

'Thank you. You can leave Private Farrell with me and return to the guardroom. I'll speak to you later about making sure he's gainfully employed.'

Tate inclined his head, turned smartly on his heel and left the room, closing the door softly behind him.

Edmund looked at George's pale face with its expression of puzzlement. The lad was filthy, shivering. He would have to discipline him, but not until he'd recovered his equilibrium. 'Right,' he said. 'Make yourself useful and brew up some tea, would you? I need to get on with these bloody reports.' He went to the bed beneath the window at the back of the room, picked up his haversack, extracted pen and ink and then settled back down at the table to write.

George went over to the stove where the water in the dixie was simmering. A few roughly chopped logs were piled beside it so he pulled his damp cuff down over his hand, squatted down to open the iron door and fed the fire, feeling the glorious warmth hit him, reddening his face and raising faint wisps of steam from his jacket. He held his hands close to the embers beneath the new wood. His fingers were so numb that he could hardly feel the heat at first and rubbed and chafed them until they began to sting back into life. The bark on the logs sizzled and spat as the flames began to take hold and he pushed the door shut and stood up close, the smell of wet wool mingling with the smell of wood smoke as he waited for the water to come to the boil.

George thanked God that he was in B Company and not under Carey. He wondered what extra duties he would be given. He felt sure that he had been saved from being handed over to the military police, at any rate. He thought how strange it was to be here, alone with Lyne who was unaware of the link that existed between them. Edmund's head was bent over his work, his forehead resting on his hand. Watching him writing, his broad shoulders and the way his hair, untrimmed, had already begun to curl over his collar, George felt a strange intimacy in observing him unnoticed.

George tipped the mixture of dusty tea and sugar straight into the pot and stirred it round, allowing his eyes to wander over to Edmund's belongings. On top of the lumpy bedding roll and folded army blankets lay an open book: a copy of *The Longest Journey*. A lanyard with a whistle hung from a nail in the wall, and underneath the bed were a bucket and some rolled-up puttees. George cast his eye over everything again, this time noticing that in the window embrasure above the bed, pushed well back beside a candle stub in a bottle and a pair of reading glasses, was a green tin box with a card or a slip of paper propped up against its side. As soon as he saw the box, he realised that he hadn't only been indulging his morbid curiosity about Edmund Lyne, but had, all the time, been looking for the place in which Edmund kept his letters from Violet. He felt sure that the tin contained them. The pangs of jealousy and longing that shot through him were closely followed by a hot and bothered feeling that left him confused. It was more than a sense that in looking for something so private he had been disrespectful to his commanding officer. Lyne had gone out on a limb for him and he had every reason to be grateful. In fact, not only *was* he grateful, he had to admit that he felt an admiration for Lyne's sense of fair play on his behalf, and for his openness in speaking to Captain Hunton, that made him see his own behaviour as underhand and a little shameful. He forced himself to stop looking, turned back to his task and poured the strong, scummy brew into one of the chipped, enamel mugs that he took from a shelf beside the stove.

He took the tea over to the table and set it down. 'Here you are, sir.'

'Thank you, Farrell. Have one yourself,' Edmund said without looking up. 'And sit. I shall be through these shortly and you can take them to the quartermaster for me.'

'Thank you, sir. Of course, sir.' George filled another mug and sat down at the far end of the table, feeling his body collapse like a sack into the chair, the ache subsiding in his legs, the relief of taking the pressure off his blistered feet. He cupped his hands around the blessed warmth of the mug and sipped the scalding sweetness as if it were very heaven.

'I shan't beat about the bush, Farrell,' Edmund said as he folded the reports and put them into a pouch. 'You know you've had a lucky escape. It mustn't happen again. You understand?'

George nodded.

'You need to be scrupulous in future. That goes for everything: following orders to the letter, alertness on sentry duty, keenness to get the job done – it'll all be noted, you know.'

'Yes, sir.' George thought of Captain Hunton's beady eyes.

Edmund sighed and took a long draught of tea. He weighed up Farrell's condition: pale-faced, grey circles under his eyes, glance sliding towards the window when the noise of the barrage swelled. He looked in bad shape. If he set him to delivering ammo or rations to the lines straight away, he didn't fancy his chances. It only took a small mistake, a moment's inattention, forgetting to keep your head down . . .

'What was your job in Civvy Street?'

'I was a postman.' George was startled, wondering where this line of questioning might lead.

'Hmm. I'll have to put you on fatigues. Sergeant Tate will tell you what to do,' Edmund continued, thinking aloud. 'But whenever we can we might as well find you something appropriate, since delivery is your forte – you can run messages for me, fetch and carry mess rations, that sort of thing.' Edmund rubbed the bridge of his nose as if to smooth away his tiredness. 'Of course we may be in the line very soon. It could be from tomorrow.' At once, he felt that he could kick himself. He remembered how jumpy Farrell had been the time he'd taken a look at his newspaper and he had thought he was suffering from cold feet about active service. Yet . . . he had acquitted himself well in bayonet practice, he could shoot and he didn't hang back from unpleasant tasks; he had volunteered to help shift the wounded when they had been back at Étaples. Weak

159

nerves just didn't quite fit. There was something though . . . whenever Edmund ran across the lad he noticed a watchfulness, and an uneasy habit of gnawing on his lower lip as though he was acutely apprehensive of saying something wrong. Was he really as terrifying as all that? He had hoped that all his men might view him as reasonable; he worked hard to be approachable. He must try to get to the bottom of it; he would take a special interest from now on.

George was thinking about the officers' earlier discussion and their consensus that now everything the Germans had would be thrown at them as they strove to break through and take Ypres. Edmund, seeing his worried frown, said, 'Is there anything you'd like to ask me?' attempting his best tone of encouragement.

George said, 'Well, yes there is, sir, actually. In case . . . if something were to happen, how do I make sure that my pay will get to my family?'

Edmund considered the platitudes that he could spout: that one shouldn't expect the worst, that as long as you followed orders you couldn't go far wrong, that you had as good a chance as the next man did. He said, 'Most men make a will in the back of their pay book: you know, give names and addresses of where their pay is to be sent and any personal bequests.'

George nodded. 'I saw that there was a page for that. It's just, well . . . so you would leave your pay book with your things, I mean, not carry it on you . . .'

'Precisely.'

'Else it might not be – you know – found.'

Edmund looked at the boy, Farrell, with his earnest face, trying so hard to be a man.

'Indeed. One's commanding officer has a responsibility to write to relatives and to pass on any personal effects. I would,

160

of course, carry out that task if that were my sad duty.' Edmund's voice softened. 'Rest assured.'

There was a silence.

In an attempt to lighten the moment, Edmund said, 'Keswick, wasn't it? Your home town?' Then, as a thought struck him, a thought that brought him for a moment sweetly close to Violet: 'I don't suppose you know the Manor House out on the Carlisle Road?'

'Er . . . yes, sir. I mean I may do . . .' George was thrown into confusion. He thought that if he let slip that he knew Violet, Edmund would ask him all about her. He was no good at lying; his feelings would be bound to show.

'I know people there, you see – the Walters.'

'Oh, I always give the post in at the gatehouse,' George gabbled. 'I wouldn't know the family.'

'The post . . . of course. So, you sometimes deliver there?'

George gave the slightest of nods.

Edmund's face broke into a smile as he realised that George might very well have carried his letters to his dear girl. 'Well, well . . .' He wanted to say, 'Fancy that, my fiancée, Violet, lives there!' He wanted to ask what the house was like so that he could imagine her sitting at a window and about the gardens so that he could picture her walking there. He checked himself. Farrell was one of his men; he could hardly talk to him about such personal matters; he must keep a degree of distance. 'Well, it's a small world,' he trailed off. The boy had that look of apprehension again; he had somehow scared him off once more, despite his best efforts.

He wound the tape around the pouch containing the reports. 'Wait here while I drop these in to the quartermaster and have a word with Sergeant Tate.'

Left alone in the room, George sat still, his head awhirl with uncomfortable thoughts of Violet and Edmund: sitting close at dinner, talking together, dancing. From his seat at the foot of the table he could see, face-on, the item propped up against the green tin: a photograph. Light-headed, as if in a dream, George went to the window and picked it up.

It was a studio portrait of Violet sitting in a Queen Anne chair with a small marble pillar beside her. She was sitting rather stiffly with her hands clasped in her lap, wearing a pale dress with a rose pinned at the front, between the drooping wings of a wide lace collar. Her dark hair was piled at the back of her head; her skin was pale and her expression blank. The formal setting and dress made her look older and George could see nothing of the girl he knew. When he pictured her, he always saw her in action: walking on the fells, pausing to point out something in the view, her face always mobile – talking, smiling, frowning intently as she looked down into her camera to frame her shot. The photograph made her seem even further away, part of a world to which he could never belong.

He brought it closer to the light from the window, searching the eyes for the spark that he knew. They seemed flat and expressionless and George thought of her sitting on the uncomfortable seat, facing a stranger with a box and a black cloth and closing her face like a mask.

Then, about to replace the photograph, George suddenly recognised the scalloped edge of the tortoiseshell comb she usually wore to keep her hair in place. He felt a tenderness fill him. He passed his thumb gently over the picture.

'What the devil do you think you're doing?'

Edmund's voice from the doorway made him drop the photograph as if he had been stung. He wheeled round with his back to the window. 'Sorry, sir, I . . .'

'You weren't thieving, were you?' Edmund looked at George's

162

guilty face in disbelief. After he'd protected him from Hunton, this was how Farrell repaid him?

George held his empty palms out towards him. 'Of course not, sir.' He felt his face aflame with indignation at the suggestion. 'I . . . I was going to trim the wicks . . . of the candles . . . do something useful.' Anxious to convince Edmund that he'd had no ill intention but unable to tell him the truth, desperately he fished his penknife out of his pocket as if producing the evidence to back up his hastily conceived story.

Edmund didn't believe a word of it. What on earth had the boy been at? He could have sworn he'd had something in his hands when he'd come in. He fixed George with a keen look.

George mumbled another apology and dropped his eyes.

Edmund let the silence lengthen. At last he said, 'You'd better cut along and report to Sergeant Tate,' letting him go.

Edmund stood deep in thought for a moment. Maybe Hunton was right and harsh discipline was the only thing the men understood. Had he been too soft? He thought that he was a good judge of character but if he'd misjudged Farrell perhaps his lenient treatment would become the evening's chit-chat; he'd hate to lose the respect of his men.

He went over to his bed. His haversack was exactly as he'd left it when he'd got the ink; he was sure it hadn't been tampered with. The tin was in the same position in the window embrasure, but Violet's photograph was flat upon the sill. So – it had been the photograph that Farrell had been looking at and had dropped in fright. In a flash, everything became clear: the lad's discomfort when he'd asked him about delivering to the Manor House, his strange reaction when he had asked if he knew the Walters. Farrell clearly did know Violet and had some boyish crush on her. Perhaps he had delivered letters to her personally; perhaps she had been kind to him and maybe talked to him a little. Well, who wouldn't be half in love with her? His feelings towards George softened. He wondered whether he should mention him in his next letter to Violet; she might be fond of the lad with his puppyish affection. She might like to know that he was safe and under his care.

He propped the photograph back up in its accustomed place. What a rum do for him and Farrell to find themselves thrown together like this – but maybe Farrell had been seeking him out? He had behaved strangely right from that first time in the YMCA tent at camp . . . He thought of George's anguish of embarrassment when he'd caught him looking at the picture. He would say nothing more about it, would appear to accept the explanation given. In a strange way it was a comfort to have George here, a kind of link to his beloved. Even if there was no prospect of asking him anything about Violet's home or his conversation with her, it was still something that here in this godforsaken place there was someone who knew her.

George had left the farmhouse shaking and dizzy with nervous tension. It had been a close shave and he wasn't sure if he had carried it off. Sergeant Tate, seeing the state of him, sent him off to eat first; then he paired him up with one of the regulars, as part of a carrying party detailed to take supplies down to the fire trench, and George's anxiety took a different turn. The regular said that his name was White but everyone called him Chalky. They carried a box of ammo between them. After a few minutes, the rope handle bit into George's palm and he tried to change hands unobtrusively: not wanting to seem soft in front of the old lags. They followed on behind the others who shouldered sandbags full of rations and spades. In the last of the late-afternoon light, they cast long distorted shadows over the ground.

'Like the seven bleedin' dwarfs,' Chalky called out.

'What does that make you? Snow White?' came the quick reply.

'Nah, too big and ugly,' another chipped in among catcalls and a cry of 'Show us yer drawers'.

They entered a wood where spruce and larch mixed with oak and ash. Here and there, branches were splintered and hung unnaturally, like broken limbs. Some of the tall straight boles were gashed, exposing the tawny striations of split wood beneath the bark and some were wholly broken off, leaving jagged stumps and fallen trunks to circumnavigate. All the time the boom and mumble of distant shellfire rolled on.

Further ahead in the tree-shadows, dark-clad figures moved around small smudges of red light: some bending and straightening as they gathered twigs for their fires, some bent over the punctured tins in which the fires were set, fanning the kindling to make it catch, like acolytes of some ancient fire god. They were bearded and wore balaclavas under their caps so that they seemed to disappear eerily in the dimness as they turned away, only to materialise again as the splash of a white face, or a pair of hands like magician's gloves, reappeared.

There was an acrid smell of smoke and something sweeter, nastier, beneath it on the breeze. As they approached, a line of mounds on the left revealed itself as bunkers, raised on posts and roofed with sandbags laid on crossways boughs. From the direction of the enemy lines, pale stalks that bloomed into bright white lights rose into the sky above the wood, transforming everything with powdery light.

One of the men, seeing that they were carrying sandbags full of rations, called out, 'Those for us?'

'I wish they were,' grunted one of the forward party, sliding on the leaf mould and brittle sticks underfoot.

As they passed on beyond the support line, the smell grew stronger. George saw that there were bodies here and there, sprawled among the broken trees, their faces lent a green pallor by the Verey lights. The men around him paid no heed. They passed among them as though they were as much a part of the natural scene as the leaves that lay in drifts against their backs. The rattle and clatter of bullets in the trees ahead made George wince and shrink into his collar.

'When you's out in the open,' Chalky said conversationally, 'and one o' them flares goes up nearby, you 'as to stand very still, see, till it's gone.'

'Do we have to go over open ground to get to the fire trench?' George asked.

'Just a bit. Not too far.'

George fell quiet and Chalky added, 'We'll be all right; don't you worry.'

It had become completely dark and when the flares faded, George could see the stars in clear patches of the sky between the slow-drifting clouds. The view of moon and stars through bare branches made him think of moonlit walks at home. He tried to take himself to that quiet place where the only sound was the soft soughing of the breeze rustling the branches and rippling the lake, thinking that if he could only hold that picture in his head he might feel calmer and make a better show of things. It was no good. The noise, the shocks, the eerie bloom and fade of man-made light, the fact that every hump they passed might be debris or might be a man, kept him firmly in the present: a surreal world become reality.

As they reached the last trees, there was a droning sound above them that made them drop their loads and crouch, hands over heads. Further back in the wood there was an explosion in the canopy as a shrapnel bomb burst and spread its deadly hail of lead. The others quickly shouldered their loads once more but George fumbled as he tried to grasp the handle, his hands seeming unable to do the bidding of his brain.

'Come on,' Chalky said. 'It might get a bit lively in here if the square-heads are trying to stop more support moving up.'

From the edge of the wood, they looked out over an open field. In the ghostly light George could see, a couple of hundred yards to the left, marked by the mounded earth of the parados, the undulating line of a trench and beyond it a mess of wood and wire entanglements. As the flares died away to the right, against the dark trees he saw the tracery of bullets and in the far distance, from a dark, low ridge, a line of light bulging and swelling on the horizon as a barrage of enemy firepower boomed, roared and was answered by allied artillery in return.

'Right, here we go,' Chalky said. 'Watch yer step.'

They set off, skirting shell holes in which water gleamed. Bending low, with the weight of the box pulling on his shoulder, stumbling over mounded clods of displaced earth, George felt the sinews of his back stretch and strain. A ball of light rose into the air directly ahead and the men in front stopped abruptly, so that George and Chalky nearly knocked into them. A series of pulsing lights on rising stems followed. George froze as the light wavered, powdering his hands, his sleeves, his shoulders as if light were, in itself, a substance: motes as soft as dust. He held his breath and thought bizarrely of playing musical statues as a child, of his mother playing the piano and then stopping suddenly and turning quickly with a smile to see who was still moving. He screwed his eyes up tight. He mustn't think of Mother, mustn't think of home; it would unman him.

Another droning sound above. Should he crouch? He wanted to drop the box and throw himself flat on the ground but Chalky had said to stay still. Somewhere off to his left, the shell landed; he felt the explosion through the soles of his feet as he was rocked sideways and spatters of earth showered down. Then he was up on his feet again; Chalky was dragging the box and telling him to take the other end. He grabbed it as the lights faded once more and they half ran, half stumbled the last fifty yards to the trench.

The men in front scrambled in; one slipping and cursing as the sharp edge of a shovel caught him in the ribs. Chalky and George dumped the box on the steep mounded earth of the parados, at the rear lip of the trench, and Chalky climbed in. George crouched at the edge, caught between the naked field behind and his reflex horror of the dark slot in the ground, but hands were reaching up to pull him and he let himself slide down and come to rest in shallow water and mud. Someone slapped him on the back.

'That was a bit close for comfort,' a voice said in the darkness.

'Think we'll stay here a bit till it quietens down,' Chalky said in George's ear.

Rationally, George knew that he was safer down there but he disliked the enclosed feeling of the trench. The shallow diggings necessitated by the high water table were built up tall and sheer with sandbags and bits of wood and iron. He didn't like the steep sides, the rough traverses that cut off each section from the next, the men from the carrying party crammed together, blocking the way along it on either side of him. He felt the familiar panic rising, his breath shortening. He fixed his eyes on the open sky above him, following the drift of the clouds half obscuring the disc of the full moon.

'Who's the youngster?' a new voice said. 'Looks like he's got the wind up.'

'Farrell,' Chalky answered. 'Leave him be. He's all right.'

George shifted, trying to get a bit more space. The mud sucked at his feet with each step and he longed to get out, to go back. The lance corporal took charge of the ammo, opening the box and handing out linen bandoliers of rounds to his comrades, whilst another started hauling sandbags up to repair the damaged breastworks and parapet. George joined in with the others, handing up the sandbags, which the man laid header and stretcher to make a tight wall.

'Will a sandbag stop a bullet?' George asked Chalky.

'Not likely,' he said. 'Not on its own. You need about five feet of clay to stop a machine-gun bullet, that's why there's so much earth mounded up. It slopes too, see? That's for when there's shelling: to push the blast upwards.'

As George moved along with the next sandbag on his shoulder, he tripped over something sticking out from the front trench wall and a voice, thick with sleep, said, 'Give over. What time is it?' A man was huddled into a small hollow: bent over with his feet tucked in; he was trying to get a little rest before his watch and George had tripped over his rifle. George noticed that there were several such niches dug straight into the clay. He shivered at the thought of sleeping with the earth around you: curled up as tight as an egg in a spoon. What if the trench were hit and the walls caved in? No, you'd never get him into one of those; he would have to sleep on the fire step and take his chances. At camp when they were digging they had sometimes found shards of pottery or the occasional coin, and wondered over the detritus of other ages, men long gone. George disliked these reminders of mortality. He knew the earth was full of worms.

He stepped up and peered gingerly through a gap in the damaged parapet. Beyond the tumbled mess of earth and sandbags and the glinting strands of wire, a wide stubble field stretched, its flatness broken only by the uneven lips of shell holes and the shapes of fallen men. In the distance, like a mirror image: more wire, another trench.

At first sight, the only moving things seemed to be the rise and fall of flares but George had an uneasy sense of movement caught from the corner of his eye, the outline of the humped shapes of corpses shifting slightly as if in the bright light there were shadows where no shadows should be: dark streaks running over them . . . George shuddered.

The barrage a couple of miles to the right was growing stronger: the flashing light bellying out from the line, the noise a tumult in which the separate call and answer of enemy and defending guns was no longer discernible.

'Our lot are getting a pounding tonight,' Chalky said.

George ventured to repeat what he'd heard, that, unable to get through for floods near the coast, the full force of the Germans' resources would be thrown against them in the Brown Wood Line.

There was a silence.

'Cheery sort, your boy,' said one of the men.

All eyes were turned towards the firing.

'Well, if they break through down there and take Wipers, that'll be the end of it, they'll be through to the Channel ports in no time.'

'And if they don't, it'll be our turn next,' said another, picking up his spade. The others followed suit and returned to the task, working on until the breastworks were rebuilt. In the next section, beyond the traverse, more men with spades hoisted themselves up and crept forward into no man's land.

'What are they doing?' George hissed.

'Burial party,' Chalky said. 'Come on, time we got back and hit the sack.'

By the time they had retraced their steps back to the wood, creeping and bent double, answered the heart-jarring challenge of a sentry and trooped on past the hunched forms of men sleeping with their backs against the tree trunks, George felt transparent with physical and nervous exhaustion. He dragged along behind Chalky, thinking of nothing more than putting one foot in front of the other until they finally reached the farm. As they came level with the farmhouse an officer was approaching from the opposite direction, returning to his billet. George recognised the gait of Captain Hunton and kept his head down as they passed, hoping to escape his notice. They trailed on to the farm buildings where Chalky said he would show George where his mates would be sleeping.

Hunton picked his way over the masonry and clods of the garden to the farmhouse door. After inspecting the trenches and delivering his report, he had had a pleasant evening at HQ, where they had been served a half-respectable bit of beef and a very decent brandy. Now this. Obviously, the absentee private had been merely put on fatigues; Lyne had blatantly ignored his recommendations. He felt the onset of indigestion and knew that he would have yet another sleepless night. He cursed under his breath; the man was becoming a thorn in his flesh.

George followed Chalky into a stone barn and climbed up a wooden ladder to the loft, with the others following behind him. The wooden doors, which had been used in better times for unloading straw, were ill fitting, and the gap between

171

doors and frame yielded only a little moonlight. A chorus of groans and curses met the returning party as they stumbled around trying to find a space in which to bed down for the rest of the night.

'Mind yer fucking feet!'

'What d'you think you're doing?'

'Settle down, for Christ's sake.'

George, recognising Turland's voice joining the others in protest, edged his way across. 'Is that you, Ernest?'

'George? I thought they'd thrown you in the guardroom,' Turland whispered. 'I've got your stuff.' He sat up and pulled out George's pack from beside his feet, revealing that Rooke was sleeping back to back with him, a mutual arrangement they had hit on early in their travels as affording both a bit of extra warmth.

'What was the M.O.'s verdict on Percy?' George sank down on to the thin covering of straw strewn on the boards.

'A pill and two days' rest. He's been asleep ever since he got back.'

George fished out his blanket, rolled his greatcoat into a pillow and lay down on his side.

'Are you all right? You're shaking,' Turland said.

A voice nearby said, 'Can't you shut up and get your napper down?'

'All right, all right.'

George put both hands under his cheek to stop them trembling. Scenes from the wood and the trench kept replaying in his mind. He was glad of the chance to say nothing to Ernest. As he closed his eyes, the slow descent of pale flares played out behind his eyelids. When he finally slept he dreamt that he was lying face down, unable to move, and that something passed quickly over his hand, something that felt smooth and warm followed by a trail of something long and scaly. He woke with a start not knowing where he was. Staring into the darkness, for a moment he was terrified by the still, dim shapes surrounding him, but then he fell into a troubled sleep once more.

10

HOME COMFORTS

Kitty was late for the Grand Bazaar. She pushed the last letter through the final letterbox and set off directly to the hall; she'd promised to help and there wasn't enough time to go home. Besides, although it would have been nice to wear her best coat and the new hat that she'd had for her birthday, she felt proud to wear her uniform and of her recent, more public role of delivering the mail rather than just working behind the scenes. However much her father went on about 'men's work' she didn't see why she shouldn't do the job: she was just as quick as the boys, in fact she always took the heaviest route and didn't complain half as much as they did. Her father was fond of quoting to her the rhyme that had appeared in a newspaper cartoon under the heading 'The Development of a Suffragette':

At five a little Pet,
At fifteen a Coquette,
At forty not married yet!
At fifty a Suffragette.

It made her feel cross and even more rebellious. She rather liked the idea of turning up at the bazaar in uniform and being seen to be 'doing her bit'. She didn't see why women should try and hide the fact that they were doing men's jobs or that her rather smart, tailored uniform made her look any less feminine.

Sure enough, when she entered the hall her mother was waiting anxiously at the door and her first words were: 'Kitty, couldn't you have changed?'

'There wasn't time. The market crowds slowed me up,' Kitty said, hanging her empty postbag on a coat peg.

Her mother rolled her eyes. 'Well, you'd better come and help me at the handiwork stall,' she said, leading the way into the crowd milling around the stalls. 'There's still lots to unpack.'

The usual musty, church-hall smell was overlaid by the smell of baking from the cake table and the refreshment stand. Over the stage was a large banner that read 'SUPPORT YOUR COTTAGE HOSPITAL', a cause that had drawn together Church and Chapel and many ladies' voluntary groups in the town. Stalls lined the walls and ran back to back along the middle of the room: trestle tables pinned with swags of material in red, white and blue, framed above by poles entwined with paper flowers supporting fretwork trellises hung with goods for sale. Some stands had names; a stall piled high with baskets of apples and plums and stacked with jars of preserves had 'Cornucopia' stencilled on a sign, whilst another selling scent sachets, patriotic stick pins and penny soaps in envelopes had a sign reading 'Keswick Scouts Troop Fund'.

Kitty followed her mother, returning the greetings of people she knew and looking at the stalls selling pottery, framed water-colours, postcards and stamps. On a haberdashery stall, amongst ribbons and feather trims, she noticed some silk flowers that would look very well on her birthday hat; she would spend what was left of her wages on them when she got a chance to take a break from her sales duties. She reached the Methodist Ladies' Handiwork Stall, slipped in at the back and started laying out embroidered tray cloths and crocheted hot-water-bottle covers. Alongside these homely items, her mother was arranging others made as comforts for the troops: socks and Crimean sleeping caps. When she had finished, she let her hand rest for a moment on a pile of knitted blanket squares, patting it as if she would send her touch to all the boys like her Arthur, so far from home.

Kitty was serving a lady who was looking for antimacassars when Mrs Farrell approached with the children in tow. She gave some pennies to Ted and sent him off with Lillie; then she came over to speak to her mother. 'How are you, Mabel? Have you had any news of Arthur lately?'

'We're well, thank you,' her mother said. 'We gather Arthur's in France now. He sent a photograph of himself and a couple of friends outside the cookhouse tent.' She gave a weak smile. 'He says he's in the best of health. How's George getting on with his training? Will he get leave at Christmas, do you think?'

Mrs Farrell sighed. 'No chance of leave, I'm afraid. He's gone overseas – somewhere in Belgium is all we know.'

Kitty looked up sharply from giving the lady her change. 'I thought he was in camp! I thought you couldn't go overseas until you were nineteen! What on earth did he want to go and do that for!'

'Kitty! Shush!' her mother said, seeing Mrs Farrell's face

falling. 'I'm so sorry, Maggie.' She reached over and touched her arm. 'Believe me, I know how difficult it is.'

Seeing George's mother's bereft expression, Kitty stopped short. She shut the little metal cashbox with a clang. She had *told* him that he shouldn't join up, that he wasn't the fighting kind. Hadn't she *said* that he didn't know what he was getting into? How could he be so daft! The thought of him in a trench somewhere, maybe even under enemy fire, gave her a horrible panicky, powerless feeling. Now she would have both George and Arthur to worry about. She muttered, 'Stupid, idiot boys,' under her breath.

Her mother said, 'I think we could all use some tea. Maggie, why don't you come and take my place and I'll fetch some.'

They exchanged places and George's mother sat down heavily on the stool next to Kitty's. As Kitty automatically refolded the antimacassars that the customer had picked through, she was aware of her curious sidelong glances.

'We haven't seen much of you lately, Kitty. Have you been busier than usual? You know you're always welcome to visit any time.'

'It's all the letters going back and forth from the Front,' Kitty said. 'It seems as though the post's doubled since the war started. I'd rather be busy than sitting around worrying though, even if it is pretty hard work.'

'I expect you're busy in the evenings too, now you're courting. George tells me you have a follower?'

'Not so much, nowadays,' Kitty said quickly, regretting the lie she'd told George so hastily in retaliation when he had hurt her by shutting her out. 'I mean . . . oh dear . . .' She felt herself blushing to the roots of her hair. 'That is, we've parted ways.' She took out another pile of linen from a basket beneath the stall and busied herself in untangling the snarled threads of the price tickets.

Maggie looked at her sympathetically. She hesitated and then said, 'Were you very angry with George for going away?'

'Well, I felt he should have told me before, not just gone and done it without a word to anyone. If he'd talked to me about it first I might have had a chance to persuade him out of it. Although I don't know why I should think that, given that he told me it was none of my business . . .' She yanked at the tickets, pulling some of them right off, made a sound of annoyance and dumped them back on to her lap.

'Are you still angry with him?'

Kitty bit her lip and nodded.

Maggie sighed. 'I don't mean to interfere but George is very fond of you, you know,' she said mildly. 'He always asks for news of you in his letters.'

'Well, his letters to me are about a paragraph long and limit themselves to the state of the food and the weather,' Kitty said tartly, 'so he obviously still doesn't feel inclined to confide in his oldest friend.' She picked up the mess of cloth and price tags and stuffed them back into the basket. 'Sorry,' she muttered. 'I don't know what gets into me these days; I get a bit over-tired with all the extra work and then when I stop I'm wondering about Arthur, and now there's George to worry about too—' She broke off as her mother returned with teacups on a tray. Kitty stood up to let her have a seat. 'Can you spare me for a few minutes?' she said.

She left the mothers talking and walked slowly around the hall looking at all the goods for sale. She cast an eye for the last time over the bunch of silk flowers with its cluster of red berries that would make a fine hat trimming but then moved on until she found a stall selling comforts for the troops. Amongst the chocolate and tins of biscuits was a little Oxo trench heater with half a dozen Oxo cubes and lighters. It would

178

be useful. It would help keep him warm. She bought the heater and then went back for a tin of Needler's Military Mints as well and had them both wrapped.

When she returned to the stall, George's mother had just left to find Ted and Lillie and take them home. Kitty caught up with them all at the door, where Ted was trying to get Lillie to put her arms into her coat sleeves. 'Do you send a box out to George?' she said, out of breath.

'Every fortnight or so,' George's mother said.

'Could you put these in with the rest, please?' Kitty pushed the parcels into her hands.

'Don't you want to send them yourself?' she asked but Kitty was already turning away. 'Do come and see us, Kitty, whenever you'd like to . . .' she called after her as Kitty threaded her way back into the crowd and disappeared from view.

Violet inspected the table settings: silver and crystal gleaming on a field of white damask cloth, pink roses and dark fern in a low display in the centre with candelabra either side.

'Change the candelabra for the tall lamps with the amber glass shades,' she said to Mrs Burbidge. 'They're just as elegant and they won't obscure the guests' view of each other.'

Two days ago, out of the blue, her mother had received a letter from her father saying that he was bringing a few people down for the weekend, for some country air: business acquaintances and their wives. They would arrive by motor, in time for dinner, and arrangements must also be made to accommodate valets, ladies' maids and the chauffeurs.

The news had thrown Violet's mother into a spin. Not content with leaving Mrs Burbidge to marshal the domestics, she had marched around the house demanding that windows be washed and carpets be beaten, until Mrs Burbidge had looked so red in the face that Violet had thought she might go off like a fire-cracker. After a morning playing havoc with the household, however, her mother had tired and Violet had been able to persuade her that since time was so short she could better spend it in resting, so she would be fresh for entertaining her guests. She had retired to consider her costume for dinner and left Violet to quietly oversee the essential preparations and drop the inessential from Mrs Burbidge's itinerary.

After two days of frantic activity by the servants and extra staff engaged from the village, the rooms had been made ready, provisions had been supplied and a massive amount of cooking and baking had been accomplished: cold meats, pies, potted fowl, Dundee cake and macaroons filling the shelves of the pantry to groaning point. The table lighting was duly changed and Violet released Mrs Burbidge to oversee preparations in the kitchen and ensure that the staff were tidy and ready to greet the master of the house.

Violet's feelings about seeing her father were mixed. He hadn't visited for over two years. Granted, he was often away in Europe looking after business interests in logging and textiles but Violet had seen the London postmark on his occasional letters to Mother and deduced that he was staying at his club. He wrote rarely to Mother, letters that made polite enquiries about her health and longer enquiries about money: the estate accounts, inheritances, her allowance. He never wrote to Violet. She told herself that she was only curious to know what brought him home, with people in tow, and that she was only nervous about impressing unaccustomed guests. She tried to ignore the curiosity she felt about whether he would notice her at last as a full-grown woman, and struggled to silence the voice of her neglected child-self who still craved his attention. Despite her best efforts at rationality, she couldn't help but wonder whether the visit might mean some kind of rapprochement and that something might change.

They arrived at seven, motor cars crunching over the gravel sweep to draw up in front of the house, maids bobbing curtseys in line outside the porch as Violet and her mother stood in the doorway to welcome their houseguests. The clear October evening smelt of wood-smoke and cold as the party swept into the wide entrance hall, laughing and talking with the relief of having arrived, unwrapping themselves from cashmere coats and fur wraps and clustering around the fire, whilst behind them the servants unloaded boxes and valises and scurried to and from the trade entrance. Violet, whilst enquiring about the nature of the journey, saw her father kiss Mother fleetingly on the cheek and ask her how she was and then turn away without listening for the answer. He looked older, his hair and beard whiter, although his solid build and colour still suggested health and vigour.

'May I introduce you all?' He raised his voice and presided over a great deal of hand shaking. 'Linton Dempster, one of my business partners, and his wife Hebe; my friend of long standing, Oliver Ryland, from the War Ministry, and his wife Juliet; and Eustace Haydon who is at the bank, with his lovely wife of a mere two months, Allegra – my wife, Irene, and my daughter, Violet.'

Violet stood close beside her mother, whose cheeks were flushed with excitement as she murmured a welcome to each guest. She caught the hint of an American accent in Linton Dempster's greeting, noticed the stiff formality of the Rylands', who were an older couple, and was caught by an envious feeling as she saw the way that Eustace Haydon kept his hand at the hollow of his wife's back, an easy familiarity between lovers that brought back to her a longing for Edmund's touch that was almost a physical pain.

The guests were shown to their rooms to dress for dinner, and Violet, after checking with Mrs Burbidge that all was well, and the motors garaged, was grateful to withdraw. She wondered at her father's motley selection of guests and what they had in common. The men all members of the same club perhaps? Otherwise what on earth was he up to? She hoped that the weather would stay clear so that they could walk or shoot. If not, she would have to suggest bridge or an impromptu concert to keep them entertained.

At dinner Violet was seated with her father on her left and young Eustace Haydon on her right. At first conversation was general: the progress of the war and the difficulties in Belgium; the effect that conscription would have on the labour market and the suggestion that women might play a greater part. Violet noticed that her mother looked bemused and was covering her lack of involvement in the conversation by continuously sipping her wine. She was glad when Juliet Ryland admired the portraits in the room and began to ask Mother about the history of the house. Her father continued talking to Oliver Ryland about the war, long after the subject had moved on, and Violet picked up snatches of the conversation: 'the length of the supply chain', 'tonnage per acre', 'shipping and distribution costs'. She idly wondered what deal her father had his fingers in with the War Office, and then, noticing that everyone had finished their soup, signalled to the maids that they should clear.

She allowed herself a moment of satisfaction as she surveyed the scene. The room had come to life, filled with guests in animated conversation, the lamplight falling on the ladies' satins and silks, wraps of velvet or diaphanous chiffon, and hair dressed with jewelled combs and flowers. The men too looked well and relaxed, leaning back in their chairs, evening dress shirt-fronts starched, smart in neat white ties. A good fire glowed in the hearth and the side tables were laden with serving dishes and wine coolers. This was what the room was meant for and she felt proud of her home and her household.

When the covers were removed and the duck was served, Father finally broke off his conversation, set down his glass and turned to her with a mischievous look.

'Well, Violet. Have you completed your education? Are you well and truly finished?' He looked her up and down with an appraising eye.

'I've been home for a year, Father,' Violet said.

'Ah, indeed. And is it suiting you? The country life?' He glanced around as if to include the nearby guests in the conversation. 'Any gentleman farmers coming to call, eh? Anyone looking for a good brood mare?'

Violet blushed at his boorishness.

Eustace Haydon said quickly, 'I believe your mother was telling me that you have an interest in photography? Tell me, have you tried developing your own prints? You can produce some very interesting effects.'

Violet turned to him in relief and found him an attentive and charming dinner partner. As they talked of books and music, she was keenly reminded of the evenings she had spent with Edmund. How she missed him: the way he leant forward on his elbows when he talked to you, the way he would engage you in ridiculous debates on the relative merits of writers or composers – Dickens or Austen? Chopin or Sibelius? – the way that when he told a joke he embroidered it so much that he sometimes forgot the punch line. In her mind, she said a prayer that he was out of the line and safe and that the war would soon end.

When the talk of the table turned once more to general topics, she daydreamt for a while of a future when Edmund would be here and everything would be different. The place would be transformed. They would have Edmund's family to stay; she would arrange for croquet on the lawn, just as they played at Elizabeth's, maybe even tennis parties if the grass could be rolled smooth enough. She pictured them sitting in the bamboo tub chairs in the colonnade, taking tea. It would bring Mother back to life too, even if Father did stay away. He could stay away forever for all she cared.

As dessert was cleared away, talk turned to musical theatre and the latest West End shows. Mother invited the ladies to withdraw, to leave the men to smoke, and as the men rose absentmindedly to their feet, Father was enthusing loudly about a performance of *Our Miss Gibbs*.

'I tell you, it was stunning,' he said to Linton. 'A real spectacle.'

'What did Dodie make of it?' Linton said in a voice that was clearly audible to Violet above the scraping of chairs.

'Oh, we both loved it . . .' Father said, but then trailed off as he saw Violet staring at him in disbelief.

'Let me show you to the drawing room,' Mother was saying to the ladies who followed her. Juliet Ryland, who had pursed her mouth at her father's comment, quickly started a conversation about how much she looked forward to seeing the grounds tomorrow if Irene felt able to show them around, and wondered if the others would care to join her.

They all know, Violet thought. Father has a mistress and he has brought his friends, who all know about it, to this house. She felt savage. The men, to cover their embarrassment, were making a great fuss of passing cigarette cases and cutting their cigars. She hung back as the ladies left the room and stood folding her napkin, as if deep in thought. She leant across to her father and in a low voice and a conversational tone, said, 'You truly are a hateful man.'

For a moment he looked taken aback; then he gave a snorting laugh and shook his head. 'You have your mother's sensitivity, I see.'

'I have my mother's trusting nature and, I hope, my mother's manners,' she replied.

She bade the other men goodnight and left them.

At last, after what seemed like hours of small talk, all the guests had retired and after a quick conversation with Mrs Burbidge about tomorrow's breakfast and luncheon, Violet was able to retreat to her room. She told the maid that she didn't need her and undressed herself, letting the pale grey satin dress slip from her shoulders, stepping out of her petticoats and laying the clothes aside over a chair. She turned over the events of the evening as she finished undressing and brushed out her hair.

Poor Mother, she thought. What a betrayal. She could only hope that Mother hadn't heard and that Father would watch his words more carefully for the rest of the weekend. Everything made sense now. No wonder they never saw him, he must have another home, another life . . . She stopped brushing. Maybe other children? Could she have half-brothers and -sisters somewhere? She felt queasy with hurt and worry. Always aware that she had been a disappointment and that her father had wanted a male heir, she thought what a fine irony it would be if he did in fact have a son who, for propriety's sake, he couldn't acknowledge.

She wondered whether her mother knew about his infidelity but chose to ignore it for the sake of her dignity and position. Instantly she knew that she would never be able to ask her;

they didn't have that kind of intimacy. That too made her sad. All she could do was stick close to Mother this weekend and try to steer conversations into harmless waters.

She laid down her brush on the dressing table, opened a drawer and took out Edmund's last letter – her only safe haven. The paper had thinned almost into holes at the creases. For the umpteenth time she read:

My darling girl,

I'm writing this very early in the morning; we had a muster parade at six a.m. (presumably to avoid the enemy finding us in bed). I'm sitting in the parlour of the farmhouse where we are billeted and for the moment it's peaceful with just the sound of a blackbird singing outside. If I close my eyes I could be in England, in some secluded spot, with you . . .

I hope and trust that you are well (and that your mother is better too). We are still in reserve so no need to worry. We are quite comfortable and keeping our spirits up. Mallory gave a little concert last night, playing the melodeon, and we have cards and conversation too. The men keep cheerful and are a steadfast lot on the whole.

I spend a lot of my time filling in returns and orders, which seems boring on the face of it but which I hope will bear fruit eventually, as the powers that be need to know that unconscionable numbers of shells are duds and some of the rifles you wouldn't want to rely on in a tight spot.

There is no prospect of leave for now but I'll write as soon as I have news on that score. We could meet in London, your mother's health permitting: we would have more time together and could make every hour count. I miss you. I ache to hold you in my arms again. My thoughts of you are my joy and sustenance, dearest Violet.

I'm told there is a mail about today so I am hopeful that
I may get a letter from you. I shall carry it with me as my
good-luck charm: your loving thoughts next to my heart.
    Ever yours,
    Edmund

Violet folded the letter and pressed it to her lips; then she got into bed and put it under her pillow.

She ran through the plan for the next day. The ladies were to be shown the gardens, the lake and the little church and would play cards in the afternoon but the men had opted for Hodges to take them up into the woods. Violet thought this strange as they weren't hunting but only walking and there was not much that would interest them, the view being obscured by the thick planting. She felt rather peeved to be obliged to show the gardens when she would so much rather walk in the woods. They were beautiful this time of year in russet and gold, although Father, with his logging interests, would probably say that one tree was much like another.

As she relaxed towards sleep, her mind made a sudden connection to her father's conversation with Oliver Ryland, whom he had introduced as working at the War Office. *Tonnage per acre. Shipping costs.* Suddenly wide awake, she felt sure that her father planned to sell the timber for the war effort, their beautiful trees felled for trench supports and pit props.

Her mother had been so excited at the prospect of his visit; she too had harboured the same old hope that something might have changed. Now the real reason for it was clear. She wished the weekend could be over. She wished he would just go.

11

PLAYING CARDS

The worst thing for George about being on fatigues, apart from the relentless slog, filling sandbags for the sappers or winding wire on to poles, was that whenever he got any break it was likely to be interrupted by Sergeant Tate sending him off somewhere. If he had ten minutes to spare, he liked to sit quietly at the edge of a group and sketch what he saw: the farrier sergeant murmuring to a horse as he unhitched it from a wagon, a private asleep with the farm cat on his lap, Turland and Rooke sharing a billycan. There was never enough time for painting but catching an expression or a man's typical posture with a few quick strokes and a little shading gave him immense pleasure. On this occasion he had hardly taken his sketchbook out to draw Haycock blowing smoke rings when the sergeant whistled him over. He put the book away reluctantly, heaved himself back on to his feet and was sent off with the officers' evening meal.

When George arrived at the farmhouse, laden with a dixie of stew and a sandbag full of potatoes, the officers were sitting around the table, playing cards. Candles were set in the window embrasures as well as on the table, their flames guttering and dancing in the draughty room, making the shadows of the men, intent on their game, jump and start on the walls and ceiling. The smell of whisky and cigarette smoke was in the air, and several bottles, one still half full, stood on the table amongst a muddle of enamel mugs and an empty sardine tin in use as an ashtray. George felt relief as Edmund nodded to him before returning his attention to the game.

George put the dixie on the stove to reheat, tucked a rickety three-legged stool between the stove and the woodpile, found a bucket and sat down to peel the potatoes. The night's shelling was beginning to build as the batteries of field howitzers behind the billets fired, and were answered by German guns seeking the guns and ammunition dumps. Sometimes they were nearer, sometimes further away; there was no telling when the next might come or how close it might fall, and the unpredictability made them impossible to ignore, keeping the men in a constant state of fearful anticipation that stretched the nerves.

'I'll see you,' Hunton was saying. 'Come on, let's see what you've got.'

One by one, the others laid down their cards. Carey was last and turned his cards up slowly as if confident of a win. Hunton fanned his cards out and tapped them with his forefinger. They all paid up. Hunton, his face impassive, leant over and scooped the money towards him saying, 'Let's double up this time, shall we?'

189

Carey groaned.

'Come on!' Hunton said. 'Don't take all night about it.' He picked up the bottle of whisky, poured a shot into each mug, and then took a slug and topped his up again.

Carey put up his money, saying under his breath, 'You'll clean me out at this rate.'

Edmund noticed the hesitation of Mallory and Parks, who, as lower ranks, had less pay to throw around. He put his money in and said lightly, 'I'm out after this round, I'm afraid.'

Hunton looked at him sharply for a second before pushing a mug towards him, saying, 'Drink up, Lyne.'

The others added their francs to the pile and Mallory took his turn to deal but kept on losing his place. Hunton ignored his slurred apologies, took the cards from him, irritably tapped them back into a pack and handed them to Carey, who dealt with quick, competent hands.

They played on and George was glad of their concentration. He peeled steadily and kept his head down in case Hunton's eye should fall on him. He didn't trust Hunton's mood. The game was just ending, this time in Carey's favour, and he was gathering up both cards and money when there was a whining sound from the pasture between the farmhouse and the wood and Carey's hands stilled. As the shell came down, the sound reverberated around them. George's stool skittered on the flagstones. Plaster dust and tile fragments fell down through the gaps in the boards of the ceiling above them, sprinkling their hunched shoulders and the table, so that Hunton cursed and put his hand across his mug of whisky. The sound died away and a swag of cobweb, shaken loose, hung down from between the floorboards, white with dust.

Mallory, slurring his words, said, 'Oh Christ, oh God. I

thought that was it. I really can't stand it. What on earth are we doing here? It's not safe; we should be further back . . .'

Parks said, 'Shut up, Mallory.'

'It's the noise; I can't bear the noise . . . and we're not even in the line yet. I don't think I can do it, just wait there like a sitting target: no one should have to do it . . .'

Mallory moved to stand up and Edmund put his hand on his arm, saying, 'Mallory, get a grip on yourself.'

Mallory subsided back into his seat and put his head in his hands.

Hunton brushed the dust from his sleeves and Carey set a candle straight and began slowly to gather up the cards again.

Hunton said testily, 'Let's just play, shall we?'

Edmund said, 'I think I'm going to pass, if it's all the same to you.'

Hunton carried on as if Edmund hadn't spoken, and reached for the bottle, saying, 'You deal, Parks.'

Edmund said, 'I'm sorry, sir, but I can't match the stake. I'll have to go broke.'

'You'll stop when I say stop,' he said. 'You can play for what-ever's in your pockets.'

Edmund glanced at the others. He was down to a handful of coins himself and he hoped that Mallory and Parks had had the sense to tuck some of their pay away elsewhere, and not to be carrying it on them. Mallory was clearly drunk and could hardly keep his cards to himself and Parks's mind wasn't on the job; it would be like taking sweets from a baby. Whatever was the matter with the man, the way he toyed with them, always putting them to the test? Edmund tried to stop his irritation showing in his face. He had seen Hunton drink like this before and it wasn't advisable to cross him. If he carried on long enough, he would simply fall asleep where he sat and one of the others,

191

usually Carey, would rouse him and take him through to the parlour, which he had to himself as a bedroom.

Edmund picked up his cards and spread them out. It was the best hand he'd had and he wondered if he might be lucky this time. He had nothing to lose and the sooner he could get the game over the sooner he could excuse himself and get some useful work done before supper. He shrugged, laid down an eight of clubs and picked up a queen.

The play continued. Carey passed round a pack of Wills and Edmund noticed how he glanced quickly at Mallory's and Parks's cards as they leant forward to light their cigarettes at the candle. He saw Hunton notice too and give a brief, sneering smile. Edmund began to play seriously for the first time that evening. As if sensing Edmund's renewed interest in the game, Hunton lengthened out his turns, giving every decision close consideration, his expression inscrutable.

George, noticing the intensity of their play, was drawn to watch despite his caution. He stood stirring the stew automatically. Parks kept grumbling about his awful hand, Mallory was barely playing but Carey, Edmund and Hunton were leaning forward into the pool of candlelight, avid for the next card.

Edmund decided to call. He had picked up a queen at his last turn to add to the two he already held and he felt that this was the best he was going to get. 'I'll see you,' he said.

Parks showed his hand with a grunt of disgust. Mallory and Carey turned theirs up, Mallory with his boyish, high-pitched laugh, Carey craning forward to see what Hunton and Edmund had. Hunton, with a self-satisfied smile, turned his over with deliberation, one by one. Four kings.

Edmund had been beaten. He laid out his queens saying, 'Aah, so close.'

Edmund dug in his trouser pocket and pulled out a handful

of centimes. He scooped them on to the table; a couple landed on edge and rolled across to the other side. Suddenly it struck him as funny that they had been playing so intently over so little and that Hunton should end up with all his useless loose change: he struggled to control a grin as he said, 'Sorry, sir; that's it, I'm afraid.'

Hunton, without missing a beat, said, 'What about your jacket pocket?'

'My . . . Not much in there, sir,' Edmund said, remembering only a stub of pencil, postage stamps and some string. He started to unbutton the pocket flap and then paused. He felt the crackle of paper and a chill travelled down his back. Hunton's eyes were on him like a cat at a hedgerow. Edmund put his thumb and forefinger into the pocket, digging down to get the pencil and odds and ends without disturbing the letter: Violet's letter that had arrived today and that he had been saving to read as soon as he could get a chance to be alone.

'That's everything in your pocket, Lyne,' Hunton said coldly. 'It's been won fair and square. I'm sure you wouldn't want to break your word.'

Edmund drew out the letter and put it down beside the oddments. He could feel that he still had a stupid smile on his face, the drink slowing him down so that his expression hadn't caught up with what was happening. George, seeing the blue envelope and familiar writing, involuntarily took a step forward and then stopped. Hunton's hand stretched out and took the letter.

'Come on, sir; that's private,' Edmund said, still clinging to a light-hearted tone as if by treating it all as a joke he could make it so, even though his angry blood was rising to his face, giving him away.

'Oh, I say,' Mallory said. 'That's not right. A chap's letters . . . you know. That's from Lyne's sweetheart!'

Parks nudged him to be quiet.

'What?' Mallory remonstrated. 'It's not right! Play the game! He's besotted . . . keeps a picture by the bed and all . . .'

Hunton glanced over at the embrasure by the bed. 'Ah yes, I noticed Lyne had a bit of skirt.'

Edmund rose, his hands clenched into fists.

Hunton looked at him with an amused expression. 'What then, Lyne? Is there something you want to say?' He smiled. 'Or do? I think we've discussed court-martial offences on a previous occasion.' Without looking at George, he continued, 'The trouble with you, Lyne, is that you have no discipline: neither self-control nor control over your men. Perhaps this will help you learn some.'

Edmund, trembling with anger, pushed his chair aside and strode out of the room.

Hunton raised his eyebrows and looked at the others. He folded the letter in two and buttoned it into his own pocket. 'Get Mallory to bed,' he said.

Parks heaved Mallory up out of his chair. He was still shaking his head and muttering about 'a man's personal affairs'.

'Come on, old boy. A bit of shut-eye for you.' Parks put Mallory's arm over his shoulders and led him over to the scullery where they had their beds. He pulled the curtain across the doorway and didn't re-emerge.

Carey said quietly, 'Are you going to return it, sir?'

'Oh for God's sake, Carey, I've a perfect right to read any letter I like, to censor them, to destroy them if I see fit.'

'But still, sir . . .'

'He had a lesson coming.'

Carey fell silent.

Hunton said, 'You can serve the food now, Farrell.'

George complied, avoiding eye contact. As he waited for the men to finish eating, he covertly watched Hunton: his thick moustache laden with greasy gravy, his cold, watery eyes, his concentration on his food and the precise way in which he cut his meat. He couldn't bear the thought of those thick, stubby fingers touching Violet's letter; it filled him with disgust. He wondered where Edmund had gone. In the moment that he had stepped forward, when Hunton took the letter, he had seen Edmund notice him and put out his hand as if to stop him. Had it been a gesture to keep him out of Hunton's way? Alongside his outrage and his hatred for Hunton, George felt relief that Edmund seemed to have wholly put aside his suspicions after finding him looking at his things, and accepted him again.

When the officers had finished eating George began to clear away. As Hunton rose to leave he said to him in passing, 'Don't think you're off the hook. Your name will be on my list one of these days.' Carey followed Hunton out.

By the time he'd cleared up, he found that the stew had dried out and was sticking to the dixie. He added water and was scraping at the sides of the pan when Edmund came back.

'Ah, Farrell, it's you.' He looked relieved to find only George.

'Would you like some food, sir?' George asked tentatively. 'The others have eaten.'

Edmund came over and glanced into the pot. 'Is that what it is? Well, I'll have some anyway,' he said with false jocularity.

George dished out a portion but Edmund sat without eating, his face drawn.

'Do you think we'll be going forward soon?' George ventured.

195

'I wouldn't be surprised if we reserves weren't brought forward tomorrow night.' Edmund sought the man-to-man tone he'd used to reassure the boy before. 'I shall be right there with you men. Don't worry, we'll be all in it together.'

George felt a mixture of excitement and apprehension. Terrifying though the thought of an attack was, he was sick of the waiting game and hoped that he might at last fire his rifle instead of cleaning it. He thought that he would write home tomorrow and say that they should watch the papers for a mention of his regiment involved in action. At the thought of the family, he remembered his conversation with Edmund about making sure his mother would get his pay, come what may. Chalky had told him that when they knew in advance that there was going to be fighting, a corporal came round with a sandbag to collect everyone's valuables. A sandbag. It didn't seem very secure to him. 'Would you look after my pay book, sir?' he blurted out. 'I should feel better about it if I know you have it, rather than it being all muddled with everyone's stuff in a sandbag that could easily go missing.'

Edmund looked surprised. 'Of course, Farrell,' he said. 'If it would ease your mind.' He wondered what the family's circumstances were that gave Farrell such a bee in his bonnet about making sure that the money would reach them. He had talked to infantrymen who said the dire army food was better than they got at home: maybe for Farrell as for so many others civilian life was a struggle of a different kind. Well, God knows he had learnt tonight what it meant to lose something that was important to you. He took the pay book, poured himself a whisky and said, 'I won't be needing you any further tonight. Go and find yourself a drink.'

'Thank you, sir.' George turned to leave and caught sight of Violet's picture, reinstated in its usual place. He felt a stab of misery at the thought of her letter in Hunton's pocket. He walked quickly from the room. He wanted to get out into the cold, clean air.

Edmund nursed his whisky for a while, staring into space. He still half wished that he had hit Hunton. He hated the way Hunton had looked at him, knowing he had him over a barrel. He hoped that in the sober light of day, Hunton might give the letter back. He desperately wanted to read it and be reassured that Violet was all right. Suppose she was ill or finding the loneliness and worry too much of a strain? Now he would have to wait and fret until another letter came, and who knew when the post would catch up with them? He had waited weeks before now and then a bundle had arrived all at once. It would be a bloody torment. Hunton was a vindictive bastard! The fact that the others had shown their disapproval of the shoddy trick would go against him too; Hunton would assert his authority at all costs and would now be even more incensed to feel he had been shown up. There was nothing he could do but wait.

He flicked through Farrell's dog-eared pay book. He saw that George had filled in the page marked 'Will' as he had suggested. He read:

In the event of my death, I leave my fishing rod to my brother, Ted Farrell, my prayer book that was a school prize to my father, Frederick Farrell, and all other belongings and money due to me I give to my mother, Maggie Farrell, all of Leonard Street, Keswick, except for my book of illustrated songs which I give to Kitty Ashwell of The Post Office, Main Street, Keswick.

Signed: George Farrell, Private 1893, 8th November 1914

Edmund was touched by the personal bequests of these simple belongings. He got up from the table and stowed the pay book away and then lay on his back on the bed. He found himself reading the same page of his novel over and over, his mind divided between listening to the guns and wanting Violet.

12

EARTH

The next night, as predicted, they went down to the fire trench. After labouring most of the night alongside Turland and two regulars, helping to repair a part of the trench that had collapsed, George took his turn on sentry-go around four. He looked out over no man's land, staring into the flare of Verey lights until his eyes ached and phantom after-images flowered in his head. He methodically scanned the long slope of the field for movement, staring at the monochrome scene until he knew every plane of shadow cast by the few shattered trees, every dip and crater, every hummock: khaki and *feldgrau* all one in the greyness before dawn.

Exhausted by the digging and revetting, and numbed by the cold, George's anxiety that he would succumb to sleep grew. He knew the penalty, and that he had used up any credit with Sergeant Tate long ago. He chewed the inside of his cheeks in an effort to stay awake. He counted backwards from a hundred. The rise and fall of the flares was hypnotic – he drifted for a moment and came to with a start, realising that he had been dreaming of the spluttering gas mantle of the parlour lamp at home. His father was lighting it: the gas sucking the match flame and the white ball glowing into life, casting a pool of light on to his mother's hands setting down plates on the table. He jerked his head upright and hastily scanned the field again. He took his Imperial Service badge and put the pin through his collar without fastening it, so that it rested against his neck: if his chin dropped in sleep, it would jab him and wake him.

Turland and two of the regulars, Smith and Wilmott, were talking quietly about the rumour that the Prussian Guards, who were reputed to be crack shots that fought to the death and took no prisoners, had replaced the Bavarians in the enemy line. Everyone agreed that an attack would come soon: the previous day, Taubes had flown over the rear areas trying to spy out the guns and estimate the range for their artillery. The ensuing bombardment left everyone in no doubt about the enemy's intentions.

George peered into the gloom, working his way along the entanglements in front of the trench, looking for German scouts sent out to check the state of the wire. A patrol had gone out earlier to mend any gaps and the awareness that he must take time to discriminate between friend and foe made him hesitant and jumpy.

A quick movement, seen from the corner of his eye, out to his left among the bodies, made him hunch and recoil. The Alleyman's snipers were positioned in saps, dug from their lines out into no man's land, and he feared that one had crawled forward to lie behind the cover of the bodies of the dead. In the moment that he took aim, a flash of something round and white rose in front of him. Before he could loose off a round, he saw not a human face but the flat heart-shaped face and dark eyes of a barn owl as it swooped towards him and passed silently above his head.

He let out his breath with a sound that was half a laugh and half a sigh of relief, and turned to see the bird glide away to resume its quartering over the ground between the line and the wood. It slid into the mist, undisturbed by the warring factions below: men reduced to the level of creeping, burrowing creatures. Its freedom made it seem eerily powerful. His mother called it 'the white old woman of the night' and believed that an owl perching on the roof of a house meant that a death would follow. He had felt the draught of its wings in its low flight. Did it mean something that it had passed him so closely?

He told himself that such a close encounter was hardly surprising; the plague of mice and rats supplied rich pickings to attract such hunters. Men now slept in the barns and outbuildings where the owls used to nest, forcing them into the broken cottages and burnt-out homes that families had deserted. Both men and birds were displaced, adapting to an unnatural world changed by war. He tried to shake off his sense of foreboding but found himself continually listening, hoping that he wouldn't hear the bird's hoarse and dismal cry.

He was glad when, shortly before dawn, the corporal came down the line to rouse everyone for stand-to. George stamped his feet, trying to get some blood back into them, and flapped his arms against his body. Men who had been sleeping in the straw-lined 'caves' under the parapet crawled out, emerging with faces dirty and frowsy with sleep. They hawked and spat, passed along the bucket to piss in, jammed on their caps.

Further along the trench, the corporal was having trouble waking Addison, a small, sickly man who had been an estate agent's clerk in Civvy Street. He prodded him with his boot until he stirred and then hauled him out, set him on his feet and pushed his rifle into his hands before carrying on around the corner of the traverse.

The men checked over their weapons, working the bolts and fixing bayonets: the clicks and scrapes of metal on metal the only sounds save for the occasional crack of rifles further down the line, like the last crackle of a dying fire. The ensign followed in the corporal's footsteps with a mess tin of rum and the men took their measure gratefully. George shook his head as the spoon was offered.

'Go on, lad. It'll warm you through,' Smith said to him.

George laid aside his promise to his father, which he had only made in order to reassure him that he wouldn't get into trouble. Well, he couldn't get into much more trouble than this. He spluttered and coughed as the strong taste took his breath away. Smith laughed at him and slapped him on the back. His stomach rumbled as the warmth spread through him and he longed for the relative shelter of the wood and the chance to fry up some bacon. Even the most basic comforts of a coke bucket and a rasher or two seemed a refuge.

They took their places at the parapet, spacing themselves equally, and laid their rifles on the lip of the trench. Haycock and Rooke were out of sight, somewhere beyond a series of tight traverses. George was between the two regulars, Smith and Wilmott; Addison and Turland were further down with regulars whose names he didn't know spaced in between them. Even from here, George could see that Addison was shaking. He hoped that the tremor that he could feel inside, a kind of breathless shivering in his chest and guts, wouldn't spread to his hands and knees and show on the outside. Beyond the traverse on the left he could hear Edmund's voice as he worked his way down, speaking to each man in his section. George tried to get a hold of himself and checked for the umpteenth time that he could easily get to the clips of ammunition in pouches and pockets.

The sky was lightening to a foggy grey dawn, revealing more clearly the stubbled ground at the trench edge and the barbed wire beyond it, beaded with dew. A milky mist lay over the field, thicker on the lower slope where the land dipped away slightly to the line opposite. The enemy guns started up, shelling the woods to stop support coming through. Shrapnel shells passed overhead, with a noise like steam escaping under pressure, to explode and rattle amongst the trees in puffs of black smoke like ink blots against the whiteness. The sound was rolling along the whole length of the line, the air growing thick with lead and steel. At an order, the sentries kept their posts but the others got down, taking cover and burrowing into the funk holes. George squatted on the fire step next to one of the hollows with his arms over his head. He stared at the walls of earth, barely held back by posts: sticky clay soil, compacted by the weight of sandbags, bulging between supports or in places fallen away and collapsed into the wet trench itself to form a viscous sludge. He was frozen with fear.

He felt someone shaking his shoulder and looked up to see Edmund standing over him. His mouth was moving but George couldn't hear or even guess what he was saying. Edmund moved on to talk to Wilmott. The sentry was shouting something, and around him the men were taking up their rifles and climbing on to the fire step. George followed suit, checking again that the bolt would move and was free of mud.

The wailing shriek of shells continued as the enemy pounded the woods and the line, seeking to clear the way for their advancing infantry. Down on the left a shell found the trench, the sound of its detonation followed by shouts and a high-pitched screaming. George squinted at the thick mist that covered the lower part of the field; something darker was moving within it, like the greyness of a wave behind its foam. It began to take form and the shapes of men were discernible: lines of men moving shoulder to shoulder as one body. They broke through the mist, moving at a trot. There was no spacing out of the line, no ducking or weaving, but a continuous wall of men coming on towards them. They seemed massive to George; their packs and greatcoats rolled up together gave them bulk and their spiked helmets added to their height. They came on, with line after line following behind. He couldn't understand why they didn't attack in extended order. They would have no chance bunched together like that. It would be a blood bath. Along the Front, as far as the eye could see, came a solid forma-tion of thousands of men, the sound of their cheering reaching him between the banshee wailing of the shells. He looked back at Edmund for direction. Edmund's face was red and sweating, his cap pushed back from his brow. He was holding his pistol up in the air, his other hand clenched in a fist.

'Hold your fire!' Edmund shouted and George realised that he hadn't even taken aim, had been staring at the advancing men as if mesmerised. He got his rifle up to his shoulder and braced his knees against the wall of the trench.

As the oncoming troops broke into a run, the staccato sound of cheering lengthened into a longer, lower note: a roar that built like an avalanche.

'Fire!'

Rifle fire crackled along the trench with a sound like burning thorn. George couldn't hear his own fire as he loosed fifteen rounds a minute into the lines of men. He couldn't hear himself shouting, although words that he didn't know he knew were coming from his mouth. Men fell in the swarm of rifle bullets and rattling machine-gun fire as easily as if a ripple of wind were running through corn. As the first line toppled, the next climbed over their sprawling bodies and came on.

George felt his guts turn to water; there were too many; they would soon be here . . . He fired on, his gun growing hot in his hands. A shell fell short and George saw wire, men and mud rise into the air. He dodged back as debris rained down into the trench: stones, clods of earth, decaying and newly smashed gobbets of flesh. Sick to his stomach, eyes staring, George fired wildly into the smoke. The wire had been blown into disarray. Nearby a body hung across it, twitching, and George saw Smith take aim and shoot the man in the head before returning to raking the line.

Suddenly, through the smoke, a figure loomed over him. Before his mind even had time to register that he must shoot, Wilmott swivelled round and fired. The German soldier seemed to halt for a moment at the lip of the trench, a stiff silhouette, before pitching forwards, his helmet knocked askew by George's shoulder as he toppled face forward into the trench bottom. George turned to look along to the traverse, in dread of finding that they were over-run, but the others were still firing. He took his place once again at the parapet. The line of advancing men thinned in front of their section, and George could see that they were wheeling left to put pressure on the stretch that was nearest to the wood. Soon, all that was ahead of him were piles of bodies and a German who staggered with his hands to his head amongst the dragging and struggling of the injured.

On the other side of him, Smith was slumped with his arms out straight on the parapet, as though collapsed at a bar, half of his head blown away. George stepped down from the fire step and round the body of the dead German to lean against the back slope of the trench opposite the funk hole. His breath was coming in wheezing gasps. Edmund was talking to Wilmott, patting him on the back, both of them with filthy faces and uniforms.

Edmund came towards him, mouthing, 'Well done,' the words lost in the noise of the never-ending bombardment. George framed the words 'Thank you, sir,' but nothing would come out from his hoarse throat except an incoherent stammer. Edmund reached forward to squeeze his shoulder; he had blood on his hand and more was trickling down over his wrist. In the moment that George opened his mouth to say, 'You've been hit, sir,' there was a terrific whining sound: the drawn-out scream of a shell that was coming straight for them.

'Cover!' Edmund bellowed down the trench and pushed George in the direction of the funk hole. For a split second – a moment's hesitation – George froze. The dark hole in the earth yawned before him and his feet simply would not move. He knew he was going to die. Then Edmund tackled him, shoving him down into the gap, his shoulder barging him so that he was squeezed backwards into the hole and the smell of soil and damp straw. Edmund squatted down directly in front of him; he curled up with his hands covering his head. There was a stupendous crump that shook the very ground, and then utter darkness.

George was choking on earth. It was in his ears, in his nostrils, in his mouth, which he had opened in a scream. Part of the roof of the funk hole had caved in and crumbled around him. He gagged and spat. When he moved his shoulder gingerly, he felt soil move and settle behind it. Slowly, slowly, he worked his hand free, brought it up to his face and wiped it over his eyes and nose. He held his forearm across his brow to keep the earth off and with the other hand, reached forward. His fingertips touched something firm and textured: Edmund's uniform. He moved his hand down and found the shape of an elbow. He pushed at it but there was no response.

At first, he couldn't understand why there was no chink of light around Edmund's form; then he realised that he too had been buried, in earth and sandbags thrown up from the lip of the trench. In panic, he pushed and clawed at Edmund but as he moved he could feel the sliding behind him and he stopped, afraid of further collapse: less space, less air. The sounds of battle were muffled and distant as though he were under water. Oh God! Oh God! It was no good shouting for help; no one would hear him. He cried silently, afraid to sob, enduring the pressure that was building in his chest, swallowing it down. He moved his fingers up Edmund's arm; the material of his jacket was wet. At the top, the earth was looser in the crook between shoulder and neck. He knew that he wouldn't be able to shift the weight of both man and earth, it was too heavy and the walls of the hole too fragile for him to brace himself against. Instead, he must work slowly at the earth above Edmund's crouching shape and try to make a gap at the top of the entrance. He began to scrape with one hand at the earth, bringing each handful down between his knees and compacting it beneath him. As he worked, images flickered in his mind: the swinging light hiding his father's face from him as they journeyed into the mine and the sense that he was squeezed inside a vast mass of rock; the flare of a match in a dark railway carriage, his hands over his ears, the rhythmic struggle and the horrible sound of the trapped horse screaming. He worked on, his breath fast and shallow, his body fixed in its unnatural stance, his shoulder muscles agonised by the awkward, repetitive movement. At length, after what seemed like a lifetime, he felt his hand reach into air – free air! He pulled his arm back and scrabbled at the hole, greedy for a great gasping breath. The cold sharpness of it was like a draught of iced water. He carried on scraping, making the gap bigger, got his arm . . . his head . . . one shoulder through and was able to dig then with both hands. He pushed away the fallen sandbags and hauled himself up, climbing over Edmund, his knee and then his foot on his back: to light, to air, to life.

He stumbled out, his legs weakened by the length of time cramped in one position. The trench was empty of living men. There was a crater in the field just behind them, about twelve feet across, the debris of displaced earth fallen in a rough circle: solid ground splattered as easily as if a marble had been dropped into a bowl of flour. The parados had been destroyed by the blast: earth, sandbags and shell fragments blown in on top of them. The sounds of battle continued: the moans of the injured nearby in no man's land; the screams and shouts of hand-to-hand fighting within a few hundred yards; shells falling, more distant now. George began to scoop armfuls of earth towards him, trying to uncover Edmund. The second in which he had hesitated came clearly before him: Edmund's shout, his own fear, time suspended as the shell raced along its trajectory towards them and his legs had refused to move, Edmund's face, his mouth opening in a yell as he launched himself towards him and covered his body with his own.

He dug, frantically, not knowing how long he might have before the fighting moved towards him or death fell once more from the skies. His palm touched metal. He cleared the earth around it. A shell splinter. The jagged metal protruded from a massive wound in Edmund's back, a bloody mess of flesh and pale knobs of spine beneath. If only he could get him on his side, free his face, see if there was breath . . . He pulled away the split sandbags, levered up a splintered prop that lay across Edmund's shoulder and scooped the debris away until he'd made a space. He hauled him over, pulling him by the arm, which fell limply to his side as soon as he released it. Edmund's face was smeared with earth. George took hold of his jaw and turned it towards him. His eyes were open, fixed in a stare. Small crumbs of soil adhered to them, speckling the whites and irises. George sat back on his haunches and put his hands over his face. He rocked himself back and forth. How could he be dead? His mind wouldn't take it in. He couldn't just leave him here; he started digging again; he would get him out . . .

He heard voices approaching – German voices. They were in the trench; they were coming his way. He scrabbled frantically at the earth; then, glancing behind him, he scrambled to his feet, grabbed his rifle and fled from them, stumbling along over bodies, packs and sandbags until he reached the communication trench and could run more freely, back towards the woods and the reserve line.

As he ran, he heard the sharp patter of Vickers guns from the edge of the wood, confirming that his section must have withdrawn to strongpoints there. Their new line would be the support trench, a shallow ditch dug amongst the trees. The communication trench between the two was incomplete and petered out twenty yards from the treeline. Flat on his face, with his rifle before him, he pulled himself along by his elbows, the stink of decaying flesh in his nostrils as he used the littered bodies as cover from the zing of bullets in the air above him.

He reached the wood and crawled in over brambles and dead bracken. He got behind the bole of one of the larger trees and looked around, trying to get his bearings. Ahead of him, trees were burning; one had fallen against another and wedged in its forked trunk, which had caught alight; flames crackled in the new wood and licked along the branches, smoke rolling from the skeletal outline. The sound of firing and shouting came from beyond them. One Vickers gun had stopped; they were being over-run. Bullets cracked and ricocheted among the trees and George hastily checked his rifle. It was badly fouled with mud from the collapse. Bloody useless. He threw it down in disgust; he would have to find another. Muttering to himself in fear, he cast about for an abandoned weapon. Bodies lay amongst the tree roots, rolled into the bracken or half covered in the dark mulch of leaves. George, searching amongst them for a gun, found they had been stripped. Their pockets had been emptied: rings and watches gone.

He went back and picked up his rifle, fixed the bayonet and set off, bent double, making for the place where he thought the support trench started. Ahead, and to the left, men were moving amongst the trees in quick, crouching dashes, and then taking cover, standing upright, plastered flat against a tree trunk before edging round to take a shot. George ran from tree to tree towards the trench, cursing the brambles that tripped him, the useless gun, the fucking war.

As he came level with a clump of spruce, he heard a branch crack. The hairs on the back of his neck rose as he felt eyes upon him. He wheeled round and found himself face to face with a German soldier. His senses heightened as adrenalin coursed and time seemed to lengthen and slow. The German wasn't much older than George, well built, with a thick neck and shoulders, fleshy features and the stubble of several days on his chin. He had lost his helmet, revealing close-cropped brown hair through which the pale scalp was visible. His grey uniform was filthy and a badge hung, half torn off, from his collar. In the half-second that they stared at each other, George took all this in; he saw the man's pupils dilate, the movement of his larynx as he swallowed, his grip tighten on his rifle. As the German lunged towards him, George threw himself sideways and his bayonet caught George's arm, slitting his jacket and the skin beneath. His head filled with fear and rage, George sprang forward and was on him with an upward thrust to his chest. The man clutched at George, holding on to his arms, his mouth working as if attempting to speak. George tried to pull away; he had driven too deep; the blade wouldn't withdraw easily. He squeezed his eyes closed as he tried to fire a round to free it, as he'd been taught, but the action jammed. George pushed the man backwards as hard as he could and he fell to the ground. As the blade came free, blood followed it, spreading over his chest and soaking through his tunic. His body became slack and his eyes vacant.

George stood over him for a moment. He felt numb. He stooped and wiped the red blade on the bracken; tiny fragments of golden-brown leaf stuck to it. He was empty and felt nothing. He turned and ran for the trench.

George lay in the trench with the others, keeping up a desultory fire to stop further troops from coming into the wood. He had tied a field dressing around the flesh wound in his arm but it ached with every flexion of the muscle. It began to rain. Fat drops fell, pattering on the leafless branches, streaking the bark and dripping on to the leaf mould beneath. George was wet, shivering and exhausted.

They were told to keep their positions whilst a counter-attack was mounted and they heard fighting as an attempt was made to take back the trenches further along the line. From where he was, as the afternoon went on, George could hear the sound of digging as the Germans hastily started to reverse the trench and build a fire step facing the wood. The men around him doubted that the trenches would be retaken. Ground had been lost as well as lives. They had been driven back and miserably faced the prospect of starting work again, deepening the reserve trench to become the new fire trench.

Late in the afternoon, they were relieved by the French and trooped dismally further back into the woods to regroup beside the line of bunkers. Those who could, squeezed into the rough shelters; others slept with their backs resting against the trees, heads on their knees in the pouring rain, seeming as insensible as the bodies around them.

Captain Hunton came to speak to them. He said that the counter-attack had not been successful but that they should all feel proud of what had been accomplished. They had stopped a force that was far superior in numbers from breaking through. They had held them back from Ypres, and he believed that whoever held Ypres would eventually win the war. Afterwards he spoke quietly to Carey, telling him that the shelling had destroyed their billets at the farm: farmhouse, barns, stables, all wrecked. He asked him to take charge of the men while he sent for further orders.

George sat alone on a fallen tree. He was glad to see Haycock when he arrived but he couldn't trust himself to speak. He smoked the cigarette that Haycock gave him, holding it between his thumb and forefinger inside the hollow of his hand to keep it from the rain. Only when he smoked it down to a stub and burnt his fingers so that a raised welt appeared did he realise that his hands were completely numb with cold.

Turland hobbled back with a sprained ankle, leaning on Rooke. When Carey took a roll call only half of the platoon answered. George listened dully as the names Smith, White, Wilmott were paused at and passed over. Carey asked if anyone had seen Lieutenant Lyne. George said nothing.

13

THE RUINED HOUSE

The battalion had been moved south into a different part of the line. From their trenches at the edge of this new wood, the monotony of flatness was much the same, save for the fact that here it was relieved by the distant view of a ruined church spire, ugly as a broken tooth. In the foreground lay a scatter of burnt-out cottages, one of which, just behind German lines, was used by the enemy as a forward position for machine-gun and sniper fire. No man's land was a wide ploughed field, its crop of beets spoiled. The mud was strewn with hundreds of bully-beef tins full of shit, lobbed by both sides into the open space as a means of relieving themselves without risking a trip to the foul and collapsing latrines. On one side of the field, a scatter of wooden crosses stood in haphazard remembrance, vastly outnumbered by the corpses of unburied men. They lay in the positions in which they had fallen, awkward as the carcases of the cows that lay with swollen bellies and stiff, ungainly legs. Both stank.

In the wet November weather, the water table had risen; the fire trenches were half full and men stood belly-deep in yellow ditch water and Flanders clay. The churned mud had a slippery consistency that made movement treacherous over the shell-pocked land. It clogged boots and matted the rough goatskin jerkins that they wore for warmth when in reserve in the woods; it weighed down the skirts of greatcoats. All movement was laborious. Impeded by the weight of water in the trenches and sodden clothing out of them, the men moved slowly. Even when travelling the corduroy paths through the trees – rough-hewn branches nailed on to trunks laid on the ground to provide dry standing – they moved as if sleep-walking through the days.

Defeated by the common enemies of rain and cold, both sides had been forced to dig in. There would be no Big Push, no war of movement, no quick victory. As the weather grew ever wetter and colder, a sense of hopeless stalemate crept over them and the memory of expectations that they would be home before the year was out seemed a hollow dream, a false and naive optimism that belonged to a different world.

George had withdrawn into himself. When he was in the trenches, pumping or baling, he worked like an automaton, using the repetitive movements as a way to block out thought. When at rest, he went with Haycock and the others to the warm estaminets; he saw their spirits revive with food and drink. Once he would have taken the opportunity to sketch the animated faces of the men, capturing their laughter over ribald jokes or their intense concentration over the roll of a pair of dice. Now he could raise no interest; after the horrors of the day of the attack, everything was overlaid by a cold numbness. He had not put pencil to paper since and his sketchbook now lay at the very bottom of his kitbag. The pictures of home that he tried to call to mind were ousted by images of the ruined land of the battlefield: the colours of hills, pasture and sunlit water smeared into a muddy morass and a shattered wood. He couldn't imagine ever wanting to draw or paint again.

The men's talk of long-anticipated letters and speculation about Christmas comforts for the troops swirled around him, hazy and inconsequential as the fumes from the stove. He envied them their ability to live in the moment, to take the blessings of fire and food and forget. He said little, drank steadily and hoped for the kind of sleep that brought oblivion.

But the dreams still came. Repeatedly he dreamt of digging with bare hands, trying to free a body from the sticky soil. Sometimes he woke, sweating, before he could get it free, sometimes he lived again the moment when he saw Edmund's terrible wound, sometimes when he turned the body over and saw his face, instead of a dead stare, the eyes were open and conscious. Eyes full of pain that looked to him for help. Waking among the sleeping men in the farm shed that was currently his billet, he would cry out and flail around as if still searching for something lost. Coming to himself again, heart thumping, hoping that no one had woken, he would sit up, wrap his arms around himself and rock to and fro trying to block out the voice in his head that berated him for his weakness, his fear, his cowardice.

Unable to sleep, he remembered Violet's face when she had received the letter to say that Edmund was to go overseas. He had thought her tears had hurt him then but now he saw his pain for what it was: merely a wound to his childish ego. Over

215

and over, he imagined her getting another letter, the letter that would come from Edmund's family and how her face would fall in disbelief then crumple into grief. It was his fault and he couldn't bear it. It was all his fault.

He lay on the brick floor with his head on a sack of barley straw, unable to achieve the sanctuary of deep, undreaming sleep. Some time around dawn, as others began to shift and turn in discomfort, he would fall into an uneasy sleep where other deaths returned to him: the pale ovals of faces seen through water; the look of surprise on the young German's face as he clutched George's arms. He always woke at this point with a strange feeling that there was something important that he'd forgotten. It stayed with him throughout the day, however hard he worked, however blank he tried to make his mind. He remained restless and disturbed, running through the short encounter second by second, feeling that if he could only remember the missing detail it would somehow begin to make sense.

As December crept in, a new enemy stretched its fingers over the land, turning the trees to white spectres and furring each twig with crystals. The churned soil in the fields hardened under deep frosts that silvered its surface, freezing it in choppy waves that crunched and broke underfoot. As the temperature plummeted at night, thin plates of ice formed on the surface of the water in the trenches at the edge of the wood, and crackled and broke as men moved through them on legs stiffened to stilts by the cold. Unable to haul themselves out at the end of the night's watch, the relief would help drag them out, their hair and beards rimed white, their faces with a blue, cyanotic pallor.

When at last a thaw came, returning them to the slime and suck of mud, orders immediately came that there was to be an

216

attack all along the Front. Their specific objective was to capture the burnt-out house used as cover for German Maxim guns and Hunton was to lead half of their company out, Carey having been hospitalised when he developed an infection that turned his foot into one huge, hot, red blister. George was unsurprised to find, when the corporal came down the line to muster the troops who were to take part, that, along with Rooke's, his name was indeed 'on the list'.

Along with the other men, he followed the corporal back to the command trench where Hunton explained to them that their particular brief was to take the sap trench just to the right of the building, which the enemy was using as access.

Lieutenant Mallory asked, 'Has the wire been cut yet, sir?'

There was a pause. It was too dark to see Hunton's face. 'Lieutenant Mallory will take you out,' he said. 'Once my section has secured the house, Lieutenant Parks's platoon will support and we'll consolidate our position. That will be all.'

George cowered down with the others on the fire step, still knee-deep in water, as shells fell behind and on the wood. Earlier, the howitzers had pounded the German line and Mallory had affected a bombastic manner and said that the barrage would send the German troops 'scuttling for their reserve line like ants under a stone'. Now, the Germans were returning fire, seeking out the heavy guns. The noise broke through George's numbness, the strange detached state that he had sought through working to the point of exhaustion and shutting down his mind until he existed only in the movement of the moment: the lift of a shovel, the hammer of a nail or the press of a pump. Now, in this enforced inaction, the boom of the guns filled his head until he had nowhere to turn, vibrating through his whole body as if it were a tuning fork struck again and again. He began to shake.

A shell burst nearby with an ear-splitting crash and a rending of wood, and Rooke, who was a little further down, threw up his arm as if in a ridiculous attempt to ward off a blow. A second later, the same thing happened; his head seemed to turn of its own accord, followed by a wild jerk of his right arm in exactly the same pattern. The man on the other side of him said, 'Watch out! Keep your fists to yourself. What's the matter with you?' George jumped down on to the sole of the trench and waded along to Rooke.

'Are you all right?' He climbed up beside him.

'Got the twitches,' Rooke said through clamped teeth. In an effort to stop it, he grabbed hold of the sleeve of his right arm and pulled it tight against his body. His head strained round as if the devil were over his shoulder, before snapping back straight. George, ashen-faced, motioned to him to check his rifle but he stared at him in incomprehension. George took Rooke's hands and put them in position, forcing them to check the bolts. The familiarity of the action took hold, as if Rooke's brain had short-circuited and recognised the automatic routine; as long as he moved through this well-known sequence, control was returned to him.

'It'll be better when we move,' George bawled into his ear. 'We'll stick together and run like hell.'

When the whistle blew, the corporal who was standing beside one of the ladders pushed the first man towards it and then put his hand on each man's back as they put a foot on the lowest rung, as if counting them out. George scrambled to the top and over the bags that moved and shifted underfoot, propelling him down the slope of the parapet and out into open ground, with Rooke close behind him. Crouching low, they moved as best they could through the mud, towards the spot to the right of the roofless house with its charred walls. The bright trace of bullets flashed in the air around them as they wove around the obstacles of dead men and beasts. The Germans were sending up flares and the greenish light reflected from standing water and the litter of tins. George was aware of Rooke as a dark shape at his shoulder; he had the bizarre thought that it was as if his shadow had broken away from his feet and ran alongside him.

The rattle of machine-gun fire started: a line of dots puncturing the night. Men fell in front and they veered away, bending double. Ahead, glinting light warned of a shell hole half full of water and, ducking and weaving, George swung to the left of it, back towards the burnt house. A dark mass of men seemed to be collecting around it, obscuring the flash of the machine guns, and George realised with a jolt of terror that the wire was intact and that men were caught upon it. The bright flash of an explosion was framed in a window as one of their bombs hit home; the machine-gun rattle stopped abruptly and rifle fire took over.

Suddenly he missed Rooke's presence. He glanced back and saw that Percy and some of the others had gone right. His figure, slight among the older men, was bowed as he ran. He saw Percy stumble at the lip of the shell hole and put his hand down to the ground, but instead of righting himself, he pitched sideways towards the water.

George gave a shout and then ran, his breath tearing at his chest. He slipped and slid around the perimeter of the crater. Throwing himself down on hands and knees, he crawled towards the spot where he judged Percy to have fallen. Two bodies lay sprawled together at the rim of the shell hole; one was unknown to George, the other proved to be Addison. Of Percy, there was no sign. George stared in horror at the unbroken surface of the muddy water of the shell hole. He crouched alone by Addison's body, shivering.

Bouts of machine-gun fire still spat from the trench. There was no sign of Mallory. Not one of their men had made it to the objective, not even to the wire, which George could see clearly remained unbroken. The only thing he could do was to work his way left, towards the key target of the burnt house and try to join Hunton's outfit where the main fight was still going on. His mind refused to take in the fact that Percy was gone. How could he be? It wasn't possible. He had spoken to him only minutes ago, had felt his body behind him, close as his shadow. Crab-like, he edged along, giving a wide berth to the drowned pit beside him, its stench telling him that others had fallen there, to rot in the mud.

The stretch of ground between him and the house was pockmarked with craters from abortive attempts to destroy the improvised strongpoint. From two of those nearest the building, his fellows had taken cover and were firing on the house. As a flare lit the scene with its powdery glow, George fixed his eyes on the nearest crater; then, as the light died away, he gripped his rifle and struggled towards it. Suddenly he felt a searing pain in his right calf. He let out a cry and dropped to the ground. He curled up, grabbing at his leg, which felt as though a hot skewer had been driven into it. He heard himself moaning. Firing was intensifying around him as the German soldiers in the sap trench, relieved from the pressure of attack, turned their whole attention to the men now coming up in support of the attempt on the house. He couldn't stay where he was.

He began to pull himself along on his elbows through the churned mud. Slowly he made for the nearest crater. No shots were being fired from it so he had little hope of finding help there but his first and most urgent need was to get under cover.

The crater was wide, with a pool at the bottom, but the slope of the sides was sufficiently shallow to allow a man to lie against it and remain out of the evil-smelling water. George slid in sideways on a slather of mud, digging his heels deep into the soft earth wall to stop himself from slipping further down.

A few yards to the left, a swollen body was sprawled face down, almost bursting out of its clothes. On the other side, further round and nearer to the house, two men lay. The first was clearly dead; he was as slack as a sack and half in the water, but the second had wedged himself above him, his feet braced against the dead man's back, and was making feeble movements. George lay still for a minute, recovering his breath and trying to master the pain as a flare died away. Below him, the reflection of the new moon floated like a silver sickle in the dark water. The pain in his leg was burning hot. He pulled himself into a sitting position and gingerly unwound his puttees and began to roll up his trouser leg. The skin was dark and slippery with blood; he could feel it trickling down over his ankle and his foot felt wet in his boot. With fingers made clumsy by cold and shock, he fumbled for his field dressing. He found the excruciating centre of the pain, a small hole beside his shinbone and a larger exit wound in his calf; the bullet had passed right through. He tied the dressing round as tightly as he could and then rolled his sodden trouser leg down over it. Behind him, the firing continued. It seemed nearer and louder and George wondered if the support had come up and prayed that there would be stretcher-bearers and that he would be found.

The injured man on the other side was bulky, heavily built, and every now and then, he made a spasmodic movement, arching his back as if to push himself further up before subsiding again, reminding George of the helpless efforts of a beetle caught on its back. Slowly and carefully, by lifting his wounded leg with his hands and shuffling sideways inches at a time, George began to move towards him but was forced to pause every yard or so. As he lay back to rest, George stared up at the night sky; clouds and stars showed in the gaps between the wavering trace and bloom of flares and the detonating flashes of shells.

When he was a couple of yards from the wounded man, a flare went up close by and he saw his face in profile: the eyes closed, a thick moustache, the mouth open in a grimace of pain. It was Hunton. He had lost his cap, revealing his balding head, a tonsure of pale skin laid bare. George stopped; the man had tried to harm him at every turn; he hated and feared him. He didn't want to go near him.

As if sensing his presence, Hunton lifted his hand a few inches from where it rested on his stomach. His mouth moved. George made himself shuffle closer. There was something very wrong with the shape of him. His other arm, the sight of which had been obscured by his torso, had been completely blown away. His uniform was soaked with blood and he had bled out on to the mud, a dark slick against the yellow marl. The word that his lips were forming soundlessly was *water*. George searched him for his water bottle, shuddering as he reached over his shattered side, but he couldn't find it. He undid his own, put his arm under Hunton's head to lift it and poured a few drops into his open mouth. Hunton's hand jerked up as he gagged and choked and the water ran uselessly down his chin. George, feeling sick and light-headed, took a swig of the water himself, forcing it down despite its contaminated, petrol taste.

As the night wore on, he stayed in the same position, trying at intervals to feed Hunton a dribble of water. His breath steamed on the air and the chill from the earth beneath him struck up through his bones. He felt no animosity towards Hunton now; he felt only glad of the warmth of the body beside him and that he was not alone.

At length he heard several explosions, as of grenades, a great deal of shouting and then the firing died away. He hoped it meant that the house had been taken and that a party might be sent out to gather up the injured and bury the dead. The body beneath Hunton had slipped further down and Hunton's feet were now in the water. George started to talk to him as he laid his head back on to the mud. 'We're going to get you out of this, sir. We're going to get up nearer the top so I can call for bearers; don't you worry.' Painfully, George moved up behind Hunton's shoulders and tried to drag him further up but his injured leg was useless; his joints had stiffened and there was little purchase on the clay; it simply smeared under his weight. It was difficult even to get himself very far. 'Don't give up on me, sir,' he said as he heaved. 'Come on . . . don't . . . you . . . dare . . . give up on me.'

He tried again, fitting the fingers of one hand under Hunton's belt and the other hand inside his collar. The skin felt cold and clammy. He heaved to no avail. When he let go, Hunton's head lolled forward and George bent over to see his face. Hunton's mouth hung open and his lids were no longer squeezed shut in pain but smoothed and strangely flattened. The looseness of his face told George that he had been trying to haul the dead weight of a corpse. He let go of him abruptly and cast about him as if unable to believe that now he was entirely alone. He took Hunton by the shoulders and shook him roughly. 'You bastard! What you go and do that for? Stupid bastard!' he shouted in the dead man's face.

He sat staring at the water for a while. A thin rain began to fall. He watched it dimple the surface and ruffle the edges of the sliver of moon. It ran down his face, wetting his eyelashes and making him blink. He no longer felt cold. His leg hurt but it was as if he was somewhere distant from it, aware of pain yet somehow detached. He very much wanted to sleep, and drifted in and out of a dreamy state in which he remembered odd scenes and snatches of sound: wheeling Lillie in her toy cart; Kitty playing the piano as he stood waiting for her in the parlour doorway; lolling on his bed talking to Ted while his mother called up, 'Do you want some supper, boys?' Random scenes floated by him and dissolved like bubbles as his mind reached for them. Only when a breeze blew up and the rain grew harder and found its way down his collar and into his sleeves was he dragged away from the sensation of stealing warmth.

He shook himself. Hunton lay beside him like a slab, rain plastering his scanty hair to his head and draggling the ends of his moustache. George suddenly saw him not as an officer but as a mere man: someone's husband, someone's son. He reached across and undid the chain that carried his identity disc; then he slipped his hand into his tunic pocket and pulled out the contents: the smooth surface of a photograph, a folded letter several pages long, a blue envelope. He stuffed the others into his trouser pocket and sat turning Violet's letter over in his hands. The remembrance of Edmund filled him with despair. He thought that if he ever got out of this he would return the letter to Violet. But how could he write? What could he say? She would still be hoping . . . He couldn't break the news to her in a letter. No, if he ever got back he would have to go and see her, tell her face to face, like a man.

He put the letter into his inside pocket and began to drag himself back towards the lip of the shell hole. He knew that he had lost a great deal of blood and that he was too weak to crawl further, but since the firing had stopped, if he could just get to the edge, there was a better chance that he would be found. He would be able to watch for movement, for a burial party, to call out . . .

Twice he almost made it to the top, only to slide back: the rain had loosened the surface of the clay to the consistency of soft butter. The third time he moved left and found a foothold on a tumble of bricks. He reached the broken earth of the lip and looked out. The cries and moans of the wounded went unheeded. The shape of a man trying to pull himself along, crab-like across the ground, collapsed and lay still. No man's land was otherwise deserted. No firing came from the sap trench or from the burnt-out house. The occasional flare rose, like the last squib on Bonfire Night, revealing a scene of desolation. The dark windows of the house were like eyeless sockets. George stared, straining his eyes. Was that a movement? Had they taken the house? It seemed empty but he couldn't be sure. He could get no further; he put one arm up over the edge and got his shoulder up but he hadn't the strength to pull himself right over the lip. His legs and arms felt warm and floppy; he could barely stop himself from slipping back. The thought came to him that he was unlikely to get out of this, that he could die in this stinking pit, that his human frame would be covered, like Percy's, by water and his body left in the mud like carrion. He felt sure that he would die here, alone.

As a flare went up, snaking into the sky, he took out Violet's letter and opened it, laying his hand where hers had touched. The envelope dropped from his stiff fingers and the breeze caught it, fluttering it away from him, a pale shape tumbling over the dark, waterlogged ground. Then there was a crack, and brightness, whiteness, snow-blindness, and then nothing.

PART THREE

BLIGHTY

14

CHRISTMAS POST

George was hot, horribly hot. Sheets and blankets pinned him on his back in a bed and he was aware of cloth tightly swaddling his head and face, and of *pain*. The pain in his face was like an animal gnawing, as if a creature was trapped behind a mask and was trying to escape by the softer route through his flesh.

Sometimes hands would lift his head and a china spout would be placed between his lips. He would drink from what he imagined to be a teapot, cool water trickling down his parched throat. If he moaned with pain, a pad would be held over his nose and mouth and he would breathe in a chemical smell; then the animal would stop its frantic gnawing for a while and let him sink into a half-sleeping, half-dreaming state.

Sometimes two people would come and take off the covers and a blessed draught of air would flow over him as they lifted his body and spread dry coolness under him, or moved him from his back to lie on his right side. He heard their voices around him but couldn't make sense of them; he was aware only that they echoed as if there was a high space above them, as if they were in a concert hall.

In the time before here, there had been only pain with no respite, and movement that made the pain worse. First, the hard boards of a cart and jolting and jerking. He had tried to cry out but his mouth and throat had been full of liquid, salty as seawater, and he'd been unable to do more than make a strangled, gargling sound. That was a long time ago. There had been aeons of time since then, time when he had lain somewhere cold with men moaning around him and someone had bandaged his leg, and then his face and head, covering his eyes. Next there had been an agony of movement as wooden wheels passed over pavé roads and he had been jostled and shuffled into a close space in a train that sped, rattling and shaking and smelling of coal smoke. There had been voices, calling out for water, or for *pinard*, to drink. A woman's voice in the background had said words he didn't understand: '*les blessés*', '*les mutilés*'. Later, he had been lifted again and carried up a long slope and into a place that smelt of disinfectant, where his bed rose and fell with the swell of the sea for a long weary time and where there had been the sound of someone weeping, on and on, refusing to be comforted. Then there were the sounds of a dock, more carrying, more rattling: this time over tramlines through noisy streets, until they reached a place where he was unloaded once more and wheeled through corridors and into a room with many voices and the smell of ether.

Hands had unwrapped his face, picked the folds of cloth apart with thumb and forefinger, as gently as picking up a butterfly. A rubber mask was held over his nose and mouth until there was blackness. Then the consciousness of pain once more, gnawing away when he was left alone, excruciating when his wounds were dressed. Hands held his arms and pinned his head still while the gauze that had knit into blood and serum was peeled away. There were days and nights of burning heat when he was stripped and sponged with cloths until the rigors that shook his body ceased. At last he lay sweating under the weight of bedclothes that he had no strength to throw off, hearing busy footsteps that echoed in the high place.

It was night next time he woke. It was cooler. He remembered the agony of having his dressings changed and hoped that they would last a while and not soak through. One eye was free of bandages and he forced it open a crack, blinked and then opened it wider. A light was moving steadily towards him, illuminating plain white walls and tall, shuttered windows, set so high that no one could look in or out, their tops disappearing into shadow. He moved his head slowly as if turning to the sun. Above the light was a woman's face, surrounded by an angular white shape. The light advanced towards him, revealing, on either side of a wide aisle, rows of red-blanketed beds and sleeping men. The woman, who wore a long white apron, paused occasionally to look more closely at a sleeper before padding on.

George ran his tongue over his dry lips. The bandages passed across the left side of his face, covering his eye, and were wound tightly over his crown and under his jaw, as he remembered being tied up when he had mumps as a child. As the figure approached, he tried to say, 'Nurse,' but his voice emerged from

231

his long unused throat as an incoherent groan. The woman, however, hurried over, holding up the spirit lamp to get a good look at him before setting it down on a small wooden table beside the bed.

'Welcome back!' she said in a low voice. 'How are you feeling?' She pulled up a stool and lifted his wrist.

'Pretty ropey.' George's voice was gravelly. He studied her while she took his pulse: her dark hair was parted in the middle and pulled back under the white starched cotton. She was, at the most, mid twenties, and had a plain, kind face, broad and soft, yet at the outer ends of her thick, straight eyebrows, George noticed tiny lines like commas: the marks of anxiety and distress.

'Good, good,' she said, looking down at the fob watch pinned at her breast. 'Not so thready – there's a definite improvement.' Further down the ward, a man cried out and a nurse came out of a side room carrying a basin and went to him.

'What is this place?'

'You're back in England, at the Third London General,' she said. 'You've been out of it for quite a while, I'm afraid. My name's Nurse Patterson.' She leant forward and looked at the tag that was pinned to George's pyjamas. 'Can you tell me yours?'

'George Farrell.'

She nodded as if he had passed some kind of test.

'What happened to me? My leg . . . It smells bad.' He tried to sit up but his head spun and he sank back against the pillows again.

She put her hand on his arm. 'You've had a high fever; the wound was infected but we're hopeful that the leg will be saved. It's looking much cleaner. When you're stronger we'll move you out to the veranda for an hour or two where we can get some sunlight to it.'

232

She moved as if to rise. By way of a question, George lifted his hand as if to touch his face and she stilled. After a pause she said, 'There is some tissue damage. The eye is intact but we'll have to wait to know whether it still has sight.'

George's hand moved again towards his face but she caught it in hers and held it. 'It's a miracle you're here at all,' she said.

George took his hand away and, again, brought it up to his face. He felt upwards with his fingertips, over the grainy texture of the bandages. Beneath the small ridges where they overlapped, there was a wide indentation where his cheekbone ought to be, a hollow, as if a punch had caved in his bones like paper. She watched him as his fingertips explored the mask of bandages, and he saw her struggling to hide her pity and assume the non-committal expression of professionalism. The flesh around his eye and brow was swollen hard and despite the thickness of the dressings, he could feel that there was a dip at the bridge of his nose, where no dip should be. He held the good side of his face with his other hand, its familiar planes and angles fitting his palm and fingers as it did each night when he settled down to sleep. He felt again, finding the edges of the map of pain that made up the left side of his face. Right side . . . left side, his fingers compared. Right side . . . wrong side, his fingertips told him. Wrong, all wrong. He took his hands away and placed them palm-down on the blankets, spreading his fingers over the fuzzy surface so that they wouldn't tremble.

'Dr Bailey has done all he can,' she said gently. 'He was able to close up the wound at least. That isn't always possible.'

'Yes. Thank you,' George heard himself say in a dull voice.

'The main thing we need to concentrate on now is getting that leg better.' She stood, picked up the lamp and moved to the end of the bed. She tucked the ends of the covers more firmly under the mattress, straightened up and then paused. 'You can see the gardens from the veranda; it's beautiful in the frost. You'll like it.'

'Yes,' George said, unable to take in her words.

She patted the bedclothes. 'Try to get some sleep.' She turned away and the soft velvet darkness fell around him as she moved on with the lamp held high to shed its pool of light over other beds.

This is retribution, George thought. The bleakness of no man's land came over him: Edmund and Percy somewhere beneath the mud; the German soldier's face slowly being covered by leaves. He stared into the dark imagining how it would feel if, when his eye was uncovered, he found that he could see nothing but blackness. Would his eye be cloudy, the blue iris milky and dim like the eyes of the blind man who sold matches in the street at home? He wondered what a face looked like after a bullet had passed through flesh and bone.

Nurse Patterson had joined her young colleague tending to the man at the far end of the ward. He was retching into the basin while the women supported him so that he could sit upright. Suddenly, both women exclaimed. The younger woman stepped back sharply, her apron splashed with red, and Nurse Patterson spoke to her in a quiet, urgent voice until she nodded and ran from the ward. George watched, horrified, as blood continued to bubble from the man's mouth and the nurse held him and spoke to him, trying to give him comfort. The young nurse returned with two others carrying a stretcher. They lifted him on to it and bore him away, with Nurse Patterson following. The door swung shut behind them and the nurse immediately began to strip the bed, her movements quick and efficient, a practised routine. Her shadow moved behind her, tall against the high white wall. George shifted and turned his head away against the pillow. The smell from his leg was faint but sickly. It reminded him of the smell of water in which flowers have been left to rot.

He was woken by the creak of wheels on the tiled floor as a nurse arrived with a trolley piled high with folded sheets. She turned on the lights and a row of hanging glass globes sprang to life, their brightness making him blink. As he got used to the light he saw that the place was decked out for Christmas; from the centre of the ceiling, festoons of greenery extended to the corners: branches of yew, holly and mistletoe. At the end of the long room, above the main doorway, hung a huge Union Jack, which flapped each time the door was opened, as if insisting that it be paid attention.

An orderly arrived carrying a long pole and hooked it into a catch in the top pane of each window, and then deftly lifted and pulled so that it pivoted open a crack. He reached the window next to George and repeated the operation, letting in a shiver of air. The man in the bed on his right groaned loudly and pulled the blankets up around his ears, muttering, 'Bloody fresh air. What are they trying to do? Kill us with pneumonia?'

George caught the smell of the outside world stealing through the fug of fumes made by the stoves: fog, wet trees, damp earth. Men began to wake; those who were able to sat upright; one or two got out of bed and started shuffling down the ward. Nurses arrived to deliver bedpans and left again with them covered by cloths; others moved among the beds checking the patients or changing the bed linen. George listened to their high-pitched voices as they spoke with the patients or conferred with each other; he watched the movement of their small, quick hands and the way they walked – he had almost forgotten the way a woman walked.

An orderly came round with cocoa and the man in the next bed, on his right, sat up, his mousey hair tousled. His skin had a waxy pallor like an old candle. He took the mug saying, 'Is it hot this time? Yesterday's was lukewarm, you know.'

The orderly ignored him, took another mug from the tray for George and carried on. George, who could hardly bear the pain in his face and didn't want to move his jaw to drink, for fear of starting up an agony of throbbing, left the mug where it was.

'Wellings,' the man said, holding out his hand; then, as George turned towards him: 'Christ, what happened to you? You look like a bloody mummy!'

George said nothing.

'Got it in the face, did you?' Wellings dropped his hand.

George stared.

Wellings was undeterred. He lifted the blankets, pointing to the paunch beneath his army-issue blue pyjamas. 'Appendix,' he said. 'Bloody painful but worth it to get out of that hellhole. I should have another week or so before I get sent back, with a bit of luck: warm and dry, proper Christmas dinner, a few of the chaps are even putting on a concert.' He tucked the covers back around him. 'What have they done for you then, the stone-cutters?'

'I'm sorry; I don't know what you mean . . .'

'That's what they call them, the surgeons who patch up the faces as best they can. You're not the first, you know. There's been others through here but they don't tend to hang around; they don't like everyone staring, see, so they stick together, in a group, like.' He swung his legs out of bed, feeling around with his feet for a pair of shiny-looking carpet slippers. 'Where are you from, anyway?'

'Oh. Cumberland.'

Wellings nodded but looked as though George might as well have said Borneo. He drained his mug. 'Well, I hope you'll enjoy being at home in the bosom of your family while the rest of us are toiling away in the mud.'

George said, 'I'm sorry, I don't get your point.'

Wellings said with false bonhomie, 'Of course, you're the lucky one really, that's the point. You won't be going back, will you?'

George's heart began to thump. 'Why do you say that?' he said angrily. 'The nurse said they can save my leg! What do you know about it?'

'I'm not talking about your leg, sport,' Wellings said, looking straight at him. 'With your face smashed, you're not exactly a good advertisement for the war, now are you? Not exactly a *morale booster*. Even the ones who get masks made for them don't go back, you know.'

He put one hand to his abdomen as he stood up; then he bent to take soap and a towel from the shelf under the table and shuffled off towards the bathroom.

George tried to take in what he'd said. Surely it was ridiculous. If he were lucky enough to recover and be passed as fit, surely he would carry on as before: he'd return to the battalion, be with the others again, be of some use, have a chance to make amends? Gradually, the realisation came that what had been so crassly verbalised was true: what officers would want their soldiers to have to work alongside the scarred men, a living reminder of the power of lead and steel and of the horrors that could befall them? It would be the same at home for everyone with husbands or sons at the Front, trying to keep hopeful. Who would want to see the men with war engraved upon their faces?

George lay down on his good side and brought his forearm

up in front of his face so that he wouldn't have to talk to Wellings when he came back. The noises of the ward went on around him: the low babble of voices, the squeaking of shoes on the shiny floor, the clinking of cutlery and tin plates as breakfast was served. George didn't want a part of any of it. He lay with the pain like a clawing hand on his face, longing for sleep, a respite from thought and feeling. He wished he could sleep and never wake up.

Over the next week, George hardly spoke. He ignored Wellings, who eventually gave up and started to talk to the man on the other side of him, Cook, who had shrapnel wounds but was also expecting to return to the Front. George said as little as he could to the nurses too, answering their questions in mono-syllables, or muttering his thanks. Most of them soon learnt to leave well alone and carried out their duties, cutting up his food into tiny manageable pieces, changing his dressings, or his bed, without the cheery conversation they tried to keep up with the other patients. Only Nurse Patterson, by dint of sheer perseverance, managed to get anything out of him. She asked him questions about what it was like living in what she jokingly called 'the frozen North' and what he had done before the war. When she asked about his family and if he would like to write to them and tell them where he was, he shook his head and clammed up for the rest of the day.

The next time she saw him, she started on a different tack. She told him that every time he put up with the pain of having his leg wound washed in saline and painted with iodine was a stride towards being able to take real steps, and that the day when he could walk again would surely come. The garden was lovely, she said, the trees and bushes sparkling with frost, the carp in the fish pond moving slowly beneath the sheets of ice, salmon-pink and grey, flame-orange, burnished gold. He would see it soon, very soon, but he must drink and he must eat and he must not turn his head away.

One day she arrived early, still in her nurse's cape, and said that she had been checking the postroom and that some post had finally found its way to him. She brought out two letters from her apron pocket and put them into his hand. One bore his mother's handwriting and the other Kitty's. He looked at them but made no move to open them. An hour later, when she returned, they were still unopened on the table next to him. 'Would you like me to read them to you?' she asked, mindful of the difficulty he might have in managing with one eye still bandaged. He shook his head.

It was only when Wellings clumsily knocked the table, tipping over a glass of water that George snatched up the letters and held them tight. Wellings fussed around mopping up the spillage and then settled back to his newspaper. George waited until the quiet time, after lunch but before ward rounds, before opening the letter from his mother. Reading with only one eye was difficult: the words blurred and faded. He screwed up his eye and squinted at the date. The letter had been written two weeks before.

My dear George,

I hope this finds you well and not suffering too badly with the cold and wet that you wrote about. Did the knitted chest-warmer and chocolate that I sent reach you safely?

We have been busy at church this last Sunday starting preparations for the carol concert, and Lillie is to be in the nativity play. You will recall that Reverend Morgan encourages all of the children, however small, to join in. Lillie is to be a shepherd, wear a cloth on her head, and carry a toy

239

lamb. She is not well pleased, as she would far rather be an
angel. She was rather a crosspatch in the rehearsal; she sat on
the edge of the stage, refused to give her gift of a lamb to the
baby Jesus, and kept a firm hold on it. I was rather mortified
but could see the funny side afterwards, as the Virgin Mary
(Mrs Towers's little girl) was pulling with all her might on
one end while Lillie hung on to the other for dear life!

Many people have been asking after you, Aunty Elizabeth
and Uncle Ivor and the cousins, and at church, Mr and Mrs
Kettlewell, the Barnwell family, Thomas and the others.
None of the Ashwells were there on Sunday so I was unable
to give Kitty news of you. I hope they haven't gone down
with the cough that has been going the rounds. Fortunately,
we are all in the best of health here. I am sorry to harp on
about it but do make sure you wrap up well; I don't like to
think of you out in all weathers and do please take every
care and come back safe to us. We all miss you, and Father,
Ted and Lillie all send you their fondest love, as do I,

your loving Mother xxx
And these are from Lillie XX

George slowly put the sheet of paper back into the envelope.
Tears pricked his eyes. He imagined his mother writing at the
parlour table, and remembered how he used to sit there with
her when he came in from work: the chipped cups on the
threadbare tablecloth, the smell of drying washing mingling
with the taste of sweet tea. It seemed another world, almost
impossible to comprehend how it could still exist when the
world he carried with him was one of guns and filth and blood.
It hung on him like the pounds of mud that had weighed down
his greatcoat; it had seeped into him like the freezing water
that had soaked through his clothes.

He didn't know how he was going to tell her what had happened. He'd been barely conscious when he was brought in, too badly injured to sign a Field Service Postcard with its blunt printed note: 'I have been admitted into hospital.' He hoped that no one had yet informed his parents in similar vein on his behalf. Mother had told him not to go; he had caused her incalculable worry. How could he tell her that her fears had been realised? She would break her heart over this. He had let her down.

He picked up Kitty's letter. He felt so low that he didn't think he could bear another stiff little note. There were worse things, far worse things a man could do than fail to confide in a friend. He rested his eye for a minute by focusing on the middle distance: the greenery that decked the ward, the polished holly leaves and feathery yew mingled with the long fingers of mistletoe and dots of pale berries. They made him think of being out of doors, of the churchyard with its quiet yew shade, of alders over running water and the open hillsides with soft grass as fine as an animal's pelt. What a balm it would be to the spirits to be on a fell somewhere, completely alone.

With a sigh, he opened the letter and saw that it was dated a couple of days after his mother's.

Dear George,

I'm so sorry to write with bad news and I know we haven't been on the best of terms lately so maybe you will not welcome my letter but I have no one else to turn to and I hope that for the sake of our long friendship you will bear with me. We heard last week that Arthur has been killed. His company came under heavy shellfire near Arras and was virtually wiped out. It hurts me so to write these words. He was my brother, my only brother, and now I'll never see him

241

again. I cannot tell you how much it hurts. I keep remembering all the times we argued and I think of words I spoke in anger when he decided to enlist. I would do anything to have him back and do it all differently.

Mother and Father are in a terrible state. We had a couple come to take over the post office for a few days but Father insisted that he was all right to carry on and now they are gone. He is not all right. He is always at the counter to save Mother from the long line of enquiries and condolences from customers, and sometimes I think that he is clenching his teeth so hard his jaw will break. Mother hardly speaks to me when we're in the sorting room. She disappears upstairs and comes back with red eyes and at night, through the wall, I can hear her weeping and Father trying to comfort her. It's awful. There's nothing I can do; they have shut me out. We don't even have Arthur's poor body to bury or anywhere to go to remember him.

I'm so sorry to be writing this to you. I know it isn't tactful when you are out there too and in all manner of danger but I knew you would want to know about Arthur. No, that is not it; if I am truthful I am just so desperate, George, and you are my only real friend. I know that I was angry with you when you wouldn't trust me with your reasons for leaving but it was only because we have never had secrets before and I do so value that openness between us. In any case, I have no right to take the moral high ground as when I told you that I had a follower that was sheer pique. I suppose my pride was hurt at being left out of your confidence. I hope you have forgiven me for not trusting more and accepting that you must have had your reasons. Well, you may think that we have grown out of telling each other everything, and perhaps you do not want

this much honesty, but I have bared my heart in any case. It
was too full for me to carry alone. I wish that I could see
you and we could talk as we used to, and all could be as it
was before. Write to me. Let me know when you might get
leave to come home. I hope and pray that you are safe and
well and continue so.

    Your dear friend,
    Kitty

George felt a lump in his throat. Arthur had been good
to him; when he first started work it had been Arthur who
showed him how to swing the mail bags up on to his shoulder
without losing his balance and who had distracted Mr Ashwell's
attention when one of George's many initial delivery mistakes
had been about to come to light. He remembered how Arthur
used to get bored and irritated when the post office was quiet,
reading motor magazines and travel brochures under the
counter, always dreaming of speeding off to far-flung places.
He used to say that the motor car had opened up Cumberland
to the world so why shouldn't it open up the world to him?
George found it hard to believe that he was gone: like Edmund,
like Percy, like so many others, part of the long line of men
gone into the dark.

His heart went out to Kitty. He should have written properly
before this, not responded in kind to her stilted letters. He
should have seen the hurt that lay behind her reserve. It must
have cost her to write to him like that and to admit that she'd
told a lie in anger; he knew how proud she could be. The thought
of her misery made him feel agitated. He must write to both
Mother and Kitty straight away.

He called over to Patterson and asked if he could possibly
have something to write on. She smiled and hurried away,

returning with a pen and some postcards. They bore a sepia picture of the hospital and George was surprised to see that it was a huge three-storey building with heavy towers and gothic turrets set in wide grounds and with a separate chapel standing nearby. He had had no sense that he was within a building larger than a cathedral and wondered at the number of sick and wounded men that must be housed here. The caption said simply '3rd London General Hospital, Wandsworth', a place he had never heard of. He wondered whether there were city roads or parkland beyond the bounds of the photograph and felt again the pang of longing for open space and grass. He was glad that the caption did some of the job of communication for him.

To his mother he simply wrote:

Dear Mother,
I am safe in England again and I'm making a good recovery. No need to visit. The train is too expensive and they will probably let me come home in a week or two to convalesce . . . He wrote: *depending on* and then crossed it out. *I am being well looked after and send you and the family all my love and happiest Christmas wishes.*
Your loving son,
George

He rested his eye for a minute or two and then wrote again on the other card.

Dear Kitty,
I'm so sorry about Arthur. It must be awful. I hope to get home soon and be what comfort I can. I have been hit in the leg and in the face. It looks as though my leg will be saved but

my eye and one side of my face is in pretty bad shape. There,
I've not held anything back from you but don't tell anyone as
I hope to spare Mother worry. I'm sorry I upset you, Kit.

    With love and sympathy,
    George

The next time that Patterson passed, he gave the cards to her and asked if she could post them. She said at once that she would and George felt relieved as she walked away with them, as if a small part of his burden had been lifted. He settled down to write another card to Haycock and Turland to let them know what had happened to him. He addressed it to Haycock and then wrote:

Dear Tom and Ernest,

    I'm a bit shot up but am in London getting put back
together again – gammy leg and still waiting to see what
happens with my eye. I feel bad about being here when
you're still slogging it out. Write to me at 26 Leonard Street
as I will convalesce at home.

    I'm so sorry Rooke bought it. It was awful to see. He
should never have come with us overseas. I hope everything
is <u>*quiet*</u> *where you are.*

    Your old pal,
    George

Exhausted, he put the card on the table to pass on to Nurse Patterson and sank back against the pillows.

A few days later, it was decided that George could be moved out to the veranda for an hour or two each afternoon. It was a glassed-in, green-painted wooden structure that ran along part of the south-facing wall of the hospital. Alongside other men, George sat in a wheelchair, a rug tucked around his knees and his injured leg bared and propped on a stool to let the sun shine on it, for the sake of its antiseptic properties. Although the shin and calf remained red and inflamed, the wound was clean and almost dry, a far cry from the slimy green and scarlet mess that had smelt so awful.

Every day, men chatted, read or nodded in sleep around him but George just gazed out at the grounds. In the foreground was a rose garden, the thorny stems and old brown flower heads all furred by frost, outlined in white. Beyond this, a long sloping lawn with elm and beech trees was bounded by a laurel hedge bordering the road. At visiting times, when patients were sometimes wrapped up well and wheeled around the grounds, George watched enviously as they exchanged the stuffy, disinfected atmosphere of the hospital for cold sharp air and a clear blue sky.

At last, the day came when Patterson said that she was so pleased with his progress that she intended to stay behind at the end of her shift so that she could take him into the garden. George said that he wouldn't want to inconvenience her and there was no need. She looked at him with a sceptical expression and said that they both knew that he was only being polite, and in any case, a promise was a promise.

She wrapped him in so many blankets that he resembled a fat cocoon, gave him some other private's cap to wear for good measure, then put on her long cape and manoeuvred the wheelchair over the threshold and through the veranda doors.

The freezing air was heady as they explored the gravelled paths of the rose garden and every sensation seemed magnified after the dullness of indoor living: the sun too bright, the crunch of the wheels on the small stones loud, the smell of leaf mould musty and pungent. As they came level with an evergreen shrub, he asked if he could stop and pinched the foliage between his fingers to smell the green, piny scent.

The fishpond had a wall with a wide stone rim and a central fountain that was reflected in the dark water below. A stone shell was supported by verdigris-covered porpoises but no water flowed from the pipes that protruded from their mouths. Slices of broken ice floated on the surface like tectonic plates. George saw a quick flick of orange in the water and bent forward to follow it but his bandaged reflection distracted him and the fish was gone, lost amongst the waterweed below the ice.

They passed on to the paths that circumnavigated the broad lawn and Patterson told him of the plans for the concert that was to be held in the refectory on Christmas morning. The VADs had their own choir, convalescent officers had formed a quartet and some of the other ranks had formed a barber's shop chorus.

'Shall you come, do you think?' she asked.

'Oh, I don't know,' George said, his mind elsewhere.

'It might do you good,' she ventured. 'It's important to be sociable. All part of moving towards normality, you know, getting involved in life again.'

George didn't want to be with other people. He couldn't see how his life would ever be normal again. 'I'll think about it,' he said.

Early on Christmas morning, George was taken to a cubicle where he was told that his bandages would be taken off for good, and that Dr Bailey would remove his stitches and examine the wound.

A nursing sister whom he hadn't seen before, a small, middle-aged woman with a sharp voice, supervised a young nurse while she carefully unwound him. The dressings were stuck to dried blood in places and had to be peeled away painfully. He gritted his teeth and bore it as the nurse repeatedly apologised and the sister directed and criticised by turns. George held tightly to the arms of his chair. It seemed to him that through his closed eyelid, as the bandages thinned, he could see light. Hardly daring to breathe as the layers fell away, he tried to open his eye. The skin around it was so swollen that he could open it no more than a slit, yet the brightness of the room was blinding. He shut it and then tried again, blinking until he could make out the strangely doubled image of a rectangular window and the dim form of the figures moving in front of it.

'I can see light and shapes!' He grasped the nurse's hand.

'That's marvellous,' she said, squeezing his hand in return. 'I'm so glad for you.'

'Will I see detail again eventually?' George asked the sister.

'Blurred vision is perfectly normal at first,' she said briskly. 'Take the bandages to the incinerator please, nurse, and tell Dr Bailey we're ready for him.' She set out a basin and some implements on a table covered with a white cloth.

Dr Bailey had very pale skin, as though all his time was spent indoors, and long slim hands. He wished George good morning, congratulated him on the discovery that his eye was functional and reassured him that his vision would slowly improve. He examined George's face, saying to the sister, 'The maxilla, the nasal and zygomatic bones are all compromised, of course, but the mandible is wholly intact.' George winced as he began to remove the horsehair stitches, dropping them into the basin, tough and dark like the bristles of a shoe brush. To George he said, 'Hmm, there's some puckering at the maxilla where the wound was closed. Otherwise the scar tissue looks healthy and as the swelling goes down you'll lose some of the puffiness and shine and be a little more comfortable.'

When he'd finished he passed the basin to the sister and stood back to survey the overall effect.

'Could I see?' George asked.

The sister and doctor exchanged a glance and then both spoke at once.

'We discourage it. We don't have mirrors on these wards for that reason,' said the sister.

'It's early days,' Dr Bailey said.

George's eye was watering and he put his hand up to wipe the wetness away.

'Oh, you mustn't touch it,' the sister said. 'Absolutely not. It could still become infected, you know.'

George let his hand drop and tried to ignore the irritating tickle as it ran down over his cheek.

Dr Bailey said to the sister, 'Let me know if any problems arise.'

He looked at George and gave a faint smile. 'Good luck,' he said.

As the nurse wheeled George back through the draughty corridors, the air felt chill against his newly naked face and the salt tears from his watering eye stung his raw skin. The nurse glanced quickly behind her to check for the sister and produced a white folded handkerchief from her pocket. George dabbed at his eye. When they passed the corridor that led down to the refectory, the sound of men's voices reached them, singing, 'Till the Boys Come Home'.

The nurse's steps slowed. 'Oh, I say, it's the Christmas concert! I didn't realise it was that time already.'

'Would you like to go?' George felt obliged to ask.

'It sounds awfully jolly. They've got a tombola and everything. We could just slip in at the back.'

'Well, better wait until this number finishes.'

The nurse turned the chair round smartly and wheeled it up to the arched doorway into the refectory. A burst of applause and shouts of 'Encore' greeted the end of the song and the nurse opened the door and wheeled him through. Tables laden with trays of teacups lined the sides of the room and chairs were arranged in rows facing the far end where an officer sat at a battered upright piano and four others were gathered around it, holding sheet music in front of them. All were dressed in uniform for the occasion, although they were clearly not ready to be discharged, as all had bandages, slings or crutches. The room had been hung with flags and red and yellow Chinese lanterns, and the smell of greens and a faint haze of steam mingled with the scent from a large display of hothouse lilies on the table beside the performers. The room was packed, the front row full of VADs ready to take their turn as the choir, and behind them staff and patients sitting in groups with friends. George spotted Patterson near the front. She raised her hand but couldn't move, being hemmed in right in the middle of a row.

The nurse bent forward to speak to him over the hubbub of conversation that had broken out while the singers found their next number.

'Would you mind dreadfully if I went to sit with my room-mates?' she asked. 'I can put you wherever you like.'

George looked around. Wheelchair cases and the worst injured, some of them with nurses in attendance, were grouped together at one side. 'Don't worry, you go,' George said. 'I can manage.'

She gave a quick smile and slipped away down the central aisle. He pushed down on the wheels to move the chair along and made his way through the tight space between the wall and the back row. As he murmured, 'Excuse me,' to get people to shift forward a little, they turned in their seats and he saw their expressions change. Some registered shock and quickly looked away, some looked pitying and made a great meal out of moving their chairs, as if bending over backwards to be accommodating. A few heads turned to each other in conversation after he'd passed. Near the end of the row, George saw Wellings and Cook. As Wellings turned round there was a split second when he failed to recognise George, then he laughed in an embarrassed way and coloured up. As George passed on behind the row he distinctly heard him say to Cook, '. . . gone to sit with the other droolers.'

George pulled his chair up behind the others, his head pounding. *They should have shown me, if I look so awful. They should have told me.* He held the folded handkerchief up to his eye as if to dab it, then kept it there, half covering his face. A man beside him had a massively swollen brow and a huge, flattened nose, as if he had been broken and someone had put him back together who had only the most basic knowledge of the lineaments of the human face. His own instinctive recoil horrified him. Another had part of his jaw missing, his tongue lolling out, and further over a man had marks like train tracks running from his ear to the base of his neck. George remembered what the French soldiers called those with such disfigurements: scar throats.

The piano player found the page and played the opening bars of 'There's a Long, Long Trail a-Winding' and the singing began again, swelling in volume as the VADs joined in on the chorus and some of the audience followed them.

> There's a long, long trail a-winding
> Into the land of my dreams,
> Where the nightingales are singing
> And a white moon beams.
> There's a long, long night of waiting
> Until my dreams all come true;

251

Till the day when I'll be going down
That long, long trail with you . . .

The uproar echoed in George's head. His eyes were aching from trying to focus. He couldn't stay here; he wanted to get out. He pushed the wheels backwards and shunted into a table, making the cups rattle in their saucers and the teaspoons chink against the china so that people glanced round at the racket – dark eyes in blurred faces, mouths opening and closing as they sang. He jerked the chair round, his armpits damp from the effort, and as the song ended and applause and stamping began, he wheeled it back towards the door, bumping on chair legs and catching his fingers painfully between the wheel and the wall. A porter swung the door open for him, his eyes still fixed on the show, and George emerged back into the blessed coolness of the corridor.

He sucked his grazed knuckles and then set off for the veranda. He wanted to be alone. The wheels moved easily over the polished floor and he became more confident and moved along faster. He knew what he was going to do.

Only a few men were in their usual places, reading and dozing; most had taken up the welcome distraction of the concert. He picked up a couple of rugs and arranged them over his knees; then he asked one of the men, Miller, who was recovering from a broken arm, if he could manage to open the doors for him.

'Are you sure? It's freezing out there,' Miller said, looking curiously at him. George gave no explanation but merely nodded and Miller pushed against the door with his back until it swung open.

The going was harder on the gravel paths. George's shoulders and collarbones ached as he shoved the wheels round, making

252

laborious progress through the rose garden. The keen air made a dry, scratching sound as it passed through the rose bushes with their few shrivelled brown leaves. George's eye began to stream. He seemed to have dropped the handkerchief somewhere and wiped his eye instead on the sleeve of his pyjama jacket.

George reached the fishpond and rolled the chair right up to the wall. He bent forward and looked down into the water, blinking until he managed to focus. It was as if he were looking through a ripple distorting his reflection, as if one side of his face was dragged down, yet the surface of the water was calm. He peered closer.

His flesh was swollen and darkly bruised, red and purple, in a panda-like circle around his eye, which was crazily slanted: the skin pulled down beneath and drawn into a puckered indentation where the roundness of his cheek used to be. Lines radiated from the central point like creases in a drawstring bag and a long scar ran from this crater round to the side of his face. He traced it with his finger out towards his ear. Turning sideways, he saw that his nose was flattened at the bridge as though a bite had been taken out of it, and a ridge of scar tissue led from there as well, down to the site of closure of the wound. His body became rigid as he took in the whole effect: it was as if a sculptor had grown frustrated with his work and smeared it with his thumb, a long smudge from nose to ear.

He no longer recognised himself. He refused to look away; he stared and the stranger stared back. Beneath his reflection he was aware of depth and darkness, the slightest streak of flame and hint of movement, slow and streamlined, as the fish passed to and fro, alien, infinitely strange.

15

TIN

Nurse Patterson worried about Private Farrell. Ever since she had found him outside, on Christmas Day, his teeth chattering with cold, he seemed to have slipped further into decline. Although his healing had come on apace since then, he seemed very uneasy in his mind. He had fallen into the habit of failing to get up for breakfast, endeavouring to stay asleep for as long as possible rather than face each new day. It took all her powers of persuasion to convince him to shave and to eat a little porridge.

He had been moved from the surgical ward to a convalescent ward, which was a mark of recovery that usually boosted the men's spirits. She had thought that the progress of graduating at last from the wheelchair to crutches would have cheered him and given him more freedom to roam the hospital, or visit the chapel, but he used them only to go down to the veranda, and there he stuck, talking to no one, maybe reading only a page or two before returning to gazing out of the window.

Although he'd received post, no visitors had come, and she privately wondered if he had been less than candid about the seriousness of his injuries. She was delighted on his behalf when a parcel arrived at the postroom: a rectangular, battered-looking package in brown paper tied up with string that she imagined to be another Christmas box from his home, delayed by its journey to Belgium and back before it found him. She hurried down to the veranda to deliver it.

George was reading a book, in a corner by one of the stoves, as far distant from his fellow patients as it was possible to get. He sat with his elbow on the arm of the wicker chair, his hand cupping the damaged part of his face. Patterson had noticed this tendency to cover his face whenever he could. She thought that the time had come to tackle it head-on.

She sat down in the chair opposite. 'I'm on my break so I thought I'd bring you this.' She put the parcel down on the table between them. 'Is it a gift from home?'

George closed his book, keeping a thumb on his page. 'I should think so.' He made no move to open the package.

'Perhaps it's more books, or . . . or a cake?' she said encouragingly.

'Probably more knitted stuff,' George said. 'Socks. Scarves. Mother is keen on knitting. Perhaps she could knit me a balaclava.' He gave a strange little laugh. 'I could wear it back to front.' He looked at her, challenging her to say anything.

Sister Patterson took time to pick her words. 'It's healed very well,' she said mildly. 'The swelling has all gone now.'

'And that's made a difference, has it? Really?' George took

his hand away and turned to face her. The livid colours of the bruising had faded to blue and a dirty yellow and the swelling had dissipated, but this only accentuated the droop of the eye, its red inner rim exposed, its expression immeasurably sad. In his cheek, the puckering at the centre of the radiating folds was a knot of red tissue, the skin around it taut and shiny. George jabbed at it with his forefinger. 'People stare without seeing *me*. They just see this. To them, I'm hardly a man.'

Patterson leant forward as if to remonstrate.

'Oh, I don't blame them,' George went on. 'It's the first thing we're able to perceive, isn't it? The human face? Did you know that the focus of a baby's eyes is exactly the distance from its mother's breast to her face? And faces are the first things we draw, aren't they? Symmetrical. Two dots for the eyes . . .' He poked twice at the material of his trouser leg. 'And a line for the mouth.' He drew his finger across in a slash. 'Even clouds' – he gestured towards the sky through the window – 'when you sit and watch for shapes in them, that's what appears most easily: faces.' He stared out of the window.

Patterson watched his shoulders trembling. She wished she could put an arm around them. She sat, still and quiet, waiting for him to get a hold of himself. Eventually he mumbled, 'I'm sorry. I seem to have let it all get on top of me.'

'I wonder . . .' she said, watching him carefully, aware that she must broach the subject sensitively. 'It's not nearly as bad as you think, you know . . . but if you *feel* that it is . . . I wonder whether you might consider a prosthetic?'

George turned towards her quickly. 'What do you mean?'

'Well, there's a department here that makes them. Not masks that are heavy and ugly,' she rushed on. 'They're thin and painted to match the person's own skin tone and they just cover the injury, not the whole face. Not everyone feels the necessity of course; it's entirely up to the individual.' She stopped to watch his reaction.

He considered for a moment and then said, 'How do they stay on?'

'With spectacles. Like this.' She curved her fingers around the top of her ears as if putting on a pair of glasses.

'And it makes you look more . . . normal?'

'From a distance, at least.' She knew that she mustn't give false hopes but she desperately wanted to help him. 'The patients I've seen with them have felt more comfortable with themselves, I think.'

'Would they be able to make one for me?'

'I'm sure they would. Shall I make an appointment?'

'Thank you, that would be very kind of you,' George said, recovering his dignity.

Patterson put her hands on her knees. 'I must get back in time for the ward round. Will you be coming up for your lunch?'

George nodded slowly.

She levered herself up, saying, 'Enjoy your book.' As she passed him, she let her hand rest momentarily on his shoulder before walking away.

George sat, looking at his page but not reading. He felt absurdly grateful for that momentary touch. He realised that he already assumed no one would have any fellow feeling with him, far less want to touch him in sympathy. How quickly that assumption had taken hold. Damaged faces unsettled people, making them unsure how to act. He wondered if he would ever have the courage to do the things that others considered normal everyday exchanges: offer a handshake to a stranger or say farewell to a relative by turning a cheek to be kissed. Losing a limb made you a hero, losing the symmetry of your face made you an untouchable.

257

He felt too restless to read so he looked out of the window for a while. It was a cold, clear January day with a gusting wind that scudded the clouds along. He watched the sparrows flitting in and out of the evergreen shrubs among the dead roses. The wind ran over the ground, rolling dead leaves along and then dropping them again, reminding him of the questing dart and forage of the creatures of no man's land. Leaves, he said to himself. They're only leaves.

When George returned to the ward, a nurse informed him that he was to go to the prosthetics department directly after lunch. He told himself that he mustn't pin his hopes too firmly on this but he found himself eating his poached fish and greens quickly, itching to get going. He put the parcel, still unopened, on the shelf beneath his bedside table and set off on his crutches, tap, swing, tap, swing, through wards and corridors.

Arriving, he knocked and heard the distant sound of a woman's voice calling, 'Enter.' When he opened the door, there was no one there but the sound of running water was coming from a galley kitchen to one side. The room was brightly lit by a large window and at first George thought that snow must have fallen, such was the quality and intensity of the light. Then he saw that the walls were all covered by the plaster casts of faces, brilliant white in the winter sunlight. They hung from battens at regularly spaced intervals, like death's heads arranged on shelves in a charnel house. Some were horribly disfigured: noses reduced to a dark hole, like a skull, faces with no profile beyond forehead and lips, more ape than man, jaws askew, or become huge, bulging protuberances, or completely shot away. Others were sculpted models of perfect faces. They looked serene with their closed eyes, like ancient Greek statues, the corrected patterns from which masks would be taken.

A woman came in, drying her hands on her apron, and George turned towards her. She didn't falter but looked straight at him, smiled and said, 'Welcome. Isn't it nice to have a little sunshine at last?' She wore a white blouse with a grey bow at the neck and had her hair coiled up in a net, which didn't suit her long face but which George imagined was eminently practical.

'Do you have any pain?' she asked, indicating that he should sit on the couch.

He laid down his crutches and sat on the edge of it. 'No, it's all healed up – well, as far as one can describe it as healed.'

She looked at him sympathetically. 'May I?' She held out her hands and George stayed very still while she gently felt the contours of his face. 'The first thing we have to do is take a cast. It's not terribly comfortable. Do you feel up to trying it?'

'Will it cover right over my nose as well? I'm not very good about having my face covered; I don't like being shut in, you see.' George despised himself for the same old panic. Look where it had led. Could he not control it even now, after everything that had happened?

'We make holes for the nose, don't worry, but you have to stay very still with your eyes shut while I cover the whole of the rest of your face. Do you think you can do that?'

George nodded and she helped him to lie back on the wooden couch and put a cloth beneath his head that was prickly with dried spatters of plaster. She mixed water into a bucket of white powder, beating it to a smooth, creamy consistency.

'You have to get the bubbles out,' she said. 'You need a completely even finish.' She dipped pieces of bandage, soaking them in the mixture then began to lay them on to his face, trailing like seaweed. 'Very still now,' she said as she smoothed them, tight and wet over his skin, up to his hairline and down over his chin and neck. All the time, she talked to him and he concentrated as hard as he could so that he wouldn't think about the smothering stuff that was covering him, sealing his eyes and mouth, encasing him.

She told him that the sculptor would make a clay squeeze from the cast she was taking; it would be an exact portrait of his face, including the injury and his closed eyes. He would use it to copy the uninjured side of his face to produce a mirror image for the mask. 'The bit that seems almost magical,' she said, 'is when the sculptor opens the eye. It's as if a sleeper is woken.' She painted more of the mixture over the plaster bandages to make it thicker and tougher and he forced himself to remain still despite the drips running into his nose and ears. After a few suffocating minutes, he noticed that as the plaster began to harden it was also getting warmer and he marvelled at the reaction taking place. It was as if skin was turning to bone.

The woman was standing back, waiting. 'The mask itself will be made of galvanised copper, and terribly thin – thinner than a sixpence, so that it's not too heavy. We want them to fit as closely as possible, you see, and the thinner the edges, the closer the blend to your skin.'

The plaster had hardened off completely. George remained immobile, keeping his breathing light, and tried not to think of words like *death mask* and *sarcophagus*. He was greatly relieved when she looked up at the clock and then took hold of both sides of the cast and began to release it. Agonisingly, some of his eyebrows and eyelashes came with it but he was so glad to be free of it he barely even flinched.

'There,' she said, holding it up carefully. 'A neat job and no bubbles.'

George looked at the smooth white model of his face. As

she turned it to inspect it from all angles, he saw first one side and then the other: his old self, his new self, an eerie duality.

She laid it gently on a bench, saying, 'The mask will restore the symmetry. Never fear.' She washed her hands and gave him a basin of water and a cloth to wash with. As his hands passed over his face, he thought that he would be glad to hide this ugliness from the view of others but that he would never be able to forget what lay beneath the sheet of metal.

'We'll let you know when it's ready for fitting,' she said, and held out her hand in farewell. He took it: damp, cool, perfect skin.

That evening, as the ward settled down, men making desultory conversation or writing letters, he remembered the parcel and retrieved it from the shelf under the table. The handwriting wasn't his mother's but he assumed it had been repackaged when it was sent on. In the absence of scissors, he worked the string towards the corner until he could slip it off and then started to unwrap the brown paper, envisioning knitted gloves, writing paper, a Christmas card, maybe cocoa. When he pulled the paper away, what met his eyes was Edmund's green tin, with its incongruous picture of the boating party, the lid scratched and dented. He stared at it in disbelief. A string around it bore a tag that said, 'Pte G. Farrell, No. 1893. Pay book enc.'

He prised up the lid. On top, like a memento from another life, lay his pay book. Beneath it was a wad of letters; beneath them, a muddle of small objects. Someone must have found it in the tumble of bricks that was once the farmhouse billet, he thought. They had found it and looked no further than the pay book for an owner. He picked up the dog-eared book. A picture of Edmund as he handed it to him for safekeeping came vividly into his mind: his hair ruffled up on end where he had been leaning his hand on his forehead; his tired, patient face. He thought about all the ways that Edmund had shown his sense of responsibility to his men: how he had taken trouble to get to know small things about them, asked about their families, listened to their problems, made sure they kept their bedding dry and their feet oiled. And what had he, George, done in return? He'd got lost in the polders so that Edmund had to go out on a limb on his behalf with Hunton; he'd lied to him about knowing Violet and spied on him by looking at the studio portrait. If he hadn't been so weak, such a coward, if he'd obeyed a command with the snap-to-it immediacy, the reflex efficiency they'd all been trained to deliver, Edmund would still be alive.

George lifted out Violet's letters and placed them aside. A gold pocket watch gleamed amongst the sepia photographs. He opened it: a beautiful half-hunter with a heavy gold chain. Inside the case were inscribed the initials E.L. followed by: 'Fugerit invida Aetas: carpe diem – Envious time is fleeing: seize the day'.

He thought that it must have been a gift; the inscription was a woman's touch: maybe Edmund's mother or sister, maybe Violet. The thought of all the people who loved Edmund and would miss him so sorely filled George with despair. When his father said that death was not the end, he meant that the spirit went on, that there was an afterlife. George also knew that death was not an end, oh no, the pain of the final moments of dying were in reality a beginning: the stone in the pool that starts ripples of grief spreading outwards through the hearts of others; the agony of empathy for the suffering of a loved one, the aching to see, to hold, to speak together again, the terrible, never-ending loss.

As though the tin had come to him as a penance, George continued taking one thing after another from it and laying them

262

on the blankets around him. A set of keys led him to thoughts of Edmund's family home; a half-used pack of cigarettes brought back the smoky farmhouse kitchen near Ypres.

A tiny, exquisite dance-card holder with a minute ebony pencil he felt sure was a gift from Violet. He opened it. Inside on the first page was a list of dancing partners' names: *Lucien, Albert, Peter, Harold, Lucien*, then *Edmund, Edmund, Edmund*. For a moment it hurt him to think of Edmund dancing with Violet, his arms around her, their heads so close together . . . There was no escape from it; she had been completely bowled over. The dance-card holder had been given to Edmund – why would she keep it? She was never intending to dance with anyone else. He checked himself, stamping on these feelings; he had no right to think of Violet in that way. All that was gone. She had loved Edmund and he, George, had been the cause of his death. He had ruined her life.

He shuffled through the photographs: the calm faces of Edmund's parents and the good-humoured faces of brothers and sisters; he wondered what lines were drawn upon them now. The telegram would have read *Missing in action*, as no body had been recovered. Would they have accepted its implied message? Oh God, would they still be hoping from day to day that better news might come? He knew that he would have to see Violet, face to face, bringing the news she dreaded to hear. He owed it to Edmund; he owed it to her. The thought of telling her was unbearable.

Something small and shiny was tucked in the corner of the tin. He picked it out and laid it in his palm. Tiny imperfections at its centre were like specks of fire caught in golden liquid. Another love gift from Violet: a heart carved in amber. He held it in his hand.

*

263

Over the next few days, as Patterson had instructed him, George moved around as much as possible on his crutches, trying to overcome the temptation to hop on one leg. He must place not just his toe but also his heel to the ground to attempt to stretch the tendon, which had shortened in healing. He did small errands for the nurses, taking messages or delivering newspapers to patients. Those whom he saw often began to get used to his appearance and no longer reacted to him in the same way. When he met someone new, he braced himself for how their eyes changed and then slid away; he tried to think of his scarred skin as rhinoceros hide, a tough layer through which hurt must not be allowed to pierce, telling himself that at least he was doing something useful.

As the January freeze made way for a wet, cold and dismal February, George found that, at last, he was able to manage on one crutch and then none. He had a limp, as he was still not able to straighten his leg completely, but he was moving around a little better each day. When his leg ached badly, rather than succumbing to rest he pushed trolleys for the nurses, taking some of his weight on the handles so that he could carry on the process of exercising and strengthening his wasted leg muscles. By the time that he was asked to return for the fitting of his mask he was walking unaided.

This time, when he visited, it was the sculptor who greeted him. He looked very much the artist rather than one of the medical staff, with his unruly, dark hair and pointed beard and his artist's smock, its grey cloth paled by clay dust and daubed with smudges of paint.

He asked George his name and then went to a chest with a series of small drawers, each one labelled in tiny handwriting. It reminded George of the chests that stored the collections at the town museum back home: each drawer lined with blue

264

velvet and opening to reveal butterflies pinned on cards, the whorls of ammonites or miniature, crystalline pinnacles of quartz. The sculptor took an object from a drawer and brought it to George in his open hands, carrying it as carefully as he might a bird's egg.

The mask had a pair of round, wire spectacle frames attached to it and was made of a piece of thin metal designed to cover the top left quarter of his face. From top to bottom, it extended from just above his brow to just below his cheek. From side to side, it covered the upper portion of his nose and extended to the hinge of his jawbone, blending into the skin beside the ear. The aperture for the eye was sculpted with painstaking detail; even the creases in the eyelid were present.

'It may take a little getting used to,' the sculptor said. 'Let's see how the fit is, to begin with.'

George leant forward to accommodate him as he placed the mask over his scarred features and hooked one arm of the spectacles over his ear. The other side had a long wire attached that reached all the way around the back of his head. The sculptor fiddled with a catch that linked it to the first so that the whole mask was fixed firmly in place. It was cold to the touch but fitted like a glove.

'How does that feel?'

'It feels . . .' As George spoke, he felt the stiffness of the mask against his lower cheek, its unyielding substance. 'It feels strange but not as heavy as I thought.'

'Good. Good. It'll be about four ounces though, so you may find you don't want to wear it all day. You may be more comfortable without it when you're in your own home, for instance.' He took a mirror down from a high shelf and held it up. It took George by surprise and he gasped as he remembered the shock he had felt when he first saw his naked face; he had not looked at his reflection since. This time, however, what he saw was a transformation, instant and amazing, the sudden recognition of the correct pattern of a human face. It was as though Midas had passed his hand over part of his face and then taken his metallic touch away. The expression was wooden but it was a proper, evenly proportioned human face – like looking at a sculpture of oneself.

'Thank you,' he said. 'It's . . . It's remarkable.'

The sculptor nodded quickly as if embarrassed by thanks. He returned his attention to the catch behind the ear. 'A little too tight, I think.' He fiddled with it until he was happy that it was no longer cutting in but was still secure. 'Now we shall paint you.' He took George's shoulders and turned him this way and that until he was happy with the way that the light fell on him; then he fetched brushes and a palette with worms of paint to mix flesh tones: titanium white, cadmium red and yellow, burnt sienna, ultramarine blue.

'I try to match the subject's colouring as closely as possible,' he said as he started to work. 'But it's bright in here so there's a danger of using tones that then appear too highly coloured on a dull day. One has to strike a range somewhere in the middle.'

The rich, nutty smell of oil paint was cloying in George's nostrils and he stifled a sneeze. The sculptor smiled and stepped back. 'Feel free,' he said, 'better get it over with than risk an eyeful of paint.'

George put his handkerchief to his face, his hand meeting flesh on one side and metal on the other. He sneezed and they both laughed. The sculptor applied the paint in tiny dabs of colour, standing back frequently to assess his handiwork or tipping George's face to see it from a different angle.

'What's the blue for?' George asked.

'For the lower area of the cheek – here. To capture the tinge of blue where you shave.' He worked on, telling him about the process and how to take care of the mask as the paint was prone to chip. When all the colour had been applied, he fetched a card to which strands of human hair were pinned and held it up beside George's face. 'I use real hair for the eyebrows and lashes,' he said. 'Even the lightest, most feathery strokes of the brush look too flat. So . . .' he finished, picking a strand out, 'I will apply the hair and send the completed prosthetic down to you.' He removed the mask, holding it by the edges with his fingertips and placed it on the bench. 'You'll be ready to go home then, I imagine?'

George's heart lurched. 'I don't know,' he said. 'No one's told me.' Terror gripped him as he thought about going out into the streets and walking among strangers.

The sculptor patted his shoulder. 'It won't be so bad, you'll see. Where there's life, there's hope, eh?'

George felt that he had barely got used to moving within the small world of the hospital among those who had some cause for sympathy. Outside, surely he would be seen as a freak. He told himself that his mask made his face far more acceptable, that he must just carry it off with aplomb and that if he made no reference to it, neither would anyone else. He would think about it over the next few days and try to prepare himself for the change.

When he returned to the ward, he had a further shock. On his bed was his uniform, neatly folded, and underneath the bed were his boots. He opened out the jacket and then the shirt and trousers. They had been mended as far as possible. The trouser leg that had been torn by the bullet had been slit up the front and had a large area of fabric removed. George reckoned that they must have had to cut it to get at the wound.

It had been patched from inside and carefully darned, albeit in a darker thread. He lifted the jacket to remove the ticket with his name and number that was pinned on to the collar. There was a smell, faint but unmistakable. The mud may have gone, the clods and the clots of it, but he could still smell in the fibres the very particular type of Ypres mire: soil mixed with latrine water and dead things, the odour of corruption. He dropped it on to the bed with a noise of disgust and then looked around to check that no one had seen him. He sat down on the edge of the bed, slowly refolded the garments and put them underneath the bed on top of the boots.

The next day a sergeant came with George's discharge papers, wished him good luck and left him sitting on the edge of the bed in his dressing gown reading through the sheaf of forms. George finished reading and put them aside. He sat on, looking at his uniform but still couldn't bring himself to put it on.

Patterson arrived bringing him an envelope. 'Here's your rail warrant for your ticket home,' she said cheerily. She glanced at the folded clothes. 'Is everything all right?'

George made a huge effort. He *would not* seem afraid. How could he possibly be afraid of a small thing like taking a train? And he dreaded appearing ungrateful after everything that had been done for him, everything *she* had done for him.

'It's all right. I'm all right,' he said.

'Only I'm on my day off tomorrow and I didn't want to miss saying goodbye and the chance to wish you the best of luck.'

'So it's for tomorrow – the warrant?'

'Yes – here.' She passed the envelope over. 'Nurse Moss is bringing your prosthesis down. You should maybe wear it for the rest of the day. Get used to it, you know.'

George remembered his manners. 'Thank you. For everything,' he said.

'Oh, that's all right. Only doing my job.' She stood up and he followed suit. 'Look how steady you are on your feet now!' She looked him in the eyes. 'You're going to be fine.'

They shook hands and he watched her walk away down the ward and out of the door.

The next day he made himself put on his battle clothes. He strapped on the mask and packed his kitbag with his few belongings, his pay book and Edmund's tin, which he carefully rewrapped. The duty sister filled out his hospital discharge papers and got an orderly to find him a cab.

George sat shivering, pressed against the seat as they joined the stream of horse and motor traffic, as if to get as far away as possible from the onslaught of noise and cold: the bright, brash outside world. At the station, it was not too bad if he kept moving but standing in the queue for tickets he felt exposed to the blatant scrutiny of every passer-by.

He bought a newspaper so that he could hide away behind it in the corner of a carriage. Nothing had changed in the paper's determined optimism. He read about 'some progress' on the Western Front, 'current consolidation' and hopes for a 'Big Push' in the spring. He knew the reality was hardship, stink and stasis.

When he changed trains at Crewe, there was going to be a long wait so he ventured out to find the Station Hotel. The waitress took one look and seated him in a corner away from other customers, as far away as possible from the window.

16

26 LEONARD STREET

As George made his way along Leonard Street, the pools of yellow light from the street lamps lit a fine drizzle of rain falling upon shining wet cobbles. His leg pained him badly after walking from the station; his limp had become more and more pronounced and he made slow progress, stepping carefully on the greasy surface. When he reached the front door of number twenty-six, he paused and leant against the doorjamb.

The parlour curtains were not quite closed and he looked in at the lamp on the table with an open newspaper beside it, the small fire in the grate and the wooden clock on the mantelpiece. He wondered whether it still showed half past four as it had done for as long as he could remember. Nothing had changed. He had a strange detached sensation, as if he was looking into someone else's life. He almost expected to see the real George Farrell walk into the room, pick up the newspaper and settle himself in the fireside chair. He took a deep breath and rapped on the door with the knocker.

His father hurried through from the kitchen, came up to the window and pulled back the curtains to look out. In a reflex action, George shrank back out of view. He heard his mother calling out, 'Who can it be at this time of night?' as his father drew back the bolts and opened the door.

'Yes?' he said. There was a moment's silence as he took in the sight of his son. 'George!' His voice broke on the word. He drew him into the room and threw his arms around him. George closed his eyes and breathed in the familiar smell of pipe tobacco as he hugged his father. When he opened them, his mother was coming out of the kitchen, wiping her hands on a towel. When she saw George, her hand flew to her mouth.

'It's all right, Mother, really it is,' George said as he saw her eyes fill with tears. His father let him go and he dropped his kitbag on to the floor and embraced his mother. She squeezed him tightly and he could feel that she was crying. He said, 'I'm back safe, remember. That's all that matters.'

She wiped her eyes on the towel. 'Oh, your poor face! Whatever happened? Why didn't you tell us?' She took his hands and made him sit down by the fire. 'You're so cold! Frederick, build the fire up a bit.'

George's hand went up to his mask, patting it automatically to check that it hadn't been knocked askew. 'It's just my nose and my cheek,' he said. 'I can still see. I'm better off than a lot of the others. Well, my leg caught it as well but it's healing up; it'll be as good as new eventually.' His voice had a pleading note.

'But your dear face! Can I . . .?' She put out her hand as if she would take off the mask and attend to his wounds, as if she could bathe and dress them as she had so many times tended to grazed knees and burnt fingers: the cut on his forearm from a rusty nail from squeezing through a gap in a fence, the broken finger he got when he came off his bike and trapped it between brakes and handlebar. Childhood injuries.

George gave the slightest shake of his head. His mother let her hand fall. She pressed her lips together as if trapping the words she wanted to say. His father put his hand on her shoulder. 'I expect you'd like something to eat, wouldn't you, son?'

George nodded. 'The train stuck at Penrith for ages. I thought I'd be there for the night.'

His mother squeezed his hand and went to make him some supper, her face white. Frederick glanced after her. 'Give her time. It's a bit of a shock, that's all.' He looked gravely at George. 'Tell me what happened.'

George told him a little about the attack on the burnt-out house and that he'd fallen foul of a sniper but mentioned nothing about the deaths he'd seen, the conditions, the awfulness. He told him that he'd been lucky. He tried to smile as he said it. His father opened his mouth to ask more, but then nodded and let it rest.

George ate the soup and bread that his mother brought. She fetched a pair of pyjamas for him and he touched the cotton, softened and floppy with washing. He held it to his face to inhale the clean, fresh air smell. 'Don't bother washing my uniform,' he said. 'We'll have to burn it.'

'The shirt looks all right,' she said.

George shook his head. 'Lice. You always think you've got rid of them but you never have.' He chewed ravenously on the hunk of bread. 'The little buggers hide in the seams. Sorry – soldiers' language.'

'I'll get something for you to wrap them in,' she said hastily.

Despite his hunger, George could barely finish his meal; his eyes kept closing of their own accord. His mother brought some brown paper and string and suggested that he get some rest.

His father carried his kitbag up for him and George followed him wearily upstairs. When his mother brought a hot-water bottle, saying that his bed would need airing, he came out on to the landing, took the warm stoneware bottle from her and hugged her tight. She rested her head against his shoulder and then patted his back saying, 'You know, I think you've grown?'

'Well, that's a miracle on bully beef and biscuits!'

'You're all length though; we'll have to feed you up. Get you well again.'

George kissed the top of her head. 'I'm so sorry,' he said quietly. 'You and Father were right; I shouldn't have gone.'

'I can't tell you how glad I am that you're back . . .' She put her fingers to her mouth as if not trusting herself to speak further, squeezed his hand and left him.

He moved around quietly in the bedroom so as not to wake Ted. When he got into bed, he turned to face the wall and put a pillow behind his back so that he wouldn't turn over in the night and find himself facing his brother. He took off his mask and put it under the corner of his other pillow, his hand upon it as he fell asleep.

George woke with a start when a neighbour's back gate slammed shut. The sharp noise brought him bolt upright, his hand reaching down beside him for his rifle, heart pounding and body prickling with sweat. His fingers clutched a smooth handful of sheets and he let out his breath in gasps as he came to and found himself not at the edge of a dank wood lit by

273

ghostly flares but in his own bedroom with light shining through the thin curtains. He put his head in his hands for a moment while everything rushed back to him and then felt quickly under his pillow; with shaking hands he put on his mask, hooking the spectacle arms behind his ears and fiddling with the catch.

Ted was lying on his back, his arms up behind his head in the abandoned pose of a sleeping baby. George envied him that kind of sleep. He ran his eyes over the books and games on the shelves; they were all still there undisturbed but below them, the wall was covered with newspaper clippings and drawings. George peered over and saw headlines: 'Off To War!', 'Germans Still Falling Back', and maps: pages taken from an atlas and marked with a red line, a ribbon snaking from the Belgian coast around the bulge of the Ypres salient and on across France. Still feeling sick with jangled nerves, George saw it for a moment as one huge trench full of water and foulness and death – red, red, running with it . . . The thoughts kept coming: countless men pouring into the battle line, disappearing into it like grains of sand falling into a crevasse. Lives spent carelessly as loose change on a war that was unwinnable. He put his hands up to his ears and held his head very still.

He tried to remember what life was like before he went away; he used to fit into it, part of a jigsaw with edges that sat tight against each other to make one smooth whole, a complete pattern. Now he would be the piece that didn't fit; he was bent all out of shape. Nothing about him was the same. He would have to act a part.

Ted stirred and then opened his eyes, staring at him unseeing at first as he struggled to consciousness. He gasped and sat up to face him. 'What's that on your face?'

'It's to hide where I got shot.' George was matter-of-fact.

274

'Someone shot you in the face?' Ted said wonderingly. 'Did you kill him?'

'No. I was rather taken up with the pain,' George said dryly.

'Did you kill *any* Germans?'

'It's not like that,' George said shortly. 'Most of the time it's two sides hurling shells at each other and nobody knows what the outcome is. The people firing can't even see exactly where they fall, and the people they fall on don't know they're coming right for them until they're virtually on top of them.'

Ted took a moment to digest this.

George said, 'How did you get on with my rod?'

'Quite well. Two pounds was my biggest. I suppose you'll want it back now.'

George tried to imagine himself fishing. The picture it brought to mind of standing in clear water with sunlight through alders and willow seemed bizarre. 'You keep it,' he said gruffly.

'Does it hurt much?' Ted said in a small voice.

'Aches a bit.'

Their mother called from downstairs. 'Ted! Are you up yet? You'll be late!'

Ted called out, 'Coming!' He slid out of bed and pulled his pyjama top over his head. George looked at his brother's thin chest, his bony ribs. He thought of Rooke in the queue for baths, all the men lining up naked, their hands clasped over their crotches. Their white skin, their fragile flesh.

Ted was pulling on his trousers. 'Aren't you coming?' He looked at George uncertainly.

'Mmm? You go on. I'll see you later.'

Ted finished dressing, grabbed his satchel from the bedpost and racketed off down the stairs. George lifted his bad leg with his hands around his thigh as he moved round to sit on the edge of the bed. The injured leg was thinner than the other, the muscle wasted. He began to massage his calf between his hands and pushed down with his heel to stretch the tendon that felt solid as a pole, having stiffened overnight. He must get himself moving; there was so much he needed to do: he must go and see Kitty and be what help he could, find out at the post office what work they could give him (he must work or he would go mad), he had to get out to Bassenthwaite to visit Violet . . . At the thought of seeing Violet, his stomach turned over. He was afraid. Afraid of bringing such devastating news, of her reaction, of his own inadequacy to deal with it. Mixed in with this was a different kind of fear: he was afraid that she would find him repulsive.

He hobbled over and opened the wardrobe door to look in the mirror inside it. He tried a questioning look, a frown, a smile. From one side of his face all the life and vigour was lost, giving him a strange, lop-sided look. There were no creases when he smiled, just an eerie smoothness. He was a stranger to himself.

He looked at the sparse range of clothes hanging up. There were no uniforms now: the postman's uniform was gone and his soldiering clothes were tied up in brown paper at the bottom of the bed. There was nothing to help tell him who he was. He could hardly go visiting in the rough clothes he kept for fishing and chopping logs. He put on his Sunday best: stiff collar and tie, trousers, waistcoat, wool jacket. Was he to be his Sunday self every day? It made him look conspicuous. He would wear his overcoat and a cap when he went out. His polished brogues felt light after army boots, the leather supple. He used to wear them to go dancing.

He thought of the dusty church hall hung with bunting, the band all pink and sweating, music leading your feet so that

276

you could lead your partner, the girls in their graceful dresses, animated, and smiling. He looked at the dark slim figure that he cut, topped by a china face.

By the time George came down for breakfast, the parlour was empty and the fire burning low. George put on one of the logs that were stacked on the far side of the coal box. He could hear Mother and Lillie in the kitchen. Mother was saying, 'Don't do that, Lillie. You're getting under my feet,' and there was the noise of wheels over tiles and the tinkling sound of the bell on the collar of Lillie's pull-along dog. George remembered that he had some chocolate that he'd bought from the hospital trolley that brought round comforts for the troops. He would fetch it for Lillie as soon as he'd had breakfast.

The table was spread with the detritus of breakfast: plates with kipper bones and congealed bits of egg, crumbs on the cloth and the odd smear of jam. There was toast left over though, and the teapot was still warm. He poured himself a cup, buttered some toast and gazed absently out of the window at the blue-grey stone of the matching row of terraced houses opposite. Mrs Laramie had canaries in a cage on a table by the window, and George let his mind empty by watching the random movement of the scraps of yellow, flitting from perch to perch.

He heard footsteps and half turned in his seat. Lillie was standing just inside the door, looking at him, wide-eyed. She had grown since he last saw her; skinny wrists stuck out from the sleeves of her grey woollen dress. Her hair was squashed flat and matted on one side where she'd slept on it. One stocking had fallen down in a roll above a buttoned boot. There was the sound of the log settling in the grate and George turned quickly to check that it didn't roll out.

Lillie began to scream.

'Lillie!' George half rose to his feet.

Her arms were rigid by her sides, her eyes scrunched up as if to shut out a horror. Mother came running, saying, 'Whatever is it?'

'Lillie! It's me; it's your George!' he said, holding out his hands helplessly.

Mother knelt beside her, saying, 'Lillie! It's only George. It's only George come home again.'

Lillie hid her face in her mother's skirts and sobbed.

Mother glanced at George as she held Lillie close. 'Oh dear. Oh George, I'm so sorry.' She scooped Lillie up, and she clung with both arms tight around her mother's neck and her face turned away.

George slumped back into his seat and put his hand up in front of his face. 'She's frightened to death,' he said.

Mother stroked Lillie's hair, trying to soothe her. 'She'll be fine; don't you worry. She'll soon come round. Look, today's my day at the guesthouse anyway so I'll take her off there. I'm waxing the floors today so she can have a little cloth and follow me around. She'll be right as rain by the time we come back; you'll see.'

'I terrify her,' George said. 'She doesn't even recognise me.'

'No, no, no, she just wasn't expecting to see anyone, that's all. You took her by surprise.' She swayed Lillie from side to side in her arms and shushed her. 'Can you . . .?' She gestured towards the table.

'Yes, yes. You go. I'll tidy up.'

She took Lillie into the kitchen and George sat with his head down, listening to the crying subsiding into hiccuping sobs and then the back door closing behind them.

He felt as though he was shaking inside, a tremble deep

within him that he had to keep down. He started, very slowly, to scrape the breakfast scraps on to one plate and to pile the others up. She finds me hideous, he thought. Why had he imagined that Lillie would just accept him with childish openness, perhaps curiosity? She finds me hideous and she has every right to, he thought. Children's reactions were the honest ones with no overlay of politeness or social grace. He thought of how she used to run to him, yelling to ride on his shoulders, the way she'd fall asleep in the crook of his arm when he read her a story. The trembling inside was like a tuning fork vibrating at an impossible pitch. He carried the crockery through to the kitchen, piece by piece, stacking the china plates into the sink very carefully. One by one, he washed the breakables and laid them down, oh so gently, on the wooden drainer.

Mrs Ashwell opened the side door at the post office to George as he stood in his cap and muffler, hunched into his overcoat. The spectacles almost made her think it was a stranger; poor boy, thank goodness she had paused and had a chance to recognise him by his stance or she might have turned him away as some travelling salesman. She ushered him into the passageway saying, 'Come into the warm. It's awfully chilly today.'

George took off his cap and held it tightly in his hands. 'I'm very sorry about Arthur, Mrs Ashwell.'

Her voice deserted her and she found that all she could do was nod.

'He was very good to me when I started here,' George said, 'and I'll always remember him with affection.'

'Thank you, George,' she managed. 'It's very hard . . .' She waited for the tide of feeling that threatened to overwhelm her to ebb a little. This was how she thought of her grief, as a vast moving sea; sometimes she could skirt along its edge, sometimes she waded laboriously through the day, sometimes the waves ambushed her and swept her away. She lived on the shoreline, watching for the swell.

She led George through to the sorting room where a girl, whom he had never seen before, was thumbing through the mail and shuffling it into the pigeonholes. She glanced, gawped, and then, seeing him notice, returned to her work assiduously.

Mrs Ashwell went on towards the post office. 'I'll get Mr Ashwell. I expect you'd like to talk about your position.'

George heard Mr Ashwell telling someone to mind the counter for him and then he strode quickly into the room. His demeanour was as irritable as ever but he seemed smaller, and older, his skin lined and greyer, his moustache somehow too big for his face: shrunken. He eyed George sharply, taking in the prosthetic and the way that he leant heavily on the sorting table, supporting himself to take the weight off one leg. 'Are you invalided out?' he asked abruptly.

'Yes, sir. I couldn't do a full round; my leg's not up to scratch yet but I could do some deliveries and work up to it.'

Mr Ashwell said dubiously, 'It sounds as though you're not really fit. We don't really have anything suitable.'

'There must be something,' George remonstrated. 'I could take the cart to the station as Arthur did . . .'

Mr Ashwell's face closed over. 'We don't have any openings at present.'

George looked around him at the trough and pigeonholes filled with letters and the mailbags in the corner as yet unopened. 'I could help with the sorting to start with and then build up to taking on a round again.'

Mr Ashwell looked surprised at George's temerity. When his wife nodded as if to say, 'There's the solution,' he glared at her. 'I'm sorry but we don't need anyone. We have Lizzie now.'

The girl, Lizzie, was trying not to look as though she was listening and was sorting very slowly through a handful of envelopes.

'But, sir, I thought you would hold my job open.' George pulled at his stiff collar. 'That's what most employers are doing.'

Mr Ashwell stared. 'You didn't ask my permission to go; you didn't wait to join the Post Office Rifles, or follow correct procedure as Arthur did . . .' He paused, his mouth working. 'Arthur did everything right, and now . . .'

Mrs Ashwell moved towards him as if she would put a hand on his arm.

He glowered at George. 'Well. Now here you are back again. You should be glad you got back in one piece.'

'Geoffrey!' Mrs Ashwell looked shocked and the girl, Lizzie, glanced round at George's face. There was a horrified silence.

Mr Ashwell threw up his hands in a gesture that said 'To hell with all of you' and went back through to the counter, pulling the door smartly shut behind him.

'George, I'm so sorry. He's terribly upset over Arthur; I know it's no excuse . . .' Mrs Ashwell looked close to tears.

George, lost for words, and worrying about how he would manage to pay his way at home, shrugged. 'I was wondering if I could see Kitty.'

'Yes, yes of course. She's not here at present; she's out on deliveries. Let me think, let me think . . .' She tapped her knuckles against her mouth and then rushed on. 'She'll be over by the park by now, somewhere along Greta Street or the Penrith Road, I shouldn't wonder. Yes, I expect you could find her there. She'll be so pleased to see you . . .' she tailed off.

'Thank you.' George put his cap back on. 'I'll see if I can find her.'

Mrs Ashwell followed him into the passageway to see him

out and fumbled with the door catch, the other hand nervously at her throat.

George said, 'If I miss her, could you let her know I'm back?'

Mrs Ashwell nodded and let him out into the street.

As George followed the route of his old delivery round in search of Kitty, each house was familiar. He passed the garden where ancient Mr Cleaves was often pottering and would come down to the gate to take his letters and have a chat. Next there was number thirty-three, where the strange man lived who shouted that he'd set the dog on you if you tried to get in. It was a big bull mastiff that threw itself against the door as you approached and you had to put just one corner of the letters through the letterbox, otherwise the dog would chew them up. Then there was the Copthorne family who lived ten in a house; there was so much coming and going that the door was always left half open and there was always a baby carriage in the hall. George felt regret for the loss of his old job and its familiar routine amongst people who knew him. Yet another link to the past had been cut; yet another way in which he defined himself was gone. He would have to start again, become something else, face strangers.

As he rounded the corner of Station Street, he saw Kitty at the gate of one of the tiny front gardens further down Penrith Road, looking at a sheaf of letters in her hand. She was wearing a navy uniform and carrying a large postbag over her shoulder. He walked down the street towards her. When she glanced up and caught sight of him, she rushed towards him and George opened his arms. She launched herself into them and clung on, the postbag, which had slipped from her shoulder, hanging awkwardly from her elbow.

'It's so marvellous to see you,' Kitty said, her voice muffled in his shoulder.

'Here, let me take that,' George said. He pulled the bag on to his own shoulder. 'Look at you, all smart in your uniform with red trimming and buckles. Brass buttons and everything! However did you persuade your father to let you go out on the rounds?'

'He couldn't really do otherwise. Two of the boys enlisted after you so we were short-staffed and had to take on girls. I even get to drive the cart from time to time.'

'Shall we go to the park?' George said. 'Do these later?'

She took his arm and they crossed the road towards the street of guesthouses that led down Station Road towards the park. He tried to keep in step with her and make his limp less obvious but she noticed straight away and went more slowly. She kept glancing sideways at him until he said, 'It's awful, isn't it?'

'No, it isn't,' she said and squeezed his arm.

They passed through the double wrought-iron gates into the park. There had been days of rain and it had poured again earlier in the morning: puddles had formed in the ruts in the paths and as they walked under the ornamental trees, the branches released a flurry of fat drops every time the breeze caught them.

They found a bench away from the trees, beside the bowling green, and George used his handkerchief to dry two patches as best he could, so that they could sit down. Before them stretched the green, soggy and waterlogged, the pavilion with its eyes shut, boarded up for the season. In the borders next to them, a few crocuses grew from the dark earth, yellow and violet like gas flames.

'How are you feeling?' George asked. 'How is it at home?'

Kitty pulled a face. 'The memorial service was pretty awful. Before we even got there Mother burst into tears because she couldn't find her gloves and Father shouted at her. Nobody told me that I had to walk behind them into chapel so they both glared at me and afterwards no one knew what to do, because there was no graveside to go to, and Mother and Father hadn't arranged for anyone to come back for something to eat so everyone just drifted away. We walked home and Father shut himself away doing paperwork and Mother shut herself in Arthur's room and wouldn't let me in.'

'What did you do, Kit?'

'I just sat in the parlour waiting for Mother and had a bit of a weep.' She turned her head away. 'I keep thinking it would have been better for them if it had been me.'

George took her hand. 'That's not true. Don't say that.'

'I keep having the most awful nightmares. Arthur's always somewhere I can't get to, like a rock in the sea, or a burning building, or a boat floating down to a weir, and there's nothing I can do about it, and then I wake up and I know I'll never see him again . . .' She put her head in her hands and George put his arm around her while she cried.

At length, Kitty felt in her pocket, looking for a handkerchief. 'I'm sorry, loading you with all of this,' she said, sniffing, 'but I can't tell you how glad I am that you're back and I'll have you to talk to every day.'

George braced himself and told her what her father had said about his position at the post office. '. . . so I've lost my place,' he finished.

Kitty was indignant. 'That isn't fair! He's so bitter about Arthur he's just taking it out on you! I'm going to speak to him about it.'

'No, don't bother,' George said. 'It'll only make things more difficult for you. He's not going to change his mind, and anyway, it would be uncomfortable being where I know I'm not wanted. I'll just have to look for something else.'

284

'But when will I see you?' Kitty said mournfully.

'We'll just have to meet after you finish or at weekends,' George said. 'We can go walking as we used to, can't we? And the evenings will soon be getting lighter. I've got to try and build my leg up, so you can encourage me along.' He straightened his leg out and rubbed it. 'Actually, I think perhaps we should walk again before it stiffens up completely.'

She stood and held out her arm to help him up. They set off across the park towards the river. The place looked forlorn: the nets all gone from the tennis courts and the fence beaded with bright drops; the little wooden hut, from which racquets were hired and ices sold, was covered in grey-green algae and had a sign that said 'Closed until April'.

'What kind of job will you look for?' Kitty asked.

'I don't know,' George said. 'I wouldn't want to work in a shop or with a lot of other people. You wouldn't believe how people stare at you, or the comments they make.'

'It's more difficult when it's out of season, otherwise there would be the boats to and from the hotel.'

'It's still customers, though, isn't it?' George sighed. 'Even if I could put up with it, I can't see many employers wanting me to be the person greeting their summer visitors.'

As they approached the river at the edge of the park, the noise of its rush grew louder. It was in spate after the recent rain and at the limit of its banks: a torrent, brown with mud brought down from the hills. The tumult was deafening as they walked on to the bridge, and they stood watching the debris of branches and sticks swept along at great speed in the relentless flow, under their feet and away downstream.

17

BREAKING

When Violet had received Elizabeth's letter telling her that Edmund was missing, she had been unable to accept the possibility of his death. She could not – *would not* entertain it. She had swallowed the cold fear down and had written back to tell her she was sure it was a mistake, that he had probably become separated from his unit and that she was certain he would surface again soon. Nonetheless, she waited at the gatehouse every day for the new post boy and despite being wrapped in coat, scarf, hat and gloves, she shivered as she stood there, carrying the cold inside her.

When days passed and no word came, from either Elizabeth or Edmund, she wrote to the Red Cross, styling herself as his fiancée. Their answer gave a general account of the action on the day of his disappearance, which said that by 8p.m. the enemy had captured the sector and that further enquiries this side of the German line would be useless. They could only help by watching, with close care, the prisoners' lists coming in from Germany. The mention of prisoners had been enough for her to fashion a fragile shelter: he had been captured and was safe out of the fighting, albeit in enemy hands and unable to write, or maybe he had been injured and was recovering unidentified in a German hospital; news would reach her eventually. He could not be dead; she would know if he were; she would feel it in the stones underfoot, in the smell of the rain, in the very air around her.

She evolved a set of rituals to guard herself against the doubts that assailed her: piercing draughts finding their way through her house of sticks, rattling branches and opening chinks if she stopped, even for a moment, weaving and strengthening her shelter. Every afternoon, she walked down to the little church by the lake. She let herself in, her breath misty in the still, gelid air of the tomb-like interior. Above the pulpit, an hourglass was fixed to the wall, an ancient measure for a cleric's sermon. Violet swivelled it over so that the sand began to run; then she knelt and prayed in her own fashion: *Keep him safe. Bring him back to me*, over and over, as she watched the grains run through. She rocked herself as she knelt on the freezing stone floor until her bones ached and the sand ran away.

The strain of carrying on as normal in front of her mother and the servants began to tell and she was forgetful and irritable. When Mother had suggested that she needed a holiday and suggested another trip to visit Elizabeth, Violet had been startled into saying that Elizabeth's brother was missing so it wasn't a good time to go. Mother had said, 'What a shame,' and Violet had been forced to turn away and busy herself in tidying an

arrangement of winter jasmine, feeling that she had betrayed
Edmund by speaking of something that was cleaving her in two
as if it were trouble as distant as an unknown name on the
casualty lists.

Sometimes, alone in her room, she took out a pair of evening
gloves that she kept hidden away and put them on. She had
bought them in Carlisle: a cheap fix when her white ones were
ruined by spilt wine. They were crocheted in a matt ecru thread,
without the lustre of silk, and had lumps in the finger-ends
where the thread was drawn, starbursts replacing the whorls of
her fingertips. At the elbows, they had picot edging: small pale
fans that spread flat against the creamy skin of her arms. She
had worn them at the garden-party dance on the night that
she and Edmund had become engaged. He had held her hand
so tightly when they danced that the crocheted fishnet pattern
had impressed itself on her palm. The thought of how, in the
dimness of the garden, he had gently taken off the gloves so
that they could hold hands, skin to warm skin, made her ache
to touch him once more. She kept the gloves under her mattress,
spread flat with all the wrinkles ironed out. Each night she
imagined their open palms and fingers beneath her as she slept,
cradling her back, supporting her shoulder blades and buoying
her up through the dark wash and slap of her dreams.

As months passed and there was still no word, Violet wrote
regularly to Elizabeth, telling her not to give up hope, using
the expression of this encouragement as a means to stiffen her
own resolve. She wrote again to the Red Cross, only to receive
the same letter, though signed considerately *with sincere
sympathy in your suspense.*

On a wet late afternoon in February, Violet was keeping her
mother company for an hour or so, as usual. She was

conscious of her mother watching her as she read aloud to her.

'You don't look *well*. Are you eating properly?' her mother asked peevishly, drawing her bed jacket around her shoulders.

'Of course I am.' Violet looked up, as if in surprise, from the copy of *Weldon's Ladies' Journal* on her lap. Eating was an issue that caused friction between them. Her mother no longer came down to the dining room at midday, claiming that she disliked the smell of cooking and that the large room was too cold, reasons that Violet knew were specious. She simply wanted to hide away. It was left to Violet to entertain any visitors or to sit in solitary splendour, 'keeping up standards' and ensuring that all was ready if her father should arrive unannounced. On this day, the vicar had visited on Church business and Mrs Burbidge had served a beef stew at lunch, although it was true that Violet had eaten very little. Violet glanced meaningfully at the tray that still stood on the table beside her mother's bed, and which carried the remains of a piece of toast and a boiled egg.

'You know these new tablets do away with my appetite,' her mother said.

Violet looked at her tired face, her hair loose to her shoulders, grey and coarse against the pillows, her lips pale. 'Do you think they're working though? Were the pains any less fierce this time?' she asked. 'Maybe you should mention it to Dr Cooper if he's visiting today?'

Her mother sighed. 'I don't think they made much difference. I feel terribly washed out afterwards. Transparent.' She put both hands up to her face and pushed her hair back from her brow. 'Have you asked Mrs Burbidge to order the new curtain linings? The ones in my sitting room have split at the folds. Ask her to check all the rooms that catch the sun. And ask Hodges to spare one of the men to help the parlour maids to take down the drapes in the drawing room for cleaning in any case, whether they need repair or not. I know they're short-handed, with so many enlisting, but we can't let everything slip.'

Violet added a note to the list she already had: check with Hodges that the farm accounts were near completion; find out from Mrs Burbidge when the sweep was coming to stop the dining-room fire from smoking, and ask her to make a raised pie to see if it would tempt her mother's appetite. Only by reassuring her mother that the house was running like clock-work could she get her into a less fractious state and encourage her towards some small endeavour or interest.

'Shall I dress your hair, if the doctor's coming?'

Her mother got out of bed and placed her pale, veined feet into slippers. She sat at her dressing table, a clutter of objects strewn before her: a glass powder bowl, silver-topped perfume bottles and blue medicine bottles all muddled together, a scatter of hairpins, a shoehorn and an ebony dressing-table set. She watched Violet in the mirror, noticing how she gazed out towards the lake. Was she such a burden to her daughter? She only saw Violet for an hour or two in the late afternoon, and an hour after supper for a round of gin rummy or a chapter of a romantic novel. Surely she could produce a little more conversation. She seemed to be always yearning for the outdoors, wandering down to the church or the lake with her camera, or out on the hills in all weathers.

Violet picked up the soft bristle hairbrush and gathered her mother's hair in her hand to brush the ends first and untangle them, to avoid the tugging that Irene couldn't bear.

'I do feel worried about those linings. I don't want the same inferior stuff again that Mrs Burbidge gets from Green's,' her mother said irritably.

'I'll see to it.' Violet gently brushed her mother's hair from the roots. She coiled it around her hand and began fixing it expertly into place with pins.

Her mother put her hand up to her temple as if it was paining her.

'Do you still have a headache?' Violet loosened the last pin a little.

'You know how I suffer with my head.'

Violet longed to be on her own and not have to keep up her patient cheerfulness. If only the rain would stop, she could get out and walk, maybe climb the fell and take some more pictures. Lately she had been thinking that although she may not be able to travel to all the places she dreamt of, she could still send a few of her photos out into the world, maybe to *Country Life* or *The Field*. Perhaps she could record what she saw in words too, like nature notes, or a column . . .

She had discovered a place on the fell side where you could look down on all the rooks' nests in the wintry trees and she longed to take pictures of the sculptural shapes of the angular stick nests amongst the bare, laced branches. When she was seeking out subjects to photograph, or composing her shot – concentrating on how to frame it, the best angle for the light, the effect of different exposures – she could lose herself and forget everything for a little while in the pleasure of capturing something that she thought beautiful.

George would have liked to see the view of the rookery, she thought. His painterly eye would have appreciated its stark beauty. She wished that he would write and let her know where he was and how he was faring. Assuming that he would have joined the Post Office Rifles, she had written to make enquiries but after an age of waiting had received a reply saying that he was not amongst their ranks and that she should try all the local regiments. She had sent out letters; so far to no avail.

Her mother put her fingertips to both temples and rubbed them in slow circles.

'I'll get Mrs Burbidge to bring you some lavender water before the doctor comes,' Violet said. She smoothed back the hair that she had drawn into a neat bun and held up the ebony mirror behind her mother's head. 'There,' she said.

'Thank you,' her mother said grudgingly. 'Lavender water would be nice.'

Violet rang for the maid to come and take the tray away, and asked her to take a message to Mrs Burbidge; then she helped her mother back to bed and kissed her on the cheek. She closed the door quietly, her face resuming its customary expression of worry, and retired downstairs to the Small Drawing Room and the relief of being alone and without the need for pretence, to wait out the rain.

George, after having caught the Keswick Coach, the afternoon horse-bus, from the town, walked slowly along the drive to the Manor House. It had taken days to steel himself to make the visit and he felt a deep dread of the duty before him. He was afraid of witnessing Violet's grief at his news and knew that it would crush him with guilt. Rain drizzled from a grey sky and dripped from the canopy of ancient Scots pine and larch and the glossy leaves of the rhododendron bushes. A gardener with a barrowload of muck crossed the path in front of him and stared, as if unable to place him in the category of either servant or visitor. As George drew nearer, the man gawped and then wheeled his barrow through a doorway into a walled garden and set it down beside a wide border, half dug over. George had never seen through the door into the garden before and glanced in at the broad lawns. A colonnade ran along one side of the garden, looking out over a bed of roses, towards an ornamental knot garden and a stand of prunus in the foreground, and beyond an orchard and a row of painted beehives. The house was even bigger than he'd thought, with grey slate roofs and many chimneys. The pale stucco walls were finished with red sandstone coigns, the contrast emphasising the building's solidity. Rows of windows looked out blankly, shaded in deep embrasures.

He saw the trade entrance at the side but walked on until he reached the corner of the house with its fine bay windows and followed the sweep of the drive to a large gravel area, more lawns, then the fields and the lake beyond. He braced himself; he was here to visit Violet and must make sure that he wasn't fobbed off and turned away. Stepping underneath a wide porch supported by a row of pillars, he straightened the sleeves of his coat. He pulled the white-porcelain bell-pull and heard a chime echo somewhere inside the house; then, noticing that his shoes were mud-splattered, he bent and rubbed each foot with his handkerchief.

Mrs Burbidge answered the door, looking stern in her black, high-necked dress.

George took off his cap. 'George Farrell, here to see Miss Violet,' he said.

Mrs Burbidge took in the cap, the overcoat that was slightly too small, the brown shoes worn with black trousers. 'Is Miss Violet expecting you?' she asked.

'She's not expecting me but I think she would like to see me as I have news of a friend,' he said carefully.

There was something about George's grave manner that stopped Mrs Burbidge saying, 'Miss Violet is not at home to visitors today,' as she'd planned. He seemed somehow familiar, but it was hard to tell with that eerie-looking mask. Instead, she found herself saying, 'You'd better follow me and wait in the library.'

She led him into the entrance hall, where a bright fire burned in a generous grate and a massive carved crest stood on the mantel. The room was high, with wide cornices and plaster mouldings. A huge display of daffodils and foliage stood on a polished oblong table. She stood waiting beside him, and George was unsure what to do until she held out her hands and he realised that she wanted to take his hat and coat. She hung them on a large oak stand and led him through the hall. George had a glimpse of the access to the servants' quarters as they passed a green baize door that was half open: a whitewashed corridor with a row of bells. Mrs Burbidge hurried past and showed him into the library, telling him to wait.

As he hadn't been invited to sit, George stood looking about him. The room was heavily wallpapered and carpeted, giving the impression of being muffled from the outside world. A desk with a green leather top stood in the centre and two thickly padded red leather chairs stood either side of a wide fireplace where a good fire was lit. Apart from the chimneybreast, which housed a dark oil portrait of some worthy ancestor, the walls were lined with books. George marvelled at the number of them, each one a treasure in its own right, bound in calfskin and tooled with gold. There were so many that they had been divided into categories. Gilt lettering adorned each shelf with words that George thought must be a foreign language: 'Metaphysicks', 'Poesie Parabolical'.

A huge marble bust of a Greek god stood on a high shelf; with a furrowed brow and open mouth, it looked down on him with a sorrowful expression as if wondering what a person such as George could possibly be doing in his sight.

The door opened and George turned as Violet entered. She looked thinner. The leg-o'-mutton sleeves of her dress with their tight-drawn cuffs accentuated the boniness of her protruding wrists. Her hair, caught back in its usual chignon, had lost its shine and dark half-moons beneath her eyes told of restless nights. George found it painful to think that he had been the cause of the worry that had made her ill.

'George?' Violet took a step towards him holding out her hands; then she stopped, her face full of concern. 'Your poor face – what have they done to you?'

In a reflex action, George turned his face to hide his mask.

Violet dropped her hands helplessly. 'Where did you go? Why didn't you write? I found out that you'd joined up but I couldn't get any further. Didn't you join the Post Office Rifles? I wrote but they seemed to have no record of you. I kept thinking you'd be sure to write soon . . .'

George took a deep breath and said, 'Edmund . . .'

Violet's expression changed. She looked at him as though she feared him. She slowly shook her head as if to tell him she wouldn't listen.

'Why don't we sit down?' George took her hands gently and led her to sit in one of the chairs beside the fire. He pulled up the other chair so that he could be closer to her. 'I'm so sorry—' he started.

Violet broke in. 'It's very good of you to come to tell me; I heard from Elizabeth that he was missing but I'm hopeful – we're all hopeful . . . Or maybe . . . Did you meet Edmund? Have you seen him?' She leant forward.

'He was my C.O.'

Violet's hands tightened on the arms of the chair.

George hesitated. 'I'm terribly sorry. I'm afraid he was killed.'

'How can you know that?' Violet whispered. 'He's missing; that's what the Red Cross said.'

George rubbed his forehead. 'I was with him when he died.'

Violet sat very straight and very still; her face a ghostly grey above the lilac dress. 'I see.'

295

Rain blew against the glass in sharp squally bursts and George was aware of the clock on the mantel ticking and the crackle and spit of the fire.

'He was a wonderful officer,' George said. 'He was defending our position against an attack. He died trying to protect . . .' He couldn't bring himself to say 'me'. 'He was protecting his men,' he said instead.

'How? How was he killed?'

George paused, looking for a way to say the unspeakable: Edmund's body deep in soil, his spine broken in two.

Her eyes met his. 'I have to know.'

'It was a shell. A direct hit. He wouldn't have known anything.'

She turned away from him, stared into the fire. All this time, she thought, all this time I was hoping, and he was already gone, even before Elizabeth's letter, maybe even before his last letter reached me. How could that be? Tiny tongues of flame from the white-hot embers licked the edges of new wood and hovered and flickered above it. Consuming. Her clumsy shelter a funeral pyre.

George watched her miserably, not knowing what to do. The moment had passed and he hadn't said what was in his heart: that it was all his fault, that Edmund had saved him; he hadn't given her an opportunity to blame him and be angry. Once more, he knew himself a coward. 'Can I do anything? Can I fetch anyone for you?' he said. 'I'm so sorry; I can't tell you how sorry. I would have come before but I was in hospital and I couldn't do it in a letter; I had to see you.'

Violet heard George talking but she couldn't take in what he was saying. There was a sensation, a physical tightness somewhere between her stomach and her heart; she wanted to double up with the pain of it. 'George,' she said, folding her arms in front of her, holding it in, 'could you leave me? I'd like to be alone.'

George stood but remained uncertainly before her. 'I'm truly sorry. I'll call again, shall I?' When she made no response, he said, 'I'll come again.' She sat so stiffly that he dared not even put out his hand to touch her. He went to the door, looked back at her bent head and the tense hunch of her shoulders and then went out, pulling the door softly closed behind him. Silence. He stood with the doorknob still in his hand. A sound came from the room, a long, low moan that built to a heart-breaking wail.

In the corridor, the green baize door flew open and Mrs Burbidge came out, her face red and anxious.

'I'm sorry to have brought bad news,' George stammered. 'She wouldn't let me help.'

'See yourself out,' Mrs Burbidge said, hurrying past him. The sound of Violet's sobbing filled his ears. Mrs Burbidge shut the door firmly in his face.

When George arrived home, the house was empty. He dragged himself upstairs, his bad leg as stiff as a poker after too much walking. He levered his shoes off without undoing the laces and lay on the bed.

His kitbag hung on the footboard, a corner of Edmund's tin making an angular poke in the fabric. That morning, he had decided not to take the tin to Violet. He had wanted to break the news to her gently and feared that the finality of being handed Edmund's possessions would be too big a shock. Now he thought bitterly that he had failed entirely: he hadn't known what to say, the effect of his clumsy words had been brutal and he had been unable to give any comfort.

There was nothing he could do to make this right. He felt ashamed that he hadn't told Violet that Edmund had saved his life. 'Honesty is the best policy' was the creed on which he'd been raised and it troubled him to deceive her. But confessing would make no difference, he told himself. It couldn't bring Edmund back. Carrying the burden of knowledge himself would be part of his punishment.

He shivered and rolled himself up in the quilt as the lantern show of memories began to turn again, a sequence of horrors at the back of his mind, always ready to begin the moment he let his guard down. With an effort of will, he forced himself to look forward rather than back. He would visit and offer his company and a listening ear: a chance for Violet to talk about her lost sweetheart to someone who had known him, even if his knowledge of the circumstances of Edmund's death would mean that her grief heaped coals upon his head. In a few days, he would visit again and hope that Mrs Burbidge wouldn't refuse to let him in.

George closed his eyes and thought of the way that Violet had said his name when she first entered the room, before he'd said the words that had taken away all her hope. For a moment she had been pleased to see him, as she used to be when they walked together and she was glad of his company. Now those innocent days were gone and he would have to accept that it could never be like that again. All he could do now was to be a loyal friend and try to look after Violet as well as he could. He looked the truth hard in the face: it was all his fault that she had lost the man she loved and nothing he could do would ever be enough.

George woke hours later to the sound of his mother building up the fire in the parlour: the crunch of logs pushed together and the rattle of slack tipped from the coal scuttle. He should have banked it up before he came upstairs, he thought; he could at least have done that.

He went down and found his mother on her knees sweeping

the hearth. She let him take the pan and brush from her and stood up, dusting herself down. George asked where Lillie was; he had been trying to keep out of her way as much as he could, only coming down in the evenings after she had gone to bed.

'I had to carry her from the guesthouse; she was dead on her feet, poor lamb. She's fast asleep beside the range, all balled up in my coat.' She looked at George's rumpled clothes. 'It looks as though you've had a nap too. It would've been a good idea to take that jacket off,' she said mildly. She went over to her shopping basket, which she'd left on a chair by the table and took out a newspaper. 'Here you are. You said you wanted to get another position as soon as you could so I got you today's *Reminder*.'

George tipped the gritty coal dust into the fire, where it hissed and crackled. He thanked his mother and then found his father's fountain pen in the drawer, sat at the table and opened the paper. He scanned over the stories of local men who had gone to war: news of a field card received by a father telling him that his son was a P.O.W., of a family who had five sons in service, of a soldier who had received a Military Medal for good work done in the advance on Polygon Wood – men who had served, or were serving, honourably in the field – not uselessly stuck at home. With a bitter feeling he turned to the page headed 'Situations Vacant'. He looked down the list of advertisements: 'Barman', 'Draper's Assistant', 'Tobacconist', 'Waiter', 'Street Sweeper'; the list ran on. Many of the jobs he discounted as requiring the employee to be constantly on their feet or to be dealing with customers. His leg wasn't ready for the first trial and his courage wasn't ready for the second. He circled 'Railway Apprentice' and a position as a travelling salesman for the pencil factory in the town. The advertisement for the railway apprentice went on to say that it was track work. Walking miles, he supposed, and he had no experience of sales, which would probably involve pounding the pavements too. He put a question mark by both.

Lillie appeared at the kitchen door with her thumb in her mouth. George pretended not to have seen her, thinking that if he turned round she would probably cry. He bent his head over the paper. Mother picked her up and he heard Lillie say indistinctly, 'Make the man go 'way,' and Mother saying, 'Don't be silly. You come by the fire with me and keep warm.'

She sat down with Lillie on her lap, who pulled up her feet as if to make herself into the smallest possible ball and turned her head in towards Mother's bosom.

George looked over and said, 'Shall I take this upstairs?' but Mother put her finger to her lips as if to say, 'Let's see what happens next.'

He ran his finger down the columns again: 'Lady's Maid', 'Navvy', 'Porter' ... He put a circle around 'Projectionist's Assistant'. He wondered what that would involve. He didn't like the thought of being indoors all the time but the idea of privacy, away from the public gaze, was appealing and the Alhambra Cinema was just a few streets away. Without thinking, he began to doodle in the margins of the paper: a tree with bare branches, a series of little fluttering birds based on Mrs Laramie's canaries, over the way. Ever since Edmund's death he hadn't painted or even picked up a pencil to sketch; he'd had no desire to record anything in the world he'd inhabited, where everything had turned to ugliness and death. Becoming engrossed, he drew a bird pecking at the ground and added dots as crumbs around its feet. Glancing up he saw that Lillie was watching him and he looked quickly down again. He wondered whether to hold up the paper to show her his drawings but didn't dare. Better just to rejoice in the fact that they were in the same room and she was tolerating his presence. He would leave the paper on the hearthrug when Mother took her into the kitchen for her tea, and maybe Lillie would see it when she played by the fire later. Drawing a scruffy-looking dog with one ear turned inside out, he became so involved that he jumped when Mother tried to lift Lillie down and Lillie let out a cry and clung to her.

'All right, all right,' Mother said, scooping her up on to her hip and rolling her eyes at George. 'It's only your brother, Lillie. He's as soft as a brush.'

George went back to his sketching and drew a jack-in-the-box on a long curly spring. He added a picture of a mouse peeping out of a hole in a big wedge of cheese and then placed the paper on the rug, next to Lillie's doll.

18

THE ALHAMBRA

George came out of the office at the pencil factory and closed the glass-paned door behind him, sensing the buzz of conversation starting up among the office girls. It had taken only moments for the officious assistant manager to turn him down. They were looking for someone who would be happy with train travel and overnight stays, he'd said. George had been agreeable to both. They were looking for someone used to dealing with customers. George had said that he'd done his stint on the counter at the post office. The man had stared at him in an obvious fashion and said that they were looking for someone 'presentable'. George had no answer to that which he could articulate in a lady's hearing, so he had said good day.

He walked back through the town with his cap pulled well

down over his ears. Passing the post office, he wondered if Kitty was inside sorting or out on a round. He considered going in to find out but quailed at the thought of Mr Ashwell's expression, which would surely say that he was making a nuisance of himself. He would just have to wait until Sunday when they had arranged to go for a walk together, when Kitty was free after church. No backsliding, he said to himself, go and see if the cinema job is still going; at least have a try. Get it over with, more like, he answered himself.

In the market place, posters were pasted on the walls of the buildings urging 'Britons, Join Your Country's Army!' and 'Remember Belgium!' Notices beneath them gave details of halls and schools pressed into service as recruitment offices. Everywhere he looked there was evidence of the war: some shop windows were decked with flags, others proclaimed proudly 'Suppliers to the Army'. George paused before a poster on the side of the Moot Hall that depicted a man and woman dressed in homespun working clothes, the woman holding up a rifle and gesturing behind her at a horizon where buildings were burning. The caption read: 'Will You Go or Must I?' He turned from it, feeling unmanned, and slipped away down an alley.

A group of boys were hanging around at the back of the baker's shop; three had climbed up on the high wall and were sitting with their legs dangling, sharing out a grubby looking half-loaf. Two others were lounging against the wall, passing around the nub end of a cigarette. As George went by, they fell silent, and he could feel their eyes on his back as he made his way past the back entrances and dustbins of the shops and pubs. There was a sudden burst of laughter and he turned to see that one of the older lads was following him, staggering along in an exaggerated version of his limping walk. The boy stopped as he met George's eye, freezing as if it were a game of statues, adopting a position with one leg dragging stiffly behind him and screwing his face up into a grimace. George turned away. They're only lads with nothing better to do; ignore them, he said to himself, but as he rounded the corner out of the alley there was a further shout of laughter as another boy joined in the mimicry. 'Hey, Peg leg!' he shouted out to George as he walked on.

The Alhambra was opposite the gospel hall; the name was carved in stone above its glossy red-painted glass doors, its frontage seen as brazen showiness by most of the congregation, who favoured sobriety and decorum in architecture, as in all things. To George, even the name was exotic and mysterious: conjuring palaces and Moorish kings, dark-skinned sheikhs and dancing girls. When he had held his position at the post office, he had occasionally been able to treat Ted to a Saturday matinée, where they had hooted with laughter at the antics of the *Keystone Kops*. Once he had come with Kitty to see *Arizona* and they had thrilled to the fighting of cowboys and Indians, Stetsons and feathers raised perilously over rocky cover as the two sides slugged it out.

George went in and approached the box office, where Millicent, a bleached blonde whom his mother considered to be 'forward', was polishing the cash register while sucking a boiled sweet. She looked at him with open curiosity as he introduced himself and explained why he had come.

'Aren't you the chap who used to deliver our post?' She winked at him. 'I never forget a young man.' She slipped from her stool and went to fetch Mr Mounsey, who was both owner and manager.

Mr Mounsey was a small, dapper man in his fifties who affected a theatrical look by sporting a coloured bow tie, a different shade for each day of the week, and a matching silk handkerchief, which he folded and tucked into his top pocket in such a way that two immaculate corners peeped out.

'You've come about the job, I gather,' he said to George. 'We've had a few enquiries. Have you any experience in this line of work?'

'I'm afraid not, sir, but I'm very willing to learn,' George said. 'I'm reliable and a hard worker.'

Mr Mounsey looked him up and down. 'Good shoulders. You need strength and stamina for hand cranking. You've been in the forces, I presume?'

George nodded and held himself more upright.

Mr Mounsey scrutinised his face. 'Pardon me for asking but is your sight good?'

'Yes, thank you, sir. I was very lucky not to lose my eye; it's totally unaffected.'

'Hmm. Very good, very good.'

Millicent passed them and opened the doors to the auditorium, releasing the sound of the closing bars of a piano piece and a rising hum of conversation as the matinée audience began to spill out into the foyer. People from the balcony seats began to trickle down the stairs and the two streams slowed as they queued for the exit and filed past, their stares making George feel conspicuous.

Mr Mounsey put his hand on his arm. 'Let's get out of this crowd,' he said and led George through a door marked 'No entry. Staff only'. They climbed a narrow, steep stair lit by a tiny window on the side of the building.

'We'll go and see what Thorny has to say about you. That's the projectionist, Mr Thornthwaite to you,' Mr Mounsey said. 'I'm an old soldier myself. Served in the African war, y'know.'

He glanced back at George. 'Bad business, this war, a very bad business.'

George said, 'Thank you, sir. It's much appreciated.'

Mr Mounsey tapped on the door at the top of the stairs and went straight in, so George followed behind him. The room was dim with thick walls, painted a very dark grey. Two large, box-like machines with wind-up handles stood on tripods looking unstable and top-heavy, like travelling trunks laid on edge on a camera stand. They were set up at apertures to project the film and cables snaked from them and tangled on the floor. Metal boxes stood under a workbench on the other side of the room, which was cluttered with disc-shaped metal tins, a lamp, scissors and a magnifying glass. At one of the projectors, an oldish man in shirtsleeves and waistcoat, with close-cut white hair and spectacles that sat on the end of his nose, was laboriously turning a handle to rewind the film on to a reel.

George found the room rather close and oppressive. He wished there was a window. A square hatch between the projectors had a sliding shutter that was closed but George thought that it must open for the projectionist to see the screen, and that looking through it would help you not to feel so shut in.

'I have someone to meet you, Gilbert,' Mr Mounsey said. 'This is George Farrell, ex-army, interested in cinematography.'

Mr Thornthwaite stopped winding and stretched with his hands against the hollow of his back.

'Arthritis bad today?' Mr Mounsey said. He turned to George, 'Thorny's getting a bit long in the tooth for cranking the machines; he needs an apprentice to provide a bit of elbow grease. Suit someone not afraid of hard work.'

George stepped forward to shake hands and saw that Thorny's sharp eyes had spotted his limp. His heart sank.

Thorny grinned at him. 'Don't worry, lad. It's the halt and

the lame here. Long as you've got a strong back and a good pair of arms . . . here, have a go.' He gestured to the other projector. 'It's all laced up for the next showing. Go on, give it a try.' He turned on the lamp, saying, 'The most important thing is to keep up a good steady speed. Prints are nitrate based, you see, so if the film runs too slow the heat of the lamp can make 'em catch fire.'

George rubbed his palms together, took hold of the cranking handle and began to turn. It was much lighter than he'd assumed; it flew out of his hands and spun round with a clicking noise. Thorny caught hold of it and kept it turning. 'Have another go – it's not the weight of it you need your strength for, it's the length of time you have to keep it going.'

George started again.

Thorny said, 'That's it. Just a little bit faster.' He put his hands over George's and showed him the speed. 'Now, can you keep that up steadily? It needs to be the same speed the film was shot at, see? Sixteen frames a second.'

'Or twenty on Saturdays when you've got two showings to get through,' Mr Mounsey said and both men laughed.

Thorny said, 'What am I thinking of? You'll want to see the fruits of your labours.' He leant past George's shoulder and lifted the shutter on the hatch beside him. George looked down the wide shaft of light, alive with dust, over the shadowy depths of the auditorium and rows of empty seats. Magically, on the screen, jerky figures moved: on a wide balcony, a man in a tuxedo dancing with a woman, her dark mouth moving in speech, her long scarf fluttering in the breeze. Fascinated, he cranked faster and their movements became a little more natural and fluid. He turned back to the others, his face registering his delight.

'Looks as though I've got myself an assistant,' Thorny said.

307

'Be here at eleven o'clock sharp tomorrow and I'll teach you how to change over at the end of a reel.'

On Sunday afternoon, George and Kitty, bundled up in overcoats, hats and mufflers, set out to take advantage of the bright, clear February day. They walked the field path at the head of the lake listening for the chaffinch trying out the first notes of his song and watching the first sailing boats of the season tack across the water between the islands.

It had been so long since they'd had an outing together that at first there was shyness between them; at times they both fell silent and then both started to speak at once. When they met couples, arm in arm on the narrow path, and had to draw close to let them through, their movements were self-conscious: stepping apart again as soon as they had passed, Kitty turning a little pink.

Once they had left other walkers behind, gradually the conversation gathered momentum. Neither of them spoke of the war. When George's thoughts turned to the guilt he felt to be walking somewhere peaceful and beautiful when Haycock and Turland were still 'out there', he didn't speak them out loud. When Kitty remembered the newspaper she had read the day before, full of the rebuilding work going on in Scarborough and Whitby following the bombing of previous months, she talked instead of harmless church gossip or asked him to tell her the stories of the films they had been showing at the Alhambra. They were tender with each other's feelings, each instinctively mindful that the other needed a place of safety, however temporary, away from all the awfulness.

George cut himself a thumb stick from a hazel bush and managed to walk as far as the second landing stage. Kitty said that they should keep on the flat but walk a little further each time, but he found it frustrating to be walking at the foot of Cat Bells, its green slopes beckoning, and not to be able to climb the winding sheep path as they used to do. He wanted the sense of openness, the uplift of the view from high above the lake. Kitty, growing more comfortable and finding her old tone, told him that he must be patient and build up to it. When he could walk the distance between the boat-hire shed and the third landing stage at the foot of the fell, then they would try the easiest path on the lower slopes. 'Just a little way, mind, at first,' she said. George observed that she would make a good nurse – that she was certainly bossy enough, and she replied that if all patients were as cussed as he was, they would deserve all the bossing they got.

When George tired, they left the path and scrambled down the stony shore to sit side by side on a weathered grey stump. Weak sunshine lit glinting patterns on the cold lake and picked out the bright green lichened trunks of the island trees and the tinge of colour from buds and catkins. Every part of the scene was overlaid with memory for George. He drew them to him, the ghosts of their former selves: children building dens on the islands, wigwam shelters of wood and bracken against the rain; Kitty in petticoats and he with his trousers rolled up, sitting, legs dangling, on the landing stage throwing crusts to the ducks; later, Kitty demure in longer skirts and he with rod and reel, taking an oar each and almost losing them as the pleasure boat caught them in its wash. For a moment he held the pictures clear, and recognised who he used to be; then they slid away, dissolving into gleams on the water.

Kitty said, 'Do you remember the first time we climbed Cat Bells? And we decided to carry on to Maiden Moor?'

George smiled, remembering the long hot climb, the way that they had grumbled at each other about blisters and feeling thirsty, and the satisfaction of finally reaching the top with the world spread out before them. 'Whose idea was it anyway?'

'Yours, I think. You wanted to reach the cairn. Our stones must still be there. Do you remember? We scratched our names on them and put them on the top in such a ceremonial way!'

George nodded. 'They must be far down the pile by now; the cairn looks twice the size it was.'

Kitty said, with a catch in her voice, 'When I told Arthur what we'd done, he went up with Fred Anstey to do the same. So his must be in there somewhere too.' She stared out over the lake.

George laid his hand gently on her back. 'In a way that's a good thought, isn't it, Kit? That Arthur left his mark and that it's there still?'

She blinked hard. 'Yes,' she said, 'you're right.'

'One day we'll go up there, if you'd like. We could put another stone on or pick some flowers and lay them there . . . I'll keep working on my leg, I promise, and even if I'm slow, as soon as we could make it up and back in a day, we'll do it. How would that be?'

She made a wobbly attempt at a smile. 'I'd like that. Thank you.'

George felt a warmth steal through him. He'd almost forgotten what it was like to be able to help, to be needed. It made him feel proud to be relied upon. Worthwhile. Gazing out at the boulders strewn in the shallows and the breeze-combed ripples on the water, he thought of all the times that they had done this walk before and how glad he was, despite everything, to be here again: to be feeling the wind on his face, to be with Kitty, to be alive.

He picked out a flat stone from the pebbles at his feet, went a little way towards the water's edge and, with a deft flick of his wrist, skimmed it over the water. It hopped once, twice, three times and hit one of the boulders with a clip.

'Bravo!' Kitty said, coming to join him. 'I've never really mastered that.' She picked up a stone and threw it low over the water to splash once and disappear. They both laughed. 'As you can see, mastery is a long way off.'

'Here.' George picked out a good stone and gave it to her. 'You have to hold it really flat, see, and flick it – like this.' He stood behind her, took her hand from beneath and moved it in an arcing motion. Instead of stepping forward to make her throw, Kitty stood still letting her hand rest in his. George felt acutely aware of their physical closeness, their bodies touching, his arm supporting hers, the flat stone between their palms, warmed by her hand. He had the strangest desire to put his other arm around her, to encompass and hold her and simply lay his head against hers. As if she sensed his mood, for just a moment, Kitty let her head rest back against him and her shoulders drop. Then she twisted round and looked up at him. 'I'm so glad you're back, I can't tell you how much I missed you,' she said, putting her hand on his arm and giving it a squeeze.

She stepped away and went forward to the edge of the water, swung her arm back and released the stone. It dipped and jumped over the water, clipping drops from the surface that shone as they flew.

'Encore!' George called out. 'Encore!'

She looked back at him triumphantly with a wide smile: the expression he had known since she was eight years old; yet here was Kitty, a grown woman, with a different kind of challenge in her eyes, a flash of awareness of the effect her smile could have. It touched George in a way he couldn't explain and sent him looking for more stones, just to see that look again.

*

311

There was no matinée at the cinema on a Tuesday so George took the horse-bus to see Violet again, vowing that this time he would do better, would try to bring her some comfort, at least give her the chance to unburden herself. He must carry whatever weight he could. He stood under the porch with its grand pillars, steeling himself to take hold of the bell-pull and shatter the peace of the place, where the only sounds were those of birds calling from the woods. He rang and Mrs Burbidge answered the door once again. She stopped straightening her apron as soon as she saw him, and said, 'You! Back again!'

'I was wondering if I might see Miss Violet,' he said.

'Miss Violet is not at home. Good day to you,' she said firmly and shut the door.

George didn't believe her. As he turned and walked back past the front of the house, he saw the flash of her white apron as she stepped back from the dining-room window.

He walked a little way into the wood so that he was hidden from view, picking a spot where he could see the door, in the hope that Violet would take her customary walk. The horse-bus wouldn't return for some time so he could afford to wait and watch. He sat down at the foot of one of the big Scots pines, where the massive roots spread above the earth in complicated inter-lacings of polished wood.

After half an hour of shifting position between sitting and standing, in order to ease the stiffness of his leg, the front door opened and Violet came out wearing a shapeless brown overcoat that was too big for her and a pair of muddy button boots. She cut across the gravel sweep in front of the house, as if she intended to avoid the path and walk directly down across the fields towards the lake. If he followed her, he would be in full view of the house so he stepped quickly forward and called her name.

She turned slowly, as if she couldn't believe her ears, her body tight with tension. Her shoulders dropped as she recognised him and she hurried over. A strand of her dark hair trailed loose at the side of her face, emphasising her pallor.

'Are you all right?' George asked. 'I didn't mean to scare you.'

'It was just . . . well, a man's voice calling my name. I thought it was another one of my imaginings. Never mind.'

They fell into step together and took the path that led through the trees, away from the lake. Violet kept her eyes on the puddles and grit of the track. George glanced at her anxiously: her face had lost its softness; the curve of her cheekbones was more angular, her chin more pointed.

As if wrenching herself from her thoughts, Violet said, 'So, tell me about your war. How did you get injured?'

An image of the shell hole flashed upon his memory: the flares rising, the desolation, his certainty that he would die there. He could almost feel the paper of her letter between his fingers. 'A sniper,' he said. His hand went to the mask in an instinctive movement to check that it was in place.

Violet looked directly at him. 'Well, we're two poor broken things, aren't we, George. How are you finding settling back into civilian life?'

George thought of his avoidance of public places, of the tremors that came with the slightest shock and the way that there was no escape from dreams. He said carefully, 'Oh, it's not so bad.' He recounted how he had met a reverse in being refused his old job at the post office, and how no one wanted him anywhere near their customers, but that he had eventually found a place at the cinema. He told her about the work, finishing by saying, 'I find it difficult being so much indoors but at least I don't have to see people.'

'The family must be glad to have you home,' Violet said gently.

'Oh yes. Kitty too . . .'

Violet looked at him curiously. 'You've never mentioned Kitty before.'

George found himself unaccountably embarrassed. 'She's an old school friend,' he said; then, feeling that this was too small an expression to describe his relationship with Kitty and that he had somehow been disloyal, he added, 'My oldest friend, actually.'

'Ah,' Violet said.

From up in the evergreen woods on the slope of the fell, the sound of an axe rang out, its sharp report making George flinch. Violet looked at him in concern.

'Sorry,' he said. 'Not too good with loud noises.' In his pockets, he made his hands into fists to stop them trembling. The sound of the blade chopping a V into the trunk of a larch echoed, ricocheting among the other trees. Its top shivered with each blow.

'They've stepped up the felling,' Violet said.

'That's a shame.' George noticed for the first time that there were indeed gaps in the dense cover of fir and larch.

A pause in the axe-fall was followed by voices shouting, and a creaking, straining sound. The conical crown of the tree shifted to the side as it began to lean; then, with a splitting, splintering rush, it tumbled, branches bouncing and catching on its neighbours, on its way to the ground.

'They're taking them for pit props,' Violet said, and George felt the reach of the war fall even here, its grasping hand gathering and spending.

They walked on under arches of branches where, in places, a mist of green seemed to hang: the faintest haze of first buds. The sky beyond was blue with small clouds forming and shredding in an easterly breeze. Clumps of daffodils and narcissi

314

were scattered along the margin of the wood and George pointed out that the first green shoots of bluebell leaves were beginning to show in its interior.

'Does it seem strange to you that everything goes on as normal, as though nothing has happened?' Violet said suddenly. 'I feel as though it should have all cracked apart, yet here we are: another spring, all this growth. It seems so . . .'

'Indifferent?'

'Heartless.'

They reached the road and crossed over to join the path that meandered through the woods where the foresters were at work.

'Did you see very much of Edmund?' Violet asked.

George felt his heart beating faster. 'B company was his, so he was responsible for us: inspections, orders, discipline, making sure we had supplies and knew what we were doing, that sort of thing.'

'But you never saw him on his own?'

George cast about for an answer. 'Well, I did, actually. Rooke and I got into a spot of bother because we got lost and were missing overnight. Edmund . . . Lieutenant Lyne saved my bacon with the captain, who was a rather "hang 'em and flog 'em" type.'

'He got you out of a scrape?'

'Yes.'

'How very like him,' Violet said. 'What happened to Rooke? Did he save his bacon too?'

They're all dead, George thought. Edmund, Percy, Hunton – all gone. Whatever kind of man each had been, they were all now part of the Ypres mud over which armies still uselessly fought. 'Rooke was lucky on that occasion,' George said. 'But his luck didn't last.'

'Oh! Oh, I see. I'm sorry.' Violet paused. 'It sounds as though

Edmund looked out for you though. Did he know that you knew me?'

'No, I didn't tell him; I didn't like to presume.'

'Well, I'm glad he took you under his wing.'

George winced. Soil. Sandbags. White bone in a red wound.

Violet was looking at him strangely. 'You were fond of him, weren't you?' she said.

'I . . . well, I certainly admired him.'

The sound of sawing began as the loggers started the work of taking off the branches. The seesaw noise grated on George, making his flesh crawl. The living wood, parted from its roots by sharp metal, would be hauled to the sawmill, stripped of its bark and then run on to a huge circular saw to split it into lengths. An industrial process, he thought. Each one the same. Uniform. Pit props. Canon fodder. Suddenly he felt angry with everyone who didn't know what it was like out there in the line, even with Violet. 'He had a photograph of you,' he said. 'He kept it by his bed in the farmhouse where he was billeted. It got bombed after.'

Violet was looking at him; her eyes filled with tears. His anger dissipated as quickly as it had come and he felt ashamed of himself and disturbed by the way he had reacted to the strain. 'Let's turn back,' he said abruptly. 'I can't bear that noise.' He led the way back along the narrow path to the road, with Violet following silently behind. He glanced at his watch; the horse-bus was due in five minutes and he quickened his step until he reached the road.

He didn't want to leave on this strange note, his feelings all confused and jangled. 'I'm sorry. I don't know what's the matter with me; I haven't been any use to you at all.'

'It's the war,' Violet said. 'We're all coping with things we have no experience of. And you are a help, George, please

316

believe me. I sometimes feel I shall go mad if I have any more of my own company.'

'Look, my bus is due; I'm sorry I can't walk back with you all the way,' he said. 'Will you be all right? I could come again next Tuesday if you feel it would be any help.'

Violet nodded. 'There isn't anyone else I can talk to about Edmund. No one else knows, you see. Thank you for coming.' She held out her hand in farewell. George took it and gently placed his other hand on top of it. She clasped tight and then broke away, walking quickly across the road without looking back.

19

CAT BELLS

All through March and April, under Thorny's tutelage, George learnt his trade until he could time a showing almost to the second, and cranking at the right speed became second nature. Sometimes he would fall into a reverie about Violet, planning his weekly visit and thinking up new ways to distract her. One week he had taken her to see a squirrel's dray he'd noticed in one of the Scots pines and they had watched two males chasing each other, chattering, through the branches. He had tried to persuade her to take up her photography again but she arrived every time without her camera, her hands thrust deep into the pockets of the old brown overcoat as if she were determined not to touch anything, as if the outside world was not to be trusted.

George did his best to respond when she asked about Edmund but there was so much that he had to avoid. He told and retold what he knew: his easy manner with the men, his directness in dealing with his fellow officers, his loyalty to his company. He avoided all mention of Edmund's record in the field for fear that it might lead back to the way he died. When Violet alluded to his death he felt wary, his expression tightening and becoming closed, his whole face becoming fixed like the mask.

On his last visit, he had taken her a gift, a gilt brooch set with green and red brilliants; they were only paste but they sparkled like emeralds and rubies. The surprise had roused her from her introspection. She accepted it and said that he was very kind but when she held it against the dark fabric of her coat, it had looked all wrong. Her hand had fallen away from her lapel and, as they walked on, she had slipped the brooch into her pocket.

Nothing seemed to work; he watched her becoming more subdued and defeated as the weeks went on and the full meaning of 'never again' sunk in. Time was meant to heal but Violet said she felt there was too much time, aeons of it, to be endured. She said that there was nothing George could do; there was nothing anyone could do. Edmund wasn't coming back.

After this, George came to dread the repetitive labour of cranking the film; it was sufficiently automatic to allow the mind to wander and his thoughts went round and round with the cranking handle, endless and unresolved. He found the darkness and the close air of the booth oppressive too. Whenever possible he tried to keep busy with other tasks: filling in the shipping forms or poring over the newly delivered reels, with a lamp and a magnifying glass, to check the film for dirt and the sprockets for tears. In the breaks between jobs he had to distract himself by talking to Thorny or watching the film on the screen, anything to take him beyond the cycle of his thoughts and the familiar panic, the sensation of being inside a box.

Entombed in the projectionist's booth all week, he came to look forward with fervour to walking at the weekend. Despite the pain of pushing himself to overwork his bad leg in order to strengthen the muscle, and the day of stiffness afterwards, he longed for fresh air and open space. Kitty had been encouraging him to walk further each time they met and he had managed first the fields at the head of the lake, picking his way around the boggy places, and then added the path through a scrubby copse that led on to the second landing stage. Finally, he had won through to the beech woods and the joy of colour: spring green, slopes of orange, sandy soil leading down to grey pebbly beaches and the third landing stage. When he was outdoors, among lakes and mountains, he felt like a fish wriggling through an angler's hands to return to the water.

On a warm Sunday in April, Kitty and George had decided to try out the lowest slopes of Cat Bells. They caught the boat across the lake and walked back from the landing stage at the foot of the fell, skirting the steepest slope, which had been chosen by two climbers with rucksacks and walking poles, to approach instead by a less vertiginous route. They reached the softer slopes of close-cropped grass and scree, where the path wound back and forth to provide a shallower ascent and took detours around outcrops of bare rock. Beyond the bulk of the fell lay the higher incline of Maiden Moor where they used to explore together, as youngsters, in summer holidays that had seemed to last forever.

Kitty pointed to a place where the path disappeared behind a grassy outcrop. 'Do you remember where we had a picnic once, on the way back, near some boulders? Shall we aim for that and have a good rest before we come down again?'

George agreed and they set off with Kitty leading the way at a sedate pace. In places, small loose stones were strewn on the path; they moved underfoot and George found that his leg tired quickly. They stopped at the first bend, where the track looped back on itself for a new ascent, and looked back over the ground they'd travelled and the fields and woods of the valley beyond.

'Look how small the sheep are already,' Kitty said. Below them, sheep strayed and gathered in random knots, the ewes wandering slowly and the lambs making haphazard dashes away, only to run back moments later and butt at their mothers to make them let down their milk.

'I wish I had their energy,' George said, moving his weight on to his good leg.

'Don't worry; I'll have you leaping up here sprightly as a mountain goat in no time. Come on, look lively.' Kitty settled her straw hat more firmly on her head and they set off again; this time George went in front so that he could reach out a hand to steady her over the patches of loose shale: her boots with their little square heels weren't ideal for such terrain. As they went, they talked in a desultory way about the past week. Kitty had been upset by having to deliver telegrams to several households who had lost someone in action. She told him how the relative receiving the message would often refuse to believe it. In their shock, some would refuse to touch it and ask her to read it to them; others even claimed that they recognised the handwriting of their loved one on the telegram, even when Kitty knew that she had taken down the message herself. George, thinking that it must hit very close to home for Kitty to take such messages, said that she should get one of the post boys to do them instead. He told her that Thorny had shown him how to operate the stage curtains and the lights, and how it felt strangely powerful to hear the hush fall on the auditorium, as if you turned on the dark and it fell like snow, muffling everything to a whisper.

Mr Mounsey had been pleased to see this and had clapped him on the back, saying that he should learn as much as he could about the workings of the cinema. He had asked if he had any knowledge of accounts, and George had wondered whether his apprenticeship might be expanded and felt a rush of hope at the prospect of advancement. Kitty paused when he told her what Mr Mounsey had said, and looked up to him, her face lit up with pleasure.

'You see! Fortune favours the brave. I knew good things would come of this.'

George was surprised by a rush of pride, a warm feeling he had almost forgotten, kindled to life by Kitty's good opinion.

As they reached the last turn of the path before the outcrop, the gradient became steeper and he had no breath left for talking. His calf muscles were burning and he began to sweat with effort. He wiped his brow with his sleeve but could do nothing about the irritating dampness that had formed under his mask. He glanced back at Kitty. She had pushed her hat on to the back of her head and her face was red. She waved him on. 'Nearly there,' she said. 'We can't give up now.'

George paused to take off his jacket and roll up his shirt-sleeves. They carried on, George slapping at a horse fly that followed him, landing on his forearm and annoyingly escaping every slap. At last, they rounded the outcrop and found the spot they had visited before, a grassy level with a few tumbled boulders. George spread out his jacket for Kitty and sat down on the grass beside her. Twenty yards away on the left, a face of rock fell away and the view was of a deep valley, patterned by dry-stone walls, and the range of hills beyond. On the right was the steep side of the fell, where the first bracken shoots were pushing through, with views over the whole of Derwentwater. They looked out over the water; the densely wooded islands had greened over and lay like a scatter of cushions on the glossy surface of the lake.

'It's another world up here, isn't it?' Kitty said as they watched the steamer, shrunk to doll's-house size, cut a wake in a white curving line, and sailing boats drifting lazy, white and slow. The climbers who had gone up ahead of them were dots in the distance, leaving them alone on the hillside. Kitty slipped off her boots, emptied a tiny stone out of one of them and rubbed her stockinged feet.

'Here.' George took an apple from his pocket, cut it in two with his penknife and passed half to her. He stretched out his legs and leant back on his elbows to gaze at the blue sky and the white clouds stacking high above the hill tops.

Kitty touched his arm and pointed to the wall of rock where a stunted rowan tree grew from a crevice. The end of a branch shook as a bird alighted, black and glossy – a rook? No, as it settled its wings he realised it was too big – a raven then. They watched it hop to the end of the branch and take off, sailing out over the vast drop to the valley floor, soaring in wide circles. Suddenly its mate appeared and they looked on, spellbound, as the two birds circled together, one below the other at first, and then changing places, riding the thermals and gliding on a sliding wind. At last, their circling began to shift westwards. George and Kitty sat on silently together as the pair gradually moved out over the centre of the valley, knowing that they had witnessed something marvellous, following them until they were just black dots caught in the gyre of air.

323

George screwed up his eyes and ran his finger under the edge of the mask; it felt heavy and the skin beneath felt itchy and clammy.

Kitty was looking at him curiously. 'Is it uncomfortable?'

'A bit.'

'Why don't you take it off?' she said.

George turned towards her. 'Oh, I don't think I should.'

'I don't see why not. Go on. There's no one here to see you. Only me.'

George hesitated. He thought about how he waited for Ted to go to sleep before he took it off at night, how Lillie ran away from him. 'Are you sure?' he said. 'You wouldn't be frightened?'

Kitty scoffed, 'I wouldn't be frightened.'

Still on one elbow, George fiddled with the catch with the other hand. When he got it free, he turned away from her and slowly took it away from his face, blinking as the breeze blew over him, cooling the damp skin and touching his eye. Kitty leant over in a businesslike way, took the mask from his hand and put it down carefully on the jacket between them. He turned reluctantly towards her.

Kitty was looking at him with her head on one side.

He forced himself to keep his hands away from his face. 'What does it look like to you?'

'It looks tight and shiny . . . like skin that's healed after being burnt.'

'Horrible.'

'No,' Kitty said. 'I can sort of see past it to how it was before.'

'I don't see how; I can't do that myself.'

'Oh, you know what I mean: the way that people who knew each other as children and meet when they're grown up say, "You look the same as ever." It's like that with old married

324

couples. In their heads they always keep the picture of each other when they were courting; they can sort of look at the ageing face and see the young one still there.'

George laughed. 'Are you saying we're like an old married couple?'

Kitty went to dig her elbow in his ribs and he caught her arm in play. He looked down into her upturned face and her expression became serious. Her eyes were hazel, grey-green irises with tiny orange flecks, not blue, as they had been as a child. Her face was like Kitty but unlike her: he had always thought of her as having blue eyes. How could he not have noticed that her eyes were hazel? And so beautiful?

She reached up and laid the flat of her hand along his cheek as though the coolness of her palm could soothe the scars. George stilled at her touch. He wanted to lean his face against her hand: to give himself up to the sensation and rest there, trusting, dropping his weary defences. She leant forward and kissed him lightly on the mouth. George was so surprised that he stayed stock-still. Her lips were warm; he found that her kiss felt strange yet familiar to him, like a traveller who has almost forgotten his way suddenly stumbling across the path home. His pulse quickened.

Before he could reach for her and hold her close, Kitty drew back and looked at him questioningly; then the blood began to rush to her face and her eyes filled with tears.

The crunch of feet on stones and the sound of voices reached them and they pulled away from each other. Kitty scrambled to her feet and retreated to sit on one of the tumbled rocks. George, searching around for his mask, which had slipped into a fold in the lining of his jacket, found himself face to face with a party of walkers who had come up, like them, by the easy route. They rounded the outcrop in a tightly formed group:

325

young women and older men with thumb sticks and knapsacks, one of them with a rolled-up travel rug, obviously intending to picnic. When they saw that the popular spot was already taken, they rejoined the path again and filed past. George felt as though he was sitting there naked, the way they stared at him. Two of the girls giggled and when they bunched up again as the path widened, George heard another say to her companion: 'Did you see that poor man?' The reply was lost in a burst of conversation.

Furious for letting himself become vulnerable, George searched for the mask, fumbled with it against his face and couldn't get it comfortable, took it off and started again, and finally managed to feel for the hook and loop and get it done up again. He stood up and brushed down his jacket as though he was beating a carpet. Kitty said, 'George . . .' but stopped as she saw his expression.

'I'm going back now. Are you coming?' he said abruptly.

Kitty retrieved her boots and sat on a low slab of rock to put them on and do up the laces. George set off down the path, ignoring her calling after him to wait. 'There's the boat, look!' he shouted over his shoulder as an excuse. 'If we hurry up we'll catch it.' He went on as best he could on the loose stones, his leg aching, his face hot and his feelings a confused jumble of surprise, longing and shame.

He sensed Kitty following as she trailed down behind him, keeping a distance between them. He limped on, panicking about what he should say, how he should act. The strange sensation that their kiss was the most natural thing in the world, as inevitable as the earth turning to meet the sun, faded into fear and uncertainty: a disturbing feeling that it should never have happened. Kitty was a warm, generous-hearted person, he thought; she had been overcome by a momentary burst of

326

tenderness and had kissed him out of . . . out of . . . What had that girl among the walkers said? *That poor man.* Pity, in other words.

By the time they reached the road, Kitty looked hurt and angry. 'You could have waited,' she said. The boat was just coming in, its wake frothing as it made the tight turn to dock. Walkers and day-trippers disembarked; the queue along the landing stage shuffled forwards and they hurried to join it. They stood together in an awkward silence.

On the boat, Kitty saw a girl she knew from her street, and slipped quickly into the bench seat beside her. George took the seat behind, sliding along to the side of the boat; he stared out across the water with his face turned away from the other passengers. When they arrived at the stop for the town, the boat emptied and the three of them walked along Lake Road among the Sunday-afternoon crowd, noisy with holiday spirits. They reached the point where their ways divided and paused while folk streamed past them. The girl tactfully withdrew a little way to give them a private moment and waited for Kitty, pretending an interest in the boats on the lake.

George felt acutely uncomfortable. After what had passed between them, he had no idea how they should part. Kitty was fiddling with the strings of her hat and George imagined her to be deeply regretting a moment of womanly tender-heartedness. The fear that this could change things between them, that it could jeopardise their friendship and return them to the distant formality that had resulted from him going off to war, made him tongue-tied. 'Kitty. . .' he started, but then stumbled as she refused to look at him. 'Thanks for getting me to walk up the fell,' he said, trying to find their old, friendly tone.

She glanced up at him. 'You certainly came down fast enough,' she said sharply, and then turned and walked quickly away. She linked arms with her friend and set off without a backward glance.

George stood there for a moment. He was used to Kitty's tart responses when she was disappointed in him but this was different, she had gone without arranging to meet again. He imagined her berating herself for the folly of a moment's softness, wishing that it had never happened; she was so desperate to get away. He walked home slowly, his anger at being persuaded to take off the mask and put himself in such a vulnerable position leaching away to be replaced by a sadness and a sense of loss as he remembered the way their kiss had made him feel: light, weightless, like a bird circling up into the higher air.

20

PASTE BROOCH

Violet sat at her writing desk in the Small Drawing Room, answering a letter from Elizabeth. They had exchanged several letters since Violet had written to let the family know the news of Edmund's death, a duty she thought one of the hardest things she had ever done. Each time she wrote, she attempted words of comfort that she couldn't feel, words that sounded hollow to her ear even as they left her pen.

Elizabeth's most recent letter invited her to come and stay. Violet knew she didn't have the strength. The place would be full of Edmund's absence: empty chairs where he had sat and talked to her; boots, overcoat, tennis racquet, everywhere something he had touched. The photographs that stood on the grand piano were now a series recording a frozen youth: boy, student,

329

soldier . . . a stopped clock. In the garden, the flowers around the arbour where they had exchanged their promises would be in bloom again. She would think only of the voice she'd never hear again, the hand she'd never hold. She wrote to say that, sadly, her mother was too ill and couldn't spare her.

She sealed the envelope and sat back in her chair. Beside her, the glass cabinet that housed her china collection stood, dusty and long unopened. Inside, crowding the shelves, were vases of turquoise and cobalt blue, porcelain baskets with intricate latticework, china owls and brightly painted parakeets, a hoard of treasures kept safe behind glass: bright and dead as the past.

From the French windows, sunshine fell across the clutter on the desk: stationery, ink bottle, pen wiper, a little inlaid box in which she kept her stamps and the funny little brooch that George had given to her. It caught the sun, tiny red and green points of light in a setting of twisted gilt wires.

She felt sorry that she hadn't been able to respond to his gift as she should. It had looked so bright as she held it against her coat, obscenely bright, and placing it there had reminded her suddenly of the corsage that she had pinned so carefully at her breast when dressing for the dance, thinking with such great hope and anticipation of seeing Edmund. She had slipped the brooch into her pocket and seen George's earnest look turn to disappointment.

Violet had always known that George cared for her. She had thought it touching: a boyish crush that he would soon grow out of. She had been in control, able to manage their conversations so that they both enjoyed each other's company and friendship. She had been very careful not to encourage a romantic attachment: that would have been unfair, and she was confident in any case that George was well aware of the social distance between them. But with Edmund's death, she sensed that something had shifted. Her reliance on George's visits as a link, however tenuous, to Edmund, and an opportunity to release a little of her pent-up feelings, had changed the balance between them. She felt that she was taking advantage of his caring for her and letting him cast himself as her comforter, even though he was still so young and had his own injury to deal with. She had leant on him. Weakness on my part, she thought. Her grief was selfish and all-consuming; it left no energy to consider others. She could offer him nothing now, not even the cheerful companionship they had once shared. It wasn't right to keep letting him prop her up, however much she depended on his visits as a way to unburden herself, however lonely she felt in the days in between.

She picked up the brooch and turned it back and forth. It was roughly made, the fake stones crudely cut, unlike the jewellery she kept in a box upstairs: fine work with tiny-clawed settings that let the light shine through the stones. She wondered, nonetheless, if George had been obliged to save for it, and the thought made her ashamed. She shouldn't have accepted it. It was a gift for a sweetheart. Who was it that George had mentioned? Katie? No, Kitty; that was it. She opened one of the tiny drawers in the bureau, took out a piece of tissue paper and wrapped the brooch carefully.

She knew that her constant questioning about Edmund made George unhappy. Of course it would; it brought the war and all its horrors back; it didn't let him heal over. There was something more than she could fathom, though, about his feelings towards Edmund: a closeness that puzzled her. When she asked him about Edmund's death, he would always finish by saying, 'There was nothing I could do,' in such a tone of despair that she felt she could ask no more. She couldn't imagine what it must be like to see someone die, to wonder why a shell

331

chose someone else, not you. Perhaps it made you blame yourself in some obscure way; perhaps it made you feel guilty just to be alive.

She needed the relief of speaking about Edmund; it was the only link with him that she had left, and even the pain was better than nothing. Yet she knew she was pulling George down with her, like a ship foundering and taking down its tug. She slipped the brooch, wrapped in the soft paper, into the drawer. She shut it gently.

George had decided to brave a visit to chapel on Sunday, in order to see Kitty in the hope that it would help ease them back on to familiar ground. He dreaded returning to the congregation, despite the fact that almost everyone had known him since infancy, and didn't know which would be worse: people asking him about the war, or people studiously avoiding the subject and ambushing him with sympathetic comments for which he had no response. He asked the family to sit at the back, where he shifted uncomfortably on the hard oak seat, unable to stretch his leg due to the closeness of the row of chairs in front. He could see Kitty's straw hat up at the front: Mr Ashwell insisted on punctuality for chapel, as for post-office business, which always meant they got there early and had the pick of the seats.

The Elder finished the service with a blessing and stationed himself at the door to speak to people as they left. Some of the congregation spilt out on to the pavement, others formed groups in the aisles; there would be chapel business, social niceties and gossip for half an hour before the place would clear. George started moving towards the front but was intercepted by Alderman Rowe, who was standing talking to Mr Gibson. 'What do you think, young man?' he said. 'You've just been out there. Gibson here was moaning about the number of farm hands he's lost and I was telling him how much they're needed in the lines. They should be training them up now to have them out there by the winter. We need every hand we can get, don't we?'

Mr Gibson replied before George could speak. 'You won't be saying that when we're lambing in bad weather and we can't get the beasts down off the fells because there's no one to fetch them in.'

George said grimly, 'With respect, sir, pouring men into a winter stalemate would be pointless. They'd just sit and freeze in trenches waiting for the next bombardment. I don't think people realise . . .'

'Come, come, that's hardly the spirit!' Rowe said.

'. . . you go down with pneumonia, or your feet rot, or you get typhoid. It's like living in one big latrine,' George finished.

Both men stared at him.

Rowe said, 'Surely we can muster a little more grit? The BEF are the best soldiers in the world – look at the attacks they've seen off, with the enormous odds against us!'

'I don't doubt it, but you can't fight the cold with a bayonet,' George said sharply. 'Excuse me, there's someone I must see.'

As George stepped away, edging between the knots of dark-suited, shiny-shoed men, he heard the conversation resume. Gibson said testily, 'Well, I can't spare any more labour right now, that's for sure,' and Rowe replied, 'You may have to, whether you like it or not. If we push forward in France there's bound to be wastage; recruits will be needed and plenty of 'em.'

Wastage. The word hung in George's mind. Like an inevitable expenditure that has to be budgeted for in advance or some factory off-cut that's a necessary part of an industrial process.

Not Smith slumped over the parapet or Rooke's slim form stumbling, falling.

He rubbed his hand across his brow and blinked at the room, bringing back into focus the familiar chairs and hymn books. Scanning the noisy congregation, he found Kitty again and began to make his way between old folk who had remained seated to chat with their neighbours and families handing fractious babies between parents and siblings. Kitty seemed to recede every time he thought he was getting near her. She talked to first one acquaintance, then another, and always seemed to have her back to him so that he couldn't catch her eye. In the end, he moved sideways along a row, excusing himself to those still sitting in it, so that he could arrive beside her, where she was chatting with the Borrowdale sisters. He tapped her arm and she turned round. A fiery blush rose immediately to her cheeks.

'Oh! George,' she said, as if she was surprised to see him, although George felt sure that she had caught sight of him and had deliberately turned away.

'Kitty. Suzanne. Mariah.' George acknowledged them. There was an awkward silence and the Borrowdale girls excused themselves. 'I thought I'd never get through this crush,' he said. 'You're in a very sociable mood today.'

'I don't know what you mean,' Kitty said, fiddling with the button on her gloves.

George tried again. 'It's a nice day; should we go out on the lake this afternoon? I could row. We could go out to one of the islands if you'd like – have a break from walking.'

'I can't,' she said shortly. 'We're expecting visitors this afternoon; my aunt and uncle are coming.'

'Do you have to be there?' George asked. 'Won't they just want to talk to your parents?' He knew that Kitty found their conversation, about distant relatives she'd never met, deadly.

'I'm sorry you seem to think my company so dull.' Kitty picked up her bag from the chair next to her. 'I'll relieve you of it.'

Before George could take in her reply, Kitty had turned and was making her way towards the main door, leaving George unable to work out quite where he had gone wrong. He slipped out of the side door, into the alley, and hurried round the corner of the building hoping that the press of folk would slow her down and that he could catch up with her in the street. Just as he had feared, he was accosted first by one person and then another, asking how he was bearing up and murmuring platitudes about the healing properties of time, to which he had to respond politely, until he could have roared with frustration.

On the other side of the street he saw Mr Ashwell gathering up his family to leave and met his eye. Mr Ashwell glared at George as he shepherded them away. George finally managed to excuse himself and limped off down the cobbled alleyway towards home.

He flopped down into the fireside chair. He had tried, and all he'd managed to do was offend her again. Why on earth did she have to be so prickly and unreasonable! She was obviously settling in for one of her long ireful moods, as she had when he went away to the war. Sometimes women seemed a complete mystery. He felt miserable; it gave him an uncomfortable, tight feeling in his chest when she gave him that freezing look. It was no good confronting her when she was in that frame of mind, it would only lead to more sharp retorts that his heart didn't feel strong enough to bear. He would just have to be patient and keep enduring chapel, where she would at least have to speak to him and there was some hope that he could talk her round.

With a pang, he thought of the day they were missing and of the sun glittering on the lake. He had been going to row her out to the island where they used to climb trees and build dens or swim from one of the rocky bays in the ice-cold water. He had imagined fishing and making a fire to roast perch or bream in the embers, and sitting on into the evening to talk, as they always had done, while the midges danced crazily in the smoke. She was dear to him, almost a part of him. How could he have managed things so badly yet again? George stared at the stopped clock on the mantelpiece, with the prospect of a long afternoon of worry and regret stretching before him.

Someone had tucked a letter behind the clock and George, reading 'Mr G. Far—' on the part that protruded, realised that it was meant for him and wondered how long it had been there. Tutting in irritation, he pulled it out, opened it and found that it was from Haycock. He read:

Dear George,

Sorry to hear about your stay in hospital. At least it was a Blighty one and not worse. Your postcard and later letters came all together in one go. Sometimes we have no post for ages here (can't say where) then it all comes at once. Anyway, now I have your address I'll write when I get the chance – paper very scarce here and most of the time we're in the line. No four days on, four days off, here. This is our first day back in reserve for a fortnight.

It's a rotten shame about Rooke. Turland has been very cut up about it ever since. He says he's going to write about this filthy, rotten war, when it's all over. We had a kind of memorial for Rooke where we all lined up and Turland said a prayer. One of the regulars told us about reversed arms being a mark of respect so we stood resting our hands on rifles turned upside down. I thought Ernest might feel better after, but he said there should have been somewhere we could put a cross or some marker to remember him by.

We've been dug in for months here, in the rain – worse even than when you were here. The ground has been like slurry. We've lost some men through slipping off the paths but none of your pals I'm glad to say. However, we're all dreading <u>better</u> weather; you will know why. Apparently, it's due to be sunny next week, so think of us then.

Well, that's all my news, such as it is. I hope to see you, if and when there is leave (long overdue).

Cheero,
Tom

George knew exactly what better weather meant – drier ground and a push forward. He felt disturbed by the thought of his friends caught up in the maelstrom once again and the image of Rooke, stooping and then rolling, came before him as clearly as if he had turned a handle and played it on a screen. He felt himself sinking lower, weighed down by the awfulness of everything. When the family arrived, he was still sitting staring into the empty grate.

21

THE WALLED GARDEN

On Tuesday when George arrived at the Manor House, he found Violet already waiting for him and his heart was instantly filled with misgivings. She stepped forward, her pale blouse banded by the shade of the branches.

She fell into step beside him as they walked along the drive, but instead of bearing left to go into the woods, she suggested, since the weather was so pleasant, that they sit in the walled garden. Mrs Burbidge had gone into town, she explained, and the garden would be a sheltered spot where they could enjoy the sun.

They turned in through a green-painted door; the sighing of the wood dropped away and was replaced by a muffled calm and a warmer air. The high redbrick walls, which gave back the stored heat of the afternoon, were lined with the green leaves and white blossom of espaliered pear trees. As they walked the gravel path around the edge of the garden, Violet pointed out the herb garden and the fernery and said that they would walk down to the orchard where there was a place she liked to sit. George knew that he should feel reassured by this new intimacy, but the change of routine and something about her more solicitous manner made him feel that she was making an unnatural effort.

She asked him about his week and he told her that he was walking further, and that, on a walk at the foot of Latrigg, he had seen some fox cubs playing. She nodded, but seemed scarcely to be paying attention as he worked hard to entertain her by describing the antics of the cubs.

They sat down on a wooden bench in the orchard, among twisted grey-barked apple trees dotted with the first pink points of buds. A little further in were a row of white-painted beehives with pitched roofs and clapboard walls. Bees came and went from them: dark dots zigzagging. A loud hum came from somewhere behind the hives, low and steady.

'Look! They're swarming,' Violet said, and George saw that in one of the fruit trees there was a dark mass hanging from a branch, surrounded by a dense cloud of agitated movement.

'Are you sure this is a good place to sit?' George asked, worrying that Violet might be stung.

'They won't hurt us; we're too far away,' she said quickly, as though it was important that now she had got him here, they should stay. 'Anyway, they're far more interested in the queen. They're clustering around her, you see, to keep her warm while the scouts go off to find a new nest site.'

'Shouldn't you tell the bee-keeper?' George asked. 'He won't want to lose them.'

'No, no, plenty of time for that. We'll leave that to Hodges.'

She seemed agitated and George let it drop. He went back to telling her how he had followed the fox cubs and seen both den and vixen, but instead of asking him about it, she placed her hands in her lap and said, 'And how are the family? And Kitty?'

George, taken off guard, said, 'Actually, I don't think she's speaking to me at the moment.'

'Is it a lovers' tiff?' Violet said.

George felt his heart lurch at the thought of the sudden kiss. He said, 'Well . . .' and then fell silent in confusion.

'I'm sure she'll come round again soon,' Violet said lightly before George could say anything more. She looked down at her hands, one clasped over the other as if holding on tight. 'And the family? Is all well at home?'

Taken off balance, George scrabbled to explain, 'Well, Lillie is still being difficult . . . but that's not the point, Kitty and I aren't walking out, as such—'

'You see, the thing is, George,' she stopped him, 'I don't think that meeting like this is helping either of us.'

George felt a chill start at the back of his neck as dread began to spread through him.

Violet sat looking straight ahead, her chin lifted and her arms straight now, hands gripping the seat of the bench as if what she really wanted to do was to take flight.

She said, 'I know that you find talking about Edmund difficult.'

'I don't mind,' George said quickly.

'I'm finding it very hard to recover from losing Edmund, as you know, and . . . and dragging it all up each week is making it worse.' Violet kept her eyes fixed in front of her and spoke the words into the air.

'But you said it helped to talk about him . . .' George said. 'And I want to help, to be useful to you in any way I can.'

'I'm not being fair to you, George. It would be better if you didn't have this dead weight hanging round your neck.'

'We don't have to talk about the bad things,' George said miserably. 'We could just walk, like we used to, like we did before all this . . .'

Violet turned towards him then. They looked at each other, recognising the chasm that had opened between now and then, between the people they had been and who they had become. Violet took a deep breath. 'I'm sorry, George, but I'm no good to you; I'm no good to anyone and I don't think you're the best person to help me.'

George was silenced, unable to argue with this, as surely he was, in fact, the worst person, the root cause of all her pain. He saw again Edmund's face as he shouted 'Cover!'; he heard the whine of the approaching shell, felt the fear that froze him to the spot for the fatal split second that was all that it took to turn the world upside down.

Violet pressed her advantage. 'I'm going away, George, to stay with Edmund's family. I'm sorry.'

'Then I'll visit when you get back.'

'No.'

The word fell like a sheet of glass between them. George could still see Violet, her high cheekbones, her beautiful mouth, her stubborn, pointed chin, but he couldn't understand her, couldn't gauge her feelings or read her eyes. She had closed herself off from him so that she could hurt him. He knew that he should walk away and yet he sat there with his head hanging. Even as he spoke, he knew that it was useless, 'But I need to . . . I want to be able to look after you . . . let me do that at least. Please don't send me away.'

341

She clenched her jaw as though gathering herself; then she said quickly, 'I have nothing for you and you have nothing for me. I shall talk with Elizabeth about Edmund; I'll be better able to talk to another woman.'

George stood up. He waited for her to look at him but she would not. George walked away and neither of them said goodbye.

Violet looked after him as he made his way towards the door in the garden wall, his hands in his pockets, shoulders hunched. What had she done? It was unbearable to see him so beaten down! She had to look away. Her conscience told her that she had done the right thing, the decent thing, however painful, but she wished that she had not had to be cruel. It broke her heart to have to end like this, with him thinking her unkind.

She would miss him so: the way his face lit up with enthusiasm when he told her in his slow, considered way about things he'd seen on his walks, their talks about nature and beauty and art, his stories about Lillie and Ted, even just turning to each other to share a thought. What would be the point of walking without him?

She heard the sound of the door closing; now she really was alone. There would be no one to walk with, no one to talk with, no one who knew about her and Edmund and the bright glimpse of the life they could have had together, the hope that was now extinguished. There would never be anyone else but Edmund for her. Without that small relief – of keeping him with her through talking of her memories – how could she go on? What purpose did she have? She told herself that in sacrificing George's friendship at least one of them would be saved. George was young; he would find somebody to love; his life could begin again. She at least had that to feel glad for.

She sat on, blankly, watching the bees come and go in their

endless labour, following their flight paths between flowers and hive, leg pouches brimming yellow, spending their short lives gathering and storing in a useless frenzy of activity, soon over, soon to start again.

The colony hanging from the branch gleamed as the bodies of the bees moved over one another, their wings glistening. Clusters fell from it like heavy drops of syrup, only to reattach themselves and crawl upwards again. Violet found the close-packed insects strangely mesmerising, their drive for life – survival, reproduction – the same drive that was in all creatures. She thought, without Edmund I am barren. I will be without issue, there will be no heir for the house, the land, all this. Then, bitterly, Father will have a second disappointment: first a girl child and then a spinster.

When George got back to the town, instead of going home before the start of his shift he headed straight for the taproom of the Pack Horse. Some old boys were sitting in the window seat playing dominoes and among them sat two younger men, a pair of crutches leant against the wall beside them. The lad nearest to him, who had one empty sleeve pinned across his chest, raised his glass to George in greeting, welcoming him over as one of them. George touched his forehead in a brief salute of camaraderie but didn't join them. He ordered a pint of beer and downed it at the bar; then he bought another and took it to a corner table where he sat in a high-backed settle, out of view, where he could be alone and think.

She had sent him away. She didn't want to see him, didn't think his presence helped, so . . . he had failed her. He had tried so hard to make some kind of amends, to be what she needed: a confidant, helping her to keep Edmund alive in her mind, a comforter distracting her from her grief, a listener, a friend. He went over their conversations in his mind, trying to think of anything he might have said that was crass or insensitive.

Perhaps it was having to look at his face each week, his mask a constant reminder of injury – of the war that had taken away her sweetheart. No, he was being unfair to her. She had never shown any sign of revulsion.

He drank deeply, hoping for a release of the tension in his shoulders and the aching in his heart. He should never have given her the brooch. He had overstepped a line and made her feel uncomfortable.

When he had seen it in Miller's window, on a glass shelf marked 'costume jewellery', it had been lit from above and the colours had caught his eye, colours that seemed to be absent from Violet's life. The dances and soirées, the gowns and trinkets she'd once enjoyed, that her beauty was made for, all shrunk to muddy walks and a drab overcoat. He had counted the days until his pay packet and bought it, feeling sure that it would bring her pleasure. He saw now that his desire to see her smile once again had been his downfall.

She hadn't smiled. Maybe she'd seen it as an impropriety; he remembered how she had immediately put it away. Perhaps she had thought it cheap and tacky and been reminded of the difference in their stations. George looked around him at the bare plank floor, the scuffed, mismatched stools and tables, the curling strip of oilcloth on the bar. This was his world. Perhaps she had felt embarrassed for him, the country clown who hadn't the sense not to presume an intimacy with his betters. No, he should never have bought the brooch.

How definite she had been when she forbade him to visit. He felt sure that she had decided in advance what she would tell him. She was going to stay with Elizabeth. She wanted to be with her own kind and he must accept it, but it was so hard. He wouldn't even know how she was, would have no means of finding out if she was all right. How was he to make amends now for what he'd done? All he had wanted was to see her and have a chance to comfort and look after her, to do what he owed to her and to Edmund. What was he to do with this pressing weight of guilt? He would have to carry it like a great stone block, unable even to chip away at its edges by small actions of care for Violet. It would be like bearing Edmund's tombstone on his back. He would never be able to put any of it right. He remembered Violet saying how she missed Edmund, and that 'never' was the cruellest word in the language. This is my punishment, he thought.

The long-case clock beside the door struck six, and George realised with a jolt that he should have been at work half an hour ago to check the arc lamps and clean the projectors before the start of the evening performance. He drank down the last of his pint, hurried out and moved on through the emptying streets, past shopkeepers pulling down their blinds and women with baskets straggling home.

Mr Mounsey was in the foyer as he slunk in. George apologised for his lateness but he fixed him with a sharp look. 'I'm disappointed in you, Farrell,' he said.

'I'm truly sorry, sir.' George was mortified to have failed to live up to Mr Mounsey's hopes of him. 'It won't happen again.'

'Don't let me ever catch you with beer on your breath again,' he said. 'A moment's inattention with those lights and the whole place could go up in smoke, remember?' He looked at him keenly; then he nodded and let him go.

22

CASTLERIGG

April slipped into May and the draggled flags around the town that had faded and frayed in the winter weather were taken down and renewed with fresh red, white and blue as guesthouses and businesses vied for tourist custom through their shows of patriotism. As more men were lost at the Front, a rash of new recruitment posters appeared. George had the strange fancy that the town appeared, at a glance, to be preparing for some fair or circus – until you looked closer. Beneath the parade, the strain on the workings of the town was beginning to show. Bicycles and handcarts were pressed into service for deliveries as horses became more and more scarce. Girls that George had known at school served in the shops, daughters filling in for absent sons; many seemed not to recognise him – or pretended not to, paying close attention to packing his purchases or counting out his change, looking anywhere but directly at his face. Patriotic fervour drove shopkeepers with Germanic names away, leaving vacant shops with windows whitened in swirling patterns. The papers printed ever-longer casualty lists and obituaries bloomed faster than spring flowers.

As the tourist season began, the little cinema filled with visitors as well as locals. Mr Mounsey put on extra shows to meet the demand, and although he was careful never to complain, the hot, stuffy booth became even more of a trial for George.

The newsreels, with their dry, grassy battlefields, clean, well-turned-out soldiers, and tales of derring-do by ambulance men and chaplains, filled him with anger and frustration. The way the film cut from shells falling left and right to men in spotless bandages, smiling and sharing cigarettes, made him want to pull the film in handfuls from the reel.

The features were no better: grown men and women mooning and swooning over one another, the villains with sharp moustaches and too much hair oil stealing away heroines who seemed wilfully blind to their obvious ill intent, the rescues by handsome heroes against all the odds. None of it seemed, to George, to bear any relation to real life, with its mess, its random ills and its unresolv able hurts.

He went every week to chapel, to try to speak to Kitty, but she surrounded herself with female friends. If he forced the issue, she spoke to him as if he was some distant acquaintance, and when he suggested that they meet elsewhere, she trotted out a ready excuse and turned away. It hurt. He thought that she must be regretting the closeness that they had shared for a while. It was as if she didn't want to be seen with him in public: the man with the broken face. He had thought better of her. He missed her.

In a desperate attempt at self-protection, as his spirits sank lower, he stopped going. He still missed her. Staying away solved nothing. The long, sweltering shifts, closeted away from daylight, added to the malaise that his mother called his 'black study'.

Outside, the fells greened over as the bracken grew, its tight-furled stems unrolling as they reached for air and light. Like a green tide breaking on the hills it hid the sheep paths and badger trods, smoothing the contours of the slopes and ending in the soft greys and mauves of rock and heather. George's longing to get out and walk was like a thirst.

He had heard nothing of Violet; indeed, he had no means to get news of her and the difference in their positions meant that they wouldn't meet by chance. Their lives had touched for a while but now she had gone back to her own circle – it might as well be to another country.

Sometimes, when Ted was out and he had the room to himself, he would take out the tin box from his kitbag, which he kept tucked away under the bed. He would pick up each object in turn and conjure her before him; then he'd return them and put on the lid, feeling a deep sadness. Trying to make amends to Violet had given him a purpose, and a means, however inadequate, to assuage his feelings of guilt; now that he couldn't see her, there was nowhere he could channel those feelings and no one he could talk to for relief. He had to shut them away inside him, as if his heart were a box that could never be opened.

At the end of a shift at the cinema, in which he had felt that the heat and his troubled thoughts were beating in his head, he waited as usual at the top of the back stairs, willing the audience to go. He couldn't bear the sidelong glances and whispered comments as he passed so he stood listening until all was quiet and he could venture down. At last, they dispersed and he passed through the foyer and out into the dusky evening. The crowds thinned out once the cinema and the tea gardens had closed; older holidaymakers repaired to drink in the hotel bars or to play parlour games in the guesthouses. The streets were left to groups of young people and wandering couples, absorbed in each other, and George could fade into the shady side of the street and slip quietly through the town without notice.

He made his way across the scented park, where blossom breathed its perfume into the warm evening air; then he regained the road and walked until he came to Brundholme Wood. The shade beneath the trees glimmered with pale blue-bell flowers that seemed to hang above the green mops of their leaves and the first shoots of tangled briars covering the ground. He followed the path called Lovers' Lane that led deeper into the wood.

Here and there, the silvery boles of the trees were carved with clumsy, angular writing, the bark scratched through to the wood beneath. George stopped, now and then, to examine them. There were sets of initials and pairs of names: *J W loves P L*, *Bertie and Alice*, *Alfred and Ruby*. Mixed among them were love tokens, linked rings or hearts pierced by arrows. Some carvings were new, the wood a pale tan, the edges of bark ragged or peeling away; others, time had smoothed and weathered to silvery lines, partly obscured by lichen. He wondered how many of the couples had courted and wed and how many had found that their feelings cooled: the ardour that had moved them recorded only in a wooden inscription. A *memento mori* for love.

The phrase made him recall Haycock's letter and the service

they had held for Rooke. He pictured them standing in two lines, as if around an imaginary grave, an empty six-foot plot. He thought of Percy: his surprised expression, his sleight of hand at cards and his ready humour, the speed with which he could disappear into the background, his usually unerring instinct that had let him down so badly in the end. Percy had been so young, really just a boy. He would never know a girl; he had no one to record his passing. Unknown. Unremembered.

He stood in the middle of the path, beneath branches that laced overhead, listening to the sounds of the wood: the soughing of the breeze through the leaves, a wood pigeon calling in the distance. Taking out his penknife, he looked for a tree right by the path and chose a mature beech that was thickly covered with inscriptions. He made his first mark, among the hearts and initials, digging in the point and peeling back the silvery bark. In large, clear strips, he carved out *PERCY ROOKE*; then he stopped and pondered, unable to record the date of his birth. Instead, he added *BOY SOLDIER* and then stopped again.

There had been crosses behind the battle lines, thin wooden markers with tin plates that bore the legend 'Known unto God'. He no longer believed that was true. He thought of engraving *R. I. P.*, but that too was a lie. Surprised by a bullet, he was sunk in mud, his flesh dissolved, his bones disinterred as shells pocked and battered the same thin strip of ground until they floated like driftwood in a sea of earth. George carved the only thing he knew was true. *DIED NOVEMBER 1914*. It stood out, fresh and raw among the paler traceries of love.

Frederick and Maggie were worried about their son. Each night, in bed, they talked about what could be done. In the first couple of months after returning home from the hospital, they had thought that he was making a recovery, albeit a gradual and painful process: the job, walking out with Kitty, allowing himself to be persuaded back to chapel. Maggie called it 'returning to his world' and said that it was like a spiral that started with family, then widened to include friends, and then, once confidence had grown, acquaintances. He wasn't there yet, but eventually he would feel safe and accepted within his own circle and that would give him strength to meet strangers with equanimity, and withstand their slights and the cruelties born of ignorance. Something had stopped this gradual process and whirled him back to the centre where he ventured no social engagement beyond the family and spent a great deal of time alone.

At first, when he had refused to come to chapel any more, Frederick had said that it was probably a temporary setback and that they should give him time, but it had been weeks now. Even at home he was morose and, frankly, difficult, and often absented himself completely. He set off on solitary walks, who knew where, from which he returned late in the evening, not refreshed and invigorated but pale and drained.

'Maybe he tried too much, too soon,' Frederick said. 'The lad has a mountain to climb.'

It made Maggie think of the barren wasteland of boulders at the top of Scafell Pike where, ten years or so ago, a group of climbers had found the party they'd lunched with, roped together at the foot of the pinnacle: a three-hundred-foot fall. She tried to shrug off the picture of George climbing the arduous slopes. 'Talk to him, Frederick,' she said. 'Take him off somewhere and talk to him, man to man.'

One Sunday afternoon, George and his father left the town behind and walked out to the stone circle at Castlerigg, a place

351

that they had visited many times when George was a boy. They sat with their backs against one of the monoliths, taking in anew the ring of standing stones set on a green plateau surrounded by fells, as if in a bowl of hills. The huge stones, hewn from volcanic rock, leaned at crazy angles, some still upright and taller than a man, some sunk deep into the ground, all lichen-covered with patches of crusty yellow-green.

Heated by their exertions, the men had taken off their caps and rolled up their shirtsleeves. They sat for a while letting the breeze that always funnelled across the plateau find their faces and bare arms.

At length, Frederick said, 'Do you remember when I used to set you and Ted on to counting the stones?'

'We could never get the same number twice and you told us that they moved about when we weren't looking!'

Frederick laughed. 'I used to start you off from where I was standing next to one stone, and get you to count once, then next time, I'd move along one or two from where you'd set off.'

George gave a small smile. 'I caught on to that eventually; I don't think Ted ever did though. I remember feeling proud of myself when I counted thirty-eight of them three times running.'

They sat for a while watching the clouds chase their shadows across the fells, now purpled over with heather.

Frederick said, in a carefully neutral tone, 'Your mother's a bit concerned about you – that you're not getting out, other than walking on your own.'

'I'm just trying to get the strength back in this leg,' George lied. 'That's why I'm out so much.'

'Mmm.' Frederick said. He started again. 'You know, everyone would welcome you back at chapel; the Elder always asks after you.' He added, 'It's not because we mind – don't think that; it's because it would do you good.'

'I can't,' George said shortly. 'And it wouldn't.'

Frederick looked at George, wondering how much the war had changed him. Was it the things that he'd seen that had turned him aside from God, or things that he'd done? Soldiering was a stomach-turning business. He said gently, 'Don't shut yourself out, that's all I'd say. God's saving grace is for every one of us, regardless of whether we go to worship.'

He put his hand on George's shoulder. 'Is there anything you regret?'

George's throat constricted.

'Are there people you lost?'

George nodded but said nothing.

Frederick sat back and thought for a minute. 'These stones   ' he said. 'Strange, isn't it, when you think of men bringing them here, four, maybe five thousand years ago? Some people believe they're for predicting the length of the seasons. Think of all the centuries, maybe millennia, they've been used to help them to know when to sow and when to reap their crops.' He paused. 'What I'm saying is – it's such a short time that we have; don't waste it away in grief and regrets.'

George picked a piece of couch grass and wound it round and round his finger.

Frederick said, 'Think about it – if you'd died instead of being injured, what would you have missed? Not just now, but in your whole life: the things you could have reasonably expected to have if you'd never gone to war.'

'I don't know; I suppose a job, advancement, taking some leisure . . .'

'Yes, but more than that.'

George hesitated. 'Maybe a wife, and a home of my own; maybe children.'

Frederick sat back and slapped his hands on his knees. 'Exactly.

353

The things that make you a man! So . . . you weren't killed in that shell hole, goodness knows how, but you survived. Life has all these things to offer and there's no reason why you shouldn't pursue them. There's someone for everyone, you know.'

George thought not. He turned full face to his father. 'Look at the state of me,' he said bitterly.

His father held his ground. 'Believe me, there are things worse than scars. Dead faces don't make scars, George.'

'That's as maybe; I don't see the girls queuing up for a limping man with half a face.'

'Oh, I don't know. Kitty's always been a little sweet on you,' Frederick said lightly.

'What do you mean?' George said defensively.

'Well, I doubt she goes asking after all the boys from the post office who've enlisted the way she used to come round asking after you.'

'When was this?'

'Once she knew you'd gone abroad,' Frederick said slowly as though George was being an idiot. 'She was round every week on some pretext or another to speak to your mother and ask for news of you.'

George thought about the long spell at the camp before he'd had a letter from Kitty and the terse notes that she'd sent when he'd been in Flanders. He couldn't fathom it. He'd thought she'd been too angry to care about him all that time, and had only come round when Arthur died and she needed a friend. Well, he thought, as he struggled to his feet, it doesn't matter any more, the way things are between us now. He felt a flash of anger at the thought of the misunderstandings between them, the hurt, the unfairness of it all.

'It's never too late, you know,' Frederick said gently, as if he had read George's thoughts.

'My leg's stiffening up. I'm going to have to move,' George said, pulling himself up and hobbling a few steps towards the centre of the circle to get some circulation back.

'We'll go back,' Frederick said. George looked as low and beaten-down as he had done when they'd started out. He wouldn't have much of a success to report back to Maggie. Nonetheless, he clapped George on the shoulder as he came back over, saying, 'All downhill on the way back. Always easier when you're facing homewards.'

When they reached home, Frederick went upstairs to get ready for the Elders' meeting at the chapel and George, after answering his mother's enquiry about where they had been on their walk, sat down at the parlour table to write his regular letter to Haycock. Maggie was sitting in the fireside chair, mending socks, while Lillie played tea parties on the rug. She had set Lillie up with an old tin tray, a motley collection of saucers, a chipped gravy boat for a teapot and some eggcups to act as a tea service. Lillie had added some red bean flowers, twigs and leaves from the garden to serve as food. She had her bear and her doll sitting up against the hearthstone, both of whom were rather wet. Every now and then, she would take a plate to Maggie, who would say, 'Mmm, lovely sausages,' take a stem or a leaf, pretend to eat it and then put it back solemnly on the plate.

George took little notice and soon became engrossed in his letter, passing on to Haycock the comments in the paper on the progress of the war, telling him of the new fear of Zeppelins that had taken hold of the country, and venting his spleen about the propagandist news reels that folk lapped up at the cinema.

After a while, Maggie needed a smaller darning mushroom so that she could start on Lillie's socks, and went upstairs to get it. George started a new paragraph enquiring after Turland, the lads with whom they had shared a billet, Chalky and the other regulars they'd fought alongside in support. Black thoughts overcame him as he remembered the wait before an order to advance, the endless bombardment of shells, the awful randomness of it all. Perhaps it was better not to ask about the others; bad news came soon enough. A tiny noise disturbed him and he looked up in irritation.

Lillie was standing in front of him holding a saucer in both hands, clutching it close to her stomach. As she saw his set face, her chin dropped and her mouth turned down at the corners.

'No! Lillie, it's all right,' he blurted out, his voice choked. 'Are those for me?' he said quickly, trying to soften his tone. 'Can I have one?' He stayed very still.

Without taking a step forward, she reached out both hands, holding the saucer towards him. Very slowly, as if approaching some wild creature, George reached out his hand and, keeping eye contact, picked up a twig and touched it to his lips. He returned it to the saucer saying in his best tea-party voice: 'Thank you. That was very nice.'

Lillie said nothing but stared at him with huge eyes before returning to the rug and beginning to arrange the tray anew.

Mother came back in, carrying her sewing basket. She eased herself carefully into the chair saying, 'My back's not been the same since Thursday. Why the guesthouse has to have all the rugs beaten on the same day, I'll never understand.' She looked down at Lillie and then glanced over at George. 'Everything all right?'

George nodded and bent his head again over his letter, so that Mother shouldn't see him fighting absurdly with tears.

23

STONES

Violet was walking beside the beck through the fields, following it down to the lake. Feeling desolate, she looked only at the ground ahead of her. Bent by the stiff breeze coming off the water, the grass glistened in the sun; here and there feathers and down were caught in it, trembling, and brown flies settled on sheep droppings to be lifted again by the gusting wind.

She reached the church and hesitated by the slate stile set into the churchyard wall. The thought of the crucifix over the pulpit was too much to bear; she could no longer see the black, lead figure as an emblem of redemption but only as a representation of tortured flesh. *Golgotha, the place of skulls.* In any case, she thought as she turned away, I'm beyond praying.

She walked on, to the lake's edge, where the water lapped

fast against a thin shoreline of pebbles, eroding the grass line so that it cut in and out in tiny inlets and bays, the earth and turf standing proud of the stones. In places at the margin, spiky rushes grew in clumps and boulders were randomly strewn, erratics dumped by ice in an ancient age, some set deeply in the grass, some free of it, as though placed like giant marbles.

Violet sat down on one of the rocks; it was warm to the touch despite the breeze – the sun was high overhead; it must be nearly midday. She thought of sleep: deep, undisturbed, dreamless sleep. What a boon that would be, not to lie wakeful and lonely thinking of the life she could have had, not to toss and turn, longing for the dawn sound of the birds and the creaks and squeaks as the windows were opened by the maids to air the rooms. Only when she heard Mrs Burbidge's heavy footstep on the stair did she sometimes slip into an exhausted sleep for an hour or two, as she once used to sleep as a child when she was ill and Burbidge would nurse her. It used to comfort her watching Burbidge moving around the room, folding clothes, straightening cushions and banking up the fire, or simply sitting beside her, reading in her slow, flat style.

Violet looked at the expanse of water, its smoothness marked by the wind like a fingerprint on varnish. She wondered how deep it was, how quickly the bottom shelved away.

She turned away from it and looked back the way she'd come. The church, ringed with its stone wall, was surrounded by acres of green and dwarfed by the huge bulk of the fell behind: the expanse of Dodd Wood a mere frill at its foot, the treeline finishing only a quarter of the way up, and giving way to heather and grey scree, walls of bare rock. The leaded windows of the church and its little bell, suspended from an arch of stone above them, seemed insignificant – a child's toy.

Between church and fell stood the house, angled to give a

view down to the lake. Violet could see her mother's bedroom window and her own. She had a strange sense of looking back at herself as she prepared to take this walk, this morning: dressing and pinning up her hair, shrugging on her coat and putting Edmund's letters into the pocket. She could feel them against her thigh, a thick bundle of envelopes.

Where her coat fell open, a tiny blue butterfly the size of her thumbnail landed on the dark-grey material of the skirt of her dress. It opened and closed its wings as if it was new-hatched from the chrysalis and must dry them in the sun. The wind knocked it sideways but it righted itself and fluttered down to the pebbles at her feet. She bent to watch it, studying its antennae, the soft white fringe edging its wings; she felt quite calm. The wind caught it and lifted it once more and she picked up the pebble it had been blown from and turned back towards the lake.

How easy, she thought, to fill my pockets with stones. She imagined the chill of the water through her boots, her skirts darkening from the hems as it travelled up the cloth. She would feel the stones dragging at the waist seam of her dress, splashes and splatters as she walked, then freezing, numbing cold as the material clung to her legs. She knew that at waist height she would pause, unable to move either forwards or back, that there would be a moment of beauty before weariness overcame her, and she would lie back in the water despite the struggle that she knew would come when instinct would fight with will.

She sat holding the stone in her palm. Behind her, she could feel her mother's window as if it were an eye upon her back. Poor mother, in her sickness and pain; she could be watching now, wondering what took her daughter always down to the church or out to the hills and why she should sit staring out over the lake, weighing something in her open hand. Father is never coming back; I'm all she has, Violet thought, and in an instant, her resolve drained away, leaving only a great tiredness. She stood up and placed the smooth, grey pebble on top of the boulder as if to set a reminder to herself there; then she walked back to the house, as slowly as if she were wading through water.

As she came into the hall and took off her coat, Mrs Burbidge appeared and took it from her. 'Go on through to the dining room, miss. Lunch is ready for you; there's a nice bit of brisket and some good early potatoes, with an egg custard to follow.'

'Thank you, Burbidge, but I'm not hungry.' Violet walked past her and upstairs to her room. She shut the door behind her and went over to the dressing table. As if in a dream, she took the letters from her pocket and restored them to their place in the top drawer, hidden beneath her handkerchiefs and stockings. A faint pomander smell of cloves and oranges escaped as she closed it.

There was a tap at the door and Mrs Burbidge put her head around it and then came right in. 'Forgive me, Miss Violet, but you need to eat! It's all prepared. Would you not just come down and see if you could manage a small portion?'

Violet sat down at the table beside the window. She heard herself say, 'Thank you, no, I think I'll have it up here on a tray, if it's not too much trouble to make up another?'

Mrs Burbidge looked disapproving and opened her mouth to remonstrate.

'Please, Mrs B.' Violet recognised the pleading note in her voice. 'I'm not feeling quite myself these days,' she said, as she had heard her mother say so many times.

George sat on his bed with the tin box beside him; he had decided to send it back to Violet. He couldn't be sure any more whether he had originally kept it to protect Violet from grief or to protect himself from witnessing it. He knew that it didn't belong with him; he had no right to it.

He picked up the tiny ivory dance-card holder. The hinges were delicately worked in silver and when you touched a minute ebony button, it sprang open. It was exquisite. There was not, and never would be, anything remotely like it owned by the Farrell family, he thought. He returned it to its place.

Taking up the letters, he shuffled them together into a tight pack, took a shoelace from the bottom of the wardrobe and tied them together to show that they had not been read. When all was packed away in the box, he put the lid on and made sure it was tight. The picture of the placid boating scene, with fishing rod and red parasol, seemed to him to come from an innocent world that was utterly lost. He thought of the war rumbling on, like some unstoppable juggernaut, and wondered how innocence could ever be recaptured: perhaps it would only be possible once his generation had passed away. Perhaps it would take a new generation, making a fresh start in a peaceful world. This war must end at last and must surely be the war to end them all.

From his kitbag, he took out the brown paper and string in which the tin had been wrapped when it reached him at the hospital. He turned the paper, so that the Wandsworth address was on the inside, and set the tin down on it. He didn't want to write a letter; there was nothing he could say that would change her mind, but the thought of Violet opening the parcel without knowing where it came from, and with no kind word to soften the blow, was unbearable. And they had parted without saying goodbye. His father had always told him that to wish someone goodbye meant 'God be with you', so to leave without saying it was to withhold your blessing.

He took out his sketchbook and retrieved the watercolour that still lay sandwiched between its sheets of textured cream paper and its board back. He remembered painting the view over Bassenthwaite; he had started with a light wash on which to build lake and sky and the paper had puckered a little where he had made it too wet, then he had broken the scene down into simple shapes, fells and rock faces becoming slabs of colour. How easy it was to trick the eye and create an illusion of solidity, with colour only a few molecules thick. A perception could be constructed from coloured water, or a memory conjured by an image: the division between past and present so paper thin it was virtually imperceptible. As he held the painting in his hands, for a split second he remembered the boy he had been on the warm spring day when he cycled through the park with such hope running through him that he felt he could have taken on the world. Then the connection was gone. He turned the painting over and wrote in the bottom right-hand corner, *For Violet, in memory of happier times and in hope of better times to come.* His own kind of blessing.

He placed it on top of the box, folded the creased brown paper around it, tied it up with string and addressed it in bold capitals. He didn't want to take it down to the main post office where there would be a queue of people who stared and then slid their eyes away. He would go over to the little post office at Crosthwaite and the walk would take up some of the morning before he was due at work. Knowing that today would be a black day, he must try to fill every minute. Already he felt it coming over him, the deep sadness that settled on him like a pall.

24

NO MAN'S LAND

Late one evening, George was returning from walking on Latrigg, the fell behind Brundholme Wood. George liked it for its clear view of the sunset over the lake and its lack of paths, other than the faint tracks made by sheep, that deterred other walkers and left him in solitude, able to walk tall without bending his face to the ground in fear that he might startle people in the dusk with his pale mask.

As he rejoined the long, straight road that led back to town and ran alongside the park, he pulled his cap well down over his eyes in his customary manner and was about to lower his gaze once more when he saw a group of young people come out through the park gates and go on ahead of him. With a jolt, he recognised Kitty and her friend, Suzanne, walking with three men in uniform and a girl he didn't know. He noticed their even numbers.

George slowed his pace so that he wouldn't overtake them. The young men were in high spirits; one of them was holding a banknote high in the air, using his superior height so that the others couldn't reach it, whilst a disagreement went on about who had won a wager. He didn't like the look of them – they were rowdy types, and seeing Kitty with them made him feel acutely uncomfortable. He wanted to know who they were and how Kitty knew them.

At the top of the road, Kitty and Suzanne crossed over towards the Borrowdales' house and the rest of the group spilt into the road after them, still jostling and arguing. There was a scuffle as one of the men, a stocky chap with a kitbag over his shoulder, made a lunge for the tall man's arm and was repulsed with a shove and a curse. By the way both men staggered, George felt sure that they had been drinking. He pulled in hard against the park railings and moved along to get as close as he could, keeping in the deep shadow of the trees, so that he could watch over the girls.

At Suzanne's gate, the group divided. Suzanne went into her garden and shut the gate but paused there and one of the soldiers leant against the gatepost, clearly aiming to stay and talk. The unknown girl and the stocky young man paired off and walked away arm in arm, and, to George's consternation, the tall soldier moved off after Kitty, clearly intending to walk her home.

George's heart beat faster. He could hardly intervene; what right had he to say what Kitty should or shouldn't do? Nonetheless, he waited until they had walked on a little way and then followed after them on the other side of the street, slipping quickly through the pools of lamplight and lingering in the dusky shadows cast by trees and shrubs in the guesthouse gardens, the air perfumed with the sweetness of buddleia and night-scented stocks.

The soldier was talking too loudly, with what George recognised as the loose mouth of a man who has drunk his wages. He seemed older than Kitty. He walked with his hands in his pockets, which gave him a swaggering air, and he had his cap tipped back on his head and a stripe on his sleeve. George could hear snatches of their conversation: the man asking Kitty about herself and Kitty answering briefly, not giving much away. Although there was a good space between them and the man had made no attempt to get close to Kitty, George felt uneasy and as they turned a corner he hurried after them, anxious not to lose sight of her for a minute.

It was after ten and the visitors had thinned out in the town, either retired for the night or ensconced in the hotel bars and public houses that cast a glow from their windows on to the street. The sound of laughter and voices raised above the tinkling of a piano came from the Four in Hand and the soldier slowed his step and bent towards Kitty as if to persuade her to join him inside. The light from the open door fell upon them and George saw Kitty smile but shake her head and turn away to walk on alone.

George's relief was short-lived. The soldier hesitated for a moment, jingling the loose change in his pocket; then he hurried after her. As she came level with Pack Horse Court, the cobbled alleyway that led under an arch down to the inn, he caught up with her and, as she half turned in surprise, slipped his arm around her waist.

Fury welled up in George and he broke into a limping run. He saw Kitty push the man's arm away and step sideways and heard the man exclaim, 'Oh no you don't!' as he took hold

365

of her wrists and tried to draw her into the darkness of the archway.

'Let me be! I have to go home!' Kitty tried to pull away as he forced her back against the wall.

'Kitty!' George shouted. 'Leave her alone!' he panted as he limped to a halt.

The man released her. 'What the devil do we have here?' he said, taking in George's strange appearance. He held his hands up in mock surrender; then, as George, gasping for breath, bent forwards resting his hands on his knees, he lunged forwards, his fist meeting George's jaw. George was knocked stumbling into the street with blood salty in his mouth. He could hear Kitty saying, 'George, leave it! Come away!' but his blood was thumping in his head and ringing in his ears as he regained his feet and launched himself at the soldier, throwing him back against the wall of the passageway. In a move that he thought he had forgotten, he jammed his forearm across the man's throat, pinning him there, struggling for breath. He leant harder against his windpipe until the man's eyes ran and he made a choking sound in his throat.

'Don't . . . you . . . dare . . . touch . . . her,' George hissed, pressing down with each word, his face so close that he could smell the liquor and stale tobacco on the man's breath. He stepped back and the soldier fell forwards, bent double, wheezing and gagging.

'What are you doing? Come away!' Kitty pulled at George's arm. He took her hand and they hurried down the street.

The man staggered a few steps after them, called out 'Stuck-up tart!' and then collapsed into another fit of wheezing.

George stopped once they were out of view, beside a barrow left over from market day. 'Are you all right?' he asked, putting his arm around her.

'I'm perfectly fine,' she said.

George could feel that she was shaking. She put her head against his shoulder and they stood for a moment embracing. George could feel her heart racing against his own. He held her tight and safe in his arms. Lightly, so lightly that she might not even notice, he kissed the top of her head, barely grazing her hair.

She put her hand to her face as if she was wiping away tears.

'We'd better get you home,' George said.

They walked on, hand in hand. George hardly daring to speak in case the spell were broken and she took her hand away.

'That awful man,' she said.

'How do you know him?'

'I don't. We were watching the bowls at the park and the three of them just sort of latched on to us and wouldn't be put off.'

'You must be careful,' George said vehemently but stopped in case she might think that he was criticising her. 'I mean, I wish I had been there to take care of you,' he said slowly.

'Oh, George,' she said, squeezing his hand.

As they reached the post office, they saw Kitty's mother in the parlour window upstairs, as she peered through the half-opened curtains. She turned and said something to her husband, who rose and left the room.

'Quick, he's coming down; you'd better go,' Kitty said. A light bobbed in the fanlight above the side door as Mr Ashwell, carrying an oil lamp, made his way downstairs.

George said, 'I want to talk to you properly. Promise you'll meet me. When can I see you?'

She rubbed the heel of her hand across her forehead in a worried gesture that George knew well. 'Father's going to be so angry. I was meant to be home hours ago. I'll try but I don't know how easy it's going to be to get away – but Sunday . . . I'll be at chapel on Sunday for sure.'

'You promise? You won't change your mind?'

The key grated as it turned in the lock. 'Quick, go!' Kitty said, giving him a little shove. 'He won't like you being here and you look as though you've gone ten rounds.' She pulled away from him and started towards the door as it squeaked open over the hall flags. 'I'm here,' she said, as her father stood in the doorway with his fob watch held ostentatiously in his hand. 'I just got talking to Suzanne and didn't notice the time. I'm quite safe,' Kitty gabbled.

'Who's that you're with?' Mr Ashwell peered beyond her and raised the lamp to see. 'You!' He stared at George, with blood on his face, his jacket dirty and buttons off his shirt, slowly looking him up and down. 'Kitty, go inside,' he said peremptorily and Kitty went, pulling a desperate look over her shoulder at George.

George, afraid that if he tried to explain what had happened he would only get her into more trouble said, 'I'm sorry, sir. I know Kitty's late but I brought her safely home . . .'

'I don't know what's been going on but I certainly don't want Kitty mixed up in it,' Mr Ashwell said. 'I'd be obliged if you'd stay away from my daughter.'

George stood helpless as he followed Kitty in and closed and locked the door behind them.

George lay awake late into the night. He wanted so much to talk with Kitty but how was he going to get to speak with her? Her father would be watching over her closely, and she would be loath to risk his ire and slip away. Even at church, he would be keeping his beady eye on her and it would be impossible to have any time to talk alone. He couldn't bear it. He had had her in his arms; he wanted to keep her there, safe by his side. How cruel it was that she was to be whisked away just as he learnt what he really wanted.

A stiff breeze had got up and loosened a branch of the creeper that covered the back wall. It moved to and fro across the window as the wind tugged and released it. The room seemed full of sounds: the creak of boards, Ted's steady breathing and the twigs scraping over the pane. George pulled the pillow around his ears.

He was angry with himself for not putting right Mr Ashwell's opinion of him. But what could he have said about the soldier that wouldn't have made it even worse? He had left him imagining that he had taken Kitty to some rough bar, some brawling house. It seemed that he had saved her from one sort of trouble only to drop her in another.

What a fool I've been, he berated himself. He didn't make peace with her properly when he was away at the war. When he came back, she had tried in every way to help him whereas he hadn't even managed to do the one thing he had promised: to take her to the cairn as a memorial to Arthur. Worst of all, after she had kissed him and he had felt such joy and tenderness, he had let himself be parted from her through his own stupid pride. And now he would risk losing her if he was barred from seeing her. He'd had so many chances and always managed to let her down. He always let everyone down: his parents, Edmund, Violet. What a mess he had made of it all and how lonely his life had become.

Tossing and turning, he listened to the scraping of the twigs against the pane. Hot and tangled in the bedclothes, he drifted into an uneasy sleep. As the wind blew up, the sound of the branch tapping sharply on the glass entered his dreams as the crack of rifle fire and he started and called out, and then subsided once more into sleep. He dreamt that he was out in no man's land, alone. Bright moonlight picked out the glint of metal debris, the dull gleam of the weapons strewn among the dead and the shimmer on the surface of water in shell holes. He stumbled across the uneven ground, his greatcoat weighed down with mud, but never a shot was fired and no living creature crossed his path. There was no sound: not a moan from a wounded man, not the rustle of a foraging rat nor the shush of an owl's wing. The silence was palpable; it pressed on his eardrums. All around, the scene was the same, without wood or building to give a bearing: an endless, treeless, cratered plain with no sign of friendly or enemy lines. He began to look at the bodies, turning each one over with his foot, unmoved by contorted faces or shattered flesh, simply searching through them, at first methodically but then more desperately, taking hold of shoulders and rolling them over or hauling on stiffened arms.

He found the body of the soldier he had killed. He knew him not by his face, but by the badge half hanging from his collar. He saw it now, the detail his memory had strained over for so long: large, inexpert stitches along one side of the insignia, in mismatched thread – the stitches of a soldier like himself, making do, far from home.

'Is there anybody there?' he called out into the dead air, his voice muffled and weak. 'Where are you?' he called again, and the sound died away without reply.

He came to a shell hole where bodies floated and knelt beside it, leaning over to pull them towards him. Rooke was there, his face a pale oval, his form riding low in the water. He thought he saw the faintest movement, a feeble twitching of his floating hand and knew instantly that Rooke was the *only one*, the only other person left alive. He stuck his rifle in the mud and, holding on to it, leant over, further, further . . . until he could almost touch his hand. He strained forwards until he could grasp it and his fingers went through it like soft butter to the sticks of the bones beneath.

George woke to find Ted shaking him hard by the shoulders, saying, 'Shut up! Shut up! What's the matter with you?'

He gripped Ted's elbows and hung on.

Ted said in a loud whisper, 'You were shouting. What's wrong?'

George stared, disoriented, into the darkness of the room. His pyjamas were stuck to him, soaked through with sweat. 'Stay with me,' he gasped, clutching at Ted.

'I'm going to get Mother.' Ted, out of his depth, tried to pull away.

'No, don't! Don't wake her. Just . . . just don't go for a minute.' George relaxed his grip a little and Ted stood still. 'There . . . I'm all right now,' he lied. As he took each hand away, they shook uncontrollably, like the hands of an old man. 'You go back to bed now. I'll be all right.'

George lay back on to damp pillows, chill at his neck, straining his eyes to make out the familiar bulky outline of the wardrobe, the four-square shape of the chest of drawers, the softer line of the beds and the steps of the books and boxes stacked on the shelves. Where a curtain hook was missing, the curtain heading tipped forward revealing a chink of pale grey. George fixed his eyes upon it and lay, stiff as a board, watching it, waiting for it to lighten and the day to come. Half of me is lost, he thought, still in Flanders, never to be retrieved. What have I got to offer Kitty? A man afflicted by the shakes and the horrors?

371

25

WALKING OUT

The dream stayed with George the next day, and even when he managed to close his mind against its scenes, the mood of desolation remained. He carried it with him like a smell in his nostrils, a taste on his tongue.

On the way to work in the afternoon, he hardly noticed that the wind had dropped and the day had brightened. His thoughts elsewhere, he turned down the alleyway at the back of the baker's yard. The gang of boys lounged as usual against the back wall. He looked at the ground as he approached them, at the beer bottles and chip papers in the gutter behind the taproom of the Four in Hand. As he came level with them, one lad called out asking for some coppers, whilst the thin boy slipped down from his seat on top of the wall. 'Hey, mister!

What happened to yer face?' He plucked at his sleeve and George shook him off, scowling. He wanted to pin him against the wall as he had the soldier and had to remind himself that he was only a boy, a stupid, ignorant boy trying to impress his friends. He went on, neither faster nor slower, cursing his limp: their confidence that he couldn't catch them made them cocky, egging each other on to see who could bait him the most.

'Oi! Tin nose!' another voice called out. George carried on, seething. The other boys joined in, jeering and yelling, 'Tin nose!' after him. A lump of clinker from one of the ash cans landed beside his feet and as he rounded the corner there was the sound of laughter and then breaking glass, as a bottle smashed on the wall behind him, small brown shards skittering out into the street.

George turned the next corner and gained the sanctuary of the cinema. A queue was beginning to form at the box office and he slipped past quickly, ignoring Millicent's nod, not wanting to draw attention to himself. He climbed the stairs to his eyrie above the auditorium, wishing that Thorny wasn't taking the afternoon off. The thought of an afternoon in his own company was daunting.

He struck up the arc lamps on both projectors to check them, and began to lace up the first projector. They were reshowing *Atlantis*, a film that included the sinking of a liner, just like the awful *Titanic* disaster. Some people thought it in bad taste and there had been letters to the press, which had, of course, only piqued curiosity and sent folk to the cinema in droves. George had noticed that: the way that anything billed as 'shocking' produced a ghoulish interest. His opinion of the public had fallen since he'd started work at the cinema; he'd concluded that people really loved to be horrified as long as the horror was happening to someone else.

The pianist started his first run through the introductory music, a piece in a minor key, full of foreboding, as the audience filed in to take their seats. George rolled up his sleeves and readied himself for the labour of cranking a long film. The audience settled and the lights went down; the curtains opened and George set the shutter speed, turned the handle and started the film.

He knew the story by heart, about a doctor who goes abroad for respite from his wife's psychiatric disorder, a tale of personal and public tragedy and the pursuit of love. He had shown it several times and was bored with its set pieces: Angèle, the mad wife, creeping around with her scissors; Ingigerd the frivolous dancer, entrancing the hero with her performance as a scantily clad butterfly; the sinking of the ship and the hero's rescue attempt. He knew all the points at which the audience 'oohed' and 'aahed'. The part that caught his attention, as always, however, was a small scene of no consequence to the plot: the scene with Arthur Stoss, the man with no arms, who had learnt to use his feet as hands. On board the ship, the hero was taken to meet him for no other reason, apparently, than to provide an opportunity to show the armless man offer and light a cigarette *with his toes*. There were no title cards to show what conversation passed between them, and the man with no arms had no further part to play. He was not a *character* in any real sense, as he'd been given no characteristics beyond his disability. He was reduced to a curiosity, a spectacle, like a performing chimpanzee.

George, still smarting from the encounter with the ragged boys, thought his own experience very similar. To them, he wasn't a person but an oddity: 'Peg leg!' 'Tin nose!' They shrunk him down to his infirmity. A thing, not a man.

The squares and triangles appearing at the edge of the film

meant that he had only seconds to the changeover; he switched to the other projector, a smooth, practised transition, editing the reels together seamlessly so that no symbols showed on the screen.

George thought, I want Kitty and I want to be a man, nothing more. He mopped his brow on his arm; the heat in the booth was intolerable. The speed at which he turned the handle was creeping up, and the pianist, forced to play faster to keep up with the action, was glancing up at the booth in an irritated manner. What was it his father had said? A wife, a home, children – those were the things that made you a man. Nothing to do with 'manly qualities' like bravery or heroism or sticking it out. Nothing to do with fighting for your country or honour or glory. Just being seen as a person and known for yourself.

Who was he though? He didn't feel he knew himself. He couldn't join together the boy who used to bike, and fish, and sing at chapel with the man who fought, and killed, and failed everyone who was important to him. The image of Edmund's body came before him, curled over as any creature curls to protect itself, to present the smallest possible area to a predator: the animal instinct useless in the face of exploding steel. The sides of the booth seemed to press in on him – like Pandora's Box, full of fluttering evils; his thoughts seemed to fill it.

He toiled on, changing reel after reel, cranking faster and faster, desperate for the feature to reach its end. He wished he could talk to Kitty right now; he longed for the way she made him feel she understood and was on his side. He wished, more than anything he had ever wanted before, that she would say she would be his girl.

Suddenly, George knew what he was going to do; he was going to find her, and make her listen. He was going to tell her how much he wanted her to be his sweetheart and hope that although he was a broken man, and had little to offer her beyond his own self, maybe, just maybe, it would be enough. He couldn't bear to wait another minute.

The film was coming to a close, the credits rolling. George speeded it along to the end, not caring that the squares and triangles flashed and flickered on the screen, or that the pianist, completely lost, let his last piece peter out. The lights came on and the audience moved along the rows, muttering. He switched off the lamps and rushed to wind off the film, and then watched, impatient at the leviathan slowness of the crowd as it funnelled down to pass through the doors. Beside himself with frustration, George left the dark booth and looked down from the top of the stairs at the milling crowd below. Taking a deep breath, and making fists of his hands in his pockets to stop them from shaking, he set off down the stairs and into the foyer, pushing his way through the crowd, ignoring the staring faces, the girl who tugged her partner's arm and pointed at him, the man who shouted 'Oi!' as he elbowed past and out into the bright, eye-blinking street.

He started towards the centre of the town, weaving through the market-day crowd around the Moot Hall and around the obstacles of traders' carts and horses being harnessed up by those who had finished for the afternoon. Ignoring the pitying glances and idle stares, George hurried to the post office.

The side door was open and he edged past a bicycle that stood in the hall. In the sorting office, Lizzie was folding mail bags and Mrs Ashwell was wiping out the pigeonholes with a damp duster, taking the opportunity while they were empty to get rid of some of the paper dust that caught so at one's throat. George greeted her and she turned from her work with a start.

'I'm sorry to startle you,' George said, 'but I had to come. I really need to see Kitty.'

Mrs Ashwell shot an anxious look at the door that led to the counter. 'She's out on deliveries,' she said in a low voice, 'the near end of the Penrith Road and back to St John's.'

As George was about to thank her, the door opened and Mr Ashwell backed in carrying an armful of parcels. 'Tea ready yet, Mabel?' he said; then he turned and saw George. 'I thought I told you to stay away.' He dumped the parcels on the sorting table and scowled at him. 'Lizzie! Go and take over the counter.'

The girl looked terrified. 'But I've never . . . I don't know how . . .'

'You've got a head on your shoulders, haven't you?' Mr Ashwell said icily. 'Try using it for once.'

Lizzie sidled quickly past him and shut the door behind her while Mrs Ashwell stood twisting her duster in her hands.

'You're not welcome here,' Mr Ashwell said to him directly.

George stood his ground. 'I think that there was a misunderstanding last night,' he said. "There was . . . an incident. I was actually protecting Kitty. I would never take her anywhere dangerous. I always have her best interests at heart.'

Mr Ashwell snorted, 'Indeed!'

George took a deep breath. 'I came here to see Kitty and to ask if she would do me the honour of walking out with me. Depending on her answer, I was going to ask you for your blessing, but since I'm here, I'm asking you now. Will you sanction my paying court to Kitty, as someone who's known her all her life and loves her dearly?'

Mr Ashwell stared at George as if he had taken leave of his senses. 'What, exactly, do you think you have to offer my daughter?' He counted off George's shortcomings on his fat, stubby fingers: 'Invalided out of the army, no prospects, no security, no home! I absolutely forbid it.'

George concentrated hard to block out the words that had

rung in his own head for so long. 'Then you offer me no alternative but to ask Kitty what she thinks herself, and be bound by what she says.' He looked Mr Ashwell in the eye. 'I'll wish you good day.'

As he picked his way past the lumber in the hall, he heard raised voices behind him.

Mrs Ashwell said, 'Really! Fancy mentioning George's injury! You were very hard on him. Couldn't you let them have their chance?'

'Absolutely out of the question. I'm surprised you'd even consider it.' Mr Ashwell drowned her out. 'Even before his . . . his misfortune, he wasn't in Kitty's league. He's not of the right calibre.'

Mrs Ashwell, who was herself a railwayman's daughter, was stung. 'You think there'll be many young men to choose from after this? More and more telegrams coming through here every day! John Saunders, Albert and Anthony Rawlinson, Mrs Verney's boy, Christopher, our own Arthur, all gone!'

George paused at the door. There was a silence.

Mrs Ashwell said more gently, 'Don't you know your own daughter? It's always been George for Kitty.'

George retraced his steps to the top of the town and then followed the route of Kitty's late-afternoon round, cutting through Standish Street and along the Penrith Road. There was no sign of Kitty delivering, nor taking a rest in the park opposite.

He began to work his way through the smaller back streets, desperate to find her before she finished her round and went back home. Greta Street, Eskin Street, Ambleside Road: he had almost worked his way back to the cinema when he passed the church of St John and saw, between the gravestones, the flash of Kitty's navy and red uniform. She was sitting with her back to him on a bench at the edge of the churchyard, which looked out towards the lake and fells, her hat and the empty postbag carelessly thrown down on the grass beside her. He straightened his collar and then paused. Carefully, he took off his mask and put it into his pocket. He wanted her to see him as he really was, to say this properly, face to face. The air struck warm against his tender skin, balmy with the smell of lavender and dry mown grass.

As he lifted the metal latch of the gate, the grating noise startled her and made her turn in her seat. A smile spread across her face. 'I hoped you might find me.'

George walked over and sat down beside her. 'I'm glad I did. I wanted to ask you something.' The words spilt out: 'I've seen your father and I have to say he isn't happy, but I have seen him so it's all above board and your mother is an absolute brick . . . I think she'll bring him round, maybe not straight away but I think she'll bring him round . . .'

'Slow down, George!' Kitty tried to stop him, 'I can't take it all in.'

But he couldn't stop; he kept talking, quickly, before he could lose his nerve, looking down at the groundsel weeds and speed-well growing in the gravel path. 'I want us to walk out together as a couple, Kit. I'm getting better: I have work and some hope of advancement; Mr Mounsey's been good to me and wants me to learn.' He took a deep breath. 'I know my leg's shot to blazes and I have awful dreams that give me the shakes. I'm not much of a catch, all battered about, inside and out,' he said. 'I'm not sure I should even be asking you to walk out with me, when it means you'll have to put up with everyone staring, but I wish you would.' He finished and looked up at her and she looked back, with something in her eyes that gave him hope. He reached across and took her hand.

Kitty said, 'I tried to tell you, on the fell, that I didn't care about all that, but you strode off down the hill as if . . . well, as if you were furious.'

George considered for a moment. 'I was angry . . . but with myself,' he said slowly. 'It was my own fault – that people saw me. I should never have taken my mask off. It was wrong to give you the brunt of it and I'm sorry.'

Kitty glanced sideways at him quickly and then away again. 'I thought you didn't like me kissing you.'

'No, no, I did . . . That wasn't it at all!'

The smallest smile appeared on Kitty's lips and was gone.

George said, 'It was because those people felt sorry for me. No one likes to be an object of pity.'

Kitty tutted. 'Why are you worried about them? It was just their ignorance. They don't know you.'

'I suppose people's reactions are a kind of mirror, and I can tell that they don't like what they see.'

Kitty looked at him earnestly. 'But that's just the outside, isn't it? That's not really you,' she said, and George felt the warmth that he had missed so badly running like a current between them.

She leant forward. 'How's your jaw? Let me see. I'm so sorry about that horrible man.' He turned his face fully towards her and she bent close to look, touching gently with her fingertips. She drew in her breath. 'That's going to be a bad bruise.' As she looked up, their eyes met and George felt the light-headed weightlessness that he had longed for drawing him forward, drawing him towards her. He took her in his arms and kissed her, a long deep kiss, and it felt right: right as a song in two parts or a dance in perfect time; a jigsaw piece that fitted into place.

When they drew back, they smiled at one another. He put one arm comfortably around her and she leant her head against his shoulder with a sigh. Together they looked out at the hills that encircled the lake and the town.

In George's mind's eye, he could follow the tracks that crossed them: the narrow paths through bracken, the wide dirt and shale path that led along the whaleback of Cat Bells; he knew where they ran flat and where they led up outcrops of rock, sometimes in jagged slabs, like steps, sometimes presenting on their sides, riven like slices. He could close his eyes and feel the very grass beneath his feet, not meadow grass but grass with thin blades, cropped short by rabbits, growing densely like a mat. How could he know these things so well, every detail of his outward world, yet for so long not have recognised his inner landscape, not known his own feelings?

'I'm sorry it took me so long to see the obvious,' he said. 'You must think I barely know myself at all.'

Kitty squeezed his hand. 'George Farrell,' she said, looking straight at him, 'that doesn't matter. Don't you realise that I have you by heart?'

EPILOGUE

Mrs Burbidge set the parcel down on the table in her dim room at the top of the house, and sat down to take a good look at it. Who would be sending Miss Violet a package wrapped in second-hand paper, and tied with grubby string? The Walters were carriage trade; goods were always brought out to the house from the town for inspection.

She picked at the messy knots with her short, capable nails until the string fell away and then pulled the paper apart to reveal a square tin. When she lifted it, the things inside rattled and slid. She eased off the lid and saw a collection of objects and photographs and a bundle of letters that she saw were addressed in Violet's hand.

Tutting to herself, she sat back in her chair. She would not be delivering the paraphernalia of Violet's love affair to her, not when it was breaking the girl's heart. She had seen the letters that Violet hid in her drawer, the paper softened at the creases by reading and rereading, and the keepsakes she hoarded: gloves and pressed flowers; she'd found them when she turned the mattress and had put them carefully back in place.

She lifted the letters and examined the rest of the contents, taking them out one by one. Miss Violet's dance-card holder was there, which had once belonged to her mother, together with photographs, keys, postcards, and an amber heart that perhaps the poor young man had intended to give to her as a love token. The gentleman's gold pocket watch weighed heavy in the hand: that must be worth a pretty penny. As she placed it on the table with the rest, she noticed a piece of paper in the folds of the wrappings and pulled it free, thinking that it might be a note from whoever had sent the box. It was a painting, a view out over the lake. On the back, there was something written in one corner; she squinted at it but it was too small for her to see. She spread the brown paper right out but there was no letter.

A bell rang in the corridor downstairs and she listened for the sounds of hurrying feet. Nothing. Those girls were so slow; they had no sense of urgency. It might be Miss Violet needing something; she would have to go herself. She slipped the watercolour quickly into the box, piling the other stuff on top of it, put the lid on and wrapped it back up loosely.

She stowed the box away on top of her wardrobe, among the lumber of hatboxes, suitcases and old umbrellas. As she stepped away, she thought for a moment how strange it was – the little that's left of a person after they're gone: a few objects in an old tin.

ACKNOWLEDGEMENTS

I am indebted to the many soldiers of all ranks who wrote first-hand accounts of their experiences of the Great War. Sources that helped me to re-create the idiom of the time include letters from the collections of the Imperial War Museum, the writings of the war poets and of Henry Williamson, and the private diary of Edward Moore, compiled by his grandson Alan R. Moore and kindly loaned by his granddaughter, Christina Hall.

As well as the many general texts available on the First World War, two books were invaluable in researching the detail of the struggle for Ypres in the first year of the war and the topography of Flanders: *Ypres 1914–15* by Will Fowler and *The Battlefields of the First World War* by Peter Barton, which features the top secret panoramic photographs taken for intelligence purposes by the Royal Engineers and their German counterparts.

In addition, I would like to thank the following people who helped me: Laura Longrigg and Katie Espiner for their ever generous support, astute suggestions, and faith in the project, also Louisa Joyner, Jenny Parrott, Cassie Browne, Richenda Todd, Charlotte Cray and Charlotte Abrams-Simpson at HarperCollins; Janet Lambdon, Lucy Anderson, Pat Kent, Susie Freer and Katie Hill for their company along the way; and my family, near and far, for their unstinting encouragement, in particular my husband, Spencer, my sister, Louise Gillard Owen, and my father Peter Gillard. Lastly, I am deeply grateful to my mother, Isabel Gillard, who through her wonderful example first inspired me to write.